THE GARISH DAY

RACHEL BILLINGTON

The Garish Day fulfills the prophecy of Rachel Billington's growing number of fans that she would soon gain a place beside Evelyn Waugh and Graham Greene as one of England's outstanding Catholic novelists. Her new novel follows the life of Henry Hayes-Middleton from his birth in 1940 to the present day, paralleling the changing fortunes of the once mighty British Empire. Like his father, Henry is a staunch product of the right schools who seeks his career in the Foreign Office. But, unknown even to himself, Henry is also conducting a spiritual search that, in the strange ways that God works, reaches its conclusion in the presence of the one woman who would seem the least likely to influence his life.

Rachel Billington is a member of one of England's most illustrious literary families. Her mother is Elizabeth Longford; her sister, Antonia Fraser; and her brother, Thomas Parkenham. In addition to eight previous novels (the two most recent being *A Woman's Age* and *Occasion of Sin*), she is the author of plays for radio and television and two children's books. She and her husband and their four children live in London.

35,000 First Printing
$25,000 Advertising and Promotion Budget
Publication Date: May 21, 1986
Suggested Retail Price: $17.95

William Morrow & Company, Inc.
105 Madison Avenue
New York, N.Y. 10016

THE GARISH DAY

By the same author

All Things Nice
The Big Dipper
Lilacs Out of the Dead Land
Cock Robin
Beautiful
A Painted Devil
A Woman's Age
Occasion of Sin

For children

Rosanna and the Wizard-Robot
The First Christmas
Star-Time

THE GARISH DAY

Rachel Billington

WILLIAM MORROW AND COMPANY, INC.
NEW YORK

To my father
in his eightieth year

Lead, kindly Light, amid the encircling gloom,
Lead thou me on!
The night is dark, and I am far from home,
Lead thou me on!
Keep thou my feet; I do not ask to see
The distant scene; one step enough for me.

I was not ever thus, nor prayed that thou
Shouldst lead me on;
I loved to choose and see my path; but now
Lead thou me on!
I loved the garish day . . .

John Henry Newman

Chapter 1

The baby shouted, a hearty male cry of protest. Beatrice was glad that a dispute somewhere the other side of the Aravalli Range had intervened between her husband and the birth of their child. She was willing to give him everything but this moment.

"Let me hold him."

The nurse, whose dark skin was in painful contrast to her white uniform, handed over the sausage-wrapped baby. Beatrice saw at once that he had inherited her sallow European looks rather than Lionel's English blandness. It hardly mattered. He would so certainly be cast in his father's mold. It was just odd and rather enjoyable that her genes, so disregarded in their life together, should turn out to be the stronger, reproductively speaking.

Beatrice handed the baby back with a smile. At least Lionel had reproduced his own sex. His name was already decided. Henry.

It was the influence of gas and air liberally available in the little-used hospital of Udaipur which had encouraged Beatrice in such unusual disloyalty. She worshiped her husband. He had rescued her from a life of hapless gloom with a weary French mother and a drunken English father and transported her to the glittering reaches of diplomatic life. Well, at first, it had been the Indian Political Service. And not altogether glittering either.

One minute her vista had extended no farther than the wet fields and woods of her father's ill-run farm. The next, like Cinderella, she had attended a ball and found her prince. Lionel was twenty-nine at the time. It was the eve of war and he was determined to find a bride. Beatrice was eighteen, small and thin with pale skin, black eyes and black curls. She had as much in common with the large and pink debutantes at the ball as a currant does with the bun it sits in. Lionel, who had already completed four years in Rajasthan, found he could not keep his attention on the Honorable Mary Trigon nor even the less honorable but infinitely charming Miss Daisy Fielding, both suitable partners for a future viceroy. Instead he took the unknown country mouse to his bosom and whispered in her ear, "I'm going to marry you."

And when her eyes opened so wide in response that a rim of white shone round, reminding him of his favorite horse (named, inappropriately, Boxer), he knew that those words spoken in jest must be made true.

The wedding should have taken place in the country, a depressing prospect for Beatrice who wished never to return but luckily her mother caught pneumonia, so her London aunt was able to take over the festivities. Such as they were. War made the excuse for frugality. Not that anyone except Lionel seemed certain it was on the way. Beatrice herself hoped it was, in the belief that any change would be for the better.

This childlike trait, developed over years of country monotony, stayed with her all her life, and proved a useful aid in adapting to the forced marches of a diplomatic career. Indeed, it explained the extreme passivity which irritated her son and other less well-conditioned wives in His Majesty's Service. Her secret self, long immured in the novelettish dreams of her youth, continued unseen and gave her an aura of mystery, which those who were not irritated found attractive. It was this secret and almost shy self that took pleasure in Henry's physical dissimilarity to her husband. It bound the baby to her in a private and fundamental way.

It was out of this same sense that she had Henry baptized a Catholic in a dark and stuffy crypt. Even though she knew he would undergo full Anglican honors in one of the large white churches surrounded by tombs of short-lived Imperialist women and children. When the water flowed over his alabaster forehead (held over the grand alabaster font), she had felt a fierce surge of independence, equaled ironically enough by the moment Lionel had declared his intention of marrying her.

This tepid water, she felt, gave her son the chance of escaping his English island heritage. It linked him to the deep romantic pulse of European passion and history. These were the kind of words her secret self used—in extreme contrast to the diplomatic language of which her husband was the recognized master.

Some years on, during a quiet posting in Madrid, Beatrice was to write a novel which found enough of this kind of language to fill three hundred pages. Henry, who was the only one to read it, was amazed and, after much thought, likened it to the early novels of Vita Sackville-West. It suffered, however, from a curiously stilted syntax which Henry eventually identified as a maternal heritage. Beatrice had spoken French with her mother for the first five years of her life. The novel was never mentioned between them again. It was set, incidentally, at the time of the French Revolution and featured a brilliant and beautiful raven-haired girl who was saved from the sharp edge of the guillotine only to fall into the dangerous embrace of the decadent British aristocracy.

After the midnight christening Beatrice suffered a collapse. The nurse attributed it to polluted baptismal water. This made Beatrice guilty, for Henry shared in her disability, since it lowered her milk yield. But as he had been born several weeks early—indeed that was the reason she was still in Udaipur and not removed to the grand hospital in Bombay—her illness seemed quite natural to everyone else.

Lionel appeared to enjoy her weakness, encouraging her to lie back in winding sheets of white muslin. One morning it struck Beatrice that he would have enjoyed her death. She pictured him with Henry, taking him on the front of his horse, teaching him to be a man before he could walk. But the thought of Henry gave her strength, and after a couple of months she rose shakily and attended a wives' tea party. Now Lionel applauded her pluck. She took with her Henry, who slept determinedly despite the combined cooing of many ladies.

"Oh, what a jolly little fellow."

There were no bad fairies among them to forecast "Fate, Time, Occasion, Chance, and Change . . ."

Chapter 2

Henry's first memory occurred in 1944. He was, though he didn't know it, in Sri Lanka, then still called, like the tea, Ceylon. Lionel had been moved there during the war. He was attached to the Commander of the South East Asia Forces. He strutted and huddled. Beatrice wandered and plucked healing fruits from the trees. She was much struck by the information that the island was the model for Paradise. She wrote a secret poem beginning, "Ceylon is red and blue and green . . ."

Henry's first memory was very colorful, too. It took place at the graduation day for the Girls High School. This was in Kandy, above the lake and therefore some way from the famous tooth. The girls paraded on a sandy ground to the music of their own band. This included many bamboo flutes whose piercing notes much irritated Lionel, who was presenting prizes, but intrigued little Henry. He sat very upright between his parents, wearing a serge sailor suit. Although it was not the hot season, the sun shone brightly and every now and again he scratched convulsively. It may have been this unconscious irritation that fixed the scene in his mind.

The girls were dark and wore white dresses. Almost all sported long black pigtails and at the end of the pigtails bobbed scarlet bows. Around the edge of the ground sprouted smallish trees with exceptionally shining dark green leaves. Resting as lightly on the leaves as ribbons on plaits were large scarlet flowers. These were tulip trees. They were like a conjuring trick, a piece of magic to prove the impossible could happen.

"Congratulations to the High School, Duke of Wellington House," said Lionel, presenting a gigantic silver cup to the winning team. Henry leaned forward eagerly. He saw his face reflected in the gleaming curve. The distortion turned him into a fish with bulging cheeks, round hole for a mouth and no discernible eyes. Though startled, he immediately took to the image and made an announcement in the carriage that conveyed them back to their quarters.

"I am a fish!"

His parents took it fairly well, even though his inability to explain a mirror image left them unaware how the idea had risen.

"He's never seen a fish, dear," said Beatrice.

"Not seen a fish!" Lionel exploded. "This whole damn island's surrounded by fishes, impregnated with fishes. There are more fishes than humans. He could see the fishes from his bedroom window any morning of the week!"

"The water's so dark," murmured Beatrice appeasingly. "Not like at the seaside."

It was true the lake in Kandy had fishes. But what she had meant to imply by her remark was that she and Henry had never been to the sea. In fact, they never traveled at all. Lionel dashed all over the place, often to a great port on the northeast called Trincomalee where wives and children were not welcome.

Lionel's view of the sea was purely military. He saw it as an aquatic game of *L'Attaque.* He had an outstandingly good memory, visual in method, and at the word "sea" could picture the whole naval layout of the war, down to the individual battleships and probable whereabouts of German submarines. It took an immense effort to narrow his vision to his wife's tender imaginings.

"There isn't a seaside here," he said.

Beatrice gave a polite gasp of disbelief.

"Not in the way you mean. There are fishing villages. There are rows of boats with black sails on the skyline. There are men wearing only a cloth round their waists pulling in fishing nets." The urge for factual truth drove him on. "There are long stretches of white sand broken only by coconut groves."

"There you are. Long stretches of white sand."

Lionel hurumphed crossly. "And where would you live? In a fishing shack, I expect, and defecate behind a tree with the rest. You have no idea of the realities of existence."

This combination of the unmentionable and the irrefutable silenced Beatrice, so she bent and patted Henry's hand in a consoling manner meant to irritate her husband.

But he was carried away now by this theme. He had, in fact, prepared an address for the High School Girls and was frustrated by the lack of demand. Like all the best speeches it was easily adapted. "We are living on the equator. In a time of strife we live at the center . . ."

Beatrice, mind preparing to wander, thought how clever it was of Lionel always to believe himself at the center. She guessed that was what had attracted her to him in the first place. There were some, she supposed, who might have considered the damp fields of Hampshire more central than an Asian desert. Not him. Not her, Beatrice smiled.

Lionel, who had reached a diminuendo—". . . and if the forces of evil turn this way . . ." caught her smile and hesitated. He really never had a clue what she was thinking. But he could see this was a smile of opprobrium, so he hesitated. He rode in a carriage under a sunny sky with his admiring wife and his clever little boy. Being a romantic even, at sudden and unexpected moments, a sentimental man, he put his arm around Beatrice and said with choked voice and tear-filled eyes, "Oh, Bea, we're so lucky!"

Husband and wife glowed in happy unity. Henry, squashed between the two, mind still concentrated on fish, wiggled uncomfortably.

"Do we eat fish?"

Beatrice looked down vaguely. "Of course we eat fish, dear."

"I don't want to eat fish."

Both Beatrice and Lionel had forgotten their son's earlier supposition that he was a fish. However, their mood was tolerant.

"Fish have eyes."

"Everyone has eyes."

Lionel looked down at his wife and son. Beatrice was right. He had been so concerned with his work that he had not shown her any of the island. There was that chap Ridley, an archaeologist. Always borrowing transport.

"I'll contact that chap, Ridley."

Used to her husband's trains of thought, Beatrice smiled at him gratefully. She knew Otto Ridley from cocktail parties. He was very fair with a silly mustache, and the Otto was explained by a Swedish mother. He was afraid of being taken for a German. Every month or two he disappeared up north to look at some ancient cities. When he returned he was thin, sunburnt around the knees, and his pale eyes gleamed fiercely. He was not married.

"Thank you, dear."

"If I was a fish I would not want to be eaten."

"But you're not a fish."

"I am a fish, I told you." Henry was suddenly near tears. "I am, I am, I am." 7

At this point in his existence Henry had no clear idea of who or what he was. His childhood had, of course, been very different from the conventional English childhood for his class. First there were the wide golden vistas of Udaipur, the pink skies over the smooth lake, the whitewashed walls of their government bungalow and the dusky warmth of his ayah.

"Nini baba nini/Roti mucan cheenee . . ." she had sung to him and after a while his mother had taken it up, though she never got the rhythm quite right.

They had traveled from India to Ceylon partly by train and partly by boat across the short stretch of sea to Colombo. Lionel was preoccupied by piles of papers that had arrived just before they left. He sat on deck moving sheets from one side of his chair to the other.

Suddenly an evil Tamil wind lifted the top layer of one of the piles and took it over the balustrade of the ship and straight out to sea. Lionel leaped to his feet, shouting and waving his arms. Sailors and interested observers appeared in crowds. Lionel was very red in the face.

"Government documents!" he shouted.

"Lost on the high seas," contributed Beatrice, appearing from below. She took a firm grip on the trousers of Henry, who was peering down at the pulsing waves.

"Lost! Lost!" shouted Lionel, turning on his wife angrily. "What if they were found?"

At this several Indians shot off the side of the ship into the foaming waters.

"Hooray! Hooray!" cried a group of English girls.

But the ship was steaming forward steadily and the papers were already far behind.

"Help! Help!" screamed the Indian boys, whose act of bravado disguised a limited swimming ability.

"Throw them life belts!" shouted the chorus.

Altogether it had been a most amusing morning and a great pity for Henry that it had not qualified as his first memory. In later life, however, prompted by his mother's reminiscences, he recalled the event quite easily whenever he was presented by mounds of white paper.

Henry looked out of his bedroom window. It was very early, indeed, barely light. Beatrice wore trousers, an exceptional occurrence. Otto Ridley wore jodhpurs and they were setting out for the ancient city.

There was a Jeep, a driver and a servant stuffed in the back with a lot of equipment.

"Goodbye, Mummy!" called Henry, his voice sounding very thin.

Beatrice waved but didn't answer. It was as if she had already entered another world.

The trip took five days. In Beatrice's mind it lasted for a great deal longer. Otto's blondness was later reflected in the hero of her romantic novel, although she made him a good deal more handsome than he was in real life.

"Are you interested in the past?" Otto had viewed his assignment with resignation. Beatrice had seemed a spiritless type of woman without energy or information.

"I've read everything I could. The ancient kings seem so fascinating. The way they moved whole cities, just like that."

The face beside him glowed.

"They didn't move their cities. They built new ones."

"There you are. I always get everything wrong. I'm afraid it's going to be very boring for you."

Otto had given up trying to interest the wives in Kandy. Their looks of boredom and brittle laughs as they failed to pronounce Polonnaruwa or Anuradhapura properly had driven him to silence. But this was a different proposition. Here, apparently, was a ready listener, an intelligent acolyte. Beatrice's lack of spirit suddenly seemed the attitude of a thinker.

Otto settled his hat on his head. "First of all, I will tell you the history of Devanampiya Tissa, 260–210 B.C. . . ."

They reached the rest house that was to be their headquarters at dusk. The building stood on the edge of a reservoir so huge that it reached the horizon. The heat melted slowly into darkness filled with moths and far-off wailing.

"Wherever you go, there're people," grumbled Otto. "Usually wailing."

"It's wonderful," sighed Beatrice.

"Supper and bed. Up at dawn."

Otto was brisk. He had noticed a droopiness in his companion's posture which was not wholly due to exhaustion. It reminded him of the dread occasion when a Kandy wife, slightly drunk, had poured herself over him, begging, "Take me! Take me! I am all yours!" Otto didn't have much sense of humor and could never think of the occasion without acute disgust and a kind of shame.

"I'll just have a quick wash," said Beatrice, sensing his mood, but also knowing that supper could hardly be less than romantic. The tables, all unoccupied, were set on the water's edge. The moon would rise, casting its silvery light.

Lionel, in Trincomalee over a glass of beer, was having second thoughts, rather too late. He had been telling a colleague, Norman Swinock, whom he'd never liked anyway, about the terrific trip he'd arranged for his wife.

"I say, old man, you're a trusting chap. I wouldn't send my wife up among all that heat and stones with a young fellow like Ridley."

This struck Lionel unpleasantly in all sorts of ways, although least of all because he thought there was truth in it.

On the third day Beatrice discovered an ancient swimming pool. (The episode appeared in her novel disguised as the discovery of a historic sewer under Paris's Left Bank.) They woke at dawn and, fortified as usual by a drink of coconut milk straight from the shell, they drove to the area of scrub where Ridley was presently working. He had a large team of Sinhalese digging for him but he was so nervous about their doing damage that he hardly allowed them to proceed at all without his direct involvement.

After a while even Beatrice's loving attention had had enough of red earth cut away to reveal corners of gray stone. Otto hardly noticed her at all except to warn her of snakes, of which he seemed extremely frightened.

Beatrice, after her years in Udaipur, wasn't at all frightened of snakes. Soon she wandered off through the tangled undergrowth and spiky trees. Wherever she looked there was some indication of the past. Sometimes a row of sharp-edged pillars leaned out of the ground at rakish angles. Sometimes a grass-covered dome hinted at the dagoba below. Gradually the noise of the workers and Otto's anxious commands faded into the buzz of insects and the occasional chattering of bright-winged birds.

She was beginning to think of finding somewhere to sit down when she saw the swimming pool. It would have been difficult to miss it. It was enormous, divided into two halves and built in glittering granite. It might have been a mirage except that its solidity was so profound. She ran toward it, emerging from the shadow of the trees into brilliant sunlight. She stood by its side, stroking the stone. It was not overgrown at all. There were the steps, a spectators' platform, chairs carved with graceful lilies. Except for the fact that there was no water, she could have stepped into it that instant.

Beatrice dragged a reluctant Otto into the heart of the living jungle.

"Look!" she cried. "Isn't that wondrous?"

Otto, intent on a rustle to his left, took a moment to raise his eyes. When he did, he was, to Beatrice's satisfaction, simply thunderstruck. Despite the sun, he took off his hat and rubbed his head, then his eyes.

"I know," Beatrice said sympathetically. "I thought I was seeing things at first."

Without saying a word he strode toward the great mass of stone. He laid his hands on it. He walked all round, Beatrice following demurely behind.

Then he sat down. He still hadn't spoken. Beatrice sat beside him. She saw there were tears in his eyes.

"Oh, Otto!" she said, laying her hand on his knee. It was a moment of great emotion. He hardly seemed to notice the hand. His eyes stared fixedly.

"Do you see the lilies?" whispered Beatrice.

Otto turned on her fiercely.

"What a fool it makes me seem!"

"Oh. Oh, no."

"Grubbing about in the dust when this stood around the corner!" He got up and beat his fist on the granite. "What a dolt! Dullard! Idiot! What a pathetic apology of an archaeologist!"

It took him till the evening to recover. Beatrice, used to Lionel's habit of seeing everything from his point of view, soon got over her initial disappointment. By the evening Otto was prepared to lecture her on the glamorous users of the pool.

Some late washers beat saris on the edge of the tank and Beatrice picked bones out of her fried lake fish.

He said, "In my view that pool could be the place where Prince Saliya met his lover, Asokomala, for whom, since she was a commoner, he forsook his right to the throne."

His eyes glistened pale across the white tablecloth.

"Oh, yes!" breathed Beatrice. She felt this was a declaration and that she could ask no more from life.

Lionel, despite Swinock (silly oaf), took one look at Beatrice and all suspicious thoughts fled from him. There was something about her smallness, her sallowness, which seemed inimical to lust. Now, if she had looked like some of the other Kandy wives with their pink cheeks and large bosoms, he might have worried. In fact Lionel had always viewed his own attraction to his wife as somewhat eccentric and therefore could not conceive that someone else might share it.

As it happened he was right about Ridley, though for the wrong reasons. If Ridley had wanted a woman he would have picked Beatrice above all others.

Ironically, Beatrice's romantic episode improved her relationship with Lionel, for it raised her emotional level and fed her secret self.

Henry realized there was a war on. This may have been in retaliation for his mother's preoccupation with ancient cities.

The war was, in fact, getting fairly near its end. Which meant that Henry was almost five, a big boy who could appreciate that soldiers and tanks and guns were a man's province. He had also been taught to read by his ayah. This surprised and pleased Lionel and offended Beatrice, who had vaguely imagined she would be the one to hear him lisp "p" for pineapple, "s" for snake.

Lionel began to show more than a theoretical interest in his son. He drew diagrams of battles for him and, in return for intense concentration, allowed an explosive climax of bangs.

Beatrice said, when Henry had retired to bed, overexcited, "You're not a soldier, dear. You're a diplomat."

"Diplomacy is war," responded Lionel in such an important tone that Beatrice was silenced. She listened while Lionel expanded on his theme. "Von Clausewitz," he said, "got it only half right. Look at Yalta. Already the Russians are seeing Europe from a post-military point of view. Diplomacy has never been so important."

Beatrice's imagination was captured, even though he had entirely misunderstood her criticism. Lionel swelled again in her eyes. Gradually her passion for Otto, which had always been a passion for the state of romance, diminished. She saw how feeble he was in stature, particularly beside her large and brilliant Englishman. She effected a separation between her image of the blond escort in the jungle and the reality. Soon she hardly noticed his presence in the club or his absence in the jungle.

However, she had been preoccupied for some months, a long time in a child's life, and by the time she returned Henry had fled the nest.

"Right! Right! Right! Right!" The small boy, elegant in new-washed white, paraded round their bungalow. They were going for a celebration lunch at the headquarters of the South East Asia Command. The headquarters were set in the middle of the Botanical Gardens outside Kandy. They approached through an avenue of coconut trees. The trunks were so tall that however hard they craned their necks they couldn't see the leaves at the top. The effect was like moving between giant rows of posts.

"This climate is very conducive to growth," Lionel commented, in an inappropriate tone of gloom.

Ahead of them were bunting, bands, excited victorious soldiers. The war had been won.

But what was ahead for Lionel? Back to the I.P.S. and the fag-end of Empire? No wonder he sat so sternly erect. There was a battle still for him. He must move to the center if the center moved from him.

"I shall make great efforts to continue my contacts in the Foreign Service."

Beatrice looked at him, surprised. She barely knew the difference between the Indian Political Service and the Foreign Service.

"Oh, yes, dear."

Henry, snug between the two, looked up at his father. The face, foreshortened, resembled an ox. "When will we go home?"

Neither parent knew to what "home" he referred.

Chapter 3

Lionel was posted to India once more. But first of all he took his family to England.

It was the middle of winter. They stayed in Beatrice's aunt's house, from which she'd been married. It had been unoccupied during the war and only just reopened. Henry and Beatrice both turned a pale yellow from the cold, which annoyed Lionel. He went a purplish red like all good Englishmen.

"You should move about more. Get the bloodstream flowing. Don't HUDDLE!"

They sat in the drawing room. It was very dismal, since all the good furniture had been removed to the country. The gas fire made threatening noises.

This didn't worry Lionel. He lunched most days at his club and spent a lot of time looking up old colleagues or making new and, he hoped, useful contacts.

But Beatrice had neither colleagues nor contacts. Her mother had died during the war and her father had been put into a home for alcoholics. A few days after their arrival she took Henry to visit him. This was a success, despite a bad start.

"Who's that litle dago fellow?"

Henry shrank from the gaunt and ugly old man.

"I'm Henry Hayes-Middleton."

"What? Eh? Speak up! Cat got your tongue?" As he spoke, yellowish saliva dribbled out of the edge of his mouth.

Henry looked at his mother imploringly. "It's your grandson, Father. My child." She gave Henry a shove forward.

Beatrice had been told his liver was in such a bad state that he would not survive for more than a few months. This gave her an advantage over her son, who imagined him filling his world forever.

The old man leaned forward. "Do I seem very very nasty?"

Henry took a deep breath. He felt things could not be worse. "Very very nasty indeed!"

"Henry!" began Beatrice. But her horrified tones were drowned by a huge bellow of laughter from her father. This developed without words into a terrible fit of coughing. Water showered from his crevices, causing daughter and grandson to move back hastily.

A nurse arrived and hit him with great force on the back. "Been laughing again, I expect." This seemed to sober him up. Gradually he resumed his more normal size and shape.

"He loves a good laugh," she said, "but it doesn't do him any good."

Henry, watching his grandfather warily, was surprised by a sudden dropped eyelid. It was as if a monument had winked. Now he burst out into laughter. His grandfather beamed.

"Well, that's enough excitement for now." The nurse chivvied them out.

On their way back to London through an endless chain of battered buses, Beatrice tried to recall her father as a laughter-loving soul. But she could only picture him slumped in his favorite armchair, or walking with slow step toward some broken fence on the farm. But as they neared Burnt Oak, she remembered one occasion when he had laughed a great deal. It was late at night. He had arrived home drunk. Laughing. He had laughed all the way up the stairs to the landing where he'd been sick. After that he'd stopped laughing and called for his wife.

"Poor Grandpa," she said in severe tones. "So old and sick."

"I liked him," announced Henry. "When I grow old I want to be just as nasty as him."

Henry found a secret source of energy and happiness. This was a cardboard box in an upstairs bedroom. It contained cars. They were made of lead and painted in bright colors. Henry took them out of the box and set them out in rows on the carpet. He gloated over them, stroking their cold sides and rubber wheels. He did not care that many were chipped or dented or without tires. At night he lay awake picturing them driving out from under the bed in two neat lanes.

Henry lay on his stomach and rolled a yellow Sunbeam Talbot very gently forward. His eyes were on a level with the wheels so that they were magnified almost to the size of a real car. His mouth moved a little, making an experimental engine noise. He parked the Sunbeam Talbot and returned for a gray Vauxhall with a red stripe. The noise from his mouth increased, the wheels turned faster. The Vauxhall was joined by a Bentley whose door opened—the one that hadn't fallen off. The room became filled with roaring, racing vehicles. Snakes and sherbet, ayah and coconut trees, were forgotten. Henry had become a little English boy. His cheeks, sensing the change in him, became flushed and pink.

Now when Lionel came home in the evenings he looked at Henry approvingly and said, "Well, at least one of you has taken my advice. A bit of English fresh air and exercise."

"Henry doesn't like going out," said Beatrice, almost sullenly. She herself often walked through the battered streets but instead of turning her cheeks pink the walk flattened her spirit. She wished Lionel would get his posting. These desultory days in a war-ugly city squeezed out her sense of romance. There were too many stories there, too much evidence of a grand drama that she had had nothing to do with.

"I don't blame him, actually," she continued. "Everywhere is so, so squalid."

"Squalid! You call bomb craters squalid? You call noble ruins of a heroic stand against injustice squalid?"

Lionel had just become aware that he was losing his battle to avoid Delhi, so he was easily irritated. It also made him pompous because he was having to be so humble during the day.

A week before they were due to leave Beatrice's father died.

"If we hurry about the funeral, you can still leave with me," said Lionel, not meaning to sound heartless. Henry was the most upset by the death. It was discovered Beatrice's father had left £30,000. It was the figure, less his hospital costs, for which he'd sold the farm. It had sat in a bank, uninvested, unknown. They decided to use some of it to buy Beatrice's aunt's house.

Henry, face pale again with anxiety, tugged at his mother's sleeve.

"Can we buy the cars too?"

"Cars? What cars?"

Henry took his mother's hand and led her upstairs. It was a grayish late afternoon not long before Henry's bedtime. Outside a street lamp was newly lit.

Henry went to the bed and pulled out the box. Very carefully he extracted one car after another. Beatrice realized she was witnessing a ritual. She sat on the bed.

Henry put the cars through their paces. Careful observance on the street had taught him about gear changes, traffic lights, road lore. He drove off each car from his mother's feet and after a few minutes returned it there.

"Now you must play!" He dragged her down to the floor with surprising force. Beatrice found herself the driver of a Bentley with one door.

"Turn it! Rev it! Stop at the lights!" commanded Henry.

After a breathless half hour, Beatrice begged off and the cars, with much debate on proper order, were garaged.

"So, can we buy the cars?"

"Oh, I expect they count as fittings and furnishings." Beatrice smiled, although she would have preferred her son to conceive a passion for about anything other than cars.

Over a late-night supper of Welsh rarebit and treacle tart with condensed milk (Lionel's favorite) she said, "Henry has no friends."

"Want another, do you?" Lionel, with mouth full of tart, was not an inspiring sight. Besides, it was not at all what she meant. One child had increased her grip on reality just as far as she wished.

"Of his age."

"Ah, well. School will provide him with friends."

At the age of seven or eight Henry would be sent to an English boarding school. The same school, naturally, that Lionel had himself attended. He had hated it, coming, in much the same way as Henry would, from an entirely Indian background. It had given him a permanent terror of people bigger than he. Luckily, at six foot two, there were not many bigger anymore.

"There's some time yet," said Beatrice. "Delhi is stuffed with excellent English-speaking prep schools."

Henry had no memory of Delhi.

"This is Central Government," announced Lionel with the emphasis on "Central." He had grown a mustache while they were in London. It sprang blond and jaunty above his exhausted face. They had been traveling by boat and train.

Henry thought they must be somewhere very important to have taken so long to get there. They were now in an official car driving them to their official residence. It was six-thirty in the morning, a crip sunrise in March. Henry leaned forward.

"Is this a Rover?"

The driver turned round. He was a pale Indian with large sad eyes. "Yes, sir."

"What kind of Rover?"

The driver glanced at Lionel. But he was lying back with his eys closed. "Nineteen Thirty-two." His voice rose. "In the garage we have a Rolls-Royce 1922, a Rolls-Royce, 1935, a Morris and an Austin."

Henry sighed with satisfaction.

Lionel heaved. "Delhi was designed by the British. It is laid out in a logical system of grids and roundabouts. It is a showplace to the world. Driver, take us to the Palace."

"Yes, sir." Pause. "It is not on the route, sir."

"Oh, darling!" A small protest from Beatrice.

Lionel turned to her, face no longer weary. "Henry must have a superb first impression of the center of a great Empire." He addressed his son. "You have seen England for yourself now, you have seen how small it is. You have seen the scars of a war it fought and won. Now you are going to see a symbol of its pride and magnificence!"

The car turned into a straight, exceptionally wide road, bounded on either side by flat expanses of pale green grass. Lionel began telling the history of the Empire. Henry listened without understanding. He was always flattered when his father spoke to him.

In the rearview mirror he could see the driver's sad eyes. Henry said, "Who built the road?"

Lionel, interrupted in a sentence about the role of the Princely Kingdoms, was not disconcerted. "That is a very good question. The Viceregal Palace, which we are about to see—ha!—there—look ahead now!—was designed by a superb architect, Sir Edwin Lutyens. However, he had a rival, Baker, another architect, who thought the job rightfully his. Instead he got his hands on the roadway leading up to it. This road. The grand run-up to the grand palace. And he built a dip in it. So that suddenly, absurdly, without warning, the magnificent Lutyens edifice simply disappeared. Popped away. Vanished. Fell into a hole. Look. Look now!"

They all craned out of the windows. And sure enough, the Palace they had admired a moment before was no more. "It's like magic!" cried Henry excitedly.

Even Beatrice smiled.

Lionel, pleased with the effect of his story, sat back. "What a revenge! Of course, it will pop back up in a moment. But reduced, reduced."

This was Henry's first lesson in Empire.

Henry cared only for cars. Each morning now he went to school. It was a very white school—apart from a few of the pupils. A white light came in through white blinds and shone on white walls. Even the desks, which were of pale polished wood, were more white than brown. The paper they wrote on was white and they wore white overalls. It hurt Henry's eyes and his mind. He felt torn open by light. He remembered with nostalgia the dusky upstairs bedroom in London.

Since the school was several streets from their house, Shanti, the driver, drove him there each morning. This was his best ten minutes of the day. They talked constantly, testing each other's vehicular knowledge.

After such intellectual cut and thrust, school was an anticlimax. Henry found the work very easy. In mathematics he barely had to think for the black numbers to jump into the right answers. Spelling seemed quite natural and he could remember any lesson however much it bored him without stretching his brain at all. He couldn't help realizing that he was much cleverer than any other child at the school.

"Henry is most precocious," Beatrice was told by the headmistress.

"But how is his behavior?" Beatrice asked anxiously. She had always assumed Lionel's son would be clever but she had a horror of little bullies. She felt incapable of assessing his character herself. Physically, she could see, he was a thin boy, tall for his age, with her own dark curly hair and dark eyes. But whenever she tried to assess his character her gaze was fogged by his aura. It was the same with Lionel and was to be so all their married life. She presumed the aura was produced by her own deep love. But occasionally she wondered if it was a barrier to personal contact that they themselves thew out.

"Behavior?" echoed the headmistress reluctantly. The teachers were so dazzled by Henry's intellectual skills that they had not been much concerned with his behavior. She looked down at a sheet of paper in front of her. "He's never late. He has no black marks. He won a gym stripe." She came to a halt.

Beatrice waited hopefuly. These details were hardly personal.

Seeing her expression, the headmistress clapped her hands. "We will summon his form-mistress."

Beatrice and the headmistress sat silently. The matter of Henry's character weighed heavily between them. The headmistress thought rather resentfully that most mothers would have been delighted to hear their son was the cleverest boy in the school. Indeed she had been looking forward to the interview, to the conveying of good news. But now here she was confronted by a kind of determined passive resistance. The face opposite her was smoothly olive, unlike the complexions of most British wives in India, which quickly became red-veined and old. Beatrice sat upright, hands in lap, really quite like a child. What did she want to hear, after all? Whatever Henry's form-mistress could dredge up to say it was hardly likely to be very informative. After all, the boy had not even been in the school a term.

The form-mistress entered. She was a nervous woman, Anglo-Indian, particularly frightened of the headmistress, who had broken precedence in hiring her.

"Mrs. Hayes-Middleton," said the headmistress, her tone making the teacher jump, "would like to hear about her son's behavior."

"His behavior!" She looked at Beatrice, who gave her a vaguely encouraging smile.

"It's so difficult to know one's own son."

"Oh, yes," agreed the teacher, who could not imagine ever having children of her own. She thought very hard. "His mind is very quick . . ."

"Behavior," interrupted the headmistress, glad to see someone else wrestling with the problem. From this spectator point of view she decided to help out a little. "Is he talkative, for example?"

"He doesn't have many friends yet." Beatrice leaned forward. "But then he's only been with us a few weeks." Beatrice leaned back again.

"Does he seem happy?"

"He does not seem unhappy."

Beatrice stopped listening. It had been a foolish idea to ask these women about Henry. Of course he was secretive, just like she was. He would never let such people get close to him.

"Thank you," she said, getting up in one languid movement. "I'm so glad you're pleased with him. I shall report to my husband."

Lionel was working close to Mountbatten. It had been announced that India would be given her independence no later than 1948. Mountbatten was there to see it through. This put Lionel in the ironic position of destroying his own career, the career not only of himself but his father and his father's father.

However, he read *The Times* and saw that the world was a large place and that Britain had a grand place in it. Then he rejoiced that he was still young, barely thirty-seven, and that he could start a whole new career. Not for him the bursar of some insignificant public school. Not for him the fund-raising or early retirement that some of his colleagues, hardly older than himself, discussed gloomily in the club.

Lionel's sense of ambition had increased. He had lost the indolence of a man whose path is always certain. He had a hungry look. His brain was sharper. At this time, in Delhi, he suddenly found himself attractive to women. At parties women he hardly knew would come up and posture humbly as he talked of change and revolution.

"You're like the King of Siam, with your women!" Secure in her knowledge of his strictly limited capacity for romance, Beatrice smiled indulgently. He smiled too. Yet he was flattered and not unresponsive. After all, he had hardly known the society of women during his years as Political Agent or his years with the High Command. Now he enjoyed taking a sweating palm and watching the flutter in a face. He wasn't particular whose palm he held, although he preferred it to be between the ages of twenty and thirty.

Then there appeared a woman who snapped him up. Lionel was a tall, broad-framed man who was unsuited to desk work. In Udaipur he had spent much of the day on horseback. He had fallen in love with Beatrice because her eyes reminded him of his horse. Now he rode each morning at six-thirty before the heat and flies became too overwhelming. He even learned to play polo, filling Henry's Saturdays with images of slim-ankled horses and the click of hard little balls.

One evening he set out on his favorite ride. It followed the Moghul Canal, taking him past the Commander-in-Chief's house with its soon-to-be-anachronistic Union Jack. It was later than usual, the sunlight turning the sandy path peach-colored. His destination was Hans Khas, the remains of an ancient university built on the side of a lake.

As he rode, he thought of Nehru. Here was an Indian leader as democratic as an Englishman. If anything his vision was even wider. Wasn't this very idealism a barrier to the firm hand needed in such a gigantic and disparate country? Even the British had not dismantled the Princely States, yet Nehru was committed to doing that, and it was hardly the biggest of his problems. "Religion," thought Lionel gloomily, for the word itself was enough to depress him. Religious belief was India's main handicap.

Henry clapped his horse's shoulder and increased his canter to a gallop. "Tally ho." He waved the hand carrying a crop in the air. "Rule Britannia!"

It was then he saw the other figure on a horse. It was a motionless silhouette, very small against the stone tower. Unwilling or possibly unable to pull up his horse, he continued exuberantly toward it until he could make out the shape of a woman on a tall chestnut. She was not very correctly dressed for riding, with a panama hat and a short-sleeved blouse over jodhpurs.

Lionel and horse puffed in front of her. Lionel tipped his bowler with his crop. "Good evening. Fine evening for a ride."

She looked at him with clear admiration. "You're Mr. Hayes-Middleton, aren't you?"

This was both flattering and unwelcome. He had seen himself as someone more anonymous and exciting. As his focus settled down from the wild ride he saw the woman's face. It was small, sunburnt, with blue eyes and cropped blond hair. The nose was snubbed, giving her a monkeyish air.

"I felt so brave riding out here on my own." She spoke ridiculously.

"You've come out from England recently?"

"Yes. Just a few months. To be with my father. My mother died."

Lionel could now place her in the Delhi round. He could even picture her late mother, from whom she had inherited the animal nose. She had died, he remembered, from an allergic reaction to a mosquito bite.

"I'll show you round the ruins," he said, slipping off his horse.

Priscilla, as the girl was called, was not really a girl at all. She was a woman of twenty-six who had worked as a nurse during the war and had not found anything very compelling to do with herself since it ended. She didn't fall in love with Lionel, she was rather cold in that way, but she admired him tremendously and thought it would be a very good idea to have an affair with him.

Lionel first kissed Priscilla in a conservatory in Government House. It was toward the end of an official cocktail party when they could both use alcohol as an excuse for such naughty behavior.

But Priscilla didn't drink and when he had finished kissing her, she said, "Where can we go?"

The obvious inference of her words stunned Lionel. He was

quite happy to kiss and be in love. However, now that she mentioned it . . . He found himself aroused in a way he hadn't been for years.

"I don't know." He kissed her again, grasping at her body eagerly.

She pushed him away, smiling. "There must be somewhere."

He looked at her, befuddled. He wanted her undressed as quickly as possible and spread-eagled before him. This image did not sharpen his wits. He lunged forward again.

"No," said Priscilla. "Anyone might wander in. Your wife."

This had the desired effect. At least temporarily. Lionel smoothed his hair with shaking hands. "I'm sorry. I'm afraid I lost control."

Priscilla took his hand. "I want you, too," she said.

Lionel stared at her with amazement. He had never heard a woman say such a thing. "Oh, Priscilla."

"We'll have to find somewhere."

That evening Lionel slaked his lust on the body of his wife, who was gratified. She adored it when he loved her madly, crushing her down until she barely seemed to exist. Lionel, seeing he had made her happy, felt only a modicum of guilt, gone by the morning.

The next evening Hans Khas saw two figures rolling strenuously at its base. It was so simple that Lionel could and did laugh. Two sorts of exercise from one expedition. He felt elated and tender and alive. He thought he'd been living in a kind of fog which making love to Priscilla had miraculously cleared. He looked back to London with amazement. He and Beatrice and even Henry had moved about like blind people, feeling their way, terrified of stubbing their toes against something. How tentatively he had sounded out his career prospects, how humbly he'd approached his future!

Now he felt strong, dominant, self-aware. He saw people notice it in the office. He was bolder in his advice, clearer in his summing-up. His energy level rose, his weight dropped and he even talked more quickly. Before he had been admired at work for his ability to marshal facts; now he was seen as a man who could present them, too.

Beatrice noticed the change in her husband less than anyone. His work had always been outside her understanding anyway. She encouraged his riding because she saw it made him happy. She admired his new-slimmer frame. Sometimes when he got up early and she was still in bed, he stripped off his pajamas before going to the bathroom.

Then she watched his white body through half-closed lids and felt desire for him grow in her. But she was too sleepy and passive to call him to her, so she would let him go, comfortable in the thought of ownership. He always kissed her before he left, touching her with warm hands as if she were a talisman.

Shanti was driving Henry back from school. Usually his mother picked him up and took him either shopping or to the park, where a buffalo pulled the lawnmower. But today it was very hot and Shanti had come in the car. They decided to circle the town on a car-spotting expedition.

"There's a Morris Oxford. And there's a super Rolls-Royce!" Henry leaned out of the window, making exciting reports.

"Yes, yes. And what's that little yellow one?" asked Shanti, enjoying the game just as much as Henry.

"That's an Austin and that's my father sitting in it and he's kissing a girl."

Shanti stopped the car. It was irresistible. There among the hurly-burly of afternoon shopping was a little yellow car and there also was Mr. Hayes-Middleton, just releasing a fair-haired girl whom he recognized as having something to do with the Embassy. He started up the car hurriedly.

"Who was that lady?" Henry craned round for a last view.

"No one," said Shanti, who had decided to be loyal.

"My father was kissing a lady." Henry, who had seen no particular significance in the sight, became more interested over its denial. "He was kissing her! He was kissing her!" He bounced up and down on his seat.

Shanti became upset at the repetition of such an unholy word. "I looked and I did not see. You are imagining."

"No, I am not! It was a lady with yellow hair. Perhaps it was his sister."

Shanti saw a gleam of hope. "Ah, yes. From England." By now he had driven them nearly back to the Hayes-Middleton house.

"I will tell Mother," said Henry.

A new abyss appeared. "Why you do that?"

"She'll be coming home for tea, won't she?"

"Oh, no. She say goodbye. That's why they kiss."

"But you said they weren't kissing!"

Shanti was flummoxed by youthful logic. "Why don't you look only at cars!" he muttered under his breath. He slowed down his car and turned round to Henry. He made his large eyes very serious. "This will be our secret," he said.

Henry thought about this. "Why?"

Shanti became exasperated. He stopped his car in front of the house. "Because in the other case I won't take you car-spotting again." He got out a handkerchief to wipe his wet brow. "Today it is very hot. Everybody is seeing things that are not there. Everybody is having secrets. Everybody is having sisters."

"Yes," agreed Henry docilely. Henry had very little imagination. However, what there was developed round the concept of a sister. Priscilla was only the start of it. For the overseen kiss signaled the last day or two of her Indian visits and then she was gone forever.

But Lionel's new self-awareness could not be allowed to lapse. After a few months he found a willing wife, a quiet, ordinary sort of woman whom the whole family knew. Yet Henry was quite clear when she moved into the "sister" status. He did not define it like this in any but the most muffled, childlike way. But the knowledge, all the same, was there. His father had sisters whom he kissed. It was secret, it made no sense and he did not tell his mother.

Lionel's need for "sisters" lasted during Henry's growing-up. By the time he was able to understand the reality, it was buried beyond recall in childhood love. Besides Shanti's denial of the kiss which they had both just seen as clearly as the car, gave the whole event a fantastic air, to be linked with snake charmers and fakirs who lay on nails. These feelings permanently colored Henry's attitude to women. Women could not be categorized by rational thought. Women were mysterious.

Beatrice contributed to this conclusion. The web of romance she spun round herself became even stronger as the years progressed. She developed a way of standing very close to people and then talking in a soft mystic voice as if she could not really make them out. One of Henry's schoolfriends felt moved to ask in a wondering way, "Is your mother blind?"

She was blind to Lionel's sisters. She had to be. It might have all changed, for, early in 1947, she became pregnant. There was a possibility of a real sister for Henry. After the initial shock, Beatrice began to enjoy herself. Pregnancy was an excuse for doing all the things she enjoyed most. The living room became like a theatrical boudoir, with novels and magazines piled high, shawls draped over chair backs in readiness, trays laid with cool lemon drinks. The blinds were seldom drawn and an extra servant was engaged to deal with all her wants.

She rose only to accompany Lionel to his official engagements, thus fulfilling her role as good wife, which was part of her self-image. She felt unwell but not in pain and took the obvious symptoms of fetal distress with tranquillity. When she bled, she caused no panic and only bothered to mention it if the doctor happened to visit. She was shocked when, after one of these incidents, he suggested she should forgo an afternoon on the polo ground.

"I must be there to see Lionel get the cup."

"You do not have a stable pregnancy, Mrs. Hayes-Middleton."

But Beatrice could not respond to such bold speaking. Her expression became even vaguer than usual. "Henry is so looking forward to it," she murmured. The doctor could not appreciate how much she needed these official events. This was the glitter that Lionel had brought into her passive life. Just at the moment it was the cement that held them together.

It was not on the polo ground but at a lunch party where Lionel was giving a talk on "Economic Partnership in the Commonwealth" that she began to miscarry. She was taken to hospital by the chairman's wife, who therefore missed her lunch. Beatrice kept saying, "Oh, please. I'm perfectly all right. Think of that chicken julienne." But the woman stayed with her all day and was almost in tears when the baby made its final exit.

Beatrice was amazed and touched by her sympathy. She had never had a close woman friend before but now she saw the need. The woman, who was called Bridget Kershaw, visited her every day with presents of homemade biscuits and jam. She was very energetic and talked fast in staccato bursts. Her three children were all away in England at school, so she had plenty of time to fill.

She always dressed in a khaki shirt with a khaki skirt and had plain features, with a mole on her cheek from which hair grew. Lionel referred to her as "Beatrice's admirer," which salved his conscience in a cheating way. Both Lionel and Henry had been sad about the baby but too preoccupied with their own affairs to investigate Beatrice's feelings very deeply.

Lionel now knew that Mountbatten was planning to hand back India that very summer. This was a year earlier than had been originally planned and was causing a breakdown of nerve among many of his colleagues. Those who were staying for a while could not decide if they were the lucky ones or the unlucky. Meanwhile civilian disorder became more threatening.

One day he arrived at work in a violent thunderstorm. He was soaked through in the time it took to get him from the door of the car into the door of the building. In his office he found his usual change of clothing was not here. At that moment he was summoned to his superior's office.

"Important," hissed the secretary.

I am thirty-seven, thought Lionel, not a schoolboy. And gave himself time to dry his hair and rub off his shoulders.

His superior was a man heading only for retirement. He was thus able to rise above the scrabbling of rats in the sinking ship.

"What do you know about America?" he said abruptly the moment Lionel had sat down.

Lionel refused to answer immediately. A recital of facts was obviously pointless and he had never been to the country. "What everyone else knows," he said eventually.

"Ah." His superior picked up a sheet of paper laid neatly in front of him. He pushed it across to Lionel. "It looks as if you may be learning rather more."

The independence of India was also Lionel's independence. He had been accepted into the newly formed Foreign Office and he was to be posted to America. He would be in New York, a Counsellor in the British Information Service. The light of his confidence had blazed up to those in the highest position and they had rewarded him.

Chapter 4

Lionel started in New York at the same time that Henry went to boarding school. Thus began the pattern which controlled Henry's life until he went to university. His father, extremely well tailored, tall, handsome, with the light of new dawns in his blue eyes. Himself, also on the aurora trail, but slight, nervous, with a private look in his dark eyes. In fact, he wasn't nervous with his peers. He was too clever for that. In Latin, Maths, Geography and Science he could make their failures seem absurd without even trying. In English it was different. There he was called upon to produce an opinion rather than trot out the results of a memory exercise. Faced with a passage of great prose to analyze, he felt curiously helpless and ill equipped. The words fixed in his mind but with little sense. He guessed at questions of character motivation and cause and effect. For the same reason, he read no fiction, no *Jungle Stories* nor *Oliver Twist.* Information filled and receded from his head like the tide into a beach hole. A small swill remained to mix with the sediment of his early years. His love for his mother lay somewhere there but his father, part of the tidal sea, swished most of it away.

One passion remained. When his trunk arrived at school on the first occasion, Matron was surprised at its weight. The explanation lay in a dozen or so lead cars lining the bottom. She summoned Henry. "These toys," she said, "will have to be banished."

"Toys!" exclaimed Henry with a shocked expression. He had never thought of cars as toys.

"You're far too old for toys," continued Matron. "We will send them home."

Speechless, Henry picked up the one-door Bentley.

Matron watched. "Maybe I'll let you keep just one, just for this first term. Would you like that?"

Henry could not separate one car in his mind as if it were a stuffed teddy bear.

"That's settled then." Matron became brisk. "Now off you go and finish your tea."

Henry descended slowly. The mirror sheen on floor, walls and wooden stair rail mocked his misery. There was no one to share it with. He imagined the cars bundled into dark brown paper, unloved and uncared for. He could not finish off his bread and jam, which drew the attention of the head of the table. "Jam is a special privilege, don't you know?"

Henry was summoned again. This time it was evening and he wore his regulation viyella pajamas, heavy wool dressing gown and felt slippers. Walking required an effort.

"I've locked the cars up for the term," said Matron, "since your parents live in the United States of America." This appeared as an accusation. "You will receive them back at the end of term."

Henry noted that she had not used the word "home." It was merely "your parents live in the United States." He felt this was a useful clue to his future. He was also glad about the cars. The knowledge of their presence, even if locked away, would be a support. He asked in a viyella-diminished voice, "Do I have to wear this dressing gown always?"

Matron was surprised by this query. "I thought you boys from overseas suffered from the cold."

"It's just that I can't move."

The deadly seriousness of this appeal tickled Matron's little-exercised sense of humor. She let out a single guffaw. Her round face with its small regular features turned the color of the inside of a fig. Henry watched only slightly surprised. Matron recovered and patted him genially on the head.

"You'll be glad of it when winter comes."

This laugh made Henry a favorite of Matron's. This had advantages, such as slipped peppermints, and disadvantages because it singled Henry out from the other boys. It took him only a few weeks to realize that he must build the sort of protective coloring that made one boy indistinguishable from another. He was obviously different in two ways. He was cleverer than the rest and he did not possess an English background.

His knowledge of England stemmed from his one short visit to London and Geography lessons. Luckily these lessons had been extremely thorough and he could follow with his mind's eye seaside visits to Bognor or walking tours in the Highlands. He gave the impression of a well-traveled English childhood, in which he soon almost came to believe. Only when the subject of the Empire, and particularly India, arose did he find himself trapped. He could hardly have lived through the independence of India (on which he had views) *and* basked in the security of the Home Counties. The answer seemed to be a series of interesting foreign tours not overemphasized.

His efforts to conform in the classroom were not as successful. For a full week he attempted to fail at his studies. His form-master asked him to stay behind after a lesson.

"Are you h-h-happy here?"

Henry was stunned at such a question and unable to answer. Even his mother had never asked him such a thing. To his distress, he felt his eyes bulging as if with tears.

"Y-you see, you're much too c-c-clever to be doing such b-b-b-bad work. So there must be something wrong."

"Oh, no, sir," said Henry, trying hard not to catch the stutter. "I'll do better n-now."

"G-good." Squires sounded relieved. "The games master says you have the makings of a nippy winger. Enjoy football, do you?"

"Yes, sir," agreed Henry, understanding now that uniformity could not be reached by underachievement.

Soon after this Henry made a friend with whom he could discuss or at least diminish such events. The friend was called William Salmon. He was large and blond and looked slightly like the fish of his name. He was not very clever but very English. His parents had a farm in Hampshire of which he was proud. He wanted to be a farmer when he grew up. He invited Henry to stay at half-term.

"I say, Hayes-Middleton, there won't be much to do but we can always play tricks on Sally and Jane." These were his elder sisters. Since the alternative was to stay at school, Henry accepted eagerly. When he informed his mother of this happy plan, she wrote him a whimsical letter all about the joys of an English autumn. This was disingenuous of her, since it was the time of year when she had become most depressed when stuck on her father's farm.

Henry had had no experience at all of countryside before that calm October in Hampshire. He and Salmon spent long hours bicycling to objectives that they never reached. They were not allowed on main roads, so they became intimate with the ruts made by tractors. He was so tired in the evening that he always fell asleep to the sound of Salmon in the middle of a sentence. "The tractor can plow ten times as fast . . ."

Salmon's mother, despite having four children, was not motherly. She preferred other women, who filled the house with neatly buttoned blouses and plans for local events. Sally and Jane were much like their mother. They were sixteen and seventeen and already wore stockings. They talked a lot about leaving Roedean and going to a finishing school, after which they'd be coming out.

"Where do you come out from?" Henry inquired politely.

"Sal, do just listen. He wants to know where we come out from."

Shrieks of laughter.

"It's a presentation, my dear little ignoramus, to His Majesty, King George VI, if you've heard of him."

"Thank you." Henry had heard enough.

"It's about meeting Men!" Both girls giggled coquettishly. "Men. Those creatures in long trousers with hats on."

Henry agreed with Salmon that the only point of his sisters was to play jokes on them.

Salmon delivered a note to Sal. It read, "I am mad for love of you. I beg you to meet me in the rose garden at seven-thirty. Signed, An Admirer. XXX."

At seven o'clock two pajama-clad figures took a zigzag path out of the French windows and stopped behind a rhododendron bush. Much scuffling and whispering followed.

At seven-thirty Sally, dressed in her prettiest floral button-through, strolled languidly toward the rose garden. She was followed by Jane.

"She's coming!" Rhododendron leaves rustled. Sal stopped in her tracks. There facing her was the most handsome scion of manhood. Dark, slim, he stood expectantly, looking, however, not in her direction but away to some distant eastern point.

Sal stared. Here was a flesh-and-blood man, quite unknown, standing confidently in her father's garden. She allowed Jane to catch up with her. They whispered, raising their heads now and again to admire the gentleman's elegant profile.

"He might be a burglar."

"He might be a murderer."

They approached him warily, as if stalking a wild animal. The rhododendron bushes agitated violently and a sound like an unhappy thrust penetrated the foliage.

"Do you think he's a dummy?"

The figure turned. They caught a glimpse of dark piercing eyes above a straight nose, full mustache and a pale yellow necktie.

Both girls gasped. Romance made their heads spin. They felt like holding out their arms in ecstasy. But before they could do a thing, the apparition, blowing one kiss in their direction, had, with a bound and a dash, disappeared behind the rhododendron bush.

"He's gone!" cried Jane.

Two pajama-clad boys holding a bundle of clothing took the long way round toward the house. Max, the young and handsome gardener, looking disheveled, skulked home by way of the greenhouse.

As a practical joke, it was almost too successful. Discovery would have made it perfect. But neither boy dared confront the wrath of the sisters.

The odd thing was that when Salmon got back to school his attitude to the incident gradually changed. He would not talk about it anymore, as Henry wished to, reveling in the expression on the girl's faces. He said, "Do pipe down!" and "Drop it, if you don't mind." It was as if he had become ashamed.

Golden autumn was vanquished by winter. It happened quite suddenly in the middle of one night. Henry woke up with his limbs fixed in attitudes of despair. As consciousness came, they began to shake violently. Remembering Matron's remarks, he bundled himself into his dressing gown and waited for morning, when he presumed something would be done to remedy the situation.

His horror was great when dawn brought the usual angry bell and commands for the cold wash. Moreover, boys who he knew to be no braver than himself loped off obediently. Had everyone gone mad? His fingers were bluish-yellow, and when he blew on them they were surrounded by white steam like a magician's gun.

At the door, inexorable, stood the dormitory prefect, his own towel cast negligently round his naked shoulders.

"Come on, Hayes-Middleton. It's not going to get any warmer."

Henry saw he was right. Dawn showed no hope of sun.

"Is it like this all winter?" he asked his neighbor in the cold plunge. His feet had lost consciousness early, which was a mercy.

"They say it gets warmer when it snows," replied the boy. He was a thin, frail boy and goosebumps competed with vertebrae on his back.

"Do we survive?" he inquired when a rough toweling had stimulated a flicker of life.

"I got pneumonia last year. The whole school said prayers for me." The boy paused. "It wasn't a very cold winter."

"But what's the point? Why torture us?"

The boy looked uncomfortable, a response Henry's questions often provoked. "It makes us strong."

"But you got pneumonia."

"I survived."

"But what if you'd died? I mean, shouldn't you go home?"

"It's just as cold at home."

On Sundays Henry tried to convey a sense of his new life across the Atlantic. He found letter writing very difficult. He devised a system of lists which impressed the master in charge. The main problem was that he could not believe that they were ever read. There was no indication of this in his mother's letters. No response to questions, no comment on his affairs. He knew his parents were living on the fifteenth floor of an apartment building in Manhattan, but he found it very difficult to picture it. As Christmas approached with celebrations which swamped routine, he was summoned to the headmaster's study. "I have a ticket for your sailing to New York," he said. "My sister's ship was sunk on the same crossing. But that was during the war. I'm sure you'll arrive safely."

The ship docked at seven o'clock in the morning, New York time. Henry was brought off near the beginning. It was still dark; snowflakes swirled gently among the spires at the end of Manhattan. Henry's pale face turned upward like a daisy to the sun. It was thus that his parents discovered him. Both were confounded by his smallness. So much had happened since they last saw him that they had expected nature to keep pace.

"Well, dear." Beatrice kissed him. "Four whole weeks till you go back."

Sowing the seeds of departure was not comforting but Henry kissed her bravely.

"Good crossing, old man?" Lionel patted him as he might a favored dog.

"I ate an awful lot." He was surprised to see his father there. He had imagined him too busy. "Can I go up one of those tall buildings?"

"Skyscrapers," said his father. "Don't worry, we've booked a place on the top of the Empire State Building."

Light began to filter through the snow-clogged sky. Beatrice was wearing a smart purplish coat that Henry had never seen before and a matching hat. It was styled with a military breadth at the shoulders, which contradicted his unconscious image of her as a floating, obscure sort of person with little outline. Even her face was punctuated by dark lipstick and black brows. Her hand, however, felt the same, a boneless warmth that encased his ungainly fingers, cold and itchy with chilblains.

They proceeded to the street where two cars waited. "I shall see you in the evening." Lionel signaled to his driver. "We will look at your report."

The resonance of this was destroyed by Henry's cheerful response. "That's all right, I already opened it. It's mostly jolly good!"

"Henry!" cried Lionel, bumping his head on the car roof.

"Henry!" echoed Beatrice, hoping to diminish her husband's righteous anger.

"Wasn't I supposed to?" Their son's face looked tired and innocent.

After all, this performance of meeting again was new to them all. They could hardly be expected to get it word perfect on the very first occasion. There were years ahead for them to practice receptive nuance. It had not been bad for a start. The matter of the report was shelved and Henry whisked off uptown to 300 East Fiftieth Street.

Beatrice then had half an hour or so of panic. Her imagination was not of the sort that is fired by reality. She lived the present in a wistful way and dreamed about the impossible. When Henry had been away at school she had not been able to believe in his return, although she had dutifully prepared a room for him. It was therefore a considerable trauma to find herself in possession of a small boy for four unbroken weeks. Her mind whirled and she could think of no activities that he was likely to enjoy.

His room, at least, was a success. It sat at the back of the solid old apartment, a small room with a large window that peered waist-high at other apartment buildings. Between them, most exciting, were fillets of shining gray. This was the East River, running sluggishly beyond. Henry was captivated. The snowflakes had stopped and a sharp blue sky was already pricking through the thick clouds.

"It might be a lovely day!" said Beatrice, thinking vaguely of park walks.

"It's so warm in here!" Henry flung off coat, heavy sweater and finally shoes. He climbed on his bed, which sat neatly in the angle between window and wall. "I could stay here forever. Just forever. Oh, thank you, Mummy!"

Beatrice was touched. She was not to know the extraordinary contrast between an icy dormitory and this overheated nest. She came over and kissed her son and told him how much she loved him and how much she had missed him, which suddenly seemed true to her.

By the evening, mother and son had worn each other out. Henry lay asleep, bedclothes thrown to the floor, limbs spread out in childish abandonment. He dreamed of New York and felt he'd entered Paradise.

Beatrice lay also, waiting for Lionel to come to bed. He had been to a dinner for the Indian Ambassador and was in the process of dismantling his evening dress. He did this with great deliberation in a fixed order. Jacket first, brushed and hung up. Then cufflinks, linked neatly together and put in a special box. Suspenders were then unhitched and trousers removed, brushed, folded and put in their press. Oddly, it was only at this moment he removed his tie, doing it flashily with a flourish of the wrist, as a conjurer might pull a flag from a hat. He held it up a moment before dropping it into a drawer.

This was, for Beatrice, the climax of the performance. She did not like the withdrawal of socks or the revelation of the vest. Actually she had turned against his body at the moment, knowing instinctively it was not for her. Lionel was still in his sexual-romantic phase, for which he found an *embarras de choix* in New York. Of far greater interest to him, however, was his job. During his husbandly striptease, he talked about the change in the balance of world power and the fluctuations of the dollar.

Beatrice wanted to talk about Henry but the subject seemed irretrievably remote from international diplomacy. Besides, she felt so exhausted.

"Europe must forget the war as quickly as possible," said Lionel.

"Yes, darling." Beatrice wondered at his energy. When he got in beside her, she laid her head on his chest. "What shall we do with Henry?"

"He can keep you company, can't he? And then we're going off to Maine. It's all arranged."

Beatrice tried to imagine what it must be like to feel everything was arranged. "Today we went up the Empire State Building. Even though we queued we were back in an hour and a half. Children do everything so quickly."

"I was planning to take him up the Empire State Building."

"I'm sure he'd be more than happy to go up again."

"That's not the point." But Lionel was suddenly too tired to argue. America called on his resources. He fell to sleep in a few seconds, snoring with healthy regularity.

Beatrice slept too, dreaming kaleidoscope scenes in which Henry figured, grown tall like a man. It struck her that Henry must be found holiday friends of his own age.

Belinda was nine, very fair, very neat, very knowing. She was the only child of Mr. and Mrs. Lewis McQueen II. The McQueen/Hayes-Middleton association arose out of an affair between Queenie McQueen and Lionel.

Belinda and Henry met toward the end of Henry's first Manhattan holiday. He had returned from skiing in Maine with a red face and an interest in aerodynamics. They sat on his bed while he talked around the subject.

"The forward motion of the body at such a high speed leaves a vacuum behind, which is filled with turbulence. This turbulence . . ."

Belinda, even at the age of nine, was an attentive listener. She looked like her mother, with regular small features and gleaming turquoise eyes. She dressed neatly in a miniature version of her mother's style, complete with cardigan tied with bobbles at the neck and knife-pleated skirt. She liked to sit holding a concertina of pleats while she listened. Occasionally she let them go, frilling out across her smooth knees. Henry found her fascinating.

"This turbulence tries to pull back the speeding body in order to fill the gap."

When he had finished talking, they sat in silence for a moment or two, then Belinda announced with the American twang Henry found so thrillling, "I guess I'm famished."

"We could go to the kitchen."

They went along to the small, shining room. Henry stood helplessly at the door. He had never thought of food as something he could approach personally. All his life, it had approached him or sat waiting in allocated portions on a plate.

"Let's make ice cream sodas." Belinda stepped daintily toward the refrigerator.

In the living-room Queenie and Beatrice sat at either end of a long sofa. The conversation had already suffered many longueurs.

Both women were reactors rather than initiators in social surroundings.

"Shall we see how the children are getting on?" Beatrice rose, brushing down her pencil skirt. Secretly Beatrice had thought Queenie's wool dress dull and Queenie thought Beatrice's tight two-piece sexually provocative. This was ironic, given Queenie's promiscuous nature and Beatrice's prim romanticism.

Henry and Belinda sat at the bar in the kitchen. They turned as their parents entered. Beatrice gave a gasp. Henry's face was daubed with white and red and blue. The same theme recurred on the floor, on the bar top and even on a considerable part of the wall.

Words failing Beatrice, Queenie gave a small sigh. She said with what might have been pride, "Belinda can find her way around anyone's kitchen."

"I was teaching Henry to make a soda," Belinda stated with no guilt in the accent that was at such odds with her pursed mouth.

"We got the colorings out to make the Union Jack!" cried Henry with his mouth full. He imagined some terrible punishment would shortly crush him.

"Just don't forget to clean up after yourselves." Queenie spoke as if the scene was perfectly normal. She smiled at Beatrice. "Didn't I say they'd make friends better without us?"

Henry watched his mother leave. He saw that Belinda, or perhaps it was America, brought new liberty.

"I do what I want." Belinda had understood his expression.

"Don't you ever get told off? I mean, it is a jolly awful mess."

"Do you love your mother?"

"Oh, yes." Henry could not consider such a question seriously.

"My mother lets me do exactly what I please because she feels guilty about me."

"Oh, I see. Why does she feel . . .?" Henry couldn't bring himself to repeat such an emotionally charged word as guilt.

"I won't tell you till I know you better." Belinda got down from the bar stool and stood with her hands on her hips. "Do you like cleaning up things?"

"I don't know." Henry didn't continue. It seemed feeble to admit that he had never made a mess before.

"I quite like it. With the right equipment." Belinda began to work, handling brush and mop with military precision. Her pleated skirt swung, the muscles in her calves stretched above her ankle socks. Henry felt a glow of love and excitement and sat down to watch her. She seemed as different from Salmon's large and easily duped sisters as a Sunbeam Talbot is from a tractor.

Belinda looked up. A splotch of white cleaning fluid decorated her cheek. "When you come back next holiday, I'll teach you to do the shimmy."

Henry saw that with Belinda nothing was impossible.

When he returned to England and to school, he told the boys about the Empire State Building. But it was Belinda who grew tall in his imagination.

Chapter 5

Henry, reckoning without the Foreign Office family travel regulations, assumed he would be back in New York for the Easter holidays. He imagined wonders of warmth and culinary expertise.

Then he received a letter at school.

> Dear Henry,
> You don't know me but I'm your father's sister, your Aunt Anna. We are all so pleased you are coming to stay with us for the holidays. We live in the middle of Ireland in a nice big square house that was once a vicarage. We have a mixed farm, which you will be able to work on. We have not been blessed by children but we do have horses. You will be able to feed the chickens and watch the cows being milked. Don't forget your gumboots.
>
> Love, Aunt Anna
>
> P.S. Don't forget your gumboots, dear.

Henry sat aghast at this letter. Eventually, in order to break its spell, he showed it to Salmon, who nodded wisely. "Jolly good fun, I'd say."

"But New York!" cried Henry, narrowly avoiding a mention of Belinda.

Salmon looked at this letter more carefully. "Perhaps it's a hoax," he said eventually. "Although the gumboot line rings very true."

"I thought that might be a kind of password," said Henry hopefully.

"No. That's practical advice."

Now Henry began to be schizophrenic in three different directions. There was the schoolboy who could not quite disguise the ease with which he had reached the top of his class. There was the boy who had crossed the Atlantic, first class, with energy born of eager anticipation. And there was the very small boy, carrying a very large pair of gumboots, who boarded a sleeper for a remote farmland in Ireland.

Henry was too young to appreciate the strains of his situation. But he developed a special expression of bewildered independence when he set off from one life to another. He only really felt secure in Belinda's presence because her marvelous self stood between him and the world.

Aunty Anna was obviously disappointed with him from the start. She was a strong, red-faced woman who met him off the ferry at Dun Laoghaire with an expression of disapproval. "You are a wispy little thing."

Henry burst out in despair. "I've brought my gumboots."

"Jolly good. Come on now, I've got to pick up some yeast in town."

Henry's knowledge of country behavior stemmed from his one stay with the Salmons. He felt it expedient to draw on it deeply, feigning mock experience. His aunt remained brusque. But his Uncle Johnny, although silent, was sympathetic. He provided him with books with titles like *Boys in the Empire,* which he said had come with the house. He also gave him the responsibility for looking after a Labrador puppy. This caused Henry both joy and agony. He immediately identified with the dog, which was a soft gold color with weepy brown eyes. He was happy when it was happy, bounding and slobbering and yapping in a way Henry himself had never achieved. But at night when dog went outside to its canine quarters and boy went to his cozy bed, Henry suffered agonies of self-identified loneliness. He lay awake listening to rain and wind and imagined poor Fudge, as it was called, also lying awake, cold and miserable. Eventually he cried out to Aunt Anna, "It's so cruel! Poor Fudge. All alone. Out there." He burst into tears.

"But he's not alone. He's got the other dogs."

"He misses me," sobbed Henry.

Aunt Anna sighed. She would have preferred a horse inside. "Would you like him in a basket in your bedroom?"

Henry couldn't speak. His aunt patted his back sympathetically. Previously, she had thought him almost cold in his independence. "But remember, you won't be able to take him back to school."

Johnny said when informed, "You should take him hunting. Make a man of him."

"I know, dear." Anna's sensible face grew a little misty. "I can't help thinking of him as a little orphan, so silly when there's Lionel and Beatrice."

School summer terms were different from spring and winter. There seemed to be many more boys, springing out from dark corners and spilling over the grounds. There were cricket matches almost every weekend. The only boys who seemed to do any work were the last-year students, who had to take exams for their next school. They carried piles of books around, which caused them to walk with a shuffle and heads bent. A few who had really big piles rested their chins on the top. This gave them a special dedicatory expression, as if they were looking to heaven.

One of these was Salmon's elder brother. He had the reputation of a grind. He wore glasses over his fish countenance, looking like a character from *Alice in Wonderland.* Henry thought he must be very clever.

One afternoon they found themselves side by side watching a compulsory cricket match. Salmon Senior's pile of books stood sentinel at his elbow.

Henry, daring, said, "Hello, Salmon."

Salmon looked sideways. "Hmm. Hayes-Middleton."

Henry looked at the books. The top title read: Fraenkel's *Agamemnon,* Vol. 1, *The Prolegomena Aeschylus.* The warm sunshine raised a fetid smell from it of ink and sweat and perhaps tears.

"Do you have to read them all?" asked Henry humbly.

"Not just read them," Salmon Senior spoke with feeling. "Know them by bleeding heart."

Henry, even more impressed, relapsed into silence. He wondered if his Salmon, not noted for his brainpower, would turn into this kind of scholastic paragon during his last year.

It was one of the mysteries of his early childhood that, when the school results were read out in autumn assembly, Salmon Senior had failed to pass his exam. It was only in Henry's own last year that he understood that books were a barricade against the world, piled higher in direct proportion to lack of intelligence.

Henry, of course, had no need of such props. His deprivations continued to be in the familial area. At the end of his first school year, he was back on the *Queen Mary* again. On this occasion and subsequently every summer, his parents were surprised at his growth. It was as if warmth stimulated the growth that winter cold denied.

"We have taken a house by the sea," Beatrice informed him. "We will share with Queenie and Belinda and then dear Bridget hopes to come with her children."

Belinda at the seaside! In his wildest dreams, Henry had never imagined such a miracle. The reality contained a dangerous twist. Belinda had brought a friend. The friend, who was called Lou, had a breathless way of talking, hardly above a whisper, which infuriated Henry. The girls were self-conscious about undressing on the beach and if Henry happened to look their way, shouted crossly and wrapped towels around themselves.

Henry only shone in the water where he was brave to the point of foolhardiness. While the girls jumped the little waves and screamed and ran away at the larger ones, Henry dived into them. He did this with his eyes closed, expecting each plunge to be his last but determined to be bigger and stronger in something.

His reward came in cries of "Oooh, Henry! You're so brave!" or "Look, there's Henry under again! How does he do it?"

Strangely, when Lou left, Belinda suddenly became brave too and they had great fun, jumping and diving hand-in-hand.

That summer saw the climax and also the end of Queenie's affair with Lionel. Queenie was not too pleased by the seaside arrangement. She had hoped the Hayes-Middletons would return to England for the summer, revealing some interesting relative with a house where any friend of Lionel's would be a friend of theirs. She had seen herself leaving her husband to work through the New York heat, accompanied by Belinda as the token of respectability, crossing the Atlantic to new horizons. The American coastline had little new to offer her.

Lionel, understanding nothing of this, thought the arrangement perfect. He loved to see Beatrice and Queenie together. In a sentimental way, he began to think of them as the two sides of the moon, the dark and the light. He even entertained romantic fantasies of a man with two wives. These disintegrated rudely whenever he came into contact with Queenie's husband, who was a substantial presence favoring brilliant shirts and plaid trousers.

Queenie found it necessary to leave the seaside for the city once or twice a week. On these occasions it was her habit to congratulate Beatrice on her inner tranquillity, which allowed her to enjoy unbroken periods in the same place.

"I'm too restless," she would say, hat in hand, case at knee. "If I stay in the same place too long, I become so jittery I make it a misery for everyone."

Lionel also praised his wife's peace of mind, both to her and in conversation with his mistress. "She has a presence," he would say as they lay together in his Manhattan apartment. Lately Beatrice had taken up tapestry work and one of his favorite sights was watching her sitting on the veranda in the big old rocking chair, clever fingers flicking in and out but face as peaceful as the picture she embroidered.

Beatrice took his compliments without comment. She did not dislike them. She could hardly fail to suspect a special relationship between her husband and Queenie but she could imagine no scenario in which she could object. They were both so particularly good to her and so careful in public. Besides, ever since her miscarriage she had carried about a nervous dread of becoming pregnant again. Since she could not bring herself to ask Lionel to take precautions, this made the sexual act a source of fear and postponement.

"My head aches, dear. The sun on the beach was so bright."

Husband and wife rolled away from each other. Betrayed wife more relieved than unfaithful husband. He still liked making love to Beatrice, finding her remoteness a contrast to Queenie's obliging accessibility. Only in Beatrice's dark dreams did her deeper unhappiness sometimes surface, causing her on several occasions to wake in tears. But this she did not tell even Bridget.

Bridget arrived halfway through the holidays and immediately the whole atmosphere of the summer altered. Her mannish attributes made Queenie nervous—even more than her obvious and immediate understanding of the marital intrigues. Those were normal. Bridget was not. She made ordinary overtures like "This is a jolly old place. D'you come here every year?" sound threatening. It was her loud tone of voice and her hairy face and the way she splayed her legs. If it wasn't for her three children, Queenie would have drawn a very modern conclusion.

Bridget chased Beatrice into corners and stood close. "Poor darling, darling, dear. Why didn't you write and tell me?"

Beatrice looked as vague as only she knew how but it was enough for her friend. "How you must have suffered! All on your own." Her expression became grave. "We must do something."

"Oh, no!" Beatrice cried out involuntarily. All her life she had worked on the principle of doing nothing.

"Why not?"

Bridget's face was so close that she could see the pores in her skin. She had never seen even Lionel with such clarity. Bruised in spirit, she slipped sideways.

Bridget did not give up easily. Her attacks tended to come early in the morning while Beatrice lay drowsily in bed. "And what about the children?"

"I believe they're going to a fair."

"You know what I mean. Witnesses to immorality."

"Oh, no. Not here."

This was a practical approach which Beatrice immediately regretted.

"If not here, where?"

Beatrice refused to answer.

"I think of poor little Henry . . ."

"No."

"Consorting with the daughter of a harlot. Herself already corrupted . . ."

"No, no!"

"With her brazen ways and slinky little body . . ." Bridget's children were stalwart and dark and deeply unattractive in serge divided shirts.

"No, no. No!" Surprising them both, Beatrice flung back the bedclothes and leaped out of bed. "Henry is very happy and Belinda is a very nice little girl." She stood defiant, trembling. "The trouble with you is you have a dirty mind!"

Bridget stared, unable to speak. The injustice of the accusation made all words impossible. Turning with dignity, she left the room.

Bridget's dignity strode over the rest of the day. The fairground trembled. Seesaws hovered neither up nor down, bumper cars failed to bump, the Waltzing Matilda wound down to a slow fox trot. Her three ugly children dared not speak. Belinda giggled and said, "I've never seen a grown-up in such a temper."

Bridget's dignity gave way to rage. Lionel stared at her in amazement. Since he was not naturally observant about people, this showed how much she had altered.

"What's the matter with your friend," he asked Beatrice. Receiving no answer beyond a faint twitching, he later addressed the question to Queenie. "What's the matter with Beatrice's friend?"

"Change of life?" suggested Queenie. Bridget's evil looks didn't accord with her ideal of the gaiety of life. She counted the fifteen days more of the holidays and decided, not without regret, that the affair must be terminated.

Beatrice also counted the days. So did Bridget. So did Bridget's children. They didn't like the heat. They didn't like the overfull house and they didn't like Belinda.

Only Belinda and Henry were happy. And Lionel, of course, whose essential happiness depended on work and not women.

"Next time I come it will be winter," sighed Henry, legs buried in burning sand.

"I guess I might come over to England."

"Oh, would you! Would you! The English countryside is quite remarkably beautiful."

Belinda's eyes slid away from his, which were eager, imploring. She could already sense the end of Queenie's affair with Lionel.

She jumped up and ran to the sea. "Going, going, gone!" She splashed face first into the water.

Henry lifted his legs slowly one by one and watched the sand run off on either side.

Chapter 6

School. New York. School. Ireland. School. New York. The pattern held strong for several years. Henry grew taller, though no broader; and Belinda, despite having passed beyond him into a realm of teenage fantasy, remained his female ideal. On occasions, she still liked him, using him as a pet to calm adult terrors. When Belinda was thirteen, Queenie divorced her father and married a gloomy man who owned an impressive house in the center of Manhattan.

The pattern seeming so strong and Henry being still only eleven, any change in his life seemed impossible. One evening Henry received a handwritten letter from his father. This was so unusual that Henry didn't recognize his correspondent from the envelope and was halfway down the front page without knowing whose news he was reading.

"We will be leaving for Cairo in November, although you, of course, will join us, as usual, in December." This was the line that brought Henry to attention. It was not a long letter.

> You are old enough to profit now from the travels which attend my chosen career. I suggest you read *Seven Pillars of Wisdom* by T. E. Lawrence, H. A. R. Philby on the desert and perhaps the Evelyn Waugh novel *Scoop* for a laugh.
>
> Your ever-loving father.

Giving way to nostalgia, Henry took the letter to Salmon. Even if their interests now drew them apart (Salmon read dirty books in any spare time), he was still Henry's first friend. Possibly, he possessed a kind of simple wisdom.

Doggedly he read the letter from beginning to end. "Jolly good for your father. Promotion and all that."

Henry was not to be so easily seduced from his own misfortune. "What about me? Cairo! It's like going to the deepest, darkest bit of an African jungle."

Salmon appeared perplexed. "Surely it's in Egypt. Where there're mummies and all that ancient-city stuff. You only have to look at the titles of the books he's given you." He gave Henry a knowing look. "It's Belinda you're worried about."

Henry had always regretted telling Salmon about his beloved. "What if it is!" He snatched the letter back. "You only think of one thing!"

Salmon's voice remained reasonable. "I think you're zooming round the world while I just sit with my awful sisters in boring old Hampshire.

This rang a sympathetic chord with Henry. He had been back with Salmon for a couple more unsatisfactory weekends.

"Think of Richard Hannay," Salmon continued, "or Biggles even. They go to places just like Cairo and have amazing adventures. You know, the more I consider it, the more I reckon it's a bit of a cheek you complaining. I should be the one complaining!"

Salmon's face became red and earnest and he ended by banging his fist into his palm as he'd seen his father do.

Both boys were impressed. Henry even mumbled something about "having you stay sometime." It revealed to Salmon himself his fundamental longing to become the first white man to penetrate the swamp civilization of Outer Mongolia, a piece of self-knowledge which was worse than useless, since he lacked the will-power to do anything about it.

The bell for games came to rescue Henry. His vanity could not tolerate being too long impressed with the B-minus Salmon. However, as he jogged across frostbitten ground—it was the first week in November—he admitted to himself the excitement of desert adventure. He only wished his father had warned him, even, perhaps, consulted him. It reminded him unpleasantly of an occasion, a year or so ago, where there had been a fire in the Manhattan apartment. It had been caused by faulty wiring in his bedroom and had consumed in its flames all his books and most of his clothes. He was told only several weeks later, in general, about the fire. It was left to his next visit for him to discover his personal loss. Books he had had since India, school prizes, a scarf Belinda had given him. No one had warned him, no one thought of him, far away in England.

At this time there grew up inside clever little Henry a distinct tendency toward self-pity.

Lionel had a fine view of life during this period. As second in command of the British Information Service, he was selling the gifts of his country to this great new world power called America. Many continued to see France and Britain as the leaders of postwar alignments. But Lionel, who had lived in Europe hardly at all, had a much clearer idea of where the future lay. Britain might be noble but America was stronger. He even understood something of the rise of Russia and the need for a strong Europe. He got on well with Americans because they recognized his unusual lack of insularity. Besides, his forays among their wives had given him an intimate understanding of their way of looking at things. He understood, for example, the need for a proper name to every proper handshake and a glass bursting with ice.

If, at the bottom of his atavistic heart (son of sons of the India Political Service), he saw America as a colony, then it was never revealed. He developed a reputation for giving parties which must not be missed. Not because they were elegant or well-cuisined, but because such interesting people attended them. Happily, Beatrice turned out to be an asset at these parties. She looked very beautiful, said little and wore the most elegant clothes. Beatrice was thrilled to have a reason to indulge her interest in fashion. She spent frantic hours perfecting her appearance and then appeared at her husband's side with that glorious calm that everyone admired.

When Henry arrived in Egypt he stared at his father with surprise. "You look old!" Lionel didn't hear. Beatrice took her son's arm in a confidential way. "San Francisco," she whispered. Henry didn't understand but felt he would get no more from his mother. Her conversation, more and more, was delivered in statements standing alone and unexplained like prophecies.

Henry lay in his new bedroom and puzzled over "San Francisco." He would have liked to explore Cairo, riding a bicycle through the crowded, sandy streets. It had been cold and windy on his arrival but the sandy coating, even on tarmac roads, had reassured him of the desert all around. "San Francisco." His father's weary eyes and narrowed face. The bedroom was dark. Dark, heavy furniture, red damask bedspread, reddish-colored floor. Only the walls were white but even they were hung with dark-framed photographs.

He slid off his high bed and studied them more closely. He recognized them easily from the books his father had told him to read. The Sphinx. The Cheops Pyramid, which he had secret ambitions to climb. A photographed print of Alexandria. To the north, he knew, lay the great canal.

Henry turned suddenly. His father stood at the door. "Checking out the local talent!" He smiled.

Encouraged, Henry went up to him. "What were you doing in San Francisco?" It was the first time he'd ever asked his father a serious question about his job. Lionel looked gratified. He took a firmer stance inside the room.

"An international conference to sign the peace treaty with Japan was held in San Francisco. We were co-sponors with the Americans." Lionel glanced at his sober-faced son. "But there were problems for us. Dulles put the United States' case, more or less ignoring the British. Then our Foreign Secretary was new to the job and the Russians weren't clear till the last minute whether they planned to attend or ignore . . ."

Henry watched his father's face. He spoke energetically, enthusiastically. He soon forgot his son and expanded on his own ideas on Anglo-American relations. Henry remembered these cadences as a child, when they had been directed to his mother. He could picture the expression on his mother's face. Half-closed eyes, pursed mouth, head stiffly forward like someone bracing herself against a high wind. He didn't believe she ever listened to anything his father said. On the other hand, she had never interrupted or contradicted him and, when he'd finished, she'd open her eyes again and give him a genuinely admiring smile. Perhaps she was just stupid, Henry suddenly thought, shocking himself. Or perhaps she didn't like international diplomacy.

". . . For one thing, Mr. Bevin decided not to cut short his holiday and arrived three days late for the conference . . ."

Henry realized that Lionel had not addressed his mother in this way for several years. His memories were of Indian origin. He sat up straighter and tried to start listening again. He decided in an all-important flash, more instinctive than conscious, that he did not wish to be like his mother. He wished to be like his father. For this purpose, he had to exert personality, stop the meaningless flow.

"I don't understand," he said sharply. "What were you doing there?"

Lionel, who was taking a small breath preparatory to starting again, lowered his sights abruptly. He came over and sat on the bed. "I'm sorry. I get carried away."

Henry looked sideways. An apology from his father was embarrassing. Yet a flush of victory spread over his face.

"I plan to join the Foreign Office when I grow up."

Lionel drew his hands together. "You wish to represent the British Lion roaring at the world."

Henry thought of Salmon. "I don't want to be stuck in England all my life."

This didn't seem to impress Lionel. "The world has changed a good deal. When I moved over from the I.P.S. I had such high hopes . . ." He broke off. His eyes rested on the Sphinx. "Take Egypt, now . . ."

Henry saw he had stimulated a new lecture. He frowned with determination to concentrate.

"The only time in its history it's been properly run was when the English did it before the First World War. Anything decent they've got was started then. But what's the position now?"

"Nasser," answered Henry.

"Revolution, riots, enmity. Particularly enmity against the British."

"So what's your aim here?"

"Compromise. Treaty. Friendship." Lionel paused but this time there was no interruption. He held his son with the gleam in his eye. "Protect British military and economic interests. No doubt you've heard of the Suez Canal . . ."

Lionel liked to travel round Egypt. In America, visiting other areas had been part of his job. Now he was theoretically a desk man, a writer of reports putting a pen on the pulse of the nation. This did not suit him so well. As in Delhi, he took to horseback and found every excuse possible to take trips. Henry accompanied him, leaving Beatrice at home.

At first they explored Aswan, Luxor, the land around the Nile. Then Lionel heard about ancient Coptic monasteries deep in the desert. Henry imagined them like islands in a great sea of sand. A plan was made for a New Year's visit to St. Anthony's Monastery, which lay not far from the Gulf of Suez. It would be Henry's last trip before returning to England.

He woke to the usual winter Cairo light, sharp and cold. It was hard to imagine the glaring sun of the midday desert. He dressed quickly and went to the kitchen, where the servant had laid out breakfast. He ate porridge, scrambled eggs and toast with marmalade but neither of his parents appeared.

Henry went to the window and looked out. To his surprise an ambulance drew up.

"I'm afraid your mother's not too well." He turned to his father's voice. Lionel stood in the doorway with a hectic look of impatience. It did not fit with the idea of someone ill.

"I'm afraid it means our trip's off. Sorry, old boy."

Without waiting for any questions he left the room. There was a shuffling and scraping noise in the hallway outside but Henry stayed by the window. He felt angry, hurt, left out again. He watched his mother carried out on a stretcher. His father attended her, still wearing the same energetic agitation. He got into the ambulance with her and the doors were closed.

Lionel returned at lunchtime. "Your mother will have to stay in hospital a few days." He wiped his forehead as if it were hot in the house, though actually it was quite cool.

"Then we can go off!" Henry said joyfully.

"No. No." Lionel was distracted but then suddenly concentrated. "Aren't you worried about your mother?"

It was an accusation. "Yes. You haven't told me what's wrong with her."

Lionel returned to distracted energy. "We must all pay her a lot more attention. We shouldn't have taken these trips without her. I blame myself." He wiped his forehead again.

"She didn't seem to want to come."

"Your mother is a very undemanding woman. Perhaps too undemanding for her own good."

Beatrice had seemed to be asleep that morning. Lionel had risen without waking her, put on his khaki travel gear with relish for the days ahead.

"Come on now!" he'd said enthusiastically. "You'll have to get up to see us off!" She was not asleep. She had swallowed thirty or forty aspirins, nearly a bottle of aspirins. He tried to remember her mood the evening before; perhaps she had been reading while he and Henry had planned their route. Now that she had gone, stomach-pumped and white-parceled to hospital, he looked round the house for clues. He found two books by her bedside. *Vanity Fair* by Thackeray and a guidebook to Egypt. He tried to imagine why she should be unhappy and was relieved there was, if temporarily, no reason for sexual guilt. He remembered complimenting her on her appearance the night before. Her youth had particularly struck him, her soft eyes and unlined skin. Just before going to sleep, he had expressed pride in Henry's development and she had agreed. Really, it was a terrible thing to happen and he could see no reason for it.

Beatrice's thought processes on that night had centered around the Coptic monastery Lionel was to visit. It was dedicated to the hermit, St. Anthony the Great, who was revered as a great worker of miracles and as a helper and consoler of the persecuted and those held captive. Before Lionel planned to go there, it had entered her imaginative life, its rich religious gloss merging with her own buried Catholicism. She imagined herself visiting it, crossing the arid desert and coming to this secret spiritual watering place. She recalled her trip into the Sinhalese jungle with Otto and her discovery of the ancient baths.

At night she dreamed of a dark chapel. On the dome, barely visible through darkness and dirt, was painted the Transfigured Christ with four angels holding shields.

Then Lionel announced he would drop in there with Henry on their way to see the Gulf of Suez. Beatrice was shocked. It was like rape. She felt probed in her most secret places. She should have shouted, instantly, "If anyone's going to St. Anthony's, I'm going there!" But she couldn't. Like an iceberg, more and more of her had slipped under the surface, leaving only the merest tip to fly the flag.

On the night before they left she said to Lionel, "Are you sure they'll let you in the monastery?"

"What?" he replied, half hearing. "As well as the hermit's cave, there's a whole clutch of churches."

"Perhaps I should come?" Beatrice's voice sank so low as to be almost inaudible.

"They'd never let a woman in."

This casual rejoinder, which she immediately recognized as the truth, crushed Beatrice. She went to bed soon after, but could not sleep. Lionel joined her, kissing her and telling her how young and pretty she looked. He was not to blame. She felt abject and worthless, a case of petty dreams that crumpled at the first light of day. She imagined waking the next morning with Lionel more like a schoolboy than Henry. Both so energetic and excited. She pictured her own lassitude once they had gone, alone with no purpose for existence. In the absolute darkness of the bedroom, she felt her way to the bathroom and shook out the pills. Then she felt her way back to bed again and lay down. A Coptic cross floated in front of her eyes as she lost consciousness.

Henry returned to England. It was several weeks before he received a letter, written by Lionel.

> Your mother is much stronger and more cheerful. We are going to take a recuperative trip in a paddle-steamer up the Nile. She sends all her love.

After that letter, Beatrice returned to the task. There was, perhaps, a slightly more loquacious and descriptive content in her pages, a livelier air. But Henry, preoccupied by entering the school rugger team, hardly noticed the change.

At last Henry was beginning to thicken as well as lengthen. Matron, his ever-faithful admirer, noted approvingly. "Just in time for senior school." She added with a dark smile, "It doesn't do to be slight in senior school."

Now Henry allowed himself a moment to realize how small and lonely he'd been at the start of his boarding school existence. He looked at the first-year boys and they seemed tiny, hardly more than toddlers. He thought with relief that he would never be that tragic size again.

Chapter 7

In the summer of 1953 Henry Hayes-Middleton was awarded the top scholarship to a well-known public school. His prep school inscribed his name on a shield of honor. By chance, that summer coincided with Lionel's long leave. He was due three months in England from July to September. Unfortunately the couple to whom he'd let their London house could not be moved out till the end of August. For July they rented a flat; August they decided to spend in Ireland. Beatrice wrote this news to Henry, adding, almost as a postscript, that dear Belinda's mother had divorced again, so they might take pity on the poor little thing and invite her over for a European holiday.

Belinda did not take a ship across the Atlantic. She flew, which did not surprise Henry at all. The family met her at the airport with a Rover Lionel had hired. Belinda walked across the tarmac. She was sixteen, nearly seventeen, more adult than child, but still in the fashion of the early fifties dressed like a child. Henry looked at the mature set of her smooth golden face, the well-brushed hair and confident stride with trepidation, but then he saw the white ankle socks below swirling pleats and took heart.

They all crowded into the Rover and, as Belinda and Henry eyed each other in the back seat Lionel began to talk about American reaction to the coronation of Queen Elizabeth II, which had taken place in June. His remarks, couched as questions—"Should we believe that the Republican spirit revolts against royal privilege?"—were addressed to Belinda. But she didn't respond, indeed showed no sign of listening to him at all.

Henry was reminded of the patronizing way she had with grown-ups and felt further reassured. Her neat mouth smiled slightly, possibly with simple satisfaction at her situation, although it reminded Henry of those exciting moments just before she suggested some really shocking form of play.

In fact Henry was interested in the American reaction to the British system of government. Lately he had begun to think history gave the clue to everything.

"Of course, they could hardly fail to be impressed by the service in Westminster Abbey," said Lionel. "Religious services are performed better in Britain than in all the rest of the world." This touched a chord in Beatrice, who up till now had sustained a bright-eyed silence. "It's television," she announced. "Such an exciting invention. Our flat has one, you know. It puts one so in touch."

Belinda parted her little red lips. "There was a Mr. Muggs on American television," she said, "during the coronation, who was absolutely lovely. He spent hours talking about coronations in the Monkey Kingdom."

"Huh!" Lionel snorted and pressed his foot on the accelerator.

Beatrice murmured a protest and Henry gave Belinda a wide smile, which was received with an unconvincing wistfulness. She'd always been a tease.

Henry had stayed regularly with his aunt since he was seven. He tried to imagine how Clayboggin would appear to others but failed. From his kaleidoscopic style of life he had developed a way of shutting each portion into individual, non-interlocking compartments. He could believe only in the existence of the one he inhabited at the present time.

It was only as their boat-train arrived at the Dun Laoghaire quayside that faint emanations of Clayboggin came to Henry—the smell of dung and silage which hung over the farm like a cloying umbrella, the wet air so that the sun shone with a kind of dripping mist which tickled the face.

They took a train to cross from east to southwest.

"It's very beautiful!" Beatrice and Belinda gazed about them in sleepy-eyed wonder.

"How many horses did you say they have?" Lionel estimated the sloping green fields and long hedges.

"An awful lot. I don't know exactly." Another memory assailed Henry. Mucking out. The first morning of his first stay, he'd woken late, descended to the kitchen, eaten soda bread and cold bacon left for him. Beside his plate lay a short note. "Mucking out. Aunt Anna."

He had eventually found her, standing amidst malodorous

straw. She had indicated a fork with prongs as long as his leg and suggested gaily, "Want to have a go?"

"No, thank you, Aunt Anna." Her surprise had the frozen quality of a Neptune with his trident or Boadicea with an implement of war.

"Then what will you do?"

Any alternative seemed preferable. "Read."

"Read?"

He elaborated. "In my room."

"In your bedroom?"

"On my bed."

The fork quivered. Fierce battles raged over the countenance. Words like "fresh air" and "exercise" nearly surfaced and then died away. She looked at Henry's spindly youthfulness. Her body heaved as a horse might after a gallop. "A bookworm," she said as if to herself. She placed the fork under a pile of droppings and with a deft flick of the wrist sent the whole lot flying out of the stable door. It landed, still in a neat group, on Henry's Matron-shiny shoes.

Lionel looked on Ireland as an ex-colony. He felt thoroughly at home there, as he had in India.

"This is an excellent holiday," he said, mounting a brute of a horse. "Excellent occupations, excellent surroundings, excellent food and excellent company."

"And what about the weather?" Beatrice liked to come and watch Lionel setting out. Her heavy mackintosh made an interesting contrast with Aunt Anna's aertex shirt.

"Temperate!" responded Lionel, giving his horse a hearty thump. "A boom shared only by one lucky hundredth of our world." He thundered off into the distance.

Beatrice watched admiringly.

"It's hardly rained at all." Henry, standing with his mother, put up a hand to shield his eyes from the sun.

"It's in the air," stated Beatrice with not displeased finality. She found Aunt Anna's company cheering, perhaps for the same like-to-unlike reason that had attracted her to Bridget. They walked together and drove into the local town where Beatrice visited the library and Anna the corn merchant.

Belinda, however, had assumed an expression of incomprehension as soon as they reached the farm. She sat in her room and wrote long letters to a girlfriend in New York. Henry read these unashamedly. One sentence rankled. "There is no one my age here."

He approached her one evening as she leaned against a wooden gate. It was a beautiful evening, low sun casting shadows from the newly placed sheaves of straw. "I'm sorry you're not enjoying yourself." He spoke airily, as if dissociating himself from her failure to take pleasure in her surroundings.

"How do you know I'm not enjoying myself?"

Henry had considered the possibility of this question. "I read your letters."

As he had estimated, she was not displeased by this. She flung herself round so that she was facing him spread-eagled against the gate. "It's not your fault. It's a question of what I do with my life." This answer shocked Henry. He relied on Belinda's state of confidence. He saw her like a country, well-governed, in good shape—not very friendly, it was true, to neighboring states but making certain special exceptions of which he was one.

"Don't look so surprised." Belinda kicked the dungy ground with her neat shoe. "Everything's planned for you. Your whole life. You need never think at all if you don't want to. But for me it's different. Nothing is certain."

Henry saw he was being accused of something that was not his fault. He looked at Belinda. Her cheeks were pink with emotion. He searched for an adult response. Risking her impatience, he said, "It doesn't feel certain to me. Going all over the world."

"Oh, that." Belinda looked bored. "That's not important. Your father has a view. I admire your father."

Henry thought it would be demeaning to ask what was this view which his father held. He put a hand on the gate next to Belinda's. "I'm sorry I'm just a schoolboy."

"I think I'll take up riding."

Henry, continuing to read Belinda's letters while she rode out on a gray gelding called O'Donnell, discovered she was looking for a man both gentle and dominating. Meanwhile she became a competent horsewoman. Lionel, revising his earlier impression, described her to Beatrice as "mettlesome." Beatrice assumed he was talking about O'Donnell.

Henry and Belinda took up their old activity of cooking. They spent many busy hours baking scones and plumping soda bread. "Cool hands are essential." Belinda liked to lecture. She waved her own cool hands about. The sun, always low, crossed through the rain-stained windows and made flour puffs in the air. The atmosphere was always theatrical around Belinda. But it seemed more so in Ireland.

Sometimes Henry would read from the Greek or Latin texts which he was preparing for his new school. Belinda soured the milk with a look of reverence. She said no one in America knew Greek or Latin, which he couldn't really believe to be the case. However, it was good to feel superior in something. One afternoon he noticed that each of the hairs on her arm was tipped by a white speck of flour. Without thinking, he leaned forward and blew. She looked at him in surprise. Their eyes met. Henry felt himself blush violently. He had loved her for so long, he had forgotten she was a girl.

He muttered something and ran from the room. For several days afterward he could not look at her, for he saw only her naked breasts and golden thighs. His averted face amused Belinda but she said nothing. After a day or two he recovered and could look at her again without reddening.

Strangely enough, his behavior was remarked on by Beatrice, and it was then she formed the idea of talking to him about his Catholic baptism. The determination was reinforced by the influence of the Catholic churches which ranged around the local town like granite mountain peaks. After her visits to the library, she walked past them wistfully. Once Aunt Anna found her, foot pointed over threshold.

"You're not going in for hell and damnation, are you?" she cried with hearty Anglo-Irish contempt.

Beatrice retreated.

After Ireland they spent a few days in London in order to equip Henry for his new school. Beatrice had been secretly looking forward to these unavoidable forays into the shops.

The morning after Belinda's departure she said to Henry with a briskness he had never seen before, "Now we must go to Harrods." She wore a cherry-red suit and a spot of matching color lit her usually sallow cheeks.

Henry said, "Yes." He was obedient, which pleased grown-ups and those in authority. "Such a mature boy," they said, though exactly the opposite was true.

Henry and Beatrice walked through Harrods. She sprang, bouncing on the balls of her feet in joyous celebration. Her eyes darted from side to side, for every counter held the possibility of endless delights. With one arm she clung to Henry, who was now almost the same height as she. His footsteps were heavy.

"School uniforms are in the basement," suggested Henry.

Beatrice didn't hear. This was a day she would live off during the future year of heat and sand in Egypt. Henry resigned himself. At least he had taken the precaution of putting *The Lays of Ancient Rome* in his pocket. It had been suggested at his school interview he might learn it.

"Lars Porsena of Clusium . . .
By the nine gods He swore . . ."

"Just feel that wool. So soft. Almost like cashmere."

"That the great house of Tarquin
Should suffer wrong no more."

"And now we want china goods."

"By the nine gods he swore it . . ."

Henry read, standing in the lift surrounded by energetic ladies.

Physical exhaustion eventually drew Beatrice from Harrods but then only as far as Derry and Toms. Mother and son sat among the rooftoop verdure. It was a warm gray day, the clouds low and ugly. Henry shifted uncomfortably. Beatrice sat with ecstatic gaze, surrounded by large paper bags. Her mind, tuned into high gear by such indulgence, began to shift on to other subjects. She sat up and looked at Henry with affection. She leaned across the table.

"There's something I want to talk about."

Henry felt himself go pale. Did his mother not realize his father had told him the facts of life a couple of years ago on one of their trips around the Nile? Belinda's imagined breasts floated in front of him.

Such thoughts caused him to miss his mother's first words.

"Of course you must never tell your father."

"What?" Henry said bleakly.

"He does not approve of Catholicism. Not that we ever discuss such things." Beatrice turned her eyes down with either regret or embarrassment.

"I'm afraid I didn't hear what you said first."

Beatrice gleamed at him again, forgivingly, glad of a chance to repeat such drama. "I told you that you are a Catholic. That I baptized you a Catholic with my own hands. I held you at midnight over a stone font in the Church of St. Mary of the Angels in Udaipur."

"I don't remember it." Henry played for time.

Beatrice laughed excitedly. "You were only four days old. Your father was away. I took you there with my nursemaid. We stood alone in the gloom . . ."

"Wasn't there a priest?"

"There may have been." Beatrice became a little dreamy. Head tilted on one side. "A priest is not necessary for baptism. If the will is there."

Henry began to wonder if she was making it all up. He had always found his mother mysterious. He thought of the little group of Catholics in his last school. They went off to Mass each Sunday on bicycles. Otherwise they seemed like anyone else. He suspected this news was not as important as his mother's demeanor suggested.

Beatrice looked at her son through half-closed eyes. She admired his dark curly hair and regular features. She could see he was not much impressed by his Catholic heritage, but she didn't really mind. It was the conveying of the information that was important, not his reaction. She felt like someone who had placed a bomb with a timer on it set in years. One day it would go off. She saw that Henry had begun to frown.

"What's the matter, dear?" Her voice was calmer.

"Do you mean Father doesn't know?"

"After we got back to the house I was ill. So were you. Really quite ill. The nursemaid blamed the baptismal water. So I couldn't tell your father then. And by the time I was well again he'd arranged a grand Church of England christening service and I hadn't the heart to disappoint him."

Henry saw this could well be true. He thought for a moment. "Why did you tell me this? Is there something you want me to do?"

"Oh, no!" Beatrice looked at him almost with horror. "Certainly not."

Henry waited.

Beatrice smiled. She drew his hand on to the table and patted it gently.

Henry waited and then said in a matter-of-fact voice, "That's all right, then."

As he finished speaking a small blob of water dashed onto the back of his hand. Henry became frigid with terror. Was his mother crying? He did not dare raise his eyes. But then another blob fell and another.

"It's raining!" cried Beatrice, pushing back her chair.

They ran, bags bumping about them, for shelter. This run wiped their conversation from Henry's mind, leaving only an image of his mother's unusual gaiety, which could be better attributed to the delight of Harrods than the joy of Catholicism.

During Henry's first term at his public school, Lionel began to write regular and discursive letters. They were typewritten and cast in diary form. Henry was surprised and touched each time he read the signature at the bottom. "Your affectionate, ever-loving father." This was Lionel Hayes-Middleton, scion of the Foreign Office.

The Foreign Secretary, on a visit to Egypt, found himself with a canceled lunchtime appointment and Mr. Hayes-Middleton to fill it. This was a stroke of luck for Lionel, who commanded the occasion with meek efficiency. The wine was excellent, the food better than usual, and he was able to tell firsthand stories about Nasser. In not so many months the Foreign Secretary would need a new Private Secretary. Lionel took the trouble to accompany him to the airport on his departure. In an agreeable chat, he implied that most diplomats were too spoiled to know about any problems outside Europe while he, who had entered diplomacy the hard way through the Indian Civil Service, had a practical understanding of international politics.

Henry had just been informed that he would be playing for the Colts rugger team when he read the letter telling him that his parents' next move would be to London. It was 1954. He was fourteen, a large English schoolboy with red cheeks and a sweet tooth. He admired his father. He had little contact with his mother. He was reasonably popular with the other boys and at night he dreamed about naked girls. On Sundays he went to church in company with the ninety-eight percent who were not Catholics or Jews. He was very conventional.

Lionel had never lived in London. He paced up and down their reacquired Oakley Street house. It was January. Henry was at school. Beatrice was out. The house was empty, hardly furnished. Their furniture would follow in wooden crates from Cairo. He was not expected to report to his new office until the following week. He looked at his watch. Four o'clock. It was a long time since he had been doing nothing at four o'clock in the afternoon. He seemed to be presented with a moment out of time which perhaps should be used for reflection, meditation, a check of where he was and where he was going.

Beatrice arrived back at five o'clock, accompanied by a man carrying a large, obviously heavy box. She found Lionel sitting in their one armchair with a glass of whisky.

"Lionel! Lionel! Guess what I've got?"

Lionel stood up when she came into the room and looked at her with mild admiration. He liked to see her animated.

The man took out a pocketknife, which he opened with great deliberation.

"Do you *see* what it is?" cried Beatrice.

"A television set."

"Put it here on this table," commanded Beatrice, "and make it work!"

Beatrice instinctively realized that television would fulfill her ambition for audience non-participation. Her mind could fly while her body sat still.

A spot of light centered in the screen. It spread outward, increasing as the full moon does on a misty night. Silver gauze swirled about, casting magic reflections on Beatrice's face.

"Aah!"

A goldfish swam very slowly from one end of the screen to the other.

The man started fiddling at the back of the set. "Line hold," he said, and a ferocious army of parallelograms imprisoned the fish. "Focus," he said, and the lines gave way to a sea fog. "Frame hold," and the screen, like Edgar Allan Poe's fourposter, squeezed downward till the fish swam in a narrow channel. "Brightness," said the man, and the fish moved from stygian gloom to desert sun. "There you are now. It's all yours."

Lionel sighed. The brightness at the center of the television had not seemed a moon to him but a whirling mass, a Catherine wheel, just like the London office, from which he could be thrown out and up, down and away or simply sucked into a bureaucratic vortex. The danger came from the proximity of the politicians.

The sight of the poor beleaguered goldfish had released Beatrice to consider her son's size, his unbearable smallness. She regretted their loss of contact, hugged to herself the memory of tea on Derry and Toms' roof garden. She said, "I wonder if they have a television at Henry's school."

The electrician, on his way out, turned back importantly. "Schools all over the country are acquiring television sets."

Lionel, staring at the goldfish, felt a vague sense of doom. Was patriotism enough? He sighed and the goldfish, as if at the exhalation of his breath, was extinguished into blackness. A torso of a man appeared sitting above a desk.

"Good evening. This is the news for Tuesday, January fifteenth."

Lionel now realized that the goldfish's particular quality had been silence.

"An Anglo-Egptian agreement was reached today on the Suez Canal base."

To Henry's surprise, he missed the visits to Ireland. It was the space, he supposed, the height of sky, the wide area of green, the sight of his uncle plodding so slowly across the farmyard. London exhausted him.

Henry was entering the exhausted age when possibilities of the future approached from the horizon in a shapeless and threatening mass. His thoughts, so well-educated into Greek, Latin, History and the Sciences, so incisive and so clear-cut when faced by a text, dissolved like crystals in water. During the holidays he escaped into sleep or books not worthy of his intellect. (He hid these from his father but not from his mother.) Long hours of lassitude, some spent with his mother in front of the television, led not to refreshment but further hours of lassitude. For the first time Lionel remarked the close resemblance between mother and son.

"He must have time to rest and be on his own, poor boy," said Beatrice.

"It's a very difficult age," said Lionel with some vague memory of himself languid under a tamarind tree.

Neither parent tried to talk to Henry. They would not have been able. Nor would Henry have been able to explain his state of mind to them. He tried once with a new school friend he'd made.

Wiggins was very unlike Salmon, who had transferred with Henry to the same public school. Wiggins was as clever as Salmon was stupid. He had come to the school on a special scholarship and was said to have Jewish blood. In fact he was Welsh, small and dark, with a flowing line in conversation and a hot response for every occasion. He was very unlike Henry, too.

Henry's attempt at baring his soul was premeditated. On Sunday morning the school attended chapel. Afterward the boys were left free to wander with cheerful consciences.

"I say, what did you think of old Hogbin's sermon?" This

opening was supposed to be a shortcut to such fundamentals as "What is the meaning of life?" and "Why should I ever rise out of bed?" Unfortunately Wiggins launched into a fluent attack on old Hogbin's view of the universe. Henry did not care about the views of the Reverend Hogbin (real name, Ogden); he saw he possessed a third-rate intellect and had long ago given up listening to his sermons. He couldn't see why Wiggins should waste his time on him. Dimly, he realized he had picked the wrong man for the conversation he had envisaged. Wiggins was destined to become a politician and was interested in principles only as they affected the working of society.

As the two boys walked along side by side, one talking, hope fading in the other's breast, they came across a master. He was Mr. Patrick, tall, thin, young. He taught Henry Classics. He was standing in the brisk morning sun, with an air of hesitancy, familiar to Henry from the moment when he chose between one translation or another of a Greek word. His face struck Henry suddenly as receptive. Wiggins's voice, rising and falling at his side, faded from his consciousness. As they came level with Patrick, still poised in immobility, Henry said loudly, "Can *you* tell me what the point of it all is?"

The sentence, inelegant in its verb ending (Patrick was very serious about grammatical grace) hung in the air between them. Wiggins's voice came to an abrupt stop.

The master, cast back into childish defense, squawked. Wiggins, irritated by the interruption, looked at Henry as if he'd gone mad.

"What did you say?"

Henry blushed so red that his skin tingled. An image of an armadillo rolled over on its back prevented speech for a second or two. "I said, can you tell me what the point of it all is? You know. Why we're here. What we're supposed to be doing while we are here."

"Yes, I see." Patrick was calm.

"Well, I don't." Wiggins still sounded cross.

"You've just come from church, haven't you?" Patrick spoke kindly.

"Yes, sir."

"Why don't you dodge back then and grab the Reverend. I'm sure he'd be delighted to help."

An explosive noise issued from Wiggins.

Henry did not meet the master's eyes. This was not a matter of religious indoctrination. "Thank you, sir. I can't just now. But thank you for your help."

Although Henry had spoken without irony, a faint look of guilt passed over Patrick's face. By then the boys were already passing by. The master turned and called after them, "*Permitte divis cetera* . . ."

Henry shouted back, "*Qui simul stavere rentos/Aequone fervido deproeliantis* . . ."

As he spoke, he saw out of the corner of his eye a woman making her way on a line that would end with Patrick. She half-ran, as if late for an appointment. A second later, Patrick saw her and started out on the same line. He, too, had an eagerness altogether different from his previous manner.

And yet, thought Henry in a confused manner, I was trying to make him think about the most important thing in the world. But the thought was only half formed, overlaid now by a sense of his ridiculousness. "*Nec cupres: nec veteres/Agitantur orni.*"

"Whatever was all that about?" Wiggins's voice at his elbow.

Henry wanted to watch the figures of man and woman come together. He felt something would be made clear at the moment of their meeting. But Wiggins wouldn't let him.

"Honestly, I can't believe old Hogbin has moved you to examine the meaning of the universe."

"Oh, it was nothing. Too much communion wine. Here, how about slipping down to the Headless Fairy." This was a reference to a pub whose board paraded a picture of a beheaded Charles I.

"Hey, do you think we dare?" Wiggins forgot Henry's idiotic behavior. It stayed somewhere in the back of his mind, however.

Years later, when he was a Member of Parliament and he was told of Henry's sudden and inexplicable change in career, he commented, "He was always moody. I remember at school once . . ." But then he couldn't remember and ended rather lamely, "Something about God."

"Hey. We're at war!" This was Wiggins, racing up the stairs. Such was his excitement that he tripped on the top step and slid back down several yards. Henry found him clinging there, shaken.

"What are you doing?" He laughed. It was always a pleasure to see Wiggins disconcerted.

"War," uttered Wiggins. "We're bombing Egypt." He recovered his breath and sat up. "We're sending troops from Malta."

"The Suez Canal." Henry sat down too. "Are you saying we've declared war on Egypt?"

"There's Israel and the French."

The two boys settled down for a serious political discussion. Wiggins's bruises were forgotten in the delicious consciousness of the government's terrifying gaffe. Henry, the acknowledged expert, found himself oddly baffled.

"Of course it's all a matter of economics," he said.

"Economics, my fanny. It's the last gasp of the Empire. And I'll tell you what, the British soldier won't be too bucked to die for economics."

Most of the senior school had gathered round the television. Wiggins immediately got into an argument with a prefect which ended with him being given punishment duty.

"Bloody Bolshie!" said the prefect to his companion.

"Bloody murderers!" shouted Wiggins.

Henry was spotted by another prefect. "Your father was in Egypt, wasn't he, Hayes-Middleton? So what would he make of this piece of nonsense?"

"It was two years ago," he said, neglecting to mention that his father had continued to specialize in that part of the world. An echo of St. Peter-like guilt iced his spirit.

That evening he spent two hours in the village pay phone. When he finally got through, Lionel was not in. Henry tried to elicit a response from Beatrice, who laughed and said, "They're just so silly! Thinking they can walk in and plant a British flag like something out of a storybook."

Henry was irritated by the laugh. "But, Mother, this is serious. People can get killed. And what about Father? Is he involved?"

This time Beatrice sighed. "Oh, well. We've had two years in London."

"What do you *mean?*"

"Nothing, dear. But I'm afraid it may not all work out too well for your father."

The weekly letter from Lionel did not arrive and a few days later Wiggins and Henry went to the local cinema. The newsreel showed some pictures of British soldiers embarking for Aden.

Wiggins jumped to his feet and shouted "Murderers!" It had become quite a habit by now. Unfortunately he had not noticed a line of soldiers seated two rows in front. They turned round, their beefy close-cropped heads terrifying.

Henry grabbed at Wiggins. "Shut up! Sit down!"

Wiggins, no fool, sat down with speed. But not quickly enough. Two large soldiers lumbered toward them.

"What did you say?"

"Nothing. Nothing."

"I heard what you said. You said, 'Murderers.' "

Heads turned in the half-empty cinema. On screen, rows of soldiers, cheery with cigarettes and quips, continued to file past.

"You called those brave lads murderers."

"Honestly, I didn't." Wiggins became so small in his seat that his head slipped below the back. The soldiers, half-silhouetted against the screen, were like giants.

Henry was not able to enjoy Wiggins's terrror because of his own fear that the soldiers knew he was his companion. Out of the corner of his eye he saw a man's figure approaching purposefully. It was the manager with a flashlight.

Both boys decided not to hang about in the cinema despite the managerial protection. It was afternoon. A bright autumn day. Wiggins, with the relief of survival, became quickly perky.

"That's the trouble about this country. You're dealing with political illiterates."

"Surely they're the people you socialists want to put in power."

"They have to be educated first."

"Indoctrinated, you mean."

Henry quite liked to bait Wiggins, but that day he did it with less pleasure than usual. At least Wiggins, though absurd and cowardly, had been a protagonist in the scene in the cinema.

The trouble was that Henry did not feel real enough to pronounce on realities. He would have had very definite views if the Suez crisis had already been in a history book. He could have written a brilliant paper on "the English role in the Middle East with a particular slant toward Egypt and the relevance of oil." Dimly, because all his training was against introspection, Henry realized that his feeling of non-reality was linked to his failure to sort out the fundamentals. As a matter of fact, he had eventually approached the Reverend Ogden with a few important questions. But, as he'd expected, the barrier of old Hogbin's stupidity proved insurmountable. In his mouth, words like God and the spirit came out sounding like bottled drinks. He himself became aware that he was not helping and his voice became sonorously depressed and depressing. Henry recognized the tone from failed sermons in church. It made him feel sorry for the man, so that the interview ended with his professing his worries alleviated and his spirits lifted.

That night Henry dreamed that Belinda came to him and he clasped her in his arms. It was glorious but a prelude to better things. Henry took her hand and led her to a secret passageway leading to a secret room with a bed where they could . . . But horrors of horrors, halfway down the passageway there was a narrow point, and Belinda, his slim, lithe playmate, was too fat to get through. She had swollen breasts like biblical fruit, stomach hard and round. She pressed up to him, desperate to get through and as he felt her body grinding into his, he woke. His pajamas stuck to him. The shame and embarrassment were so great that he blushed hotly all by himself in the dark.

There was no one to whom he could possibly mention it.

The next morning the letter arrived from Lionel. He was in disgrace. His name had been too clearly associated with the planning of Suez. World condemnation of British military intervention in Egypt resulted in Lionel being posted to Spain.

Chapter 8

Lionel spent four years in Madrid. During that time Beatrice wrote her romantic novel and Henry visited the Prado times without number. Once he went with his father. They walked together through the brilliant morning air. It was August. Henry was nearly eighteen. He had already taken his "A" levels, and when he returned to England would take the Oxford and Cambridge entrance papers. He was nearly as tall as Lionel.

"I simply can't believe you've never crossed the portals."

"I didn't say that. I said I've never looked at the pictures." The two men crossed out of the sun into the shadow of the dark building. "I've been more concerned with Spain."

Henry quickly rejected the reproof. "The history of Spain is in these pictures."

Lionel looked at him slyly, then bought their tickets.

"I have a student pass." Henry ignored the look. This visit to the gallery was supposed to show him off in an area in which he excelled. "This museum was founded out of a collection made by Charles V and Philip II. And then, of course, by Philip IV, who had Velasquez to give him a hand."

Lionel looked about in that high-headed way he had. "I've never seen so many tourists."

"Tourists adore Hieronymus Bosch. They gloat over every ghastly detail."

"How extraordinary! I'd think their style would be giant Riberas or sugary old Murillos."

Ignoring this disconcerting show of knowledge, Henry took a sharp left and said firmly, "We'll start with El Greco."

Father and son stood in front of "The Dead Jesus in the Arms of the Eternal Father." After several minutes Lionel moved to "The Descent of the Holy Ghost," "The Resurrection of Christ,"

"St. Paul," "The Baptism of Christ" and all the others. Henry waited dutifully for him to finish looking. He had more than a few well-chosen words.

Suddenly Lionel swung round. "Do you feel the lack of religion in your life?"

Henry was astonished. He had never in his wildest moment of conjecture applied the ideas of El Greco to himself.

Lionel turned back to the paintings. "Obviously a madman, of course. He's one of your favorites, is he?"

Henry stammered out the information with a sense of failure. "I've visited his house and museum."

"I don't like them, you know."

"His idea of perspective is very unusual, exciting . . ."

"You look at them objectively, I can see. But I look at so few paintings, I can't waste my time being objective about them."

"We should have looked at the Velazquez." Henry's voice was despairing.

"It's not your fault, old boy. Don't get so ruffled. I take all the blame."

They walked back along the galleries. Henry felt crushed. He should never have brought his father here.

"I'm getting old, that's the trouble. I'd never have been upset by a Spaniard's idea of Christianity a few years ago. I've been too long in Madrid." His steps slowed and he turned to look at his son. "What do you think of Spain? It's a very violent place, you know, outside the cities. The Civil War is still felt here. Sometimes I don't feel it's part of Europe at all." He sighed.

"But it's not, is it?"

The visit was not proceeding as Henry had imagined. His father introduced such grand subjects—religion, the state of the Spanish psyche—but then he did not continue to discuss them. He left them in the air, hanging above in a threatening manner. "How about a cup of coffee?"

"Why not."

As they turned for the exit, a woman, fortyish, in elegant suit and very high heels, came toward them.

"Oh, Lionel. I never knew you cared for art." Her voice was deep, with a slight Spanish accent. Her skin was dark but her hair golden.

Lionel bowed. He kissed her hand with the kind of gallantry Henry disliked.

"My son." Lionel introduced him. "The Contessa de Badajoz."

"You are the art lover, I may presume?"

"Henry is knowledgeable about everything. Perhaps you'll join us for a cup of coffee?"

"No, no." Henry noticed the Contessa flung her hands about in a way contradictory to her sober appearance. "I have a meeting here in the museum. I am on a committee."

The high heels clicked away across the polished floor.

Lionel drank his coffee down in one gulp. Then he sat silent. It was hot on the sidewalk, even under a canopy of trees. Henry felt prickles of sweat inside his shirt. He said, "Who is she?" The prickles turned into little streams.

"Who?"

"The Contessa."

"Maria Cristina. A powerful woman. Her husband's in the Spanish Foreign Service. He's related to the Royal Family. It's all part of Franco's new look." Lionel signaled for another coffee. "A beautiful woman, didn't you think?"

"Oh, yes!"

Henry now greeted the appearance of any attractive woman with intense curiosity about her sex life. He imagined the Contessa naked. Or perhaps retaining only the stockings and high heels. The sweat ran in thin trickles down his back.

Father and son walked back to their flat. Beatrice looked at them from behind a lace curtain. Their appearance of unity gave her a mixture of pain and pleasure. She was proud and jealous. Her condition was more than usually emotional because she had spent the morning with her novel. The heroine, Laura, a mere quarter of an hour before, had narrowly avoided the guillotine.

"Cooeee!" She waved. Henry looked up and waved back. Lionel didn't notice. They entered the apartment block and she went to meet them.

"Your friend David rang." She put her arm through Henry's. Writing always made her more demonstrative.

"David?"

Henry did not recognize Wiggins by his Christian name.

Lionel sat in his study, surrounded by papers. He was supposed to be writing a report on the Spanish attitude to the creation of a European Common Market but his mind was gloomily fixed on the Contessa de Badajoz. Like his son, he imagined her naked. Unlike his son, he had the aid of his memory. She had stripped for him one afternoon in her ancestral drawing room. Light, filtered through white curtains, had undulated about her like water. It had been a windy day, a hot dry wind blowing right across the plateau in which Madrid sat so heavily.

Lionel sighed. Over lunch, graciously served in a long dining room, she had whimsically described her husband as a bullfrog. Lionel had not wanted to hear such things. He found the Marquis courteous and distinguished. He was one of his best contacts in the Spanish Foreign Office. Really, he did not want to make love to his wife.

Nor had he, as it turned out. One particularly inward rush of the curtains had thrown a brilliant stripe of sun right across the room, revealing the dark figure of a maid in one corner. Lionel, still in his formal suit, was more relieved than worried. He coughed and indicated that Maria Cristina should look behind her. So she did (without losing a jot of sangfroid). "Ah, Livia. You have a message?"

"The children are back, madam. *Los niños han regresados.*"

"So late already?" She turned back to Lionel with a wry smile and began to dress again. As she bent forward a small silver crucifix swung between her breasts.

Henry and Wiggins traveled rough across the north of Spain. Wiggins irritated Henry by wearing a scallop shell, the insignia of St. James, strung round his neck. They usually slept out at night unless they were discouraged by mosquitoes, rain or rocky ground. Then they lay on the soft earth of a peasant hut, or camped under the high stones of abandoned buildings. They drank a great deal of wine.

One evening they came across the remains of a castle. As darkness fell they climbed up a turret and found a wooden floor and a roof. They had hardly settled down when it began to drizzle. Looking out they could see no light or sign of human habitation.

Wiggins unzipped his fetid sleeping bag. "This is what I call travel," he remarked contentedly.

"Yes," agreed Henry, although the rain depressed him. He stared outward. A breeze blew some drops toward him. "Why do you like traveling?"

"If you saw my home you wouldn't have to ask."

Henry didn't want that sort of response. He was always embarraised by Wiggins's reference to his background. Wiggins's father worked at a steel factory in Port Talbot. Henry moved out toward the rain again. Water swished across his face. The heavy smell of the warm wet earth mixed with the freshness of grass and trees. Behind him, Wiggins continued.

"It's quite different for you. You'll be traveling all your life. That's the reason for being in the Foreign Office."

"I don't think my father felt that. Or any of his colleagues. They take a little bit of Britain with them wherever they go. That's the whole point of the Diplomatic Service. You plant your flag in a plot in the heart of an alien country, then you behave in as English a way as possible to make sure everybody knows you consider yourself more important than the alien country. Members of a foreign service never leave their own country for one minute."

For once Wiggins came back with no ready response. Henry felt suddenly hungry. "Any of that bread left?"

Wiggins was shaking his head vigorously. "Do you think it's just the British who behave like this?"

"Oh, no!" Henry had found a stump of bread, which he waved about. "The whole Diplomatic Service is run on old-style ideas of super-nationalism."

Outside the loud swish of rain had decreased to a staccato patter. The odor of sheep droppings spiced the air round his head.

They reached Santiago de Compostela two days later. They had passed through the green rain belt and entered September sunshine. The stone of the Cathedral was golden. So was the archiepiscopal palace to the left and the chapter house to the right. Even the sky, early in the morning as it was, seemed more golden than blue. Henry and Wiggins stood in the center of the still deserted square. They were both moved by the achievement of arrival. By the beauty of their surroundings. By the towers, cupolas, staircases, statues and pillars.

"Now, you must admit we've traveled." Wiggins gave Henry's upraised face a sly look.

Henry frowned. "Your crass remark interrupted a religious experience. A particularly English religous experience."

"But it only occurred because of your pilgrim's travels."

Henry hesitated. He had not, of course, undergone a spiritual experience while standing in the square outside. He had said that merely to irritate Wiggins, who was a tourist about religion as about everything else and therefore easily impressed by deep emotion. He had felt lifted out of his body but that was due to the beauty of his surroundings, the sun, the earliness of the hour and, not least, to the dislocation produced by a hangover.

"Restitit Aeneas claraque in luce refulsit/os unerosque deo similis . . ." He was Aeneas, glowing in pure light, his face and shoulders like a god's. Spiritual moments were unusual in classical literature.

Beatrice was out of sympathy with her son. When he won a scholarship to Oxford, she felt depressed. He was so pompous. She was not to know that this was recognized even by himself as a passing phase. She found his newly broad shoulders and leathered-elbowed jackets repulsive. When he appeared in Madrid the Christmas after his triumph wearing a brown trilby she could hardly bear to look at him.

Henry came to his father in his office. He was impressed by the appurtenances of career. His gaze moved reverently over the high ceiling, large mahogany desk and two shiny black telephones. Lionel was speaking on one of them. "The preoccupations of the United States are not always the same as Her Majesty's Government." He waved Henry toward a chair.

When he put back the receiver Henry leaned forward eagerly.

"My junior," explained Lionel. "Stupid youth who sees every issue in terms of North America."

"Surely that's not far off the mark. With the Korean war barely over and Russia looming."

But Lionel, although admiring his son's intelligence, was not keen to have a political dispute with him, particularly in his own office. He stroked his mustache, which brought Henry's flow to an abrupt halt. He could not reconcile himself to that mustache.

"You've got something you want to ask me?"

"Yes. I thought I'd go to Ireland after Christmas. To fill in time before Oxford."

A telephone rang on the desk. Henry looked at it, waiting for his father to pick it up. But after a couple of rings it stopped.

"What would you do? You don't ride."

"I want to work."

"I presume you're planning to stay with my sister." Lionel appeared irritated out of proportion. He rose to his feet and went across to the window. "What about that Wiggins friend of yours? What's he doing?"

"I don't see what Wiggins's plans have to do with mine."

"No. Quite." Lionel continued staring out of the window. "Do you mean to support yourself with your work? Or will you require an allowance?"

The telephone rang again. This time Lionel crossed the room briskly and picked it up. "Hayes-Middleton."

Henry waved at his father and left the room.

Aunt Anna was amazed when Henry turned up, looking for a job on the farm. She said, "It's not as if you rode. Nor as if you needed the money."

"Yes, I do." Henry followed his uncle out into the yard, thus avoiding more questions. His uncle, up to this point, had been a shadowy figure. Shadowy in personality, that is, but corporeally substantial with a heavy red face, thick-set shoulders and enormous feet. The feet had been part of Henry's consciousness from an early age—or at least the gumboots that clad them. They stood, from nine in the evening till six in the morning, as twin sentinels at the door of the house. The mud never dried on them, even in the hottest summer, with the result that they emitted a threatening odor. Henry's first act on arrival in Ireland was to buy a similar pair. He stood them, in all their hygienic newness, beside his uncle's, a token of his willingness to get his feet dirty.

It did not take long. Henry rose in the dark, left the house with his uncle and escorted the sleepy cows from fields to milking shed. There were many, many cows marked black and white, moving like spotted ghosts through the dawn. Henry trudged, listening to the suction of hooves leaving mud. The first morning it didn't rain and the sun even rose, like a pale sliver of melon off a green plate. Everything was green-tinged, even the mud. On the second morning it rained. And on the third and the fourth too. Water filled the hoofprints as soon as a hoof lifted. Slurry ran across the yard like the underwave of a shiny sea. When Henry and his uncle came in for breakfast, their clothes steamed odorously. Their boots were indistinguishable. After a week Aunt Anna, who found that an extra hand released her for more hunting, said with satisfaction, "So you do mean to work here a while?"

"Yes," replied Henry simply. His mouth was full of bacon on fried soda bread. Butter dribbled to the corners of his mouth. The two hours' work before breakfast gave him an appetite which he suspected was akin to a sexual experience.

On his second Saturday Aunt Anna, exhilarated by a good run, announced, "There's a dance tonight in Castleloon." This was the nearest small town. "Johnny says he'd lend you the car." Lionel had written a brotherly letter suggesting his son was having a nervous breakdown. Anna was not insulted by the idea that only a nervous breakdown would explain Henry's decision to live on an Irish farm. If it hadn't been for the joy of hunting she could never have borne living there either.

Henry did not want to meet "young people," which possibly constituted a nervous breakdown. If he had wanted that sort of thing he could have stayed with school friends in London and gone to dances. He had been invited to several. Stiff white invitations doggedly followed him round the world. One had arrived that morning.

That Saturday evening the stars and moon were so bright and low in the sky that Henry spurned the car and dug out his aunt's bicycle from the shed. He pedaled along the rough tarmac road with a buzzing feeling in his chest. He rode with his head up high and he felt starlight and moonlight brushing his face. There were no other cars on the road until he reached the town. But he caught up and overtook a couple of bicyclists going the same way. At these moments he crouched forward and pedaled like mad so that the wind roared past his ears.

It was disappointing to reach Castleloon. Nor could he fail to find the town hall, since it was rocking with noise and lit up by light bulbs strung across its white pebble-dash walls. He was tempted to bicycle past and shoot out the other side of the town, but he thought, suddenly, This is a foreign country, and he felt the excitement of curiosity. He braked and leaped off the bike.

The entrance to the hall was obscured by twenty or more youths wearing dark, ill-fitting suits and white shirts. They leaned against the walls, not saying much, watching as the girls passed through in clusters of three or four. They wore very high pointed shoes under coats that looked as if they belonged to their mothers.

Henry left his bike with several others and made his way through the crowd. He realized he stood out, with his smooth face and cavalry twill, but the exhilaration of his ride stayed with him, giving him a swaggering devil-may-care attitude. Inside the hall he was temporarily nonplussed to see the sexes divided against either wall. Frankly, he felt more in common with the girls, now revealed in tight sweaters and straight skirts, their pale skin and pink cheeks infinitely appealing under the bright lights.

A band sat on the dais and below them was a trestle table set with soft drinks. Seeing this as neutral ground, he made his way toward it. He found himself standing beside a girl. She was very thin, with long red curly hair and huge purple eyes. She wore an emerald-green angora sweater, which may not have been in good taste but certainly made a dramatic effect with her coloring. She tottered slightly as she stood, which Henry put down to her matchlike legs balanced on stiletto shoes.

"You're English, aren't you?" The glorious creature had not spoken. The words came from her friend, a previously unnoticed bundle of sweaters.

"You can tell so easily, can you?"

The friend giggled and nudged the girl, causing the purple orbs to swivel in his direction. The music started with a glaring clash of cymbals, which then settled down to a loud thumping beat. Conversation became impossible. The girl offered Henry a drink. He took a gulp. It was very sweet.

He put it down and shouted, "Do you want to dance?"

She looked at her friend, face expressionless, and then looked at Henry's feet. Henry looked, too. His trousers were still stuffed into his socks. He bent down and pulled them out. The friend giggled.

A bloodless hand, with bitten nails and a few freckles, was laid on his arm. Henry took her onto the floor. All the other dancing couples were girls. She danced stiffly, with the same fixed expression she'd preserved from the beginning. He shouted in her ear, "What's your name?" She recoiled slighly but her red mouth pursed.

"Mary Ann," she whispered, setting each word in its own space.

Henry swirled her about enthusiastically, causing her face to clench convulsively.

"I can't."

"What?" bellowed Henry.

"It's my shoes. I can't gallivant round like that."

Henry stopped abruptly. She swayed like a giraffe on stilts.

"Why do you wear them?"

"Oh!" It was a cruel question. All the girls wore them. Henry put his arm round her. Her shoulders were like a game of pick-up-sticks under the soft angora.

"We can't just stand here in the middle of the dance floor."

"Sorry. Sorry, Mary Ann." He began to jog up and down again in a way she seemed to find acceptable. The hall had grown warmer and soon he saw her cheeks brighten rosily and her mouth part to pant. This show of mortality encouraged him to his usual practice of imagining desirable females naked. In her case this was not easy. The fragility and pallor of her form would not take physical shape. Breasts would sprout less easily under the mohair than wings.

This failure did not diminish his ardor. "Catch a falling star." Henry began to hum a popular song. At this point the music stopped. Mary Ann stepped back and pushed away her red curls in a self-conscious gesture.

"Would you like a drink?" Henry led her to the table. She immediately returned to her friend, linking arms, although keeping her head tilted toward Henry as if acknowledging his continuing right over her. He found them both drinks and looked round the hall.

The boys from outside had now come in, distinguishable by their glowing faces and alcohol-bright eyes. They stayed in a bunch, still leaning whenever possible but talking more in bursts and flurries. They reminded Henry of a herd of young bullocks newly turned out into a field.

"Where are you staying then?"

It was the friend. "I'm working on my uncle's farm. John Jamieson."

"You don't look like a farmhand."

"What do I look like?" Henry would have preferred to carry on this slightly flirtatious conversation with Mary Ann but the friend seemed to be the established mouthpiece. Now both girls giggled.

"Go on. Tell me what I look like."

"Mary Ann thinks you look like an Italian film star."

"Oh, well." Henry found to his surprise he was blushing. He felt inordinately puffed by the silly compliment. The room seemed hotter, brighter than ever. Suddenly he longed to be back on his bicycle, out in the dark and cold, carrying with him the image of Mary Ann and "an Italian film star." He took a step closer to her.

"I've got to go."

Her eyes blazed. "They're going to do the spot waltz." Sure enough, the band struck up and a color spotlight was switched on from the ceiling. The young bullocks moved toward a group of girls.

"You can't dance." Henry looked at her shoes.

"I'll take them off."

The friend giggled. But Henry wanted to go. He scrabbled in his pocket for a piece of paper and pencil. He wrote down his name and address. He gave it to Mary Ann. "That's where I am," he said.

"You're not really going, are you?" The friend sounded aggrieved.

"Come and see me." Henry strode back across the floor. Every now and again the spotlight struck across his head or face, turning him pink or blue or yellow. When he got outside, he heaved a huge sigh of relief. He snatched his bicycle from the wall. He could hear the spot waltz pulsing on the other side. He set off, ready to fly like the wind. Unfortunately someone had let the air out of the tires. He had no pump.

Owing to his early departure from the dance, Henry returned at just the time Aunt Anna expected him.

It was several weeks before Mary Ann and her friend visited Henry. Being farm-bred girls, they chose the moment just before milking, when the men came in for a cup of tea and a bun. It was a clear, sharp day and their noses were red from the journey. They also had come on bicycles. Anna saw their faces peering at the kitchen window.

"Does a Henry Hayes-Middleton live here?" They giggled.

Henry went out to them. Mary Ann had filled his dreams. She wore a huge rough sweater and a tight skirt, with her terrifying orange legs fully displayed.

"However did you bicycle dressed like that!"

"You just keep your knees tight together." The friend laughed.

Henry blushed. "Are you coming in?"

"We just came for the ride really." This was Mary Ann speaking.

"We haven't got any lights."

They all looked up at the sky. The sun had already gone down, spreading a golden wash to the west.

"I'm off tomorrow. I could come into town. My uncle might lend me the car."

They arranged to meet at a monument of Parnell at two o'clock.

That night Henry slept in the knowledge of his first date with a girl.

It took Henry four dates with Mary Ann before her friend had another engagement. On that fifth date he kissed her, finding her mouth delicate and hard-edged like an oyster shell. This lasted him through three more dates. Since they only met once a week on Saturday afternoons, it could not be said that their romance rushed along with hasty ardor. They spent hours talking, and Henry's main interest continued to center on her body. He was romantic about her when stuck in the ruts of his uncle's farm, but her physical presence inspired only lust. He kissed her between conversation, forcing his tongue masterfully through her lips. He had felt small breast-like protuberances under her sweater. He looked forward to the warm weather when they would be more accessible. She had never said no to any of his explorations, which gave him hope for an exciting future.

On April 1 they propped bicycles against a hedge and climbed over the gate to a soft grassy field. Henry had brought his mackintosh for them to lie on. He also had a contraceptive in the top pocket of his jacket. As a longtime symbol of manliness, it was dog-eared on the outside.

The affair opened well. Their kissing was now nicely attuned with hand under the sweater for chorus and hand under skirt for thrilling solo. This hand was normally removed by Mary Ann after a few seconds, and they would revert to kissing. Today Henry pressed his case. The complications seemed endless, but eventually her blue eyes were swimming under him and, relatively tidily encased, he plunged himself into her. Such was the work and concentration involved that he could hardly be said to have enjoyed himself. But he did feel a freedom, a lifting of the spirit.

She seemed to feel the same, for she sighed heavily and then sighed again. Her eyes were open and wet at the corners. As if orchestrated, they rolled away from each other and drew their clothes tidily together. Henry became aware of the vast sky above their heads, with clouds bunched and watching like fat giants. He wished he could sing a song at them or make a boast.

Mary Ann said, "Do you love me?"

Love had never been mentioned between them. There was no doubt in Henry's mind that he did not love her. He felt too gentle to hurt her but unwilling to lie.

"I don't know about love. Look at the sky. Just look at the sky."

"Oh." Now she looked at the sky. "I ought to go."

Henry wondered halfheartedly if she were unhappy. They were both so serious. He could feel his face stiff enough to crack. He took her hand. He tried to think of something to say. "Thank you, Mary Ann."

She got up slowly and walked toward the gate. Henry felt unable to move. As she climbed over the gate he called, "See you next Saturday." She raised a hand and disappeared.

Henry lay on the mac for so long that the damp penetrated from the ground below and the clouds above descended in evening darkness.

Chapter 9

Henry's love affair (if that is the right term) continued through the springtime. Structured into Saturday afternoons, it simmered rather than raged. Sexual contact was not always total and, although the ground grew drier under the mac, they spent less time lounging than bicycling. Despite Mary Ann's fleshless form, she was strong and athletic. Sometimes they visited villages ten or fifteen miles away. Henry liked to look at the churches there and Mary Ann liked to look at him looking. Usually she brought a thermos and sandwiches, which they ate on a tombstone.

Toward the end of May the sun shone bright and hot for several days. They decided to set off early and go to the sea. The hedgerows were still decorated with spring flowers, the leaves on the trees still freshly green. But overhead the sky was blue enough for summer. They reached the coast at a grassy headland where a wall and some stones indicated the remains of a small chapel. A hedge of wild fuchsia grew above their heads. In front, the sea stretched in a calm shimmer of blue.

They both sat down. Mary Ann began to unpack their lunch. Henry opened a bottle of Guinness.

"I'll have to leave next month."

Mary Ann became rigid. Her hands curved like white claws in front of her.

"I'll have been here six months and I've got to prepare for university and see my parents. I'll have to go to Madrid. Next month."

Mary Ann had a piece of sandwich in her mouth. Henry watched as she swallowed it with difficulty.

"Toward the end of the month," he added.

"Yes," she said.

Henry saw the horror of it. The sun seemed frilled with black. He dared not say more. He walked to the edge of the headland and looked down. There was a small beach not far below. Smooth rocks led out into the sea. He waved his Guinness bottle.

"I'll have a quick swim before lunch."

He climbed down, holding on to the tufty grass with one hand and the bottle with the other. Soon he was at the bottom, standing on a thin rim of crusty sand right under the bank. It was very hot and secret. He felt cut off from the world above where Mary Ann sat with her picnic and misery.

He sat down and swigged at the bottle. She had never seemed real enough for him to imagine her suffering. Nor did he count himself sufficiently important to cause it.

The bottle finished, he lay back. He would swim in a second. It was then his hands felt the sand and brought up something else. He held a handful in front of his face—the whole beach was made of tiny shells. Pink, pearl, lilac, terracotta, lemon, silver, lavender. Every one a different color, every one a different shape. Little furled rosebuds, curled horns, miniature saucers. He let them run through his fingers. It felt like a miracle.

But instead of wanting to share it, shout, Hey, Mary Ann, look what I've found!, he felt a selfish compulsion to enjoy it all on his own. It was his miracle, created for him, perhaps even by him. The day had been made memorable. The elegant romance of Mary Ann (whose mouth had tasted like oyster) merged into his bed of shells. In front of him rose the endless vista of sea.

Henry reached Oxford in 1959. This put him slightly ahead of the years of youth supremacy. Undergraduates still looked like juvenile versions of their parents.

Henry wore a tweed jacket with leather patches and cavalry twill trousers. He thought he looked very English. In fact, there was something foreign in his appearance. It was not just his elegant tan leather shoes bought in Madrid, nor his olive skin darkened by the Spanish sun. It was more the expression of his face, which was static and yet seemed to threaten sudden change. His voice, too, was quick with the public school accents tinged with something stranger. He had a way of being silent for long periods, which was disconcerting in one so clever. Other graduates were unsure whether to like him. Those who had been at the same school said, "Hayes-Middleton seems to have gone more off-beam."

During the first week he visited, in company with the rest of the university, the hall where every club and society lays out its wares. Henry marched stolidly past Rugger and Football and then signed for the Rowing Club, which he'd never tried. When he reached the political societies he found Wiggins, vociferous at the Labour Club. To his friend's surprise, he joined with a smile. He then moved down the line and joined the Conservative Club.

"Hey, you can't do that!" Wiggins came from behind his stand.

"Why ever not?" Henry put away his membership cards cheerfully. "I might join the Communist Club, too." Actually he had no intention of doing this, realizing it would blot his record for the Foreign Office.

"You're not serious," said Wiggins fiercely. He had been feeling important at the Labour Club, already on the road to a political career.

"Yes, I am. I want to know about both parties. Then I can make up my mind how to vote." He looked at Wiggins. "I'm not born into one camp like you."

"Yes, you are." Wiggins sulkily started moving back to his stand. "You're pure Conservative."

"Nonsense!" cried Henry with his irritating good humor. "I'm absolutely open to offers."

After this exchange he went back to his grand scholarship room in his grand college and arranged the club cards on the mantelpiece like invitations.

It was dark outside but the curtains were too ugly to draw. Henry sat down in the large comfortable armchair. He looked round his room. He had already arranged his possessions, mainly books. He did have one picture his mother had given him. It was a reproduction of a Madonna and Child. He could not place it, though it seemed somewhat in the style of Bellini.

Beatrice had come to him one night in Madrid. He had been reading in bed, waiting for the air to cool. She had worn a long robe from which something bulky protruded. Her face, so pale under the dark hair, had worn the look of mystery which indicated high good humor. She had swished toward him like an angel of the night.

"Whatever have you got there?" Henry had sat up, glad of the diversion. He had been reading Lawrence Durrell, which he found unconvincing.

Beatrice had not answered at once. She had sat down on the edge of the bed. She fixed her black eyes on a spot above his head. "Do you remember what I told you about your religion?"

"Yes," said Henry, because "no" seemed too harsh a word in the quiet. Besides, he did have some recollection linked to London and picnics in the sky.

"Then you will know why I have brought you this present to take with you to university."

Henry waited but she seemed unwilling to unveil her secret. Perhaps she wanted more encouragement from him. He said, "You baptized me a Catholic."

Beatrice smiled approvingly. Slowly she drew the picture out from her robe. She held it up for Henry to see. It was much bigger than he expected: the golden and blue shone in the dim room like an apparition. Beatrice propped it against his headboard. "I had it specially framed for you."

"It's beautiful," said Henry.

"You spent so much time in that gallery. This can be a remembrance for you."

Henry looked at his mother. This rational explanation was at odds with her earlier introduction. Perhaps even she had some misgivings about the reception to her gift.

"It's very beautiful," repeated Henry. The eyes of the Madonna were staring at him now. They had a watchful, waiting expression.

"Your father has something for you, too." She gave Henry a sly look. "It's a globe. Very beautiful, too. Over a hundred years old, with all the countries of the world in bas-relief. It has its own stand in carved rosewood." She sounded like a saleswoman but now her expression was frankly mischievous.

Henry thought, So father's giving me the world and you're giving me the heavens. But he didn't give her the satisfaction of saying it. He sat up straighter. "I shall hang your picture on my wall at college," he said with more vigor than he'd shown so far. "Thank you very much." He held out his cheek, expecting a maternal kiss. But instead she rose and draped Henry's coverlet over the picture. That done, she turned back to her son. "Here we must hide, not hang." And out of the room she swept.

Henry, left alone with his secret like a ghost at the end of his bed, switched off his light and resorted to sleep. Occasionally he wondered whether his mother was mad in a clinical sense but on the whole he considered it excessive romanticism. Her life, attached to his father's coattails, was too constrained, her imagination too vivid.

The next day he unveiled the painting. It seemed even more brilliant in the morning light. Honoring his mother, he took it to his cupboard and stuck it behind his coats. This gave him a pang. It seemed sacrilegious and was certainly unnecessary.

Now, in Oxford, it held sway on a bare expanse of beige wall. It looked distinctly out of place. His father's globe, on the other hand, looked exactly right. It might have come with the room. Its rosewood stand matched the wood paneling. It was coated with an oily patina of age just as the ceiling and walls were.

"What a fine globe!" Henry had not heard anyone enter. It was the tall, fair Julian Oats. He had an attractive supercilious air and a faint lisp. "Are you coming to Hall?"

Henry rose out of his chair. "What do you think of the painting my mother gave me?"

"Painting? Oh, you mean this. Don't go in for repro myself." He went closer to the picture. "Although I must say it's good quality. Where did she get it?"

"Spain."

"Hmm. Now, if you'd said Italy."

They went out of the room together. Down the stone steps. Henry was struck by Julian's assessment of the picture not including the subject matter. As they crossed the quad he said casually, "Do you have any particular religious belief?"

He caught Julian's fixed look and found himself blushing. He mumbled, "You know, that picture."

"You're not Catholic, are you?"

"Oh, no!" Henry defended himself hastily. "I'm nothing, like everyone else."

They reached the hall and without further words took their place in the queue for food.

When they sat down they discussed the organization of a Classics Society. Julian suggested its name should be "Gods and Other Mortals." Henry agreed enthusiastically.

During the second part of the term, Henry had a letter from Mary Ann. He couldn't think who she was when he first opened the letter. Then the memories came back, smelling of grass and sea and damp. Although he never thought of her and had no wish to see her again, he did not feel threatened by her writing. He was, however, surprised that she had found his address. But in their relationship she had been the organizer, making picnics, deciding on times. She had always been better at map reading than he.

The letter was not very long.

Dearest Henry,

I hope you don't mind me writing. It's so dull here without you. And it's already such a long time since you left. Now there's winter coming in again with the rain and dark evenings. We went right through it, didn't we, last year, and came out the other end into summer and sunshine. I think of our afternoons together. If you ever get a moment write to me.

All my love,

Mary Ann

I am thinking that I might come to England sometime.

Since the last line was scribbled in small letters, Henry didn't see it at once. He was pleased by the tone of the letter, even considered answering. He showed the letter to Julian.

Julian was impressed by its air of civilized romanticism. He gave Henry an admiring look. "What a lucky fellow!"

"Read the last line."

He did so. "That's a bit of a drag."

"I don't know how she got my address."

"Love conquers all."

"It wasn't like that."

"Oh, really." Julian reverted to his more usual, gently knowing manner. "Why is she coming to England then?"

"That's true."

Julian leaned forward and gave the globe a spin.

"Hold on! That's a valuable antique."

"I think you'll have to write a cruel letter, saying you're working too hard for any visitors."

"I don't want to be cruel. It was a dream. Perfect in its way."

"It wasn't a dream to her."

"How do you know?"

"Women aren't like that."

"My mother is." Both men raised their eyes involuntarily to the Madonna and Child above their heads.

"You don't think your girl's . . . ?" The baby stared calmly down at them.

"No." Henry was firm. "I'm no fool."

"I just thought being Irish Catholic and everything."

"No," repeated Henry.

There was silence for a moment. Then Julian started again. "In my view, if you don't write that cruel letter, you'll have her on your doorstep and then you'll be in a fix. That's my last word on the subject."

So Henry wrote the letter. It took him a whole evening and was very long and elaborate. In the middle he even put a Latin quotation. Nevertheless the message was plain. He heard no more.

There were girls, of course, at the university. Henry discovered that his relationship with Mary Ann put him ahead of most of his contemporaries in sexual experience. He developed a reputation for being a bit of a ladykiller. This was due to Julian, who got drunk and became talkative. Naturally in his version Mary Ann was pregnant.

Henry did not know about this until one evening at a bottle party an unknown girl came up to him. "I hear you've won the prize for first Oxford father." Jeans had not yet become fashionable. She wore black drainpipe trousers. Her face was made up to be absolutely white à la Juliette Greco and her bright eyes were surrounded by black pencil.

Henry, who had drunk a bottle or two, became angry. He threw Julian downstairs (Julian was too drunk to care) and shouted, "I'm a misogonist, don't you understand? A MISOGYNIST!"

A few days later the Oxford Film Society asked him to play Heathcliffe in a modern version of *Wuthering Heights.*

"I don't even belong to the Society," he objected.

But they wouldn't let him off till he'd shouted again—at another white-faced girl. This one wore black Wellington boots and had an extraordinary mass of yellow hair. Despite his resolution to be a misogonist, he regretted his rudeness and sent her a note.

I'm sorry I shouted at you. Please come and have tea.

That same day he received a telegram from his parents.

Aunt Anna died. Coming home for funeral.

Father

Henry's first thought should have been for his aunt, who had been kind to him over so many years, or indeed for his uncle, whose gumboots would stand outside an unwarmed hearth. But he had had no experience of death and therefore could not suffer for them.

Henry's room was decorated with three vases of purple chrysanthemums in honor of the second girl he'd shouted at who was coming to tea. By four-thirty it was dark. Henry lit two black candles standing on the mantelpiece. He'd borrowed them from Julian. He thought the effect, combined with the flowers, nicely theatrical. They also made the Virgin's eyes gleam.

There were steps up his staircase and a knocking at the door. Henry bounded to the door, showing in the moment of excitement more of an athlete's energy than an aesthete's languor.

Mr. and Mrs. Hayes-Middleton came into the room.

Beatrice, dressed in a luxuriant black fur coat, stopped after one step. "Darling," she breathed. "How wonderful! I never guessed." Her eyes, having taken in the general effect, now focused on her picture. "I'm so glad," she finished dreamily.

Lionel, looking tired, came further into the room. "You got my telegram, I hope, old boy." He did not seem to notice anything special about the room.

There was another knock. Henry, who was still near the door, opened it gingerly. A girl's pale face peered round for a second. "I'm so sorry." It removed itself hastily.

Henry opened the door wider. There was no reason to be ashamed of his parents. Her obvious nervousness had alleviated his. "This is the right room."

She was already in flight down the stairs. Her wonderful hair floated, billowing like a cape. He called, "Flavia!" He had never pronounced her name before. She turned. "It's me. Henry. Those are my parents arrived unexpectedly."

She returned and allowed herself to be escorted back into the room. His parents were now seated but Lionel half rose for the girl.

"This is Flavia," said Henry, "who is coming to tea."

"What a lovely idea!" cried Beatrice with the air of a child at a party.

"Tea. Excellent."

"They've traveled from Spain," Henry explained to Flavia.

She sat on the edge of a table, swinging her legs and turning her hands over and over in her lap. Round her neck she wore a long scarf, which hung down between her Wellington boots. Beatrice watched her with a half smile. Henry scurried about making tea and Lionel shut his eyes as if going to sleep. No one said anything until Henry had brought the tray to the center of the room. The sight of the teapot revived Lionel. He said, "We're booked on a flight to Ireland tomorrow morning." Flavia got off the table.

Flavia was a strange mixture. Her flamboyant yellow hair, which had attracted Henry, as it did many other young men, was the least typical thing about her. Her nature suited dark, secret colors. She liked most of all to watch, invisible, or at very least anonymous. Sometimes she thought of cutting her hair very short. But she had been told so often by her parents that it was her pride and glory that she didn't dare. Besides, such absence of hair would draw attention to her face, which was not prepossessing. It was slightly pudgy, unlike the rest of her very thin body, and the features were small. The eyes were a good dark blue, certainly, but she herself preferred brown. Flavia had a love-hate relationship with her appearance which sometimes took up more time than Beowulf or Spenser. She was reading English.

"That's a beautiful fur coat." She leaned forward to touch it lightly.

"Lionel presented it to me for my birthday." Beatrice gave the sort of proud mysterious look which only she could carry off. She was, indeed, as contented as she looked. Henry seemed at this moment more her creation than she had ever thought possible. He was grown-up, too, separate in a way that lessened her anxieties. She enjoyed the admiration of the thin girl with the dazzling hair.

"Your aunt died out hunting, you know." Beatrice looked at Henry. "A low branch swept her to the ground."

"The best hunt of the season," said Lionel heavily. He was distressed by his sister's sudden death. Death was not a subject that naturally preoccupied him. But Beatrice's attempted suicide had brushed him with black thoughts and now this sister, whose attitude had been so like his own, was carried off with such shocking swiftness. It battered his confidence.

"I expect she'd have liked to go like that," Henry commented, not meaning to be callous.

"People are always being killed riding," said Flavia.

Henry looked at her curiously. He had not connected her with horses.

"My parents are country doctors," she explained nervously.

"Terrible injuries," said Lionel, "broken necks, broken backs, internal organs wrenched, external abrasions . . ." His voice faded.

"She was killed outright." Beatrice's voice, almost gay, penetrated his increasing gloom. He did not condemn her lack of sorrow. Although not given to introspection, he understood that her nature faced death every day. She was not to be horrified by its outward appearance.

Now she leaned forward to Flavia. "What subject are you studying here?"

"English." Flavia's eyes flickered to Henry. Did he, with the superior brain of a classicist, despise those who chose to play among the human emotions? The answer, in fact, was that he did. On the other hand, he'd have been surprised and even worried if she'd said anything else.

"My father works for the Foreign Office." Henry looked at Flavia but could get no further than the yellow hair. It was like a spotlight, moving with her wherever she went and yet, instead of highlighting her, it seemed a disguise. If only he could have her all to himself! He felt a sudden despair over this unplanned foursome, saw it stretching out endlessly into the evening. At the same time he imagined pulling off Flavia's Wellington boots and slipping down her black trousers.

"We're staying here in a hotel," said Beatrice. "We thought we'd give you a first-rate dinner." Her glance included Flavia. "Perhaps . . . ?"

"I have to be in at ten," said Flavia, who was beginning to feel overwhelmed.

"Come to the Mitre about eight." Lionel rose to his feet. He was impressive in the room, tall, broad-shouldered, with bleached hair and sunburnt face. Like his son, his Englishness, so convincing in Spain, looked foreign here.

Flavia appeared to be leaving with Beatrice and Lionel, so Henry held her arm. She turned away from him, as if, he thought, in distaste at his touch. In fact, he was gripping her so tightly that she was hiding an expression of pain.

"I must go."

Henry capitulated. "I'll walk with you." They walked silently through the wintry streets. Some of the shop windows already displayed Christmas decorations. They stopped in front of one and Henry saw Flavia was trembling with cold. "Here, have my jacket."

She said nothing but allowed him to drape it across her back. It cut across her hair, giving her a short pudding-basin bob. Her face was illuminated by the shop window. It was pale, the eyes like little raisins in a pale biscuit. Henry felt a tremendous surge of protective affection.

But then she pulled out her glittering net of hair and cast it round her. She walked on with a surprisingly speedy gait.

"Do come to dinner," Henry said when they reached the gates of her college.

Flavia wanted to say, "But I hardly know you." She substituted, "They'll want to be alone with you."

"Oh, no!" Henry seemed shocked at the idea.

"I'll come if I can." The words blew round him like a mist.

Chapter 10

Lionel rose early. He revisited his old college and walked along the river. He walked briskly like a soldier. Strangely, it restored his confidence in the future. He had traveled so far already, and the very next step was Ambassador in Her Majesty's Service. He bought all the newspapers, including the *New York Herald Tribune,* and took them back to the hotel. He read them over a very large breakfast. Outside in the foyer the cleaner roared her vacuum over unwelcome footprints. He had noticed her as he came in, a pretty girl with wispy fair hair and flushed cheeks. No, Lionel thought, he was not so far along the road to death.

"Cuba's Batista Flees; Revolutionary Forces Under Fidel Castro Seize Power." That was worth reading. He made a mental note to follow up the piece with more information. He was not off duty, merely on compassionate leave. What a support are the structures of a career!

On the airplane Lionel read a report on agricultural tariffs between proposed members of a European community. He gave disapproving snorts at intervals. Henry read Sallust. He'd written a splendid essay on the Catiline conspiracy. Unfortunately, he'd now miss the tutorial at which he was to read it. Beatrice watched the clouds massing over Ireland.

"Of course," said Lionel, "our family has not been much touched by death."

He said this in the Irish farmhouse, usually so mournful, now, in mourning, so filled with people.

"The family," repeated Lionel, as if he liked the sound of the word. Indeed it was an extraordinary concept to a man who had spent all his life on pinpoints of the globe. He stood leaning slightly backward, one arm resting against the mantelpiece, the other resting on his bereaved brother-in-law's shoulder. The latter wore a dazed, good-humored expression. His open, weather-beaten face was not suited to tragedy.

Henry crashed through the house till he reached the back door. There his feet became entangled in something yielding yet inescapable and he fell heavily to the ground. By the light coming down the back passage, he saw his assailants silhouetted. They were his uncle's gumboots, the mud as thick as ever, the odor, as he lay nose to heel, as pungent. Henry felt a tortuous progress within his body. It was as if he were trying to give birth to a stone through his mouth. His chest heaved, his head throbbed, his nose swelled, he kicked the ground with his feet.

A small sob escaped into the damp night air. Despite the noise of his fall and his battering feet, this little bleat struck Henry like a gong. He was silent for a moment and then he gave another and another. He rose to his feet and walked off into the darkness. His sobs jerked around him, still painful but gaining fluency with the motion of walking. He had no memory of ever crying before.

He did not cry just for Aunt Anna or Uncle Johnny or even Johnny's gumboots—so alone, so desolate on the threshold of a hearth made of ashes. He cried for himself as a little boy in a boarding school. He cried for the lead cars he'd lost without looking for them. He cried for his mother being carried out on a stretcher in Egypt, for the young Belinda jumping through the surf, for Mary Ann, who meant nothing to him, for the Madonna and Child who sat on a beige wall in, quite honestly, a not very good reproduction. He cried for Salmon because he was so stupid, for his tutor who had a stutter, for Julian who wasn't quite a man, for Flavia's thin trembling body. He cried for the Spanish Civil War, which had knocked corners off his favorite churches, for England, which had been so humiliated in the matter of the Suez Canal. . . . There was nothing too great or too small, too public or too personal, that didn't seem a subject for tears. In fact, about the only thing, or rather person, he didn't cry about as he strode backward and forward over the wet grass was his father. He seemed strong, outside such uncontrolled wells of despair. His father had a vision of the world, in which Britain and British interests sat at the center.

Henry shuddered like an animal sloughing off sleep. His sobs and steps decreased in unison. He felt himself surrounded by the huge darkness of the sky. It was not as cold as it had been in

England. He crossed his arms over his chest and turned his face upward. A few remaining tears slid down his ears. Although they tickled, he did not wipe them away, for they seemed brave badges for what he had experienced. Already the ghosts of tragedy were becoming pale. His body, which had been so racked, was comfortable again; the bands about his head loosened, leaving it particularly light and airy, like the sky above. His eyes seemed wider open than they had ever been and he felt as if he could see into the darkness for hundreds of miles.

He stood still, savoring this unusual sensation, allowing the frantic minutes before to fade.

Then a new feeling spread from his feet upward. It was a warm exhaustion, turning his limbs into putty, finally reaching his face and half closing his too-wide eyes. He felt as if he might sink into the ground and be there in a stupor all night long. However, with exhaustion came a simple common sense which presented pictures of warm beds and four walls. Stumbling slightly, he made his way back to the house. The gumboots, splayed wide in trollop fashion, caused him no confusion. He stepped over them cleanly and proceeded to his bedroom.

After such a soulful experience, the funeral which followed the next day was certain to be an anticlimax. Nor did any hedge or tombstone disgorge Mary Ann.

Mary Ann was, in fact, in England. She and her fat friend, whose name was Gail, had both come to London. They were working as maids in a small hotel near Paddington. All morning they put top sheets on the bottom and bottom sheets on top. Oh, to work in the sort of hotel where they bundled all sheets straight off the bed out of the room!

"Putrid!" shouted Gail. "Putrid dump!"

Mary Ann gave a serene smile. She was not ambitious to make things happen like her friend. But she didn't need to be. Things happened to her anyway. Look at Henry.

"Aren't you going to look up Henry ever?" Gail had this disconcerting habit of reading her friend's thoughts.

"Maybe." Mary Ann's face became dreamy in a way that particularly irritated Gail. "Maybe not.

"He didn't reply to my letter."

Mary Ann left the bedroom hurriedly.

Gail chased after her with a rat-like expression. She was glad to have caused a show of emotion. "You love him, don't you?"

Mary Ann unlocked the door to the next bedroom. She wished

she was more educated so she could answer Gail on an exalted level. What was it, Henry had said, when she'd asked him if he loved her? Something about the sky. He'd told her to look up at it. Stars and eternity, thought Mary Ann. "Virgin Mother, Star of the Sea."

"What?" Gail came up behind her. "Oh, Christ!" She stared into the room. Both beds had been completely stripped. Blankets, towels and sheets wound together across the floor.

"Oh, Christ!" repeated Gail with more emphasis.

"It makes it so hard to tell the top from the bottom sheet." Mary Ann was relieved at the diversion.

"It was those men." Gail picked up a corner of a towel between two fingers. "Disgusting pigs."

"No, it wasn't." Mary Ann kicked gently at the pile. She thought a little smugly that Gail's particular anger at evidence of sexual fun and games was due to her continuing virginity.

Henry stood in a queue for the Classic Cinema. *Smiles of a Summer Night* was showing. It was dark, raining slightly. A poster declared: *Unstintingly Hedonistic.* He was by himself. Suddenly to his right, he saw a flare of light. It was Flavia, approaching along the pavement with her usual undulating speed.

"Flavia!" She shook her head like a pony. "It's me, Henry."

She stopped with a look of surprise. Her eyes flickered down and up again. "Hello."

They had not met since he had returned from Ireland. "I'm queuing," said Henry. "In the rain. Why don't you join me?"

"I've seen the film." Flavia still wore her surprised look.

"Any good?"

"Very good."

"Why don't you come again?"

"I don't know."

"How's your film going?"

"We've run out of money." She took a step nearer and smiled. "I was left in a bath with no clothes on."

"Oh."

They both stared at each other. Flavia's original surprise was due to the very large gumboots Henry was wearing. They were his Irish pair, hallowed by emotion. But to Flavia they presented a contradiction to her estimate of his character. She thought of him as stiff, formal, conservative and very clever. She liked him as a kind of black-tie antidote to the swagger and bluster of most of her friends. Such a man did not wear gumboots except in the country.

"The queue's moving." Henry took her arm.

Flavia remembered his reputation as a womanizer, which had become displaced under his correctness. She floundered. "I should go." His grip on her arm was strong. The line advanced toward the box office. Suddenly they were under bright lights, still together.

Flavia, who was not without will, felt herself in Henry's power. They entered the cinema.

Henry was suffering an acute case of lust. He could see her naked body in the bath, hair spread like the Little Mermaid. He imagined her breasts much as he'd seen her eyes and face on their last evening together—dark raisins in pale biscuits. He wanted to put his mouth to their hard roundness. Their sweet roundness. His grip on Flavia's arm became fiercer.

"Ow!"

"Sorry." He released her arm and they settled into their seats. "Thank for you coming."

"I don't know why I did." She gave him a tentatively flirtatious smile.

"You can always sleep." He too smiled. His lust subsided somewhat. The problem with open-air sexual encounters such as he had had with Mary Ann was that he never really got a proper look at the uncovered body. Or not in a country with a climate like Ireland, anyway. The imagination became overstimulated, overoptimistic, very probably, about what lay under the covering. Flavia in a bath was quite likely a pallid affair, too much bone and not enough padding. Her little face gave a clue to all that. His lust subsided further.

"I wasn't really naked in the bath," whispered Flavia. "I wore a pink body stocking. The color of bubblegum. I looked revolting."

Flavia, the daughter of two doctors, was a strange mixture of the practical and the romantic. Her parents had been disappointed by her concentration in English.

"But you've got such a good mind, dear," regretted her mother.

"You make it sound like something in a bottle."

She was an only child but she had a great many first cousins, with whom she spent much of her childhood. They were large and fearless and never bothered with exams. Two of the girls, whose hair was nearly as yellow as Flavia's, were already married and one had a large baby. Flavia felt ethereal in their presence. She felt her whole life lacked conviction. And yet she knew they thought her immensely strong and daring to strike the portals of Oxford. Sometimes she imagined crawling into bed and staying there for a very long time. At Oxford she had many friends but none of them were close. At night she read *Woman's Own,* followed by Spenser's *The Faerie Queene.* She enjoyed both enormously. She had tried sex because the daughter of two doctors was not afraid of that sort of thing but had found the experience unsatisfactory. The performing male had bruised her upper arm quite badly and when she'd pointed it out he'd laughed proudly. She'd decided the next time would have to wait on love. She'd never been in love. She worried that this was a serious character deficiency, suggesting coldness of heart.

Henry slept ten hours most nights, which gave him plenty of time to dream. In one of these dreams he was cast back to childhood, playing with lead cars in a large half-furnished house. The next morning he decided to pay a visit to London. He waylaid Flavia, flying along to a lecture.

She was breathless, late. He always seemed to catch her unprepared so that she couldn't think clearly. It flashed across her mind that perhaps this was love.

"We'll take the ten-fifteen train." Henry looked at his watch. "We have ten minutes." He was dressed in one of his Spanish tailored suits. It made him look older, commanding.

Flavia stuffed her gown into her shoulder bag. She was wearing a tight red knitted dress underneath. This was freedom.

"Haven't you got a coat?" Henry looked at her doubtfully. She was so brilliant.

"This dress is very warm." She gave a long involuntary shiver. She looked up at Henry. "I do that when I'm nervous."

He put his arm round her and they walked toward the station.

Henry and Flavia sat in the dining room at the Ritz. Flavia looked beautiful against the golden whorls and curlicues. Men, hands poised to pop in a delicacy, paused and turned their heads.

Henry tasted the wine and nodded to the waiter. Flavia's face was almost invisible against her sunbeam hair and flame dress. She said, "I'll get drunk."

Henry nodded. "We both will. Unless we eat an awful lot."

"I'm not hungry." Flavia peered at the menu despairingly. The admiration she was inspiring made her feel light as thistledown.

Henry remembered the rare occasions when he had been taken

out of boarding school. The object of the exercise was to eat as much as possible without actually being sick.

He said to Flavia. “You've met Wiggins, haven't you?”

“That Labour Party man.” Flavia sipped her wine like a butterfly.

“Once his parents took us out from school to a place like this . . .”

“The Ritz!”

“But halfway through the meal his father was so sickened by the amount we ate that he got up and left the restaurant.”

“How did you pay?” asked Flavia.

“His mother.” Henry was brief. That wasn't the point. “It was a treat, you see. A traditional indulgence. After our usual cardboard carcass and flooded veg. But he was a very obstinate man. He thought we were disgusting. Of course it explains a lot about Wiggins.”

Flavia sighed. She would have preferred him not to talk about food. It reminded her of home. “Eat, Flavia, eat!” were the first words she'd consciously heard.

“So this is a treat like that one. An indulgence,” he concluded.

“How lovely!” said Flavia, as her heart sank further. She could hardly shovel unwanted food into the starched folds of a Ritz napkin.

Henry ordered generously.

A silence fell while they waited. Flavia's exhilaration returned. Henry ate his roll and then hers.

Flavia said, “You don't go to any of the clubs, do you?”

“I've joined them.” Henry smiled at her. This was rather rare. Both of them were dazzled. Flavia smiled back. The wine tingled in their heads.

“I like watching the Union debates.” Flavia leaned toward him so her hair brushed along the table top. “It's wonderful theater.”

“That's the problem with it.”

“And no women!” cried Flavia. “They're such a pompous lot. In their evening dress. After all, it's nearly 1960!” Out of the corner of her eye, she saw the first course approaching. So much of it.

“You're very social, aren't you?” Henry tucked into a steaming puff of pastry.

“I do like people.”

“I thought so.”

“Don't you?”

“Certainly not!”

Flavia laughed. But she was not sure Henry meant it as a joke. Sometimes she wondered about his sense of humor.

He was looking very serious now. "I like you."

Flavia saw her chance. "You won't mind if I don't finish my"—what was it?—"this, then?" Since he didn't say no or indeed seem to hear, she pushed it away anyway.

Henry was thinking about companionship and marriage. There was something magical about Flavia. Her presence made anything seem possible. "I did like one other girl," he said.

"Oh." Flavia tried to look mature. She realized he was going to tell her about this girl he got pregnant. It would probably be in the form of a confession. Flavia thought that what she really liked talking about was her work, ideas, abstraction. She liked set subjects. "The Role of the Infinite in Two Shakespearean Tragedies."

"She was called Belinda. Still is. An American girl. We grew up like brother and sister for a while. She reminds me of you."

Flavia frowned. They couldn't talk about his work because she knew no Greek and only enough Latin to get her through the Oxford entrance examination.

"But I lost touch with her years ago."

"I see." So it wasn't that other girl. Flavia leaned back to let the waiter by with the next course. "I think Shakespeare's terribly clever about friendships between men and women. Look at the way he shakes up the usual picture by making the women dress up as men."

"That was partly the age he grew up in." To Flavia's delight Henry picked up her idea and they were off, having the sort of discussion that made her tutorials so special. . . . Flavia's cheeks began to match her dress and her main course was cleared away without her noticing what she'd eaten.

Henry took a packet of Black Sobranie from his breast pocket. He offered one to Flavia, who took it cheerfully. Neither of them knew how to smoke, so they performed the task with deference. Around them the room was nearly empty of lunchers. The waiters gathered by the door.

Henry stubbed out his cigarette and called for the bill. He had fallen into one of those silences which his friends found disconcerting.

Flavia felt vaguely guilty. Perhaps he had wanted to talk about Catullus or the position of royalty in Spain.

When they got out of the restaurant Henry put his arm round her. He immediately felt another tremendous surge of lust. The suddenness of it startled him. He had been feeling quiet before, even a little depressed. He looked round wildly. Now all he wanted was to strip off her dress.

Flavia mistook his look entirely. "Are we going to be late?"

"No." Henry was flushed now. They stood in the foyer of the hotel. He longed to say, Shall I book a room? Shall we go upstairs?

Flavia decided he was cross. "Did I say something wrong? It was a wonderful lunch."

Henry was unwilling to let his powerful emotions drain away to no avail. He said, "I must kiss you."

The urgency of his voice and face weakened Flavia, as when he'd asked her to come to London. "Yes," she murmured. "Yes."

"Where?" snarled Henry.

Flavia looked back at him helplessly. The idea of a room in the hotel never crossed her mind.

They walked slowly outside. When they reached the pavement Henry grasped Flavia and kissed her for as long as possible. It was not enough but it was something. Afterward they both felt too shaky to move immediately. Neither bothered about curious passers-by.

"I think I should like to marry you," whispered Henry. The words were swallowed up by the Piccadilly traffic. Flavia, who had turned away, one hand to cheek, did not react.

Chapter 11

Lionel had started writing letters to Henry again. As in the past, they discussed his current diplomatic preoccupation. From his unwanted position on an outer limb of Europe, he followed as closely as he was able the growth of European unity. Or rather the lack of growth. In December 1958 the idea of a unified European Industrial Free Trade Area bit the dust. A new initiative along economic lines, under the OEEC umbrella, came into being.

It was this initiative that caught Lionel's imagination. He could not know much about it but he wanted to be back in England, or, at very least, out of Spain. "It's a question of the Commonwealth," he wrote to Henry. "And America. You and I, who have lived in both"—he had begun to pay Henry the compliment of man-to-man dialogue—"can appreciate the complications of appearing to cast off both our dependents and those on which we wish to be dependent. At the same time we have to look to the future. But a future with honor. Britain has more to offer the world than narrow nationalism. Let the French win as many points as they like on that front. . . ."

Henry read his father's letters with interest. He kept them in a special drawer.

Julian sighed. "You're so lucky to have such a strong father as a role model."

"Whatever's that? A sort of train?"

"My father was a talented drunkard until recently. Now he's just a drunkard."

Henry imagined his marriage with Flavia. She flared across the pages of his books, as yet unattained but secure in his imagination of the future. One evening she gave him a new name—Harry

Hayes, instead of Henry Middleton-Hayes, which she insisted was only fit for a middle-aged banker. She said half the girls in her college were in love with him, but she didn't say she was.

A cry of exultation came from Lionel. "I have a new job concerned with economic affairs. In London. I am to be Deputy Under-Secretary. A relatively new post. Of enormous importance at the present time. The Foreign Secretary has not forgotten me."

Henry, now Harry, met his parents in London in July 1960. Since the end of the term he had been on a walking tour in Wales. Julian had accompanied him part of the way but complained so incessantly of the sun, the flies and the rain that Harry had sent him away. He spent the evenings in a farmhouse eating homemade fudge and reading a series of poems by Propertius. They were all about an ethereal girl called Cynthia who reminded Harry of Flavia. If his hosts dared to disturb him he rumbled "Epiparaclausthurion" at them and they retreated nervously.

Lionel and Beatrice had reinstalled themselves in their house. Harry rang the front doorbell for some time before either appeared. Then they were both there together. They wore the same excited, flustered air. Like children, he thought, dragging in his haversack.

"Where's that nice girl?" said Beatrice, peering behind his back.

"Oh, she'll be here." Harry had not seen Flavia for six weeks.

"You look flourishing, I must say." Lionel led the way to the drawing-room.

"So do you." Harry turned to his mother. "Both of you."

"We are!" agreed Lionel definitely. He patted an enormous pile of English newspapers.

Harry was struck by the similarities in his parents. Even their physical outlines seemed to have modified from two extremes. Beatrice, once so strangely dark and thin, now was rounder and her hair softened by gray. Lionel, who, on the other hand, had started out a large blond Englishman, was now lean in face and body with hair made colorless by gray, his rubicund English complexion made sallow by too many hot summers. At some point, unnoticed previously, they must have started growing together. They were looking at him in the same part-admiring, part-wary way.

The doorbell rang.

Harry bounded off. He flung open the door and snatched Flavia in a vise.

"Let me get in," gasped Flavia.

"Don't forget we're due at the Commons," called Lionel from the drawing room.

"What will they think?"

"I was so happy to see you." Harry smiled. And Flavia, who didn't like being pulled about, felt like kissing him after all.

They went into the drawing room. Harry, who had washed, shaved and changed, now noticed that both his parents were dressed extremely elegantly in dark suits. Flavia wore her drainpipe trousers. Surely he had told her they were going to listen to the Foreign Secretary speaking?

Beatrice said, "How very nice to meet you again. I've prepared a light lunch before we go off."

Flavia's eyes swiveled questioningly to Harry. He had not told her.

"We're still camping here, as you see," Beatrice added.

"How about a drink?" Lionel poured them all large sherries.

Harry wondered whether, when they married, Flavia would always wear those horrible trousers.

They set out in a taxi to the House of Commons. Flavia sported a linen suit belonging to Beatrice. It seemed to fit her exactly.

"The last time I was here for a debate," meditated Lionel as they reached Parliament Square, "was in 1938. Just before I married. Just before the war."

"Can you remember what the debate was about, dear?" Beatrice pushed down her window.

"Germany. Must have been at that date."

"I was only seventeen," said Beatrice with her face out of the window.

"And so beautiful!" Lionel patted her knee. "I fell in love with her, you know, the first moment we met. She made all the other girls look like fatted calves."

The taxi drew up. "It seems very odd to me,"—Flavia's voice was bright and loud— "that people in the Foreign office aren't *made* to go to the Houses of Parliament every so often. It is the center of government, where all the important things happen." She jumped out of the taxi, her cheeks, Harry noticed, bright red. Perhaps she was angry about his mother's suit. He did not imagine she seriously believed that the Foreign Office was less important than this theater they were about to enjoy, this scene of sound and fury.

Since Lionel was occupied paying the taxi Harry took up the defense himself. "The Foreign Office, as its name implies, deals with Britain's affairs overseas. The Members of Parliament, whom we are about to see, have no knowledge and no interest beyond their own petty borders. Their constituencies, that is." At this point Flavia flung her hair about and took a step away. But he was determined to finish. "Ministers, Foreign Ministers included, are chosen from their ranks not because they have specialized knowledge of the appropriate subject but because they happen to be in favor with the Prime Minister. Thus it is the Foreign Minister who must come to the Foreign Office to gain knowledge, not the . . ."

"Come on, dear." Beatrice took his arm.

". . . vice versa." Despite this lame ending, Harry was pleased by his speech. It seemed to him a fitting way to mark his first visit to the House of Commons. It placed him clearly as a man not to be stupidly impressed.

Selwyn Lloyd was making a long and complicated speech. It was his last as Foreign Secretary. It had been decided that Britain's attitude to European unity msut be clarified before the summer recess. He said, ". . . If Britain were to be regarded as outside Europe, we could not fulfill our complete role in the world."

Flavia sat forward with her chin in her hands. Although enjoying discussions about abstractions in literature, she was pragmatic in her politics. These grand statements meant little to her. She watched Lionel's absorption from across the chamber. Beatrice was also leaning forward, eyes bright like a spectator at a tennis match. At one point, her eyes met Flavia's. She smiled encouragingly. Flavia blushed. She thought her outburst in the taxi had made her seem like a child to be patronized.

Selwyn Lloyd said, "I think it would help if we could be given some indication of the attitude of the Six towards the special problems I have mentioned." Lionel seemed to nod. He took Beatrice's hand and squeezed it. Flavia looked away.

Harry was still elated. This was a special day. The Foreign Secretary's speech was an important one. He was stating Britain's determination to move, however slowly, toward unity. He searched for parallels from ancient Greece, rejected the Panhellenic League as too loose a confederacy and then the Delian League as too much under the dominance of one country. Unless you saw Athens as the U.S.A. and the other common members of the League equivalent to the Western Alliances. But that was not the Market. Harry saw himself involved in the great pattern of world events. It made sense of everything. It made everything so simple.

Beatrice whispered in his ear, "We are partaking in history."

"And Sparta is Russia," said Harry.

Flavia spent the night at the Hayes-Middleton house. There were two bedrooms at the top of the house. The furniture had not yet arrived from Spain, so in each stood a cot and a sleeping bag. Flavia felt exhausted by eleven. Selwyn Lloyd had been followed by a film and an Indian meal. She lay in her sleeping bag watching London lights through the uncurtained window. Her feet felt cold, her head hot. She could not sleep.

A figure came gliding into the silvery room.

"Harry?"

"Yes." He came over to her. He was wearing the sort of tailored pajamas seen only in old movies. She knew she mustn't make fun of him. She put out a hand.

Harry took the hand and held it gently. He wanted to lie down beside her, but there was no room on the bed. Besides, she was zipped away inside her sleeping bag. He got up and padded away again.

"Where are you going?" Flavia sat up but he didn't answer.

He returned in a moment and made her stand up. "Come along." They went to his bedroom where he had spread open his sleeping bag and laid out blankets. They lay down together.

Flavia felt comforted. She even fell half asleep. Harry said, "Don't you think government is stupendously exciting?"

"Uhnn."

Harry recognized her half-unconscious state with some alarm. He remembered Mary Ann's simple enthusiasm and quickly stifled the image. Flavia seemed to be wearing a long man's shirt. He slid his hand between the buttons and felt her skin and then a breast. The nipple hardened the moment he touched it. At once he wanted to be inside her. His head began to buzz loudly. He tried to take a deep calming breath.

Flavia turned toward him. She put her mouth to his and sucked at his lips. Harry found self-control even more difficult. He recalled a conversation he'd had with Julian about premature ejaculation. Julian had said a quiet repetition of the words themselves had a salutary effect. It was their linguistic ugliness, he thought. "Premature ejaculation. Premature ejaculation." It was difficult with Flavia's delicious leech-like kisses.

"What are you muttering?"

"Nothing." Indeed it had worked. Quite miraculously. Now he dared run his hand over the other breast and down her flank.

Flavia enjoyed the stroking lazily.

Harry put his hand between her legs. They fell apart for him.

Harry had an image of Aunt Anna's little puppy which he'd so loved as a child. He smoothed Flavia's thighs up and down, up and down.

"Premature ejaculation. Premature . . ."

"Sshh." Flavia fixed her mouth on his again.

Harry wanted to feel her all over. If only it were possible. "Will you take your shirt off?"

"You do it."

Harry undressed himself and then her. He pushed her away a little so as to see her better. Her whiteness was glaring. He wanted to tell her about their future as a married couple. Flavia held out her arms. She seemed unselfconscious, happy.

Harry stopped thinking.

Harry and Flavia were a serious couple. They worked together, walked together and talked, sometimes for hours. Harry was captivated, not because of Flavia's body, although he enjoyed it, not because of her mind, whose intricacies irritated him, but because of her aura. Her aura, which was a composite of hair and imagination and steady medicinal background, remained incomprehensible to him and therefore exciting.

On June 3, 1961, he said, "I think we should get married." She looked at him, shocked. "I'm not pregnant, you know," she said and jumped into the River Cherwell.

Since it was a hot summer afternoon, that was not too odd an action, except that she was wearing a dress. She floated on her back in the muddy water, eyes open, hair like seaweed about her.

Harry knelt on the edge of the bank. "Why do you make fun of me?"

Flavia didn't answer. She was not making fun of him. She was merely escaping the pressure of a serious future. She felt the river's current carrying her very gently away from Harry. After a few seconds watching her, he stood up and walked away. Flavia closed her eyes and fell into a kind of dream, which was only broken some yards downstream by some rude little boys throwing sticks at her.

She stood up suddenly to give them a fright and their faces were so absurd with the shock of it that she laughed and laughed. Tears of laughter joined river water running down her face and neck.

When she recovered and looked round for Harry, there was no sign of him. So she wrung herself out and squished back to college.

After this episode they did not see each other for the rest of the summer term and throughout the entire summer vacation.

Harry went to Paris and lived with a poor but well-bred family who taught him French. He enjoyed himself more after he started an affair with a waitress at the café he frequented. Like all the women he admired she was thin and fair but she did not wipe out the memory of Flavia.

Flavia spent the entire vacation at her home in a village near Marlborough. She worked part-time at her father's surgery and had no affairs with anyone. She became obsessed by the idea that she was cold and unfeeling and incapable of love. Where else would she find a more talented and interesting husband than Harry? But even the word "husband" made her cringe. Perhaps she was emotionally retarded, crippled by too much early medical knowledge. She wrote a letter to Harry.

> Dear Harry [she was not tempted to write "darling"],
>
> You must understand that I am different from other people. I can't give real love and sometimes I can't even bear to receive it. For me the most erotic moment of our relationship was a discussion we once had about the heroic self-image of the Norseman as exemplified by Hengest and Horsa.
>
> Sometimes I think that perhaps I'm an intellectual but my brain is so much less clear and well-ordered than yours. Oh Harry, I do miss you. Please let's meet soon.
>
> Love,
> Flavia

On rereading this missive, Flavia decided that the only part that rang true was the last sad appeal. But that was barred for reasons of pride. The rest seemed absurdly pretentious. She cut the paper through several times and then burnt it. This physical action gave her such pleasure that she wondered if her talent lay in the direction of manual dexterity. She used the last month of the vacation to make a great mound of paper collages.

Meanwhile in Paris Harry was in the process of a visit from Julian. Julian was jealous of Harry. He couldn't understand why Harry, who was so conventional in outlook, so rigid, so conservative, so—quite honestly—*dim,* should so persistently swim far out in the waters of experience. While he, Julian, an experimenter, an innovator, a bold free spirit, seemed in comparison to be merely dabbling his toes at the edges.

The girl in the café was not only a true Parisian and very chic but had a brother who had connections with the underworld and an ex-lover who was a ballet dancer with the prestigious Ballet Russe.

All this, which would have given Julian food for many late-night conversations, seemed as nothing to Harry. His days were pinned into a routine. He worked from ten to one at his French, ate lunch on his own at Sybille's café, took her to her flat when she finished her work until she was on duty again in the early evening. He then either visited the cinema or the theater or stayed at home and read.

"You're like an old man!" Julian's cry sounded bitter even to his own ears.

Harry looked surprised. They were having a Pernod outside Sybille's café. It was late September and the pavements had already cooled.

"What do you mean?"

"Mon Dieu!" Julian pulled on his long pink and purple scarf. "How can you do the same thing each day?"

"We'll all be going back to Oxford soon." Harry's voice was mild. He was pleased to see Julian. A few days ago he had caught sight of a small bulky figure not unlike Wiggins. His heart had lurched with pleasure, until he'd seen an unmistakably French face. The incident had shown him that he was ready to leave Paris. On the whole, after his initial surprise, he felt sympathetic to Julian's irritation.

This annoyed Julian more. "How can you be so comfortable?" He flung himself about on his spindly café chair.

"I'm not," said Harry to pacify him.

Julian gave him a suspicious look but sat more quietly. "Do you miss your Flavia?"

"Yes," said Harry. And as he spoke a gust of homesickness blew across the Channel. Tears prickled at the back of his eyes and then crept round to the front.

Julian watched him closely. "Are you crying?"

"No." Harry rubbed his eyes. "Sometimes I forget to blink."

"Ha!" snorted Julian. But he was satisfied. That evening they got very drunk indeed together and insulted Sybille. In fact they did more than that. They tore down some creepers from a wall and whipped her with them. Sybille seemed to take it in good humor. But the next morning when Harry appeared at her café she would have nothing to do with him.

"Fous le camp!"
"Mais, Sybille."
"Ça suffit."
"Pourquoi . . . ?"
"Allez-y!"

Feeling like a mouse shooed out of a kitchen, Harry retreated. His head ached and he had no memory of the whipping scene. It was Julian who reminded him. His face expressed pride, not penitence.

"Bloody hell!" exclaimed Harry and went back to bed. There he dreamed of green English fields.

Harry and Flavia were both starting their last year at Oxford. They felt in tune with autumn, sad, mellow, near the end. They met by chance on Addison's Walk. They approached down the long straight path with shrubbery on one side and river on the other.

Flavia, of course, with her hair luminous in the afternoon sun, brighter even than the golden leaves, was instantly visible. Harry watched her strangely undulating walk, which appeared so languid and yet covered ground so fast.

"Hi, Harry!"

"At least you haven't jumped in the river."

"I'm sorry."

As usual on any first meeting, lust overcame Harry. He gripped Flavia and kissed her for as long as he could without breathing.

As usual Flavia felt herself weakened. They found a bench. Their bodies tingled against the hard wood. Flavia was surprised it didn't go up in smoke. She heaved a painful sigh.

"I had such a boring summer."

"So did I," lied Harry. Sybille might not have existed.

"I made fifteen colleges."

"What?"

"Pictures out of bits of paper. When I came here I gave them to a hospital sale but they only managed to get rid of one, even after reducing them to seven and sixpence."

"That's very funny." Harry began to laugh. And Flavia, who had previously seen the rejection of her colleges as a serious personal defeat, began to laugh too. By the end of the afternoon they had decided to marry after completing school.

Harry went a little crazy. For example, he worked between eleven

P.M. and four A.M. one week, four P.M. and eleven P.M. the next week and four A.M. and eleven A.M. a third. It was only noticed when he missed a ten A.M. tutorial. The explanation that he was working did not please his tutor.

Then he took up rowing. Although he had joined the university club on his arrival at Oxford he had never yet found the boathouse. The final year was not considered appropriate, not least because he had an extraordinary natural talent.

"You do not row in your last year," said his tutor, who wanted him to get a First.

"No," agreed Harry regretfully. He was always obedient when confronted directly with authority.

Beatrice observed her son's eccentricity when he came home for Christmas.

"Have you noticed Henry drinks sherry at breakfast?" she asked her husband. She personally did not mind this kind of behavior, which fulfilled her sense of the oddness of life. But she felt a duty to inform Lionel.

"Your mother tells me you drink sherry at breakfast," Lionel accused his son, fairly mildly, as he thought.

"Yes," said Harry, without explanation. The two men were reading after dinner.

"Why?" asked Lionel rather more aggressively.

"So I don't have a hangover in the morning." Harry looked pointedly, though without reproof, at his father's whisky and soda. "I don't drink in the evenings."

"But then you're drunk in the morning!"

"No, I'm not."

Lionel retired to confer with his wife. He himself was at the office in the mornings. "No, I wouldn't say he was drunk." Beatrice gave him a sloe-eyed look. "But then young people are different anyway, don't you think?"

Lionel decided to overlook it. He had been drunk a great deal of his time at university.

Flavia, like Beatrice, was not too upset by her fiancé's more eccentric behavior. He had taken to writing her little notes, usually delivered at the porter's lodge during the small hours of the morning. When spring arrived he accompanied them with a daffodil or a wild anemone. He wrote little. Sometimes entirely in Greek, which Flavia did not understand. Sometimes a comment on the political situation. Only occasionally about her. Once he wrote a poem:

Jackdaws steal
Pursed up for life
Golden flashes 110
In the night.

It made no sense to Flavia, but she was working too hard for prolonged worry. Besides, as far as she could see, everybody round her was behaving at least as oddly. The girl next door but one had eaten nothing but pork pies for three weeks and a girl one floor down had shaved off all her hair. (Admittedly she had since been taken to hospital screaming, "I'm not a collaborator!") But everyone knew finals were a great strain and you had to give a little somewhere.

Harry's own view was rather different. He felt highly stimulated, in peak form and yet at the same time thoroughly bored. His notes, his unusual routines, his rowing were all attempts to leaven this strange boredom. He found he no longer needed very much sleep, often going for days with only a few hours. His brain was at all times magically clear and his body filled with energy. He found he could recite huge chunks of Greek and Latin without even thinking.

He couldn't understand how his friends complained of not enough time when he could read *The Times, Telegraph* and *Guardian* from cover to cover and still find the day hung heavily. He called on Wiggins, whom he had not seen for months, and harangued him on the balance of power.

Wiggins, he noticed, seemed to have grown smaller, his face sharp-nosed and the texture of his skin murky. He interrupted himself to exclaim, "You look frightful."

Wiggins's patience was suddenly exhausted. "You look and behave like a madman!"

Harry returned to his room chastened. He realized that he had been getting out of control—he, who so much valued the rule of convention, who was destined for that most orderly of places, the Foreign Office. He stayed in his room for several days, appearing only for meals in hall. Then he went to his tutor and said that he'd been overworking and would like to leave the term early.

The tutor, still hoping for that First and impressed by his self-knowledge, gave him permission.

Flavia received a letter which said, "See you in April. Ave atque vale!" She wept a little and then flung *The Pardoner's Tale* against the wall. Where was the steady, conservative figure who had dragged her from the Film Society? She tried to burn all his billets-doux in a bucket but the matches kept blowing out. The use of the bucket brought a protest from the second-floor cleaning monitor.

Harry went to London. There he found a letter from Mary Ann. Once he had remembered who she was he realized it was Fate. She was from the real world of people who did not read books and had never heard of exams.

Without unpacking, he took several tubes to Paddington.

Mary Ann had stayed faithful to her area but was working in a different, rather smarter hotel. In fact she was engaged to its proprietor, an Italian named Toni Grissini. She had written the letter in order to convey this information but she had not succeeded. Harry understood only her name and remembered their past together.

The hotel, smart but not big, was called Quattro Seasons, an effective mixture of linguistics, in Toni's view.

Harry pushed into the foyer. He felt as if he were entering a foreign land. Behind the counter stood a thin woman dressed in black.

"I have come to see Mary Ann." He hesitated, having no memory of her surname. The girl's face caught his attention. It was suffused with red, whether from the color of the light bulb above her head or the reflection from her reddish hair or some inner illness or emotion he couldn't guess.

"Hello, Henry."

"Ah." That explained it. "Hello, Mary Ann."

Mary Ann's emotional coloring was caused almost entirely by pleasure. She had, after all, been waiting for him to come back to her for three years—almost to the day, as a matter of fact. And now he was here and she was engaged. Triumphant!

As if on cue, Toni appeared from an inner room. He saw Harry. "No rooms till tomorrow."

"It's an old friend of mine, Toni. Henry, meet Toni, my fiancé, who I wrote you about."

They sat in the room behind the counter. It was very small and hot. Mary Ann sat on a high chair with her legs crossed. She wore a short black skirt, dark stockings and wicked-looking shoes with pointed toes and pointed heels. Above her head was a picture of the Madonna and Child.

"Yes," said Mary Ann, watching Harry's eyes. "Toni is a Catholic too. We'll have a white wedding and a nuptial Mass."

Harry said nothing. The flush had not subsided from Mary Ann's cheeks. She looked very desirable.

"We will have the reception here in the hotel." Toni spread his hands proudly.

"And all my relations have booked rooms." Mary Ann laughed happily.

Tea came, brought in by a young Irish girl who bore a distinct resemblance to Mary Ann.

"My cousin, Finola."

Harry shook hands, causing her to spill some tea on the carpet. A sense of despair overcame him. "I'm sorry." He couldn't cry here.

Mary Ann crouched on the floor with her hankie.

Toni said, "All our carpets are especially sprayed to be liquid-repellent." The long words brought out his Italian accent.

Finola disappeared and Mary Ann sat down again.

Crushing back tears that no one had noticed—oh, where was his youth!—he muttered, "As a matter of fact, I'm engaged too."

"What?" Mary Ann uncrossed her legs.

"Yes. I have to take my exams first." He stood up. "Well, thank you for the tea."

"We will send you a wedding invitation." Toni held out his hand.

Mary Ann went pale and then pink again. She realized he was inventing this engagement to salvage his pride. She held out her cheek for him to kiss. But he had already turned away. Through the door and into reception.

A man stood there, very tall, very wide. At his side was a girl, hardly more than a child.

"A room for the afternoon," said the man.

Harry stared. "I'm sorry?"

"I said I want a room for the afternoon," the man bellowed, enunciating each syllable with ferocious clarity.

Harry walked past him into the spring sunshine. The sudden brightness added to the sufferings of the world caused partial blindness and he bumped into one or two passersby.

"Drunken lout!"

At that moment Harry realized that a paneled room filled with books was an excellent idea. He also pictured Flavia, a mermaid of undulatory extravaganze, at his side. His eyes cleared and his step became more purposeful.

Chapter 12

Dr. and Dr. P. Morton
invite you to the marriage
of their daughter,
Flavia Jane,
to Henry William Jean-Pierre Lionel Hayes-Middleton
on . . .

Till this moment Harry had not known he possessed two further Christian names. William, he discovered, was his paternal grandfather's name, Jean-Pierre his maternal great-grandfather. In his heart of hearts he suspected the reiteration of doctor at the top of the invitation made it all seem ridiculous, but his head was now firmly in control.

In the event it was he who became calm and orderly during the exams and Flavia whose wits scattered to the winds. They had not had their results yet but Harry had few worries. He had since taken the Foreign Office exams in the same competent manner.

Flavia didn't worry either. But that was because she was making a wedding dress out of silver gauze. First, Second, Third or Fourth, she could hardly wear them like orange blossoms in her hair.

Dr. and Dr. P. Morton, both "P," being Patrick and Patricia, came up to London for a medical conference shortly before the wedding. They visited the Hayes-Middletons for a drink. When they arrived only Beatrice was there. She noted that Patricia had Flavia's light-filled hair, while Pat was black with a black mustache. But they were both thin like their daughter and possessed the same small bright eyes. Beatrice poured them exceptionally large sherries and explained her husband was in conference with the Foreign Secretary. Although normally talkative, they were impressed into silence.

Beatrice was dismayed. She said, "I expect your conference was much more interesting. Medical gossip is far more amusing than political blood and gore."

Harry entered into the silence. He had not met them before either.

Pat said, "Although we're general practitioners, we are also believers in homeopathic remedies. We had hoped to say a word or two about it at the conference."

"No luck," said Patricia.

Harry tried to imagine these were Flavia's parents. But failed.

"Flavia's going to have the whole church decorated with white flowers," said Patricia. "I've told her she'll end up with all daisies."

"What about roses?" Beatrice spoke dreamily.

"We've never been too lucky with roses ourselves. Black spot."

There was another silence. Pat looked at Harry. "You're very young to get married."

Beatrice leaned foward. "I wasn't quite eighteen when I married."

"We were young, too. We met at medical school. We waited for children, of course, till we'd both done all the exams."

"Ten years," said Patricia. "And then there was only Flavia. I sometimes wondered if we didn't wait too long."

Harry shifted uncomfortably on his chair. He did not enjoy this adult self-questioning. He preferred his elders to remain opaque, at best reflecting back his own ideas. In his view adults were fully programmed and not open to change. When he was forty he intended to kill himself.

"More sherry?" He poured another round.

Beatrice looked into her glass. "Of course, Henry," she flashed up to her son and corrected herself: "Harry is a Catholic."

"Mother!"

Beatrice smiled gently at his scandalized expression. "That is, he was baptized a Catholic."

Harry was about to expostulate further when he noticed that neither of the Mortons showed any signs of shock. This diverted him. Was religion then entirely a matter of what color flowers decorated the church? It struck him that he had not discussed this fundamental question with Flavia. She had suggested a church and he had not objected. Presumably this meant she believed in God. Or could he presume it? If it came to that did he, baptized a

Catholic as he was, believe in God? The truth was that he had not entertained the idea of an omnipresent, omnipowerful being since he had left school. In fact he could not remember ever being in a room where a serious discussion on such matters had taken place.

He put the sherry bottle on the sideboard and turned round. Was there any reason why he should not ask the Mortons where they stood on the matter of the Great Creator? Or his mother, if it came to that?

As it turned out, there was. For the conversation had moved on to London restaurants.

"It was labeled 'fresh cream' but simply stuffed with monosodium glutamate."

Harry sat down, depressed.

Pat and Patricia looked at each other. They both longed to be on their train speeding back to the country. They were prepared to take Harry's reputed brilliance on trust but his silence unnerved them. Beatrice's efforts at communication seemed to resemble a fairy waving a wand. Was it their duty to wait for Mr. Hayes-Middleton?

Lionel entered the house. He came into the drawing room with his elegant pinstriped suit and warm, loud-voiced manner. He was like the most outgoing kind of consultant, a type whom the Mortons admired without approving.

Beatrice sank back, sighed, smiled, became silent. Harry sat straighter. The evening was restored. The Mortons stayed for supper and nearly missed their last train. Lionel lectured.

"Britain has to find a new role. The world has need of our unrivaled experience in the underdeveloped countries. The future lies with clever young chaps like my son here. It is a time of change. An exciting time when we must not look back to what we have lost, but forward to what . . ."

He was not so clear as all that about what they should look forward to but everyone was impressed all the same. Confidence is catching. Harry saw his future in his father.

"It's been an honor to meet you," said the Mortons, shaking hands energetically on the doorstep.

Harry got a First Class degree and passed fifth into the Foreign Office. The day after he heard, he was approached by a man wearing a donkey jacket and smoking a cheroot. He also wore smoked glasses and carried a satchel. He was the kind of figure who inspires fantasies about sinister agents of foreign powers. Harry, standing on Charing Cross station waiting for the Northern Line, was thinking just this. Places like Lithuania sprang to mind.

"I couldn't borrow a light, could I?"

The voice was bluff, English and entirely at odds with his appearance.

"Sorry. I don't smoke."

"Lucky you."

They stood shoulder to shoulder, looking down at the empty line.

"Slow coming, aren't they?"

"Yes," said Harry.

"Just down from university, are you?"

"Yes," agreed Harry. Was it so obvious?

The lines sang and a train appeared. Both men got in. They strap-hung together.

"Going far, are you?"

"Kensington High Street."

"Coincidence! Me too."

Together they changed trains at Tottenham Court Road. Together they got out. Harry was on his way to buy a wedding ring. Beatrice had told him about a small jeweler's near Barkers. It seemed that he would be buying it in the company of this cheerful cheroot-smoking non-Lithuanian.

Harry stopped in the middle of the pavement. "Look here. Why are you following me about?"

"Christ, I'm sorry. Am I upsetting you?"

"No," Harry said, sounding very upset and childish. "I just want to know why you're following me. Perhaps I know you from the past or something."

"No, we haven't met before." The man resumed his cheerful expression. "The thing is, now you've brought it up, I'd like to have a chat with you." He looked round him. "There might be a café . . ."

"If I have this chat, will you go away?"

"I assure you I don't want to be a nuisance."

They sat in the El Sombrero, a fashionable coffee bar to which Julian had introduced Harry.

The man dropped his bluff voice and began in a hushed whisper. It took Harry several minutes before he realized that the man actually was what he looked like, a secret agent, although from England, not Lithuania. He was on a recruiting mission.

Harry thought of the implications of this and felt quite annoyed. "I fear you've not been very well briefed," his voice was at its most pompous. "I have just passed in, very high up as a matter of fact, to the Foreign Office proper." He gave solemn emphasis to the final word.

The man sipped his coffee and smoked his cheroot. His smoky glasses looked black in the low lighting.

"So I might as well be off," added Harry, pushing back his chair.

The man put a hand inside his donkey jacket. An image of a smoking pistol leaped at Harry. The hand returned to view with a calling card.

"In case of second thoughts."

Harry took the card. "Do you mind if I ask you something?"

The man nodded encouragingly.

"Why do you dress the way you do?"

"The way I do?" His words were repeated without apparent understanding.

"So that everyone looks at you. Is it a kind of double bluff?"

The man took off his glasses. Underneath his eyes were small and red, as if he had been crying or was about to. He rubbed them till Harry felt sorry for the eyeballs.

"I didn't mean to offend you."

The glasses were returned in position. "It depends where you are as to whether you stand out."

"I see." Perhaps he had just returned from Lithuania or thereabouts and had not had the time to put on his Charing Cross mackintosh and briefcase. "Goodbye, then. Thanks for the coffee." The cheroot was lifted in gloomy salute. Harry felt rather guilty at spoiling his original cheerfulness.

He did not look at the calling card till he was inside the jeweler's reaching for his checkbook. For a moment he thought he'd picked it up from the desk.

M.A.P. Pershing
Diamond Merchant
Britain-Poland-Ceylon Import-Export

Plus a very long telephone number which might have reached the furthest point of the globe. Now, if he'd only seen it earlier they might have been in business.

Harry paid a lot of his parents' money for a very small diamond and left the shop.

Flavia barely scraped a second-class degree. Her parents were most disappointed.

"Passing exams was the happiest time of their life. They thought of nothing else for ten solid years." She lay in Harry's arms on his drawing-room floor. Mr. and Mrs. Hayes-Middleton were attending a function at the Spanish Embassy.

"You passed yours." Harry stroked her white arm. She was dressed in an embroidered blouse, like a little girl. It had an elastic waistband, which Harry was longing to snap over her head. He wondered how long he must listen to talk about her parents.

"Oh, I'm not worried."

Harry put his fingers under the elastic. The touch of her warm secret skin made his head whirl. Embassy functions tended to end promptly. He must get her upstairs.

Flavia liked Harry's excitement. It made her feel powerful. Just for fun, she kept on talking about exams. Harry wound his legs round hers. She felt so fragile between them. She was glad she was being married in silver gauze.

"You're not wearing anything underneath!" Harry's incredulous voice made her jump. He had reached her breasts under the blouse.

Flavia laughed. "Women don't have to wear bras. There's no rule."

"I thought there was a medical reason." Harry's voice faded away.

"Touch me," murmured Flavia. Was their relationship entirely based on sex?

"Your skin's like gloss paint. Like peppermint-flavored gloss paint."

"Peppermint?"

"Humbugs."

"Caramel."

They should go upstairs. Imagine Mr. and Mrs. Hayes-Middleton at the door in white tie, tails and long black velvet. With a touch of scarlet. But how could they move now?

"Oh, Flavia! I can't wait."

"You don't have to anymore." She thought he was referring to something else. "Women are efficient about that sort of thing too." Flavia giggled.

But Harry had not been referring to birth control. He was in love.

Wiggins was Harry's best man. Harry couldn't quite understand how it had happened. He thought he had asked Julian. But there was Wiggins, sturdy-bodied, sturdy-faced, tailcoat more suiting a chaffinch than a swallow. Perhaps Julian had refused the honor. He had become odder even than usual after failing his degree altogether. He was working on a building site in East London. He said it was the only way he could avoid his mother. Harry visited him there one hot day. The site was an old crater not far from St. Paul's. They were building a large concrete building. Harry found it difficult to recognize Julian. He wore jeans and an undershirt just like the other workmen. He had tied a scarf round his forehead to stop the sweat dripping into his eyes. His job was to carry steel rivets from one part of the site to another. He continued to do this during Harry's visit.

"Can't you stop a moment?"

"I'm not doing this for fun, you know. Why ever are you dressed like that?"

Harry wore a suit. "I've just been to the Foreign Office."

Julian dropped a steel rivet a hair's-breadth from Harry's toe.

"Look out!"

"Sorry. What's all this wedding business?"

"You know Flavia."

"Who is Flavia? What is she? You don't have to marry her."

"You don't have to work on a building site."

On reflection, it was probably this conversation that had moved Julian out of the best-man slot. And then Wiggins was so thrilled, so champing with jolly pride.

The day of the wedding was bright and showery. Mr. and Mrs. Hayes-Middleton, Wiggins and Harry drove to the country from London. Wiggins and Lionel discussed party politics for the entire journey. Because of their fundamental disagreement on almost every point—Lionel already saw the welfare state as sapping the greatness of Britain—they could have continued indefinitely. At one point it struck Harry that neither of them ever listened to the other. They merely took turns in stating or, very often, restating their own position. This selective deafness enabled them to remain on good terms however violent their disagreement.

Beatrice, seated in the back of the car with her son, took the opportunity for a few important words. "You shouldn't be marrying at your age, dear. Everyone says so. But you've always been so independent."

Harry was surprised at this estimate of his character. He didn't feel at all independent. In fact he suspected it was exactly his lack of independence that had led him to marry Flavia.

Beatrice patted his hand. She wore white gloves, which reminded Harry of a conjurer. "I'm glad it's in church. Even if the wrong one. I would believe in ecumenicalism if I could only say it."

Beatrice had a new secret life. Over the last few years, particularly since she and Lionel had returned to England, certain things had altered. He was no longer frustrated and bitter but successful and energetic. This had resulted in an end, at least temporarily, to his *affaires de coeur.* Beatrice, with loyalty extended, had finished her romantic novel and did not intend to write another. The light in her life had become clearer. Yet she still wanted something richer.

Father Bernard was the answer. He was not a closet priest, a tremulous visitor to the furthest reaches of the soul. He had nothing in common with the Jesuits whom Beatrice had sprinkled like black stars through her book. He was a public man, the prior of an order of monks, who ran a church near the Hayes-Middleton house. Beatrice met him at a coffee morning after Mass. Lionel was in Geneva at a conference. It was the first time she had been to Mass for several years.

It was Father Bernard's simplicity that attracted her. He was Irish but had lived in England for the twenty years since his ordination. He handed her a cup of tea. "I don't think we've seen you here before?"

"No. Although I have been to Mass a couple of times."

He did not question further. "You're most welcome, I'm sure."

He was a scruffy-looking man, sandy hair growing in tufts at the front and thinning at the back. His cassock was not very clean, and he wore what looked like hand-knitted socks under open leather sandals. He was tall, red-cheeked, and bent to each visitor in turn. Beatrice would have liked to capture him all for herself.

She sipped her coffee with a half smile. She remembered that the nuns at her convent had tried to genuflect whenever a priest visited.

She met Father Bernard again at "The Spirit and the Word" meeting. Lionel was in Brussels. This was an event mostly attended by women past their prime. Beatrice made one contribution. "The word must always come second to the spirit."

This shocked her neighbor, who happened to be one of the few old men present. He coughed explosively, which, more than Beatrice's words, drew the attention of Father Bernard. He looked in his kindly way at Beatrice. "I meant," she said, "that words often lie while the spirit is ever true."

"Words separate the human from the animal." Father Bernard was gentle but firm.

Beatrice, seeing opportunity for discussion, stayed on afterward. They sat over a cup of tea until ten o'clock. When they parted, Beatrice registered a lifting of the spirit. She had intended to mention it to Lionel but he came back from Brussels with a heavy cold and a briefcase stuffed full of papers. She realized that the experience she wished to communicate was too quiet for him to hear.

So Beatrice's secret life became fuller.

It gave to Harry's church wedding a particular poignancy. She had mentioned the occasion to Father Bernard, who promised to say a Mass. He had pointed out that the Church of England marriage service was recognized as binding by the Catholic Church.

Nevertheless she felt she must mark the occasion by some reference to Harry's baptismal faith.

"The life of a diplomat's wife is never easy," she said to Harry one evening.

She had meant this as a reference to Flavia, but Harry took it as a reference to herself—rightly, as it turned out. "I thought you liked traveling," he said.

Although flustered, Beatrice remained apparently calm. "Do you remember that Coptic monastery you and your father were going to visit in Egypt?"

"On our way to the Gulf of Suez." Harry congratulated himself on his memory. And yet he did not, at that moment, recall why they had not made the visit.

"It was dedicated to St. Anthony. The Christian tradition there dates back through him to St. Mark and therefore to Christ himself. I wanted to go there so much. That was why I became ill. The Church is very important to me."

Harry was disconcerted by his mother's words, but her continuing placid manner enabled him to treat them lightly. "I'm glad," he said feebly, since something seemed required of him.

Beatrice continued. "Catholicism is the one true faith, handed down from Jesus Christ and now in the hands of his priestly descendants."

"Yes," agreed Harry.

The Hayes-Middleton car arrived at the church at the same time as a short but fierce burst of hail. They sat tight.

"In August!" Lionel frowned angrily.

"Scientists believe the weather is being adversely affected by nuclear experiments in the Sahara." Wiggins's good humor was inexhaustible.

Lionel's frown became deeper. He had wanted a London wedding at which a crowd of useful diplomatic contacts could have been invited. Anyway, he felt too young to have a married son.

A tall figure, bent against the weather, sped by the car. "That's Julian!" cried Harry. He laughed at his wedding clothes, so different from the workman's undershirt.

"I never thought he'd come." Wiggins pursed his mouth. "A pagan, not to say something worse."

Harry opened the car door and stepped outside. The rain seemed inviting. Several other figures dashed ahead of him into the safety of the church porch. Julian had disappeared inside and Harry knew none of the others. He had the strange sensation of being an insignificant guest at his own wedding. The guests talked among themselves. Flavia's name occurred several times but never his.

"I say. We thought you were making your escape." Wiggins arrived with the Hayes-Middletons.

Lionel's distinguished presence immediately altered the porch atmosphere. Here was a man on his way to a knighthood. Backs straightened, a sense of purpose directed them into the church. Now they noticed Harry as if with recognition.

"It has stopped raining," he said. Indeed a streak of sun broke through the clouds with such force that they all blinked and put up their hands.

"Let's proceeed, then," said Lionel. "Proceed, proceed."

Harry and Wiggins waited for Flavia at the front of the church. Harrry fingered the ring. It reminded him of the possibility of a secret life offered by M.A.P. Pershing, diamond agent.

Flavia, dressed as promised in silver gauze, stood at his side. The vicar, with whom they'd had several relatively interesting talks, faced them. Harry had seen in his face all the teachers, tutors and, recently, Foreign Office officials that he had striven to satisfy with his acute, well-ordered intelligence. That he *had* satisfied.

The honeymoon took place in America. An American friend of Lionel's had offered his seaside house for two weeks. Harry had not crossed the Atlantic since he was ten. Flavia was very insular indeed. She had only once left the British Isles for an unfortunate trip with a French girl who gave her father mumps.

"An airplane is my first marriage bed," said Flavia poetically. Already her wedding was becoming a roseate dream, ripe for nostalgia. From Harry's attitude to her parents—a distant formality—she guessed that the roses would soon cover her whole background. Childhood was over. "I fly away with my beloved!" she cried even more extravagantly.

Harry smiled good-humoredly. He was thinking of Belinda. The house they were borrowing was not far from the beach where they'd played as children. He recalled their own serious conversation when she'd accused him of a "certain future," proclaiming her own life as dangerously unpredictable. Last week he had received a letter from her.

> My Dear Harry,
> Welcome to the ranks of the Young Marrieds. Of course that is surely an exaggeration in my case. Tom and I celebrate our fifth wedding anniversary on Thanksgiving Day. We have a son called Pollock. Tom is a lawyer, specializing in real estate. We are planning to move from the East Coast to California as soon as we've saved enough to make a proper start. We wouldn't want to be too low down in one of those canyons. Meanwhile please come and see us on your honeymoon. I can promise to cherish you and your wife.

At this point Harry's mental pianola stopped abruptly. "Cherish" struck a discordant note. "Cherish the dear departed." It reminded him of funeral wreaths and unctuous handclasps.

He turned to Flavia. "There's an old friend of the family's living near us on the coast. Shall we visit her?"

"Oh, yes," replied Flavia, picturing an elderly woman in navy worsted.

They flew into Idlewild Airport. Darkness swept along behind their route from the airport so that the city, guttering lights multiplying at their approach, seemed like a stage set. Act One, Scene One.

Flavia, of course, was not immune to its magic but she was tired. For weeks she had been dedicated to their wedding. Frankly, she felt like a rest. A bit of cherishing, perhaps.

Harry dropped their bags at the hotel and took her out. They had dinner in a restaurant which had been Lionel's end-of-holiday treat when he was ten. Harry ordered champagne and oysters. Flavia could not eat. At midnight, five A.M. English time, they went on to a nightclub. Flavia enjoyed this part, sleeping on Harry's shoulder while he jogged round the dance floor.

In their hotel room, Harry was struck with the pride of ownership. He undressed Flavia, who by this time was more like a puppet than a human being. He undressed himself.

At this, Flavia woke up and caressed him tenderly. Her eyes, however, would not stay open, and she soon fell back on the bed. Harry, energy increasing every moment, dived upon her. Again she woke, again she slept. The steady vibration of the air-conditioning gave her a confused sense of being still in the airplane.

Harry seemed not to notice her inattentiveness. He talked: "It's a circle, you see. Or it should be. We try to complete it continually. In all sorts of ways. Love. Marriage. Work. Success. Probably children too. Art, of course. Most important. A line of perfect poetry." Here he quoted several lines from Pliny, somewhat imperfectly. "Music. Yes, definitely music." Here he shook Flavia. "We must immediately get a decent stereo. America's a very good place to buy. Music. Music." His voice trailed off. Flavia sighed and snuggled into his arms.

He ran his hand down her hip and legs. "Beauty," he began again. "Beauty!" Meditation increased to exclamation. It seemed at that moment he had the secret of life within his grasp. University career A-I. Entrance to diplomatic future at the top. Love, beauty, sent to prove the unlimited boundaries of his sexual prowess. Yet again he fell on Flavia.

Sleep was the last thing he wanted. But some outside force immobilized his limbs before he could take countermeasures, and the numbness spread to his brain. He was asleep. Outside, the lights of the city stage had been switched off. A curtain of crushed pearl hung between night and the glare of a new day.

A few minutes later Flavia woke up. It was light enough to see the time on her bedside watch. Five A.M. Ten o'clock in England. She covered Harry's sprawled body with a sheet and went to sit by the window.

She eased the slats of the blind a little so that she could watch the sun come up in orange stripes. She turned off the air-conditioning so that it was quiet. They were too high up to hear any street noises. Occasionally she glanced back at Harry. She was proud that he had felt such ecstasy the night before. She had inspired it, at least, even if she had not been able to share it altogether but they had a whole marriage to put that right.

Besides, she had at this moment, a different kind of ectascy, a soulful standing outside of her body. Oh, to be a poet! Flavia, wrapped in her honeymoon negligee, sat dreaming.

Three hours later Harry woke and bounded out of bed. He saw Flavia and embraced her fondly. He ordered breakfast, showered, dressed, commandeered taxis, airplanes, hired cars. Flavia, slight and pale, swam in his wake. She wasn't unhappy in his mastery. The energetic union between her parents gave her a romantic view of the docile wife.

They arrived at their seaside house in the early evening. It stood among trees about half a mile down a sandy track to the water's edge. The sky above the trees was a delicious pansy purple.

"Let's go for a swim!" Flavia suggested. She had a drawn look around the eyes. Her slim arms, usually so languid and graceful, looked angular and brittle.

"I need a drink." Harry made himself a gin and tonic and sat down on the sofa. The house was made of shiny orange wood, inside and out. In front of him, atop a shiny table, was a shiny television set.

Flavia unpacked her new bikini from her case. She took a towel and stood at the door. Harry looked up. "I'll come in a moment."

Flavia flitted down the sandy track. There was more light outside the trees, but it still had that theatrical purple tinge indicating the approach of night. The air matched exactly the temperature of her body, and a sea breeze gently lifted the hair off the back of her neck.

Harry turned on the television and became absorbed in remembering the rules of American football. Then he fell asleep.

It was dark when Flavia returned. She felt as if she were entering a stranger's house. Harry slept so deeply that the idea of death occurred to her. But his body when she touched it was very warm and soft. Also immobile and immovable. She left him and went to do the unpacking. When he still hadn't awakened at eleven she went to bed. Quite contentedly, she thought again of the long years of marriage ahead which would bring them close together. So passed Harry and Flavia's second night of marriage.

During the next week, Harry began to see he was a man of action. He did not like sprawling on sand under sun, near sea, as Flavia did.

Now Harry drove off every morning to collect the papers. Often he stopped for a coffee at the local drugstore. Sometimes he became engaged in conversations which he reported back to Flavia.

"America is looking for a hero," he announced one day, which was not so prescient, considering Kennedy was already president.

He liked watching television and hired a boat on a couple of occasions. He was joined by Flavia on the first expedition but she soon pronounced the experience either boring or frightening. Harry was not upset by her reaction. He appreciated her separateness. It made the nights when she lay naked in his arms more exciting. No one had taught him how to love with friendly affection. On the fifth night he noticed a little wetness around Flavia's eyes but he didn't feel it his right to ask the reason, and Flavia said nothing.

At the start of the second week they drove off together to look for Belinda. The address led them to a hinterland of smallish houses with porches, gray lawns and dark spruces. It was a particularly hot day with low clouds covering the sun and no wind. The lack of sun was probably the reason Flavia had consented to come. Her skin was now a deep golden color and her hair almost white. Harry was unchanged, partly because of his naturally olive skin but mostly because he never sat in the sun.

"There's 3022!" cried Flavia. Harry felt a moment of terror. Flavia, jumping out of the car, all white and gold, looked like some exotic moth. There was no other human visible on the street nor a car that moved. It was midday, the place as still as if it were midnight.

They stepped between the lawn to the front door. Harry rang the doorbell, and Flavia pulled at the screen door. Harry rang again.

The door opened inward very suddenly. "Sshh!" said a voice. "Pollock's sleeping." It was dark in the hall and very hot. The figure stepped backward into a sitting-room. That too was dimly lit, with venetian blinds over every window.

"Oh," said Belinda, "It's . . ." She hesitated.

"Harry."

"Harry?" She came closer.

"Henry. And this is"—he paused—"my wife." It was the first time he had pronounced the word, and he looked at Flavia for confirmation. But she merely shook her head like a pony.

Belinda laughed. "This is just great!" She stood with her hands on her hips. She wore a halter-neck T-shirt, shorts and sneakers. Her hair was pulled back into a rubber band and her face glistened without makeup. Behind her stood a television set, mouthing energetically, and a table on which a cigarette smoked. Harry and Flavia took in these signs of decadence with the same widening of eyes. They were reminded that this was another country, another culture.

“Well, sit down. Make yourself at home. Coffee? Cake?” Belinda left the room but returned almost immediately. She poured out good strong coffee and cut slices off a chocolate cake. Harry remembered how they had cooked together as children. “I usually have a nap while Pollock sleeps, so this is my get-up-and-go lunch. Coffee for the brain, cake for the body. Pollock and Tom have supper when he gets back from work and then I go out to swell the family income.”

“To work, you mean.” Harry cleared his throat. He remembered how Belinda had always swept him along with her life.

“Yup.” She sat back on her chair, stretching out her naked legs toward him. “We’re saving.” She glanced at Flavia. “To go out West. Besides, we’d be divorced by now if we spent every evening together.”

Harry felt his eyes open wider. Flavia sighed. How did people dare say things like that? “What do you work at?” she asked.

“Waiting at table.” Belinda shrugged. Then smiled. “I get my supper, too.”

There was a short pause. “So are you two having a good time?”

The strong coffee was making Harry’s heart throb uncomfortably. He could feel sweat like pins and needles around his neck and in his armpits. The room was very hot. He noticed that Flavia’s sunburn had taken on a greenish tinge. “We were hoping to take you out for lunch,” he said firmly.

“That would be just great. I’ll go wake Pollock.”

Pollock was not keen to be wakened. He appeared with flushed cheeks and small, tearful eyes.

Belinda had put on plastic flip-flops and changed her halterneck for a white blouse.

They stood in a group between the gray lawn and the car. Pollock became almost human at the sight of the car. “I guess that’s a Buick?”

“I don’t know,” apologized Harry. He remembered his passion for cars as a small boy. “It’s an American car, you see, and I only know about English ones.”

“Are they bigger?”

“Smaller, I’m afraid.”

“Are American cars the biggest cars in the world?”

“Yes. I should say that’s so.”

They all got into the car. Harry wondered about the question of reality. Why did Belinda's life seem so much more real than his and Flavia's? Was it her self-possession, her house, her child, her job, her attitude to her husband? He wanted none of them and yet there was something about it he admired. For example, it was simply impossible to imagine Flavia in a job.

Flavia, in the back seat with Pollock, fought against carsickness. Although she was glad to see a little of real America, she imagined with longing the cool sea waves.

They ate in a hamburger restaurant recommended by Belinda. The air-conditioning made it very cool and both Harry and Flavia revived. Harry drank American beer and began to talk about Cuba. Actually, it was more in the nature of a lecture.

His sense of his own reality revived. Pollock was quiet while he concentrated on his food. Belinda listened with a faraway look on her face.

"You're so clever," she said. "You always were, of course. Tom is interested in politics. The politics of making money."

Flavia said, "You make me quite ashamed."

Belinda and Harry looked at her in surprise.

"Working. Money. I never think of things like that at all."

Harry dropped his head.

"I've finished. Let's go now!" Pollock, stoked with food, found a very loud voice. Flavia's comment, ostensible praise but possibly criticism, was overwhelmed.

The hamburger restaurant had been windowless, lit in rubicund gloom. Outside they found a storm in progress. Lightning split the clouds like silver marbling. Globules of rain fell out of the cracks in alternating flurries. Pollock danced about shouting. Flavia, too, became happy and excited. "Let's go for a swim. I love swimming in the rain!"

"Where's the sea?" Harry asked Belinda.

She waved her hand. "Not far. Over there."

"I wanna swim in the rain!" shouted Pollock.

They were all getting very wet. Harry put a newspaper over his head. The drops of rain were so big that they threw up a splash as they made contact.

Flavia and Pollock ran up and down the pavement laughing. Belinda, who was watching them, suddenly looked old. She turned to Harry. "Tom likes a decent meal when he gets in. I ought to go back now. We'll come and see you over the weekend."

"We leave on Sunday."

"We'll come on Saturday."

They walked toward the car. Soon the others followed.

When they reached Belinda's house, she squeezed Harry's forearm. "I was so in love with your father."

Pollock and Flavia talked about cars in the back seat.

"I never knew that."

"You never even knew he was banging my mother," Belinda laughed.

Harry was more pained by the expression "banging" and the laugh than by the information it contained. "He always liked women."

"I'll say."

"What happened to your mother?"

"Four times married, four times divorced."

"I'm sorry."

"I wanna get out!" Pollock pushed forward Harry's seat so violently that the steering wheel wrenched at his stomach.

Belinda kissed Harry's cheek. "See you Saturday. I want you to meet Tom while I still have him."

"The rain's stopped." They both looked at the windshield, which glistened with slowly swelling drops.

"It's raining, raining in my heart," sang Belinda and hopped out of the car.

"Not a very good advertisement for marriage," commented Flavia on their way home.

"We haven't seen Tom yet," said Harry, appearing loyal. In fact he was irritated by Flavia's assumption that there was such a general state as "marriage" which could be good or bad. He did not believe in such a stupid idea or he would never have married Flavia.

Flavia was glad she was beautiful and ethereal. Harry would never love someone like Belinda. "Saturday could be interesting." Her face wore an unaccustomed expression of curiosity mingled with complacency.

Flavia wandered up from the beach, towel dragging, legs weary. From fifty yards away she saw a car, like a giant silver porpoise, come swimming up to their house. Screened by the trees, she watched as several people got out. Only Pollock in scarlet shorts and striped T-shirt was recognizable.

Harry, having a lunchtime snack of pastrami on rye while

reading the *New York Herald Tribune* in front of the television, did not hear the car arrive.

"Well, hi!"

He looked up to see a figure shining with color and energy like a cover photograph of a magazine. It was Belinda, he realized after a moment, but a very different Belinda from the one they had found in her home. This visiting Belinda wore golden curls, scarlet lips, blue eye shadow, a pink-and-white-spotted dress with a full skirt and tightly belted waist, and was perched on very high white sandals.

"Hello," he managed somewhat shakily.

"You are expecting us, aren't you?"

"Oh, yes." Harry felt himself flush. Behind Belinda he caught a glimpse of a man in a white jacket and another woman. Where was Flavia? They knew Belinda was coming and yet had not been expecting them. Number 3022, the hamburger restaurant and the storm had become myth.

The man came forward. He stuck out a hand. "Tom Fuchs. Glad to meet you." He looked round. "Nice place you have here."

Harry remembered real estate was his business. Out of the corner of his eye he saw Flavia sneak in behind their guests and race upstairs.

"And do you see who we've brought along, too?" Belinda presented the other woman like a conjurer with a rabbit.

She was, in fact, more like a marmoset. Bright inquiring eyes in a wizened little face within a ruffle of pleated hair.

"Look! He doesn't recognize me. Well, Henry, I am shocked!"

As he looked at this representative of the human species, Harry felt a profound antipathy for his race. He could think of no reason why contact with such as stood before him should be possible, let alone profitable.

"It's my mother!" laughed Belinda. "Queenie."

Harry came to life. Crushing down the dark thoughts of his soul, he made drinks, opened cans of nuts, conveyed information in a manner which was relevant. Soon Flavia appeared with freshly brushed hair and the docile expression of a good child on her face.

"I do admire your car," she said to Tom.

"We borrowed it." Belinda gave her husband a look of dislike.

"I'm kinda fond of European cars," said Tom.

"Oh, Europe, Europe!" sighed the marmoset. "How is darling England?"

Neither Flavia nor Harry felt able to answer this question.

"So, you're going West?" said Harry, after a pause.

"She told you, did she?" Tom gave his wife a look of dislike.

Harry caught Flavia's eye and looked away hurriedly.

"There's a lovely beach here," suggested Flavia.

Queenie wanted to stay in the house with Harry and talk about old times. So the party split, the girls taking the child to the water.

Queenie drank gin and tonics. Her appearance improved, her cheeks filled out and her voice deepened. Tom, too, soon seemed a good enough chap. He was thickset with broad cheekbones and a short nose. His voice had a pleasant twang and he talked about money as if it were a much-loved but difficult friend. "Last week I really had it made. It was a property on the seafront with two acres adjoining . . ."

He listened with a patient kind of patronage to Harry's account of his own career to date and his future prospects.

"So what you need is a foreign assignment pronto?" he commented very sensibly.

"And I'll get one," said Harry.

"Just like his father. Always so decisive." Queenie sighed over her gin and tonic. "So handsome."

"A fellow's got to take his chances." Tom beamed approvingly at Harry.

By the time the beach party returned, Harry felt Belinda would be pretty silly to let such a good egg slip through her grasp. He tried to tell her in a muddled sort of way. "You wanted a husband so much. I can remember that. In Ireland."

"You're drunk." Belinda gave him a stony look. "All of you."

"Oh, I say." In Harry's set it was not the sort of thing you said, however true it might be. Flavia laughed at her husband's face.

Belinda drove the silver porpoise away. Tom, at her side, gave the victory salute out of the window. Queenie and Pollock lolled in the back, one inebriated, the other asleep. Flavia and Harry watched them go.

"And I did mean to bring up the subject of Jackson Pollock!" exclaimed Flavia.

Chapter 13

Harry opted for the Arabic department of the Foreign Office. Lionel advised him against it. "You'll be stuck out in godforsaken holes. Europe's the place now, my boy. Look at me. Stuck with the Raj as if it still existed." Lionel was about to be sent back once more to Delhi as High Commissioner. "And if you're still not convinced, just remember Egypt!"

Harry was still not convinced. Europe seemed tame. He wanted a new challenge, a new language, a new world. Flavia had hardly finished furnishing a small house in Fulham—with an efficiency that surprised both of them—when he was sent out to MECAS, the Middle East College for Arabic Studies, near Beirut.

The day before they left Flavia received a letter confirming she was pregnant. She did not tell Harry. She felt uneasy that they did not talk about things like that. Their flat looked down from the heights of the city to a dazzling view of sea and sky. Bougainvillea grew round their terrace in sunset-pink clouds, and at night the blackness was decorated by garlands of silver tinsel. They hardly knew where the city lights ended and the stars began.

Despite (or because of) being the daughter of two doctors, Flavia had striven successfully to retain a romantic notion of the body. When Harry commented on her swelling breasts, she attributed it to the unusual winter warmth and sunshine. She did not want to falsify the situation, but she did not like to feel herself entirely subservient to ordinary bodily functions. She had not *felt* as if she were conceiving a baby.

Also, she feared Harry's reaction. If he was proud she would feel humiliated, reduced to an object on the long assembly line of the female species. If he was disgusted, which in a sense was the attitude she would most understand, she could hardly help being depressed.

She decided to tell him, finally, in a nightclub. Beirut was full of nightclubs. Apart from their MECAS fellow students, they soon made a great many friends. Flavia's flaring blond hair made her particularly popular in a land of dark luster. It was dancing with a Lebanese reputed to be worth twenty million dollars that decided her to break the news.

The Lebanese, who was one of the most handsome men Flavia had ever seen and spoke exquisite English spiced with snippets of other languages, leaned close and whispered in her ear, "You are *enceinte,* my dear, and so beautiful, so beautiful. . . ."

It took Flavia a moment to understand his compliment. Luckily the lights were too low for him to see her blushes. If he could see she was pregnant, then how many others? It would be unfair to allow Harry's blind English eyes to make him the last to know.

He was sitting at a table with a half-Lebanese, half-French woman called Elise. This confirmed Flavia in her decision. She had learned recently of Harry's liaison in Paris, which had led her to the conclusion that his French blood made him susceptible to Frankish charm. He said he cultivated Elise to practice his French but Flavia distrusted her soulful black eyes, spiky bosom and tightly trousered buttocks. Besides, more often than not, she spoke a deliciously accented English.

Flavia sat down beside them. It oftened surprised her that Harry had taken to nightclubs with such enthusiasm.

Elise patted his arm. "Good night, *cher* 'arry, 'appy dreams."

"You're going early."

"Tomorrow I am up early and off on the road to Jerusalem."

Elise was a journalist. She carried everywhere a large shoulder bag stuffed with assignments. Flavia had never seen an article written by her but Harry pointed out they went back to France. She was in her thirties and had been divorced five or six years ago.

When she had gone, Harry suddenly looked tired. "I don't know why the classes start so early," he grumbled.

"I've got something to tell you."

"Let's walk home, shall we? I'd like some air."

So Flavia decided to tell him under the night sky. They walked arm in arm. They could not afford to buy many drinks, so neither of them was drunk but their hearts were full of this bright new life.

Harry thought of all the cities in which he'd lived. He thought of Delhi, Kandy, Cairo, New York, Madrid, Paris, London. Yet this city, Beirut, a European island set in an Arab sea, seemed the most mysterious and magical. Elise, who had known it for years, called it the second Paris.

He became aware Flavia was speaking. She was using the voice Harry inwardly described as "mists of romance." It usually made its appearance to soften practical matters, often requests, such as the need for more housekeeping money or for Harry to put his underclothes in the laundry basket. Sometimes the mist deepened into fog and Harry couldn't understand what she was on about at all. This seemed to be one of those occasions.

". . . in a country so remote. Starting a new life without . . ."

"What?" said Harry.

"I'm having a baby," said Flavia.

They both stopped walking. "I'm having a baby," repeated Flavia and burst into tears. The double pronouncement of her personal responsibility for this creature growing inside her was overwhelming.

"You're having a baby," muttered Harry with bewilderment which even darkness could not hide. Indeed, in this first moment he did not think of linking himself with the event.

Nor did Flavia press the point. She allowed Harry to pat her shoulder with thoughtful sympathy. She sniffed and stopped crying.

Harry began walking again. She had to run a little to catch up. She waited hopefully for Harry to say something.

And Harry wanted to speak. He saw this was a moment when words would be really appropriate. But he could not find them. He thought, This is the sort of thing that happens to other people. But that made it sound like death. He thought, Frankly I just don't believe it! But now he came to think of it, Flavia had changed shape lately. For the better, too. That cheered him and gave him a line.

"That's why you've been looking so beautiful!" he said and laughed.

Flavia recoiled a little at the laugh, which seemed to lack reverence for the wonders of nature but, on the whole, felt his reaction could be considered as a pleasant acceptance. "I'm so glad you feel like that." She sighed. Perhaps they would never have to talk like this again.

Harry gave her a surprised look, again lost in the dark. He was not aware of describing his feelings. Indeed he didn't know how he felt. However, it seemed that he had satisfied Flavia. She walked beside him now with a happy spring in her step. Babies, after all, took some time to grow. There would be plenty of time to reflect on the various aspects of the case.

"Home again, home again, clippety clop." He took Flavia's arm and tucked it through his.

"I'm worn out," murmured Flavia contentedly.

Harry's judgment of the pregnancy time lag turned out to be over-generous. Flavia was already four and a half months along the way. He was busy. Weeks sped by, unnoticed. Spring made their social life even more sybaritic. Flavia spent long afternoons on the beach where Harry joined her at the end of the day for a swim. He became used to her bulge as he might a new armchair in their living room.

In May they made a trip to Palmyra in Syria. Soon after their return, Flavia said, "My mother says I should go back to England in the next week or so and have the baby there."

She sounded so unusually practical and positive about this that Harry didn't think to argue. It never occurred to him that he could be present at the birth. He was still only twenty-three years old.

The day after Flavia's departure, Harry became Elise's lover. Without Flavia's bodily presence, he simply felt unmarried. Elise, with her knowledge of the Lebanon and her questioning mind (which Harry described to himself as masculine), seemed like part of his job. She even began seriously learning Arabic so that they could study together.

The problem with Elise was that she was, like the man on the underground train, not quite what she seemed. In short, she was a spy. Not a grand kind of spy who steals valuable information, causing death to hundreds. Her simple job was to report on what might be roughly described as "atmosphere." Atmosphere being made up of people, she naturally made it her business to move energetically in many different circles. This was what made her so attractive to Harry. Her "questioning," as it were.

Elise was a French spy. Or so her country understood. Great Britain was not quite so certain. At about the time Flavia was entering a very nice maternity hospital near Marlborough, Harry was called in to the office of the First Secretary political. He had come straight from a class entitled "Arabic, Language of Disguise."

The First Secretary, whose name was Myrtle—surname, that is—shook hands in a friendly manner and indicated a chair. Although he gave no indication of it, he was thrown off balance by

Harry's appearance. He had been told to warn off a young man at 136 the start of his Foreign Office career from a potentially dangerous situation. It had seemed a routine matter in which he spoke, as it were, from on high and the callow youth bowed from low to even lower. But this—he looked at his note—Hayes had a disturbing air of confidence. Or perhaps, more exactly, independence.

He looked at the notes more carefuly. First at Oxford. Passed fifth into the Office. Clearly a high flyer. Married. Very young to marry. Wife back home having a baby. Well, that was the point.

"Your wife getting on all right, I hope?"

"She's with her parents," said Harry.

"Very sensible." Myrtle paused. He often thought his own wife had children in order to go home. They had four boys and one girl at the last count. He looked at Harry. "Lonely for you, though?"

Harry frowned, then smiled. "Not really." He was wondering when the small talk would develop into something more interesting.

Myrtle felt distinctly nonplussed. Surely no young husband admitted to not missing his new bride? He looked at the notes again. The name Hayes-Middleton caught his eye. His father. Harry Hayes, son of Lionel Hayes-Middleton. Suddenly it all became clear.

"I knew your father," he said, "in Cairo. In fact, I probably knew you." Even if he didn't know him, Myrtle thought, he knew boys like him. They all had a slightly dazed expression masked under an air of independence and competency. Myrtle, whose father was a solicitor, had a theory about it. The dazed expression appeared the first time they were uprooted from home and hearth. It became more deeply fixed with the advent of boarding school. Of course Hayes didn't miss his wife. He had taught himself at the age of eight to miss nobody and now wouldn't know how to. Poor young chap! Myrtle sighed.

Harry shifted about in his chair. He had grown up with men like Myrtle. They slipped in and out of his father's office with a smell of the second-rate hanging about them. In the old days they would have been in the Consular Service. "Was it something special you wanted to see me about?" he said rather loudly.

Myrtle jumped. So deep was he in the delights of psychoanalysis that he had forgotten his mission. "I'm afraid so." There was no point in beating about the bush with a son of the Foreign Office. "Been asked to warn you off"—he glanced at his notes—"Mademoiselle Elise. Planchette. No questions, no answers. Just take my word that it's better you stay at—er—a little more distance than—er—you have up to now."

Myrtle became aware of Hayes's very dark eyes staring rather too directly. "I presume this is not for moral reasons," he said.

Myrtle gulped. "You misunderstand me." He halted.

"I'm sorry." Harry now wore a sulky, child-like expression.

"It's matter of national security." Myrtle was suddenly cloaked in official pomposity. "Mademoiselle Planchette is considered a security risk."

At once Harry's expression changed. He had been misled by the social nature of their earlier exchanges. Now he heard the voice of the Foreign Office, he had no hesitations. "I'm sorry," he said again. "I didn't understand. I can't avoid seeing her altogether but I will do as you say."

"Thank you." Myrtle leaped to his feet. "That's a closed subject then. Now the moment your wife returns I want her to meet Emma, my wife. I know they'll have so much in common."

"Thank you," said Harry.

Harry went back to his flat. He didn't feel like classes that afternoon. He lay on a daybed on their veranda. It was very hot. He rose to pour himself a beer and then returned. His thoughts drifted. First, with some regret but no real pain, to the loss of Elise. He supposed he would have to be more careful. Unlike many young diplomats, he was not in awe of the upper echelons of the Foreign Office. He had met them around the world in his father's company. Indeed he could give them the face of his father if he cared. Yet he also remembered his father's years of disgrace after Suez. "They" had sent him to Spain. "They" were faceless, black-suited, seated permanently in London, spiders in the middle of a giant web.

Harry half closed his eyes. Had his unfortunate liaison twitched the web a little? Had the spider's eyes swiveled toward him disapprovingly? Was a hairy black leg waving in his direction? Harry shut his eyes entirely.

Flavia's eyes were also shut.

"Push!" cried the nurse with sympatheic aggression. "You've got to work. You've got to WORK to CREATE!"

Frankly Flavia couldn't believe this was happening to her. The pain was one thing, expected, after all, but the sense of indignity, of being split apart in places whose existence she preferred to forget, was a nasty surprise. She opened her eyes and cast them upward to her mother, whose doctor status had placed her near at hand.

Dr. Morton caught the appeal and squeezed her hand. "You're doing very well, dear."

"Here we go again," cried the nurse, hand on Flavia's tummy. "Push! Push! Ha, ha! Now we've got some progress."

Flavia shut her eyes again. A fleeting image of escape brought silver to the cloud. She was running light-footed across a lawn. But then the pain swelled up again.

"I think it's time for Doctor." The nurse brushed her hands together and departed.

"Second stage," whispered Flavia's mother conspiratorially.

Lines from Shakespeare began to go through Flavia's head. When the next pain came she cried inwardly: "There's hell, there's darkness, there is the sulphurous pit . . ."

And as the doctor arrived and there was hardly pause to breathe or think, wave after wave of words filled her head till she thought it might burst even before her stomach. "Howl, howl, howl, howl! O! You are men of stones:/Had I your tongues and eyes, I'd use them so/That heaven's vaults should crack. She's gone forever."

"You've a lovely baby son," said the doctor.

"Daughter," corrected the nurse, turning the baby round.

"Daugher," echoed Dr. Morton, smoothing Flavia's forehead. "A perfect little girl. Well done, darling. Well done."

Flavia smiled. Her head still rang with Shakespeare but her body felt gloriously at peace. The tempest of birth had thrown her about, but she had emerged triumphant. The baby itself, product of triumph, did not yet catch her imagination.

"Can I go to sleep?" she murmured, already halfway there.

"One shake of a lamb's tail," said the nurse, swaddling the baby with cheerful efficiency. "Then I'll settle you down. Baby first, mummy after. That's the way it'll be now, I'm afraid."

Harry met Flavia and the baby at the Beirut airport. He did not know what to expect. He knew no one who had a baby. He couldn't remember ever consciously looking at a baby. The idea of himself as a father was clearly ludicrous. The idea of Flavia as a mother was hardly less so. Yet she had produced the baby from within her body and there was no doubt he had dealt her the seed.

Harry waited in the hot and noisy airport with defensive trepidation.

Flavia appeared to Harry's eyes totally unchanged. She even wore the same dress she had left in, made out of mattress ticking.

At her side an airport official carried a small cot. She pointed to Harry. They came together. Harry put his arm round her.

"How was your journey?"

"All right. Do you want to look at Cordelia?"

"Who?" Harry's voice expressed horror.

"Cordelia. If you like."

Harry bent over the bassinet. All he could see was half a tiny pink face and a lot of wrapping. This was a relief. More than that. A joy. Half a tiny face and no body was unthreatening and beautiful.

"She's beautiful!"

"Yes," agreed Flavia modestly. "She'll probably wake for a feed soon." She caught the scared look on Harry's face and smiled. "At home. There's time to get home."

Cordelia, as she became without more discussion, was four weeks old. She had wisps of fine blond hair, small button features and pink and white skin. She was very like a Victorian doll. This likeness was accentuated by Flavia's treatment of her. She dressed her in pretty clothes and propped her about the room.

Harry never knew where he'd see her next. Once, coming in after dark, he nearly trod on her. She was leaning against the wainscoting in the hall fast asleep.

Flavia was apologetic. "I put her there when I brought in the groceries. And then she fell asleep so I didn't like to move her."

"But that was two or three hours ago." Without being critical, for after all he knew nothing, Harry felt that Flavia's approach might differ from the authorized version.

"Never wake a sleeping child," said Flavia less apologetically.

In fact Cordelia was an extremely good and contented baby. When Flavia was dressing she lay in her underclothes drawer gurgling and kicking. When she was cooking, she bounced up and down on the kitchen scales. If they had visitors to dinner she was placed in the middle of the dining-room table as a living decoration.

When Flavia went outside the flat she took Cordelia in her arms, shifting her from one hip to the other. Although she gave up breast-feeding her early on, she was otherwise as close to the baby as it was possible to be. Harry's worries for the baby, ill-defined as they were, could hardly stand up to such strong motherly caring. It was something to do with human dignity, he felt vaguely, and an image of Myrtle with his five children came into his mind.

A day or two later Flavia was walking back from the market

carrying Cordelia in one arm and a large bag of oranges in the other. It was a cloudless blue day and both mother and child wore white panama hats. Nevertheless their faces were pink and shiny.

Flavia stopped for a rest. She put down the bag and switched the baby to the other hip. When she looked up a woman was prancing in front of her. At least she moved nervously from leg to leg.

"I'm Emma Myrtle," she said, "from the embassy. I've been meaning to look you up for ages, so when I saw you down the street I couldn't resist. We saw quite a bit of your husband while you were away. What a perfectly lovely baby! Can I hold her? I've got five, you know. The youngest a bit older than this. A girl too. First girl, actually."

Flavia handed over Cordelia, since otherwise it seemed this woman might go on talking forever. She shook out her arm. How wonderful it was to be out in the sunshine carrying nothing!" "Where's your baby?"

"At home with the nurse. Coo, coo, little pretty. Has your pram broken?"

"Pram?"

"For the baby."

"I haven't got one."

"You don't think a stroller's bad for her back?"

"I haven't got a stroller either."

"Oh."

"I just didn't think of it."

Emma now saw why Harry had asked Myrtle (she thought of her husband as a surname) to ask her to give Flavia a helping hand. The poor child didn't have a clue. Probably a university graduate, thought Emma, who shared her husband's taste for analytical detective work. All brains and no sense.

"I'll tell you what. Why don't you come for lunch?"

"Yes," said Flavia, gratefully. Why ever hadn't she thought of a stroller?

Emma, who enjoyed organizing, although in a general, fairly chaotic way, soon had Flavia fixed up with a daily nurse and a large colonial-style pram. Surprisingly, the two women then became friends. Flavia told Emma about her medical background and her revolt against it, about her love of English literature and the circumstances of her meeting and romance with Harry. To Emma it all had an air of unreality, like children playing, but she supposed that was just because of the age difference. She was twelve years older than Flavia.

Emma told Flavia about her own background at a day-school convent, about her job as a secretary in a solicitor's office and her meeting and falling in love with Myrtle. "He represented to me all the romance of the great world. Still does, as a matter of fact."

Flavia admired this capability for love, which she felt a lack of in herself. She admired it even more after she'd met Myrtle. She was also fascinated by Emma's Catholicism. The rhythm method of contraception became a favorite topic of conversation.

Since Cordelia's birth, sex had become more of a duty than a pleasure for Flavia. Harry, on the other hand, was delighted to find her body unimpaired by what he understood to be a racking experience. The slight thickening at the waist and hips lasted a few weeks and then disappeared, leaving her just as she'd been before. Since he had been celibate for nearly two months, he lost no time. Unlike Flavia, he had always found sex the easiest and most relaxing of occupations. He found no difficulty in shutting down his brain and felt a delicious lack of self-consciousness which he never achieved at any other time. He loved Flavia and he loved her body but when they lay together she might have been anyone.

This made him less sensitive to Flavia's feelings. Therefore she could disguise her fundamental coolness. But the need for secrecy made her grow more separate from him. This made her unhappy and she would have liked to talk about it. But Harry's daytime self was silent and scornful of personal introspection. He laughed about Emma's Catholicism as if it were a silly woman's whim. The Virgin and Child had not come with them to Beirut.

Flavia once or twice tried to start a conversation at night but he was so comfortable with himself, so sleepily satisfied, that she couldn't be so cruel. Often now when the baby slept and Harry was out sharpening his brain, she lay across their bed in a haze of romantic yearning. Without Emma and the Beirut nightlife, which continued as energetically as ever, she would have been truly unhappy. Cordelia seemed too much part of herself to be a source of comfort.

At a simple level, she was extremely lonely.

Sometimes they went to dinner at the Myrtles. Harry went on sufferance. "Not the Myrtles again!"

"We haven't been for weeks. Anyway you're the one who wanted us to be friends."

"I wanted her to help you with the baby."

"Emma's more than a nanny. She has very deep convictions. . . ." Flavia stumbled under Harry's cynical stare. "You're an intellectual snob. That's your trouble."

Harry smiled, not at all displeased at the idea.

"Julian will have to come too."

"Julian?"

"He made his presence known at the British Embassy. I left a message inviting him round this evening."

Flavia retired to consider this. Julian's flamboyant costume and homosexual ways had made him quite a figure at Oxford. She knew he was a friend of Harry's—he had, of course, been at their wedding—but she thought they had lost touch, even quarreled. Julian and Myrtle seemed an odd combination.

Harry was curious, in a competitive way, about Julian's circumstances. Their last proper conversation had taken place on Julian's building site when he had made fun of a Foreign Office future.

"Shall I take my bow?"

Harry was under the shower when Julian arrived. Julian pulled back the curtain to present himself, a glittering figure all in white.

"Your preoccupation with clothes always amazes me." Harry came out, dripping.

"But then I'm not a naked Adonis like you."

Harry grabbed a towel, laughing. He knew he was healthy, sunburnt and working hard. Julian's face was almost as white as his suit. "You haven't been long in the Middle East?"

"This morning. Direct from the motherland. Fifty-five degrees and raining. I decided to come out last night. Congratulations, incidentally!"

"What on?"

Julian raised his eyebrows with mock surprise. "Fatherhood. So soon. So young."

Harry put down the towel and started to dress. He felt exhilarated by Julian's presence. The evening seemed full of possibilities. He liked his mocking admiration. "So you have no business here?"

"Business? I have no business in England. I am a roving arbiter of good taste. A heartwarming example of what can be achieved on a small private income."

"So the building industry must do without you?"

"Decree absolute."

Flavia found, after all, Julian amusing. She felt he might discuss the sort of things she worried about—and Harry would never talk about—even if his heart was in the wrong place. They had several drinks before they left for the Myrtles and Julian took a tray from the kitchen because he wanted to present Cordelia as if on the shield of a Great Knight of Yore. 143

"Look here, she's my child!" protested Harry.

"It's no good. You just don't have the knight-like qualities necessary." He struck a pose with tray, happily minus baby, across his chest. "You have to be swashbuckling, independent and answerable only to your inner being!" He picked up a spoon and banged the tray. "Your heart must beat like a drum and . . ."

Eventually they left and arrived in excellent spirits at the Myrtles'. There, two drawbacks to the evening immediately presented themselves. First, Myrtle's four-year-old child could not sleep and installed itself on the drawing-room sofa from where it muttered and tossed. Secondly, it was Friday and fish was on the menu, filling the small hot flat with a pungent aroma.

"Sorry about the smell," Emma apologized the moment they arrived. "It's a local specialty. Three different sorts of fish served with arrack and laid on a bed of garlic."

"How delightful!" Julian kissed her hand. "And so kind of you to have me." He then gently moved the legs of the child and sat down with a pleased and expectant expression.

"I'm John Myrtle," said Myrtle.

"But everyone calls him Myrtle," cried Emma.

"Just passing through, are you?" Myrtle offered around a tray of wine.

"Are we not all?'"

Emma hooted appreciatively. It was a line perfectly attuned to her point of view. "Our son's headmaster says he is training the boys for death."

"Very sensible," agreed Julian emphatically. "What school did you say it was?"

Julian and Emma embarked on an intense examination of the meaning of life with particular regard to the proper preparation through educational channels.

This left Harry and Myrtle to swap valuable information about the new Ambassador expected to arrive the following week. Flavia listened. Surely she had not done so much listening in the past?

The child went to sleep, the fish was burnt beyond recall, much wine was consumed and they had omelettes cooked by Julian for supper.

"Your friend is splendid!" Emma sparkled over the bubbling coffeepot. Flavia agreed. She looked from the kitchen to where the men sat waiting on the veranda. A delicious perfume coiled toward her.

"Julian's smoking something nice," Flavia remarked.

Emma sniffed, but the smell of coffee dominated. They went out.

Julian stretched his hand languidly to Harry. "Want a puff?"

Harry, Flavia and Myrtle instantly realized what he was offering. Harry declined, Myrtle stood up and sat down again in an agitated manner and Flavia smiled as if she were having a nice time all by herself.

"It's good stuff," said Julian, rather hurt. "I got it in the market this morning. Dirt cheap too. One of your embassy porters directed me. Fellow with a squint."

Myrtle seemed about to speak but before he could Emma held out her hand. "I'd love a puff. It smells like all my favorite things rolled into one."

"Better than fish on a bed of garlic," agreed Julian, who felt more at home every minute.

But before Emma could take the cigarette, a barricade in the form of Myrtle sprang up between them.

"Not in my house, you don't!" His normally regular features seemed from Harry's point of view to be dancing all over his face. Or perhaps that was the effect of the alcohol. They had all drunk a good deal.

"We're on the veranda," suggested Julian, apparently not realizing the seriousness of his host's anger.

"Oh, dear." Emma looked round at Harry. "Is it something we shouldn't . . . ?"

"It is!" Myrtle interrupted with loud voice. "What your friend is offering you is an artificial stimulant, an illegal narcotic, either hashish or marijuana, an addictive substance which has caused the downfall of millions."

"Oh, dear," murmured Emma again.

Julian looked blearily at his cigarette. "I'd never quite thought of it like that."

"Well, you'd better start thinking now!" Myrtle's manner as aggressive enough to make even Julian take note.

Harry felt he should say something sensible and soothing. "As a matter of interest, is hash illegal out here?"

Myrtle did not seemed soothed. "I would remind you that you are on British soil. This is a registered diplomatic residence. For all intents and purposes, legal included, we are in Great Britain!"

This last trumpet cry had the unfortunate effect of waking the child on the sofa, who began to scream. Her screaming awoke Cordelia, who also screamed. The noise, even on the veranda, even on British soil, was terrific.

"Christ!" Julian dropped his cigarette over the veranda's edge and looked as if he wanted to follow.

"We will leave," announced Harry. "With all apologies."

"Quite." Julian wriggled past Myrtle, who, apparently impervious to noise, stood fixed in an avenging angel's pose.

"Such a pity," murmured Flavia with Cordelia at her hip.

Julian tried to look for Emma's hand to kiss but she was almost completely submerged under whimpering children. He contented himself with a general wave. "Splendid evening, splendid. Tempered only by my crass misjudgment, for which I apologize. Many thanks to all, to both."

"Good night," Emma responded with as much warmth as her embarrassed state and the prospect of a sleepless night and an angry husband allowed her. The two women caught each other's eyes over their children's heads. What was the fuss about? Emma's eyes said. Flavia's misted over. She thought that Harry would never refer to the incident again.

That night Harry and Julian sat up till after dawn talking and drinking. Then they drove off for a swim in the sea.

Flavia, sometimes asleep, sometimes awake, wondered if this Harry, Julian's drunken friend, was the one she was looking for. But at about eight whe was wakened by her diplomat husband. Although an unsavory mottled color, he looked in every other respect as usual—organized, efficient, unapproachable.

"Julian's sleeping it off on the sofa. Don't worry, I'll make it okay with Myrtle. See you around two."

Checking to see that Cordelia still slept, Flavia turned over in her bed. She slept more easily when Harry was out of the house.

Chapter 14

Harry was due for leave. He had spent eighteen months in the Lebanon. He could speak Arabic. He felt himself part of the great worldwide organization called the Foreign Office. It was time he was given a posting.

"I shall press my suit daily in Whitehall," he announced.

Flavia, who was spoon-feeding scrambled eggs into Cordelia, had an image of an ironing board set up on the pavements of London.

"If necessary, I shall get my father to use influence. That's how the world works."

"You can ask him in person."

"What?"

"In India." Flavia put down the spoon and faced her husband. Suddenly she was near tears. He could not have forgotten they were going to visit his parents. The anticipation had been the best part of her imaginings for the last six months. They might not talk very much, he was so busy, out all day and sometimes in the evening too, but he could not have forgotten India.

"Why should we go there?"

Flavia swallowed. "They asked us. They want to see their grandchild." She did not say, Because I want to go.

Harry looked at her impatiently. Her words meant nothing to him. He knew he must be in England and had no reason to go to India. He couldn't think why Flavia presented a face of such miserable reproach. "Cordelia's much too young to go."

"You were trundled all over the world from the age of dot." Flavia was aware of her ugly expression and blamed Harry for creating it.

"And I hated it." Harry stood up. He wondered whether Flavia knew he had been born in India. They never talked about his childhood. "Anyway we can't afford it."

"Your parents said they'd pay." Flavia undid Cordelia's bib so aggressively that the child cried out. Her anger and resentment had recolored the sun-filled apartment to a purplish red. She turned her face away from Harry's. Stronger even than her wish to go to India was her need to keep her secret self hidden. Over the last eighteen months, this secrecy had become a safeguard against his strength, his confidence. Already she had revealed so much. He had revealed nothing. A hard lump formed inside her so that she could not say more. She took the baby out of her high chair and prepared her to go out. She had imagined that things would be different in India. With his parents, they would become a family.

Harry sat down again and watched her. Dimly, he perceived this moment was important but had neither the capability nor the wish to influence it. She had never been altogether real to him, even at the times he loved her most, and now he could feel her shutting herself away from him.

The sun had come out again for Flavia. She turned at the door. "I'll be back in an hour."

Harry found he could not smile or respond in any way. Just before she closed the door his arm came free and he lifted it in a gesture of farewell or appeal. But Flavia had already gone.

Harry, Flavia and Cordelia took airplanes out of Beirut. Harry's flew west to London, and Flavia and Cordelia's flew east to India. The arrangement had been concluded without discussion or analysis.

Harry was to stay with Julian in London. Flavia knew that this, in particular, meant he would not miss either her or Cordelia. It had hardened her resolve.

Harry was astonished by Flavia's beauty as they parted in the airport. She had resumed her winter pallor and her hair, brushed and free, floated about her in the way that had first captivated him. The little replica of herself she carried, eyes button-bright, made the image more piercing, more complete. His love contained no element of ownership.

Flavia waved. Cordelia waved. Then they were gone.

Harry caught his plane for London. As Flavia had predicted, once he arrived there the image of wife and child receded. The only nasty surprise was the irritation he felt for Julian. His slapdash housekeeping and disregard for time did not appeal.

After three days, Harry was ready to look for alternate digs. He was returning from a discouraging interview in the Foreign Office when he saw a stocky figure running toward him. His attention was held, despite his disconsolate state, by the contrast between the fast human action and the eternal immobility of Trafalgar Square behind him with its stone lions and column. He had begun to feel everything and everyone in London was made of stone. And yet here was that stocky, ridiculous little man, running bravely toward him as if his life depended on it.

Instinctively he stepped aside to let him pass. Instead the runner came to a halt.

"I thought it was you." Puff. Puff. "Terribly unfit now." Puff. "Sitting on my bum all day." Puff. Puff.

It was Wiggins. "You didn't have to run," pointed out Harry. "We were proceeding toward each other. By all laws of perspective we had to meet."

"You might have turned off." Puff. "I hope I haven't done myself a damage."

"I was admiring your energy." Harry realized that he no longer felt disconsolate. "Have you had lunch?"

Wiggins hadn't. At his suggestion they proceeded to a restaurant above a pub within a stone's throw of Big Ben and the Houses of Parliament.

"So you haven't lost your political ambitions?"

"Certainly not. I spend all my spare time working for the party."

"Within hearing of the Division Bell." Harry laughed but, at Wiggins's offended face, became serious. "I'm in a bad mood. After eighteen months out in the Middle East learning the bloody language, the Foreign Office still can't decide when or where to make my first posting. I should have been a don."

"You could have been, too," agreed Wiggins flatteringly.

After they had found their places at a table and ordered wine, Harry's good humor returned. "I'd hate to be a don, actually. Far too small a pond."

"You speak geographically?"

"Not entirely. What I mean is, I'm in the right job."

"Oh, I know that. We all have frustrations." This was produced with such a smug look that Harry realized Wiggins had personal news with which to impress. It turned out he had been adopted to stand as Labour Party candidate at a by-election.

"But you're so young!"

"Not *so* young. Anyway it's a safe Conservative seat. But it's a start."

"Congratulations."

"And I've got a girlfriend."

The lunch was such a success that Wiggins invited Harry around to his flat that evening. "I'd love Julia to meet Flavia."

"Flavia's in India with my parents." This news seemed to surprise Wiggins more than Harry expected but he became even more pressing with his invitation.

"Then we must spend lots of time together. Where are you staying?"

"Julian's." There was a pause. Harry decided on honesty. "I want to move out."

Harry arrived at Wiggins's flat toward six with all his luggage. Julia welcomed him. "David has always spoken about you."

"David?" queried Harry.

"Wiggins." She smiled. She was much prettier than Harry had expected. Very neat and shiny, with a short straight skirt showing off excellent legs. Her hair was smooth and fair held to one side by a blue barrette. She was, in fact, Harry's type.

They walked round Wiggins's flat. Although small, it was bright, shiny and well turned out. Harry's estimation of Wiggins rose. He would sleep on the sofa bed in the sitting room, a modern innovation of which Wiggins was, perhaps inordinately, proud.

"There you are. In, out, in, out." He insisted on several demonstrations. "No great force needed. A small woman could do it. A child. It's an economical use of space which could benefit the human race more than the internal combustion engine."

Harry looked at Julia. She was obviously not sleeping at the flat. As if reading his thoughts, she said in a voice that Harry thought of as London via the Home Counties, "I share a flat with a whole lot of other girls. We're all working, so it's quite jolly."

It sounded jolly to Harry. He had never known working girls in London. His admiration of Wiggins increased.

"You're married, aren't you?"

"Flavia's staying with his parents in India." Wiggins's tone to his fiancée was quite brusque, Harry noticed. As if she must be kept on her mental toes.

"A touch of gin and whatsit?" suggested Wiggins.

"Damn," said Harry. "I've left my liquor at Julian's. Bottles and bottles at diplomatic prices. I'd better collect it quick before he guzzles the lot."

"Good plan." Wiggins as pink-cheeked and affable in his role as appreciated host. Maturity, he was thinking, had lessened Henry's tendency to be a stiff-necked snob. "But you must tell me about the political situation in the Lebanon and thereabout and I must tell you about the revolution here. Have you, for example, seen a two-thousand-strong comprehensive school in action?"

"No," admitted Harry.

"Or an inner city precinct where before there was a traffic jungle?"

"No," repeated Harry.

"Or a multi-racial ethnic self-help community group?"

Julia, excellent legs neatly crossed, brightened the room with a lively expression of expectancy.

Julian's flat was not far from Julia's. At the end of the evening, after much discussion and a certain amount of pilaf, Harry offered to escort her home. Wiggins, who might have demurred on grounds of sexual appetite unfulfilled, approved of the plan. "Of course I tell Julia London is the safest city in the world, but she still doesn't enjoy public transport last at night."

"On my own at night," explained Julia. "I almost live on the tube—in the daytime. We all do."

"It's one of London's great blessings," added Wiggins.

Harry had no intention of taking public transport. "I'll be back soon," he said cheerfully.

Julia seemed honestly shocked when he hailed a taxi. "But you can't waste money like that."

"Why not?" Harry opened the door for her to get in. He suspected that the moment they were enclosed together in the small dark space he would be consumed with lust. He was quickly proved right.

"David says we should use public transport for political as well as economical reasons."

"Wiggins would see a political principle in a doughnut," said Harry. The words represented a significant victory of mind-over-imagination. His imagination saw his hand up her skirt.

"Why do you call David Wiggins?"

"We were at school together."

"He doesn't call you Hayes-Middleton."

"I've dropped the Middleton."

"And changed from Henry to Harry."

Harry thought this was Flavia's contribution but did not want to introduce her name at this juncture. His imagination was now starting at the top with the buttons on Julia's blouse.

She seemed determined to talk. "You don't seem a likely pair, you and David."

"We're not a pair." Under normal circumstances Harry would have found her questioning unacceptable, but the effort needed to subdue his imagination laid low his critical faculties.

Soon they arrived at Julia's flat. "Come in," she said. "Meet the gang."

This was not exactly the invitation he had hoped for. Nevertheless he followed her out of the taxi.

The flat was cavernous and on the ground floor. Many rooms led off an evil-smelling corridor. The smell seemed a composite of cheap cigarettes, cabbage and perfume. Harry thought it would make the dung-fires of India seem a purifying agent. He had a fleeting image of Flavia. Then he was struck by the incongruity of Julia's bandbox appearance and her unsavory surroundings.

She opened a door. Harry peered behind her. Huge greenish furniture sat about in a silvery gloom. The smell of cigarettes dominated the other two smells. "Oh, there's nobody here," said Julia in a surprised voice.

Harry's lasciviousness increased but then was brought under control. "Shall I go?"

"Would you like a coffee? I mean, having brought me here?"

"You sound doubtful."

"Oh, no. They'll probably be back in a moment."

The kitchen was Harry's downfall. It was the most disgusting room he'd ever been into. Dirty plates and old food were stacked everywhere. Despite Julia's carefree apology—"Excuse the mess, we do it on Saturdays. Too busy working in the week"—he felt it indicated a licentiousness in her character which matched his. While she stirred the coffee, he put his arms round her and caught a breast in either hand. They felt wonderful.

Julia squealed and dropped the teaspoon.

Harry dropped his hands. "Sorry, irresistible."

Julia turned round. She looked extremely flushed and pretty. "What would Wiggins say?"

"You called him Wiggins," said Harry. He leaned forward and kissed her on the lips.

"We're engaged," said Julia.

"I'm married," said Harry.

"Once I'm married I shall be totally faithful," said Julia.

"So you should," said Harry, kissing her again. "We're just overcome by each other's physical attractions," suggested Harry.

"Oh, are we?" Julia looked round the room in a prettily dazed manner. "Doesn't it smell awful here?"

"The whole flat smells awful."

She walked slowly back to the sitting room. From Harry's point of view, it seemed a good sign that she forgot the coffee.

They lay in close embrace on the sofa. This was pretty good for a while but not perfect. "Do you have a bedroom?" whispered Harry.

"Shared." Her voice was lost in his chin.

"What?"

"Another girl shares it."

Harry was not used to sexual preliminaries that found no consummation. After a while he drew himself apart. "They'll all come bursting in any moment?" His resentment was obvious.

Julia sat up, tumbled and alluring. His expression softened a little. He supposed it wasn't her fault. Presumably Wiggins pulled out the sofa bed at this point.

"I'm sorry." Julia began to shiver. Indeed Harry noticed the room was unnaturally cold, an unusual combination with strong odors.

"Perhaps I should go."

Julia still said nothing. Her shivering increased till her whole body vibrated.

"Are you cold?"

She shook her head. A feeling of doom and despair descended on Harry. All lust vanished. He felt very sorry for her, himself and even Wiggins. He took her hands. "Cheer up. We had a very jolly time."

"I shouldn't have." The words were barely distinguishable.

"What?"

She shook her head. Tears began to drip out of the corners of her eyes. She looked as if she were leaking. Oh God! Harry squeezed her greenish hands. "Cheer up," he said again. "Remember, you're going to be altogether faithful once you're married."

She raised her eyes. "I don't love him."

This was the first time a woman had revealed her innermost thoughts to Harry. Mary Ann had been too humble, Flavia too proud, Sybille too Parisienne and Elise too clever. Julia's honest vulnerability touched a new chord in Harry, disgust tempered with pity.

"Of course you love Wiggins!" he said with determination.

Julia gulped.

This was not good enough. "He's a wonderful man. So generous, so hardworking, ambitious, clever, an outstanding chap in every way! You're very very LUCKY!"

"He's so boring."

"What?" Harry pretended not to hear. Now he found himself bristling with defensive indignation. "Wiggins is my oldest friend—there's Julian but that's another story—Wiggins is pure gold. Pure gold." He found he had stood up. This was a relief. Perhaps he would be able to leave soon.

Julia cowered below him. "I'm sorry," she whispered.

"That's all right." Harry bent to kiss her. "Just remember you've got a tremendous man in Wiggins!"

"Yes," murmured Julia obediently and even managed a small smile.

Harry strode out of the flat in manly fashion.

Strangely enough, this not altogether successful encounter did not blight Harry's plan to stay with Wiggins.

"I hear you lectured Julia about my sterling qualities," said Wiggins a night or two later.

"Gold," responded Harry without a blush. "I said you were altogether gold."

"And your oldest friend, too." This designation had given Wiggins particular pleasure, since his public conceit was built on a jelly of personal self-doubt.

"Quite." Harry forbore to mention Salmon. It was a concession to his relationship with Julia. This, also strangely, continued. And in a more satisfactory vein. She now invited him to her bedroom at a time when her flatmate was away. The only drawback (literally) was her insistence on coitus interruptus. However, after a few practice shots, he soon grew quite proficient at the art and couldn't think why people fussed about with bits of old rubber.

Once he almost started a conversation on the subject with Wiggins but remembered just in time that it might be a little near the proverbial precipice. Instead he remarked on the importance of the second Vatican Council, which rather bewildered Wiggins.

"Been following it, have you?"

"I wouldn't say that. But there are issues there that seriously affect world politics."

"Quite," agreed Wiggins, looking more bewildered than ever.

Harry dropped the subject with some relief. He had at last been informed by the Foreign Office that his next destination would be Amman in Jordan. With this settled, he decided to pay a short visit to his widowed Irish uncle. After a few days there he received a much forwarded postcard from Flavia.

> Having a lovely time. Divine weather. Your parents very well. Such a lovely country. Lots of love, Flavia and Cordelia.

Since Harry had little to do, he studied the card with care. His original impression that it was a very odd way to write from India deepened. "Lovely time," "divine weather," "lovely country." That was just not the way any intelligent person would write from India. It must be a form of mockery, directed at him. He showed it to his uncle and explained his reaction. But his uncle, who had become morose and silent since his wife's death, failed to see the point. "God's in his heaven and all's right with the world," he recited and took a gulp of Guinness. He had also taken to evening drinking sessions.

Too late, Harry felt a yearning for his family and the brilliant light of India. Flavia should not have gone without him. After all, he thought with sudden moral indignation, Cordelia is my child too. She had no right to take her.

Lionel had entered the prime of life at the rather late age of fifty-four. He was High Commissioner to India. The two countries for which his family had worked so hard had had at last decided to pay their debts. He woke up each morning with a sense of the rightness of his position.

Beatrice, too, was contented. At first she had missed the television. But her spirits were now so bound up with her husband's that she could not fail to reflect his mood. Age had brought her confidence. This made her less in need of the friendship of bossy Englishwomen. She now made friends among the Indian community, with whom she had far more in common. Although mostly better educated than she, they looked on life with an awareness of its spiritual significance, which greatly appealed to her. Apart from television her only other regret at leaving England had been the separation from Father Bernard. But, as he had pointed out, he was merely a stand-in for God, who was everywhere.

Her closest friend was a Mrs. Amrita Mehta, who was married to the Indian Minister for Culture. Amrita had an artistic nature and involved herself in cultural projects, arranging exhibitions of new designs for sari lengths and all kinds of hand-work. She personally gave money to various projects that encouraged community craft in poor areas. Beatrice was honored to be invited to join Amrita's organizing committee. Soon she found herself busier than she had ever been in her life.

Therefore, the arrival of Flavia with her grandchild did not predominate in her thoughts. Amrita was surprised she did not show more excitement.

"But your very first grandchild! It is a miracle proving the existence of . . ." She paused.

"God?" suggested Beatrice.

"Spiritual order," said Amrita firmly. "You already have a future, at your young age." Amrita was several years older than Beatrice but had no grandchildren. "Your thoughts can take wing with such a great happening."

"It is a great happening," said Beatrice, pleased with her friend's enthusiasm. "When they get here I shall concentrate all my attention on them."

Flavia arrived in India soon after dawn. Cordelia slept in her portable bassinet. Beatrice escorted them from the hot, crowded airport to where the official car was parked. Flavia tottered from excitement and lack of sleep. The air was still crisply cool, but the vast rising red sun promised un-English heat.

Beatrice was secretly shocked by her daughter-in-law's appearance. She was so white, so thin, so nervous-looking. She compared her unfavorably to the smooth beauty of her Indian friends. She peered in the bassinet as it was loaded into the car.

"She'll probably sleep for hours now." Flavia pulled the covers back a little so Beatrice could see better. "She was awake most of the journey. She's just learned to walk."

Cordelia lay on her back, hands curled up on either side of her face. The small doll-like baby had turned into a large doll-like baby. She had perfect white skin with bright pink cheeks and pale hair.

"We'll have to keep her out of the sun with skin like that," said Beatrice. Her heart beat fast. It was the child's total abandonment that caught her attention. How could Flavia appear so casual with such a terrifying responsibility? She tried to remember her own feelings for Henry. There had always been nurses, of course.

They got into the car. "You are clever, looking after her yourself."

"I had a nurse part-time in Beirut." Flavia rested her head on the seat.

"You must be exhausted." Beatrice studied her pale tense face.

"No! No!" Flavia sat up again. She opened the window and let the air blow in her hair. "Whenever Cordelia's asleep I'm filled with this energy. I'd like to go for a walk now. Explore Delhi." She pointed out of the window. "Visit that tomb, those shops. Catch that green parrot."

"Oh," said Beatrice, nonplussed. She had planned a nice breakfast and rest. "I've found a very reliable ayah to look after Cordelia."

"An ayah." Flavia sank back in the seat again. The glorious possibility of maternal release made her languid. She closed her eyes.

Beatrice took this for disapproval.

"She's recommended by my excellent friend Mrs. Mehta, wife of the Minister of Culture." Was Flavia going to be difficult?

"That sounds wonderful." Flavia's eyes remained closed. Her voice was slurred. Her shoulders twitched and then were still.

Beatrice realized she had fallen asleep. She smiled broadly to herself. Asleep, Flavia looked young and pretty again. She glanced at the baby in the bassinet. Rosy, contented. This time she did not feel her vulnerability but her confidence. In fact, she was reminded of Lionel. The thought made her smile again. She remembered Amrita's words. "It is a miracle proving the existence of"—and once again she supplied an ending for the sentence— "the existence of God."

Flavia had never before been looked after as she was in India. There was the ayah, a small birdlike creature who treated Cordelia as if she were a god. There were servants, who cooked, cleaned her room, washed her clothes almost before she'd worn them. There was Lionel, who was so important out here and so charmingly protective. There was Beatrice, who seemed far warmer and less mysteriously remote than Flavia remembered and arranged each day so she should have the best possible time. And, of course, there was no Harry for her to look after. Her photograph stared at her from the dressing table. It had been taken on the beach near Beirut and he was sunburnt, laughing, but not for her, she now remembered. She put the photograph away.

She felt she had arrived in paradise and could not bear to think it might end. One morning at breakfast she said something like this to Lionel, who looked at her severely. "Paradise is hardly the word I'd use. India has more problems, evil problems, than any other country in the world."

But this did not shame Flavia into changing her attitude. She could hardly fail to see the poverty, since the beggars crowded her off the pavements. Nor was it just comfort and laziness. She saw something special in the country, which she tried to describe to Beatrice. "I feel as if the sheer beauty of it takes me nearer my true self."

Beatrice was sympathetic, assuming that Flavia, like herself, sensed a spirituality among the Indian people lacking in Western Europe. But, in fact, Flavia had no real spiritual leanings. Her talks about Catholicism with Emma Myrtle had centered on practicalities like the rhythm method of birth control. Her sense of beauty, despite her talk of her "true self," was much nearer a purely aesthetic consideration. When confronted by the figure of a woman clad in a scarlet sari against a backdrop of red sunset, she felt her soul expand but it did not reach out for other spheres. Amrita Mehta instantly understood this about her and soon had her involved in all sorts of "creative" work. Shyly, she revealed her attempts at painting during her last long school vacation before she married. (She left out the bit about them not selling at the hospital even when reduced.) Soon she had joined a team investigating the possibility of adapting sari designs for European consumption.

It was Lionel who unwittingly altered the course of her life. He took her in Beatrice's place to a cocktail party at the Argentinian Embassy.

"Bloody fascists, of course, the lot of them," he commented as they arrived. "That's why Beatrice won't come."

But Flavia, star-struck in Paradise, hardly listened. At the party she met a young diplomat called George di Stefano. His grandmother had been English, which explained his Christian name. He had fair hair and regular features like an Englishman but swarthy skin and a soft hissing accent. Flavia, after a couple of drinks, confided in him her feelings of disillusionment and anxiety, which she had not known about until that moment.

After a circuit separately round the room and another couple of drinks, they met again, and Flavia further confided in him her view of Englishmen. It was extremely critical, centering round coldness, cynicism and no sense of beauty. George could not know she was describing her husband.

Assuming her single and heartfree, he took down her name and address and promised to call. He left the party with an image of floating pale hair and charming youthful naïveté. Being of a romantic nature, he already felt himself in love.

Later that night Flavia comforted her daughter, who had woken, crying. Holding the baby to her breast, she thought seriously of her marriage to Harry. The anger that had spurred her to leave him and travel to India increased with documented cause for resentment. He had bullied her into marriage much too young, before she had any chance to decide what she would like to be. Their life was lived entirely round his needs. He had never discussed the child and took no responsibility for her. He cared more for his men friends than he did for her. He cared more for his job than he did for her. He had almost certainly been unfaithful to her already. With that horrible witch, Elise. He did not love her. He had killed her love for him.

Tears of self-pity ran gently down Flavia's cheeks. The worst thing of all he'd done was to make her face such crude and ugly realities. She would not do it again, for now she knew what she must do.

Flavia placed Cordelia back in her bassinet and returned to her own bed. She slept well, dreaming of a man in a sari with a parrot on his shoulder.

Chapter 15

Harry was amazed when Flavia wrote to say she would not be returning to live with him. "I shall take Cordelia to my parents, where you can visit her." He received the letter the day before Flavia was due to return, three days before they were to leave for a final short stretch in Beirut before going to Amman.

Harry sat on Wiggins's sofa bed and tried to make sense of the news. Wiggins had already gone to work. How could this have happened when they hadn't been together, had been separated indeed by thousands of miles of land and sea? Had something occurred out there? But she was staying with his parents. It was a family visit. It must be a provocative kind of fantasy. He would soon sort it out. He stood up and put the letter away. That day Harry and Julian enjoyed a very drunken lunch together. After Julian had broken two plates making a Chinese sandwich, they were thrown out of the restaurant.

Flavia was wrong about one thing. Harry loved her. He wanted no other woman in the same continuing way that he wanted her. His love made him remember their conversation in Beirut when he had refused to go to India. She had left him then. His rational self disguised the sinking dread this knowledge brought. He went to Marlborough the day after Flavia returned.

It was a soft wet day. The Mortons had a large garden filled with heavy shrubs and gravel paths. Flavia said it would be easier to talk outside. She put Cordelia's coat on and assembled the stroller. Harry watched helplessly. Flavia was bigger than he remembered her. The sunburn had strengthened the effect of her features. Her movements were quick and assured. Her hair seemed less an airy cloak than a solid wall. She, who had always been lightness and air to Harry, even irritatingly so, now was a large feminine presence.

"Couldn't we leave Cordelia behind?" he said.

Flavia looked at him with a surprised expression. "You've come to see her, haven't you?"

"Yes. But . . ." Flavia was aiming the stroller for the front door. He had come to see Flavia. Their daughter was another matter altogether. He followed her out of the door.

"Your mother found such a lovely ayah for Cordelia. She said you had one when you were little?"

She spoke as if they were casual acquaintances. Harry realized his usual method of crossing her barriers had been physical. If he could touch her, all would be settled. But Flavia was walking briskly down the path. She needed to use a certain amount of force to make the small wheels of the stroller run over the loose gravel. This task seemed to be taking all her concentration. The noise of the stones tumbling under the wheels in the otherwise quiet garden was very loud.

Harry walked a step or two behind her. He would have to shout to make himself heard.

Flavia tossed over her shoulder, "So, are you looking forward to Jordan?"

Harry didn't answer. They continued walking. Flavia was both triumphant at the power she was wielding and also acutely unhappy. This was not the way she wanted to behave. She had been forced into it by Harry. He had always bullied her. Now she was forced to be a bully in competition. Frowning aggressively, she said, "I shall find a job as soon as I can get help with Cordelia." Actually she felt no wish for a career. She felt exhausted, with a longing to be looked after. An image of George's adoring bulk made a brief appearance. Even after he had discovered she was married, he had continued to write her romantic yet formal notes. She was "a very special woman whom I will never forget." "The joy of your presence makes my life full of light." She had "an understanding of human nature more like a poet's than an ordinary mortal."

"Can't we sit on that bench?" said a despairing voice behind her.

"It's raining."

"I don't see what difference there is getting wet walking or sitting down."

"You get cold."

"Cordelia's sitting down already."

"Oh. All right." She was tired of battling against the gravel.

They sat side by side on the wet bench.

"It's stopped raining." They both looked out on the damp garden. A pigeon, sheltering under the branch of a tree, shook its feathers and flew out in front of them. Cordelia, who had been quiet up to then, held out her hands and cried out. Flavia leaned forward and lifted the child out. She put her on her knee.

Harry thought, There goes any chance of communication. He looked at the garden and saw signs of spring with the daffodils starting to unfurl and anemones growing by the roots of bushes. He looked up and saw buds starting on the trees.

Flavia played with Cordelia. She counted her fingers and played "Round and round the garden like a teddy bear" on the palm of her little fat hand. Cordelia chortled and rolled her eyes to Harry. "Da da da da."

Harry felt a sickening lurch inside his stomach. Was this child calling him "Dada"? He looked over her head to Flavia. "Does she know who I am?"

"We've lived in the same house for most of her life." Flavia's tone was tart.

"I thought she might have forgotten."

"They all say, 'da da'," said Flavia, "if that's what you're thinking."

"I see." Harry's stomach subsided. At that moment Cordelia decided to smile at him, showing off her four pearly white teeth with abandonment. But now Harry was more wary.

"Where are you planning to live?" he asked, sounding quite impatient.

Flavia immediately lost some of her energy. "I don't know. Here, to begin with. But not for long. I like traveling. Actually I prefer being abroad to being in England."

Flavia, who was thinking of India, did not find this an odd comment and Harry debated whether to point out he was just off to the East and that one of the advantages of being his wife was the certainty of much time spent abroad. "But you don't like the Foreign Office?"

"It's nothing to do with that." Flavia jerked Cordelia, who gave a protesting squeak. "We just should never have got married. The truth is you're just not my type."

"What?" Harry screwed up his eyes. He had no place in a conversation like this.

Flavia looked slightly ashamed. "Really, there's no point talking. I mean, are you trying to win me back?"

Harry's face looked even blanker. He had thought that a meeting with Flavia would prove her letter was not to be taken seriously. He had not imagined this would involve him in any positive action such as "winning her back" suggested. As far as he knew he had not "won her" in the first place.

"You're talking like some idiot out of a romantic novel."

Flavia said nothing with an obstinate expression.

"You know me. You've known me for years. What do you expect from me?"

Flavia could not tell him she expected him to change his attitudes, although that's what she wanted. She knew it was impossible, which was why she had written the letter. "Nothing. I expect nothing from you." She sighed.

"Mama." Cordelia pulled herself up into a standing position and patted her mother's cheeks.

"She says 'Mama'," said Harry bitterly, although the bitterness was not for that.

"Much better to admit defeat while we're still friends," said Flavia in the brisk tones she'd used at the beginning of the meeting.

"I don't know what you're talking about at all."

"That's a man's privilege."

"If you wanted to work, I'd understand a little. If you were ambitious." Harry thought of Julia and her girlfriends. "But you're not like that."

"I might be."

"You might be." Defeat settled on Harry.

"I just don't like being married to you. You're the wrong man. I should have swum down that river forever."

Harry did not recognize her reference to the Oxford incident. It had never occurred to him that she had been trying to escape from him. He now felt it was all over. Yet there was still an air of expectancy about Flavia, as if she were waiting for him to say something. "You really dislike me," he said gloomily.

"Yes," said Flavia. She thought he would protest that he loved her. She was steeled against it, ready armored with a list of his faults. It was disconcerting to find them not needed. It was as if the climax of their marriage, or rather its dissolution, had not been reached. She was almost provoked into introducing the subject itself. But her pride was too strong.

Head bowed, Harry made patterns in the gravel with the toe of his shoe. Cordelia wriggled down and sat at his feet. She played with the stones. After a moment she popped a round pink one into her mouth.

Now that the child was no longer between them, Harry and Flavia had a clear space to look at each other. Flavia felt herself blushing. She whisked her hair about to disguise it. She was affected by his strong male presence. He was so different from her and that difference confused her, made her unable to think clearly. That was why she had married him in the first place.

Harry saw her nervousness. He leaned toward her. She was wearing some sort of mackintosh of a light silky material. He touched it.

At their feet Cordelia scuffled. She gave a little cough.

Harry tightened his grip on Flavia's shoulder. He would tell her he loved her.

Cordelia coughed louder. Still in Harry's grip, Flavia looked down. She saw a round pink stone pop out of the baby's mouth.

"Cordelia!"

Harry stared. Flavia crouched down by her daughter. She put her finger in her mouth and two more little stones fell on to the ground. Cordelia coughed again. Her face was pink.

"Oh God!" Flavia tapped her on the back.

"What's the matter?" Harry asked stupidly.

"Can't you see? She's been eating stones. Right in front of our eyes. And now she's choking."

Cordelia coughed several more times. Her face went from pink to red. She began to cry.

"Open your mouth for Mama," said Flavia. "There aren't any more there. So why's she still coughing? And why's she that color?"

Harry knelt down. "Perhaps she's got one stuck."

"Oh God!"

Harry picked Cordelia up and started toward the house.

"Won't you shake it down doing that?"

"Your mother's a doctor, isn't she?"

Dr. Morton met them at the door.

"She's been eating the path," said Flavia despairingly.

"Hospital," said Dr. Morton.

Cordelia was now the color of a ripe plum. It had begun to rain again.

Flavia made it clear she blamed Harry. Once they were all in the car, she would not let him touch Cordelia again. At the hospital, she treated him as if he were the chauffeur.

Cordelia, still choking, was taken from doctor to X-ray room to operating room.

Harry trailed after for a while and then gave up. He bought a newspaper in The Friends stand and set himself the task of reading every line of the financial pages. He had just reached a very dull piece about the new Prices and Incomes Board when Dr. Morton put her head round the corner.

"Well!" she said.

"Uh," responded Harry, unsure of the meaning of her exlamation.

She came a little further into the room. "Well! The little madam."

"What?" Harry put down the paper.

"Nothing there. Not a thing. Clear as a whistle right down to her little belly button."

"She's all right, you mean."

"Never was anything wrong. Just started coughing and couldn't stop. Little children do that sort of thing. She probably liked all the attention to begin with. Terrible attention seekers. Anyway I'll be late for my surgery if I don't go."

Harry sat alone in the waiting room. Since he had the car, he presumed Flavia would seek him out. He tried to continue with the thoughts of Aubrey Jones, MP, who was Chairman of the Board, but the print merged into incomprehensible patterns. He got up and went to the entrance hall. There he found Flavia sitting on a chair. In her arms she held a peacefully sleeping Cordelia. When she saw Harry she said, "Oh, I thought you'd gone. I ordered a taxi."

Harry felt tears in his eyes. He half turned away. "I'm glad she's better," he said in a muffled voice. He didn't see Flavia's ashamed expression. He recovered himself. "I'll say goodbye then."

"Yes." Flavia held the child tighter. "I'll write."

"Yes."

"I'll send you photographs of Cordelia."

After all, the child had been the most important part of their meeting. Harry kissed both of them and went out through the swinging doors.

When Harry took up his post as Second Secretary in the British Legation at Amman, very few people realized he was married. He seemed to be just the sort of ambitious Oxford-educated young bachelor who was attracted by the competitive ladder of the Foreign Office. The information was on his files, of course, but the personnel officer assumed it was something best forgotten. It was also on his files about his relationship with Madame Elise Planchette, but he was prepared to forget that too. What he did disseminate was the information that Sir Lionel Hayes-Middleton was his father.

In many professions this might have had an adverse effect on his rating among his colleagues. But not in the Foreign Office. They all gazed up the same ladder and admired what they saw gleaming at the top. A few sparks of that radiance lit up Harry's humble position. He became, on the strength of it, Henry again.

This was, after all, no one who knew him as Harry. Since Flavia had chosen the abbreviation, it seemed appropriate that they should make their exit together.

Henry had a flat in the old quarter of Amman, just above a well-preserved Roman amphitheater. There was a whole Roman city called Jerash a short drive from the center of the city. But such wonders were eclipsed by his visits to the West Bank. This was 1965, and the Royal Hashemite Kingdom counted within its boundary Jericho, Hebron, Nablus, Bethlehem and a part of Jerusalem. Henry crossed the Allenby Bridge over the River Jordan several times a week. He sat in the bar at the American Colony Hotel and enjoyed that curiously nostalgic happiness that comes upon expatriates.

He was also conscious of doing something useful for the first time in his life. The Anglophile attitude of the young King Hussein gave the British diplomats a special role in helping to modernize the country. Hussein was even married to an English girl, daughter of a Lieutenant-Colonel in the British Military Mission in Jordan. When the King came to England he appeared on *This is Your Life.* His family home, on the outskirts of the city, was run more like a middle-class home in Sunningdale than like an Arab king's.

Henry enjoyed the mosques in Amman and the wailing call to prayer at dawn and dusk. But when he crossed to the West Bank, he was unnerved by the intensity of fervor. On his first visit to Jerusalem, he missed some of the great religious landmarks because he couldn't belive they were so close together.

Henry sat in his flat and read everything he could find about this area of the Middle East. He came to the conclusion it was all an impossible invention. When he saw the little King Hussein, so plucky and determined, so proud of his children and his country, he felt very old and sophisticated.

Flavia's desertion increased Henry's isolation. She had been the only person he'd ever felt close to—apart from Wiggins, who didn't count, and Julian, whose company was irritating until they were both drunk.

Henry took to sport as a substitute. He played tennis in the early morning with another Second Secretary, in the commercial department. He was better than Henry and made him dash around the court till sweat poured off his face and his legs trembled. He enjoyed the feeling. In the evening he sometimes played again, this time with a Jordanian landowner called Rahat Razzaz. He had been at Oxford during the same period as Henry but Henry could not remember him. He was intelligent and sympathetic and the nearest to a close friend he found in Jordan.

It was after a particularly ferocious game that Henry received an important letter from Flavia. He might have been forewarned by the postmark, which said Argentina. On the other hand he'd never been informed of the existence of a rival called George di Stefano.

Dear Harry,

The unaccustomed use of this name gave Henry's heart, already racing with exertion, an unpleasant jolt.

> Dear Harry,
>
> As you will see, I am in Argentina. I have met someone here whom I'm very fond of. Sometime we hope to marry. I had to tell you at once—although I realize you probably aren't too interested—because he is Catholic, so it means I must get our marriage annulled. Apparently it's not too difficult if you know the right people. And George's family's alive with important prelates, although there is some English blood.
>
> Just at the moment I've left Cordelia with my parents, so it would be a good time if you want to visit her. I'll be coming back for her soon.
>
> I hope you are well and happy.
>
> All the best,
>
> Flavia

By the time Henry had finished reading the page was splattered with sweat dripping from the nose and chin. He put the letter down and went to have a shower. He decided, without thinking too much about it, to discuss the letter with Rahat.

Rahat lived with his mother and sisters and several other relatives in a grand old house. In his preoccupied state, Henry had forgotten the drama that invariably greeted his arrival. Women scurried about among darkened rooms, offering, in an almost panic-stricken way, soft drinks, chairs, food. Eventually Rahat appeared, calm and cool in a shining white shirt. The waves of women receded.

"Welcome," he said.

"I'm sorry," said Henry.

"Sorry for what?"

Henry stood up. "I wonder if you'd mind coming back to my flat." He could not discuss his marriage in this house filled with ears.

"Certainly."

They walked back in the peculiar orange glow of the sunset above a pink stone city. "You must make a visit to Petra without delay," said Rahat conversationally.

Henry didn't answer. When they arrived at the flat he gave his friend the letter and went to make drinks.

Rahat was horrified at the evidence of the letter's tearful reception. At some points the ink was smudged beyond deciphering. Henry had always seemed so contained, so unemotional in a noble British way. Unconsciously, his opinion of his friend fell several notches. No wife could be worth such a paroxysm of grief. Perhaps it was the loss of the child. But even she was only a daughter.

Rahat received his drink and decided to proceed carefully. "This is a sad thing for you." He handed back the letter with some relief.

Henry folded it into his pocket without looking at it. He had hoped for something more bracing from Rahat. A little righteous indignation, a plague on the house of women. He had heard him hold forth on the theme often enough. "It is sad, yes. But a bit much too, don't you think? Out of the blue, expecting me to go along with this annulment lark. And giving me a last chance to see my daughter. As if I could drop everything here and run over to England whenever I please!"

Rahat cheered up. "Yes. You have every right to be angry. She has forfeited her right to your esteem. She is a woman of no sense."

"Quite," agreed Henry, sipping his drink rather quickly. That exactly described Flavia. "A woman of no sense." Even nonsense. How different from Julia, to whose wedding to Wiggins he had received an invitation only the week before. Indeed how different from all the other women who'd come and gone in his life so neatly. It seemed the worst of bad luck that he had married someone so absurdly senseless. "I suppose it proves I'm well rid of her."

"Yes." Rahat frowned. Those tears still worried him. "But," he began tentatively, "will you be very unhappy?"

"I don't know," said Henry, truthfully. "I've never thought of things like that." He put down his drink. "I'll tell you what. There might be just enough light for a quick set. How about it?"

"You're on!" Rahat jumped to his feet. " 'Women propose and men dispose,' as my tutor used to say."

Chapter 16

At the end of 1966 Lionel was made British Ambassador to Washington. It was his last posting before retirement, the crown and summit of his career. Henry was still in Jordan building up memories of the Middle East. He picked oranges in Jericho, spent two nights in a Bedouin encampment, and rode along with the Camel Corps. He was escorted by Rahat to Petra, he went with the Commercial Second Secretary to Palmyra in Syria (which he had visited previously with Flavia) and he attended many lovely picnic expeditions to the Golan Heights organized by married couples within the mission.

Then came 1967. Israeli tanks rolled over the flowery heights of Golan and Jordan became half its previous size. Henry Hayes was chucked out of the Hashemite Kingdom.

It was nothing personal, of course. He just happened to be the Second Secretary whose number came up. The most upsetting moment was saying goodbye to Rahat. More than half his estates were now under Israeli control. Such was his anger that he would not farm them, announcing that the Israeli action amounted to annexation, whatever they might say, and he would not help them pretend otherwise. He had said that at the beginning. Now he would not talk politics at all. Henry could not meet his eyes.

Beatrice wrote to Henry inviting him to stay in Washington. Henry accepted but allowed three days for a visit to London. He stayed in Wiggins's flat as before—except that now Julia was resident with a noisy baby.

"Friendship is a remarkable thing," said Wiggins emotionally on their first evening together. Julia was in the kitchen cooking supper. "When I think of our experiences since our last meeting. Your three years in an alien culture climaxed by a war. My three years of hard slog culminating in an electoral victory!" His voice rose to emphasize his point.

"Well done," said Henry good-naturedly. He could see the effort Wiggins had made to elevate Henry's experiences to his own. In fact, he preferred to talk about England. He feared his years in the Arab world and particularly his friendship with Rahat had biased him against Israel.

Henry's whole education and career in the Foreign Office might have been designed to identify and avoid the danger of bias. Intellectual freedom, so he had been taught, was best defined by the ability to see both sides. Bias suggested emotion, an even greater danger.

"And you've had a baby too," he said to Wiggins.

"Well, that's not new to you."

It took Henry a second to recognize this as a reference to Cordelia, his daughter. Frankly that whole episode, his marriage, seemed like a particularly painful dream. "I haven't seen her for three years."

"You haven't seen anyone for three years!" Julia came into the room. Henry's presence, with memories of guilty sex in stew-smelling days, made her happy and excited.

"He was referring to his daughter," Wiggins said, using his most sober accents.

"Sorry." Julia glanced unconsciously to where her child slept in its crib.

"I don't mind," said Henry. "Wiggins was just going to give me game set and match on the election."

"Supper's ready." Julia posed in front of her guest. He noticed that, although her waist had thickened, her legs were good as ever.

"Isn't your skirt awfully short?"

Julia danced about, delighted. "Oh, isn't he wonderful! He doesn't know about the miniskirt."

"Shh." Wiggins pointed to the baby.

England was in the middle of a democratic revolution. Or so Wiggins, the new Member of Parliament, assured Henry. "It is actually fashionable," he declared "to be working-class."

Henry took all this with a pinch of salt until he met Julian. Julian, of the elegant Oxford drawl, now talked with a nasal Cockney twang. He wore faded denims and his hair hung in well-washed waves to his shoulders. "It's good to see some people don't change," he said when he saw Henry. "How's life?"

"Terrible." Henry felt exhilarated by his own honesty. He

walked round Julian's room, looking upward. It was a huge glass-roofed studio which served both as flat and office. Julian had taken advantage of the sixties to become a film agent. In one corner sat a pretty girl. Earlier she had given them coffee but now she was typing with a hesitant rhythm. Through the glass window Henry could see a blustery English sky and the crisscrossed branches of a large tree.

"That's not like you," observed Julian with satisfaction. "Perhaps you have changed."

"You shouldn't judge by appearances."

"In my profession, appearances are about all that matters."

"How horrible."

"It does offend against the old school code. But then I never was too successful in that area."

"What exactly do you do?"

"Make money mainly."

Henry now saw that Julian was not nearly so languid as he used to be. "But how do you make money?"

"Bring people together. Imagine it as a sort of extended cocktail party—except jobs result, not hangovers. Well, those as well, actually."

"But that's not working." Henry sat down with a serious expression.

Julian laughed loudly, making the typist start back in her chair.

"You're such a purist," said Julian. "It certainly isn't your sort of work."

"What is my sort of work?"

"Well, first of all it despises all forms of art."

"What nonsense!"

"Then the other thing about your sort of job is its structure. There's a top and a bottom to it and a very large middle. You have offices and planners and pensions and paid holidays."

"Do you dislike civil servants? Wiggins thinks the whole country should be run by them."

"In one hour I work harder than they work in a year."

"With the extended cocktail party?"

"You shouldn't judge by appearances. I work firsthand with myself. With what I am, what I believe, even what I look like. People like you, people in big organizations, even MPs, never do more than fill in a bit of canvas. Write a report, brief a Minister, answer questions, hand out a line. It's never you, it's just your training, going through the motions. You're slaves, actually, the lot of you. And the way you console yourselves, disguise your gloomy condition, is by convincing yourselves and everybody else, as a matter of fact, that you're doing the really important work!"

"But world politics is important," said Henry, thinking of Jordan.

"Quite. But you're not important to it. You're just number 5,001 on the canvas."

Behind them the girl had stopped typing and was looking at them, open-mouthed.

"She takes too much pot," said Julian, not very softly.

"What should I do? Throw it all up and become a pop star? I'm not a very good painter, poet, musician . . ."

"Recognize your slavish condition and practice a little humility." Julian laughed again at Henry's sober expression. "Hang around another half hour and you'll see me at work." He turned to the secretary. "Sieger's coming at twelve, isn't he?"

"Sieger," repeated the girl, nodding locks of long fair hair over her face.

Sieger arrived as a clock somewhere outside struck twelve. At the same time a storm of rain broke over the glass roof and Julian switched on a full rack of spotlights.

Sieger arrived as a clock somewhere outside struck twelve. At the same time a storm of rain broke over the glass roof and Julian switched on a full rack of sotlights.

Sieger glowed in their light. He was golden-haired, golden-skinned and dressed in shades of palest gold. He removed his mackintosh with a flourish of satisfaction. "Beat it. Not a single drop."

He was American. His accent pierced Henry with nostalgia, whether for childhood, Belinda or his honeymoon with Flavia he couldn't say.

"This is an old mate of mine." Julian, who had put on a white jacket, indicated Henry.

"Harry Hayes," said Henry quickly. "I hope I won't be in the way."

"If we can hear ourselves speak at all," said Sieger, looking upward to where rain and branches thundered on the glass.

"It's a feature." Julian was laconic. "Bourbon, gin, vodka?"

"The first, on the rocks," said Sieger, sitting down. He watched closely as the pretty girl passed by to get their drinks and then turned back to his host. "So what've you got for me?"

Henry was fascinated by his directness. What he would have considered rude in a friend or colleague, he admired in Sieger. It expressed the energy, he thought romantically, of the New World.

"Phil, would I have you here for nothing?" Julian's upper-class Cockney tones had now co-opted a third, American, layer.

Sieger laughed. He accepted his drink, taking a second close look at the girl.

"So. Your throw."

"I heard you were looking for a young girl. Fresh, unspoiled. True?"

"Long ears."

"You bet. I've found her for you. Suzy. Photos."

The girl, Suzy, approached with a sheaf of photographs, which she attempted to hand over.

"One at a time. One at a time." Sieger looked at the photographs but at least half of his attention was concentrated on Suzy, who was forced to lean across him with each new photograph. Meanwhile Julian reeled off the actress's credits—theater, television—places and names Henry had never heard of.

"Very nice," said Sieger finally. "Can I see her?"

"Anytime." Julian was eager. "Anytime." Henry thought the atmosphere was more like a cattle market than a cocktail party.

Sieger now turned to him. "Are you in the business, too, Harry?"

"Harry's on the world stage," Julian smiled.

"I'm in the Foreign Office," said Henry stiffly.

"He's just been kicked out of the Royal Hashemite Kingdom."

"Come again?"

"I was in Jordan."

"The war, you mean. Hey, that's interesting. What a scene! What drama! Those Israelis are some fighters."

"Yes," agreed Henry.

"And you were there."

"I wasn't actually involved in the fighting. I was based in Amman."

"Amman," repeated Sieger, without understanding. "But you know the background, understand how it all happened."

"Yes. Israel thought attack was the best form of defense."

"This could be my lucky day." Sieger became thoughtful. His earlier playful manner was replaced by intensity overlaid by thick charm. "Let me come clean. I want to make a movie of that war."

"What?"

Julian mocked Henry's astonishment. "He wants to make a movie of your Six Day War. You can make a movie of anything you want."

"If you can get the money." Sieger leaned forward. "People aren't too keen to back a film about our war."

"Vietnam?"

"Right. But there's an awful lot of American money rooting for Israel."

"They'd be the good guys?"

"Right. What you need for that kind of film is a really good adviser. Get the facts right. How about you?"

"Me?"

"Adviser?"

Apparently an answer was expected. "But I'm not sure the Israelis were the good guys."

"Come on. The little fellow surrounded by all those oil-rich bullies."

"It's not quite like that. You've got to look at both sides."

Sieger laughed and stood up. "Not in films, you don't. I've got to go. But think about it. Julian knows how to get me."

After he'd gone Julian took off his jacket and made himself another drink. "Phew! You certainly took over that one!"

"It was all nonsense. I could never do anything while I'm in the Foreign Office."

"You didn't tell him that. Don't tell me you were tempted." Julian sat down. He was so used to slotting Henry into a cupboard of conventional attitudes that he had not allowed for the possibility that he might be attracted by show business, just as he himself was. Reluctantly, he remembered his Rive Gauche successes and that spy in Beirut, not to say Henry's short-lived marriage to the most attractive girl at Oxford. "Most insistent on 'Harry', you were."

"I liked him, that was all."

"Liked him!" screeched Julian. "But he's a monster. Didn't you see the way he treated poor Suzy?"

"That's why you have her here, isn't it? It certainly isn't for her typing. Nor for your entertainment. Unless you've changed a great deal."

"Shit." Julian flung himself about sulkily. "It's terrible to find the friend you always admired for his principles is as cynical as everybody else."

"I liked him because he wasn't pretending."

Harry, as he became again after the meeting with Sieger, was interested to see his father operating as a full-scale Ambassador. About as full-scale as you could be. The residence was an imposing house with white stucco pillars and a driveway cutting through a large garden. It had a tennis court and a swimming pool. Unlike the same kind of grandeur in India, everything was in working order.

Harry arrived early in the morning but both his parents were already busy. Lionel was having a breakfast meeting with a jet-lagged British minister who'd flown in the night before. Beatrice was planning the menu for a formal dinner the following week.

The ambassadorial chauffeur, driving a well-preserved Rolls-Royce, dropped Harry between the porticoed pillars.

"Have a good day, sir."

"Thank you."

A servant opened the door. He showed Harry to his room and informed him of his parents' activities. They would be free at nine-thirty.

Harry sat on the bed. He was reminded of all the years in which he had followed his parents round the world. He felt very young again, sitting on the bed with the brilliant sun coming through the window. In his memory they were always hot countries, although New York must have been cold in the winter.

Beatrice came and found him there. She, too, remembered his childhood visits. "But soon you'll be the one traveling around and we'll be back in England." She put her arm round her son. They looked very alike standing staring out of the window.

"How is Father?" It was the first time Harry had asked such a question of his mother.

"Pretty fit," said Beatrice. "He plays tennis quite a bit."

Harry hadn't meant that. Which Beatrice knew. After the first rush of love, she found herself withdrawing from him. She recognized his similarity to herself and was disturbed by it. She had now so completely identified her life with her husband's that she felt threatened by the idea of a separate self. He reminded her of herself as she had been in Cairo. Then she had been desperate enough to kill herself.

Yet that was absurd. Harry might take after her in looks, but in every other way he followed his father. Here he stood in front of her, frowning, a composed, clever member of the Foreign Office. He didn't have quite Lionel's physical ebullience, perhaps, nor his propensity for lectures, but neither did he have her hopeless memory, romantic yearnings and emotional instability. She was sure about that.

"Did you have a good time in London? It must have been strange after so long."

"Everybody's working very hard at being successful."

"It is the age, isn't it? Lionel's expecting us to meet him in the Blue Room for coffee. Oh, darling, it is good to have you here!"

Harry smiled gratefully. He had noticed his mother's confusion at seeing him. Perhaps she had forgotten how they had always met as strangers. Perhaps she was expecting something more. Or perhaps she was sorry for his aloneness. She had written to him after Flavia left.

> I don't understand, dear. I'm afraid I simply don't understand. She seemed such a nice girl. And that little baby. My grandchild . . .

Lionel stood in the middle of the Blue Room. "Henry!" he cried. A secretary scurried out carrying a pile of notes. He looked very grand, very confident, very energetic. "Sit down. Coffee's on its way. How was your flight? You certainly know how to pick the action."

"What?"

"Israel. Jordan. The Middle East. I'm looking forward to some firsthand information."

"It was all over so quickly," said Harry, feeling as if he were at a debriefing. "One minute they were sunbathing on the beach . . ."

"That is the nature of a surprise attack," interrupted Lionel dryly.

Harry subsided. The Foreign Office knew best. The less important you were, the smaller your piece of the puzzle. He remembered Rahat's misery. In a sense, his presence on the spot made him less able to judge the truth. His father, as an Ambassador, was better able to see all the pieces. He was allowed to see all the pieces.

Nevertheless, as they drank cups of American coffee, Harry put forward his view on the disaster that had overtaken Jordan and the Palestinians, and Lionel listened intently.

"That's it," he said when Harry finished. "Not the end of a problem but the beginning of a disaster. Well, at least I won't be around to try and sort it out. I don't expect you see any solution?"

"No. Egypt's the only hope. But it's too poor for any really lasting influence."

"It seems to me you've chosen the hot spot for your career."

"Yes," agreed Harry. But he recalled the sunny peace of his years in the Lebanon and Jordan.

"I'll tell you what." Lionel pushed back his chair. "I've got some good news for you before I leave. Have you thought about your next posting?"

"I'm due for a long leave." Harry felt defensive. His father stood above him, smiling.

"Yes. Yes. How would you like the UN? New York?"

Harry stood up too. Beatrice remained sitting, looking at her husband as she had throughout the meeting. He saw that his father had fixed it, pulled strings. "I always found New York very exciting," he said.

"And you'll be able to visit us." Beatrice spoke for the first time.

"And we'll be able to visit you," said Lionel. "Now I must be away or I'll be late."

After he had gone, Beatrice and Harry strolled out into the large garden.

"Do you realize," said Harry, "it will be the first time we've all been in the same country for more than a few weeks."

"Is that so?" Beatrice seemed surprised. She bent as if to pick a flower and then hesitated. "I always feel as if I'm stealing."

"Property of HMG?"

"Or the gardeners. They're quite fierce."

"Where's your home, Mother?"

"Where your father is." Beatrice answered quickly, eyes wide and innocent.

"Of course."

"I *will* pick this flower." They walked on arm in arm. Beatrice waved the flower around like a wand.

Harry appreciated the moment. He saw that Beatrice had recovered from her suspicion of him. Her dark eyes glowed intimately. He saw how beautiful she had been.

Beatrice felt his admiration. She still felt Lionel's waves of confidence and success. For the first time they seemed united in a family bond of love and support. She thought she would try to write of this moment to Father Bernard. Since Lionel's posting to Delhi four years ago she had seen him only once. But she had written to him constantly. It was apparently a one-sided correspondence, since she wrote voluminously and he replied seldom and with brief religious platitudes. However, as she believed he was Christ's representative on earth, they came to her as inspired words, a source of strength and spiritual growth.

"I don't really like Father fixing things for me," said Harry.

"That's only natural." Beatrice was unshaken. "Natural independence. But there's no point in fighting it. Everyone does it. It's the system." Since he still didn't look very convinced, she added, "It's a game."

"Outside the normal moral rules?" Harry was obstinate.

"Heavens, yes! They've absolutely nothing to do with the Foreign Office."

They had now reached the end of the garden and were faced by a tennis court. Harry walked forward and laced his fingers through the mesh. Beatrice stared contentedly at his back.

Harry leaned forward and shut his eyes. He realized the sun was very hot, he had missed a night's sleep and it was still only six in the morning in England. He had no idea what time it was in Jordan. The wire bit into his face. A pleasurable sensation.

"Wherever will they put the refugees?"

"What?"

"The Palestinian refugees." Harry lifted his face from the wire. "There'll be hundreds of thousands. Soldiers. Women. Children. Families."

"That's just what the United Nations is designed for," said Beatrice bracingly, although the word "families" had given her a nasty twinge. "You'll have your special interests. You can do so much *good.*"

Her tone of enthusiasm was so charming that it made Harry smile. She, who had always seemed so dark and mysterious, now seemed like a child with her optimistic confidence. Not knowing about her faith and Father Bernard, he assumed it must all come from his father. The old-fashioned belief that with a little goodwill the educated West can sort out the problems of the uneducated East. Or in this case, Middle East. He thought about saying, The world's changed. Our views don't count for much anymore. But it seemed a spoilsport sort of line. As she had said, it was only a game anyway. Perhaps, after all, she was not so childlike.

"I'm sure I'll have a lot of fun in New York."

Chapter 17

Harry's apartment in New York was halfway up an undistinguished building.

> "And when he was up, he was up,
> And when he was down, he was down,
> And when he was only halfway up,
> He was neither up nor down."

His position in the Foreign Office was lower than halfway up, but it gave him the same sense of being nowhere in particular. When he woke up in the morning and put his bare feet on the carpet beside his bed, he felt no contact. He could create the sensation with an act of will, but it seldom happened spontaneously.

His office at the United Nations was also halfway up the thirty-eight-floor building. There were those who felt exhilarated by the grand symbol of international goodwill, moored so splendidly on the edge of the East River, flying its many colored pennants with such bravura. There were those who honestly believed in its power to do good and there were those who were excited by its theatrical properties. Harry felt none of these.

He did enjoy the walk along the river from his apartment. He usually bought breakfast in a drugstore on the way, reading his *New York Times* with the communal pleasure of a city dweller. He liked American coffee, he liked their pastries—it was about this time he collected a roll of fat round his stomach—he liked the dark and oily river. When he arrived at his office in the UN, he studied the political importance of potash discoveries in the Middle East. His reports became well known for their clarity and thoroughness.

On the fourth floor of the building there was a brilliantly lit delegates' dining room where people brought tourists and important visitors. At ground level there was a cafeteria for the staff. Here Harry found hope in the middle of the day. Not for years had he seen so many dazzling young girls. The fashion for short skirts and long hair gave them a provocative aura deeply felt by Harry, who had been away from the unlicensed West for so long.

These girls were, in fact, international. They were secretaries, assistants, translators, press officers and even members of the diplomatic corps. Very few of them were as uneducated as their appearance suggested to Harry.

"Hi. May I join you?"

"Sure. Make yourself at home. This is Donna and I'm Mona."

"Harry Hayes from the British contingent."

"We guessed that. We can tell a man's nationality in five seconds flat."

"You've been here a long time then?"

"Donna's on her third year. I'm on my second. We're American, of course."

They talked alternately. Both were attractive, with Mona winning on vivacity and Donna having a sweeter smile. Really, there was nothing to choose between them.

They arranged a double date for later that week. Harry was to provide the second man. In the end he lighted upon a handsome blond attaché who, in his brainless goodwill, revived nostalgic memories of Salmon. He had already picked him as a likely tennis partner, so this killed two birds with one stone. His name was Hugo.

Hugo, Harry, Donna and Mona met in Alan's bar on Third Avenue. The girls looked at Hugo with rather too much approval from Harry's point of view. He saw that the advantage of height and fair good looks in a very crowded bar more than compensated for a dull nature.

"If you put a dollar tip on the bar," said Hugo, "every second drink is free."

"Shall we eat?" suggested Harry.

The girls looked at each other. "We ate at lunchtime," said Mona.

Hugo laughed as if she'd made a very good joke. He was beginning to irritate Harry.

"Let's go to the Hippopotamus," suggested Donna.

"What's that?"

"It's a disco," said Hugo. "Actually I'm a member."

They went to the Hippopotamus. It was a very large underground area lit by pink and green strobe lights. As they entered a voice vibrated from every corner. *"I can't get no satisfaction!"* The heat would have made Jericho seem cool in midsummer.

Harry, although keen to forget his troubles and have a good time, hovered dizzily.

The girls noticed his reaction. They looked at each other. Donna said in a kindly voice, "Don't you like loud disco?" The girls were not as similar as Harry thought. Donna of the sweet smile had been brought up in North Carolina in a Catholic household. She had left her faith behind her when she moved to the big city but it had given her a sympathetic awareness of guilt and sin. The vivacious Mona, who, although from the East Coast, had attended the University of California at Berkeley, was much less introspective than her friend. She was also a stronger feminist, though that term was not yet in common use. After all, Donna's highest ambition, until she was thirteen, was to play the Virgin Mary in the school Nativity play. Donna, despite her modern looks, still dreamed of the "parfit gentilhomme."

"We can go if you like," whispered Donna in Harry's ear.

"Won't the others . . . ?"

"No."

Donna and Harry stood on the pavement outside the club. It was an unseasonably warm October evening. They were both excited by the sounds and smells of the city.

"I used to live here when I was a boy."

"How did you manage that?"

"The Foreign Office posted my father here for a few years."

"I always wanted to live in New York. I could never live anywhere else now. It's the freest place in the whole world."

They began to walk. Harry's main aim (which he assumed Donna shared) was to get Donna back to his apartment and screw her. He did not feel the overwhelming waves of sex that he used to, but it gave him a solid objective.

They walked briskly side by side along the pavement. "What do you mean by free?" asked Harry after a while. The echo of her words had stayed with them.

"There're so many opportunities to do what I want and no one to stop me."

"But do you know what you want?"

"That's what I'm finding out. That's the whole point."

They walked on. "I suppose you're younger than I."

"I'm twenty-three."

"I don't think I had enough to drink."

Donna thought he was probably right. She was surprised by him. Most of the English diplomats she went out with were terrified of serious conversations. They usually made very correct small talk until they tore off her clothes in a rage of alcohol and excitement. They never appreciated her cooperative efforts to reveal her nakedness. It made her think English girls must behave very oddly.

But Harry made no attempt at small talk and sometimes seemed hardly aware of her presence. She wondered if, when they arrived at his apartment, he would begin the leaping, tearing routine. "Are you married?" she asked on a sudden impulse.

Harry looked at her with surprise. He was tempted to say no, not from a desire to lie but because that seemed the real truth. "Not anymore."

"I'm sorry."

Harry smiled. "My wife had our marriage annulled, so I suppose you could say I was never married." He laughed.

"Are you a Catholic then?" Donna's heart, in search of its perfect knight, leaped at the word.

"No," said Harry. He remembered his mother's story of early Catholic baptism in an Indian crypt. "No," he repeated with even more firmness.

It was twenty-three blocks to Harry's apartment. Donna found it hard going in her high heels and short tight skirt. The pavements were uneven and threatening figures tended to lurk in and out of doorways. Harry, used to the more obvious dangers of Arab-Israeli conflict, did not take any notice. Besides, his mind was worrying, in a muffled kind of way, about the concept of freedom. Donna had spoken with such confidence. She could do what she wanted with no one to stop her.

"Here. Look out!" He raised his arm as a drunk suddenly raised himself from the gutter.

Donna sheltered behind him nervously. The drunk fell back again, deflected from whatever purpose he had temporarily envisaged.

It was Donna's sense of freedom which made her brave and uncomplaining about walking late at night in uncomfortable places. For the same reason she went to bed with men she didn't particularly like and wore tight skirts which made her thighs rub together. It was all a gesture of defiance to North Carolina. Sometimes she felt quite tired and sorry for herself but then she made herself a large martini and went to bed with a magazine.

When they got back to Harry's apartment, he headed immediately for the kitchen. Donna followed him slowly.

"I'm starving!" he explained at her arrival.

She wondered whether to cook for him. It was against all the rules of independence, of course, but after such a long walk she was pretty hungry herself. While she considered the ethics involved, Harry turned on the grill and got out a large steak from the fridge. "You can have some," he said over his shoulder.

Donna went back to the living room. But she felt restless. In fact, she liked cooking and knew a good butter sauce that would revive what she judged to be rather old steak. It seemed to her that the problem for the independent woman in this particular instance was that it made her seem only a sexual object rather than a useful human being. She knew, naturally, that he was her sexual object as much as she was his, but somehow it did not feel like that.

"I know a super butter sauce." Donna stood at the kitchen door.

Harry held a plate in either hand. "I don't like sauces." He held out the plates. "Why don't you lay the table?"

After they had eaten, Harry made the coffee while Donna did the washing up. Being an optimist, she decided that such domestic intimacy gave a special quality to their relationship. She dried the glasses carefully and put them away in the cupboard.

Harry put his arms round her waist. "Has it been a very boring evening for you?"

Donna breathed a sensuous negative.

His hands slid up to her breasts. Donna wished he had waited til she had put down the dishcloth. But at least he wasn't leaping and tearing.

They went along to Harry's bedroom. Donna wrinkled her nose a little. It had a bachelor staleness to it that she had noticed seemed particular to the English. American men's bedrooms smelled of lotions and their bathrooms of mouthwash. She lifted her sweater over her head, allowing her breasts to flip enticingly.

Harry watched seriously. She was standing beside the bed on the very piece of carpet which in the morning received his feet so unfeelingly. She let her skirt drop and stood in brief panties. She had a pretty figure, with slender thighs and long sloping hips.

"Do I look all right?" It was impossible to keep the coy satisfaction out of her tone.

"Wonderful!" cried Harry. He began to throw off his own clothes enthusiastically. "I can't believe my luck."

"Don't be stupid." Donna stooped to take off her pants. "I'm the lucky one." That remark, she thought rather confusedly as they both got into bed, made up for her earlier weakness.

Harry felt himself lucky to have found Donna but he couldn't let her into his soul. She visited his bed so regularly that autumn/winter of 1967/1968 that his cleaning lady gave notice on the grounds that she'd been hired to look after a bachelor apartment, not "a couple." This vulgar word filled Harry with alarm. He did not feel coupled to Donna in any sense except the most physical. Even there he found her only adequately exciting. She was so open about it all, so efficiently on the Pill and unresistant. He liked her presence because it gave a reality to his existence. He was there because she talked to him, made his breakfast—he had given up cooking long ago—and when he put his feet out of the bed, he felt her footprints on the carpet. But "a couple" . . .

Harry said to his cleaning lady, "Do you belong to the League of Virtue by Celibacy?" She sniffed haughtily and continued to roll up her apron.

"Or perhaps you represent the Pure Homes for Pure People Association?"

"My last diplomat was gentleman. He no talk games."

"But what did he do for women?" Harry was not sure why he was carrying on such an absurd dialogue. The cleaning lady was Puerto Rican, of indeterminate age and broad outline. She was now putting on her coat and her scarf and her hat and her gloves. She was armoring herself against the streets of cold violence.

"So you won't come back?"

There was no answer. A second scarf topped the coat, muffling the lower part of her face. She seemed dehumanized. Perhaps that was part of the process. Harry tried to think of her as a woman like Donna. Perhaps that was the problem. Perhaps her proprietary rights over his sheets and toothbrush had been offended.

"Why you speak me now? You never before." Her voice was distorted by artificial fibers.

"You must be going for another reason," said Harry, suddenly wily. He tried to think why he had not spoken to her before. The answer was simple—he had never been in the apartment at this hour of the morning. Their previous dialogue had been entirely conducted through notes. "Perhaps you are disappointed at my looks? I do have a cold. That's why I stayed late this morning."

The black eyes blinked from within their helmet. "I not come back."

"I suppose you didn't think it right to give notice through a note." No answer. "Do you have a family? Children? I was given a box of chocolates at Christmas I've never eaten."

Harry went off and found the box. When he came back, Lizzie—he suddenly recalled her unlikely name—had opened the door and was standing poised, if such a lumbering figure could be described as poised, for departure. Holding out the gaudy box, Harry felt rather like a zoo keeper tempting a nervous animal—a bear perhaps, or a raccoon.

Again he wondered why he was taking such trouble with someone over whom he had never previously spared a second. Perhaps, he thought whimsically, it was her role as the first woman to leave him that inspired him. He then recalled Flavia's desertion and he was struck by an unexpected pain of loss. His cold must be worse than he thought.

"I'm not feeling very well."

"Thanks for the chocolate. You go lie down." She shut the door.

Harry was glad her last words were kind. He was suddenly feeling very weak indeed. He went back to the bed, still unmade, and got into it without removing his clothes. The room, decorated in an ugly avocado green presumably favored by some diplomatic designing wife, immediately began to spin around. If he shut his eyes, it became worse, not only spinning but tilting at such a dangerous angle that he felt terrified of falling off. He staggered to the bathroom and was sick.

He returned to his bed, shaking violently with cold. A few seconds later his whole body was scorched with heat. He tore at his shirt collar.

Between times, he wondered if what he was feeling was within the normal bounds of flu or other conversational illnesses. He could not remember being ill since his prep school. The most logical part of his brain assumed almost immediately that only death could end such violent upheavals. But a spark of optimism suggested his symptoms were perfectly run-of-the-mill. It was his aloneness that made it frightening.

An avocado telephone stood by his bed. Fighting off nausea, he lifted the receiver. A decision was then needed about whom he should ring. The most obvious candidate, Donna, was rejected because she was the root of the whole trouble. "Couple," indeed. This left a sparse choice. He dialed a number with fingers turned doughly white and soft.

Beatrice sat at her desk in the British Embassy. In a corner the television, always her love, played gently. She was looking at the day's offering of invitations. All were official functions at which she had an official role to play. She smoothed the stack of white cards with her fingers. They expressed such security for her, such success for Lionel. He, it was true, didn't think much of such things. Indeed, now that he was in a position actually to affect the diplomatic world, he found such courtly goings-on distracting and possibly unnecessary. He preferred his intimate breakfasts and his little lunches (for sixteen with five courses) and his tactical games of tennis. It was lucky for him, thought Beatrice with satisfaction, that he was married to someone who appreciated the grander scale necessary to press the case of Great Britain—even if it wasn't *so* great anymore.

All this complacent mulling, even the smooth shuffling of the invitation cards, was designed to distract her thoughts from another missive she had received that morning. It was from Bridget, of the masculine looks and protective arts. At least that was the Bridget in India whom Beatrice liked to remember. But then there had been the black angry Bridget who'd wanted her to confront Lionel and Queenie. What a mistake that would have been! Satisfaction returned for a moment. But now a third Bridget was threatening to reenter her life. A sad, ill, possibly dying old woman who was flying to Washington to see a specialist. "May I drop in for a drink, dear Beatrice, for old times' sake? I won't stay long."

Beatrice saw nothing but ill coming of it.

The telephone rang. Automatically she picked up the receiver. A voice said, "I'm afraid I'm not feeling at all well. Not at all. I wonder if you, if you could help me to find a . . . doctor."

Beatrice did not recognize her son's tones in these muttered and hysterical words. It was exactly what she dreaded from Bridget. She tried to picture herself again as the Ambassador's wife, secure and majestic enough to handle the troubles of other, less favored mortals.

"Is that you, Bridget, dear? I didn't realize your plane was arriving so soon."

Harry, who had fallen slightly away from the receiver, believed he was delirious. "A doctor. I'm ill."

"Of course, dear. Don't worry about a thing. Where are you now?"

"In bed."

"Quite. But where in bed?"

Harry fell back again. Even he could not suspect his mother did not recognize him in his hour of need. Reason told him to scream, I'm dying. Foolish optimism reduced the scream to a whine. "In my flat. I'm probably dying."

There was a pause. The whine had not sounded like Bridget. Beatrice sat up less defensively. "That is you, Bridget, isn't it?"

But she received no reply, for Harry had dropped the receiver in a second dash to the bathroom. When he returned they had been cut off. He felt too weak for further action.

"Oh God!" he murmured profanely. "Let this chalice pass from me."

Harry's fairly ordinary bout of flu lasted for a fairly ordinary five days. His secretary found him a doctor, Lizzie returned out of pity or gratitude for the very expensive Swiss chocolates and Donna popped in and out. She put down Harry's lack of response to her ministrations as the result of his illness.

Beatrice did not discover the identity of her caller until the real Bridget telephoned several days later. "So it wasn't you," she said, mystifying her friend. "Well, I wonder who else was dying? No one I knew very well or I would have heard."

Another day or two passed before she thought of Harry. She rang him up at one. "Oh, darling, I'm so relieved to hear your voice. I had this weird call which might have been from you."

"It was," said Harry. He was out of bed but not yet back at work.

"But she—that is, you—said you were dying."

"I was."

"But now you're better."

"Yes. Nearly."

This did not elicit sympathy. Beatrice began to talk about Bridget. After a while she had the brainstorm that Bridget should pay a visit to New York, staying at Harry's flat. "She only has treatment twice a week, so she could fly down in between."

Harry was feeling better but not that much better. "My cleaning lady won't have women in the apartment."

"What?"

"I'm not well enough."

Beatrice gave up the idea regretfully. "She was very kind to you as a child, you know."

"I'm sorry."

"I must go. I am glad it wasn't you."

"But it was."

"But you weren't dying."

"I didn't die."

"No. You did sound odd. What was it you had?"

"I was delirious. Flu."

"Good. Well, if you want to recuperate, don't forget we have twelve spare rooms." Her brisk tones slowed a little. "Unless Bridget invites herself."

"Thank you for ringing, Mother."

"Much love from us both." A comfortable sigh came across the telephone wires. "It's such a consolation to have us all in the same country."

"Yes. It is." Harry did not feel ironic about his mother. It was indeed a consolation to have those twelve (or possibly eleven) spare rooms only a short shuttle away. Next time he was delirious he would concentrate on such things instead of the abstracts of loneliness and freedom.

Twelve spare rooms, two parents, one girlfriend, one cleaning lady, one tennis partner, an avocado apartment halfway up one building and an office halfway up another all seemed a pretty fair amount of reality to fill any delirium.

Introspection was bursting upon Harry with the serial explosions of a pent-up force. Inaction and illness encouraged an overheated mind. Images of his mother as she had been throughout the years unrolled in filmic vision. They were usually partings or welcomings—perhaps meetings would be more appropriate a description. Her love was certainly there but under a veil which he had never presumed to lift. Perhaps it was his fault. He must have seemed a clever, cold little boy.

Harry's mind veered around to moments of emotion. Most recently there was his parting with Rahat. He had the unpleasant feeling that their friendship could no longer exist now that Rahat had entered a real world of suffering where Harry could not follow.

There were other, more intimately painful times that he did not yet dare admit. Flavia was almost entirely swept away. Only one scene lurked a little too close for comfort. That afternoon when Cordelia had sat at his feet eating gravel. It was, in fact, the last time he had seen her. Once a year Flavia wrote, enclosing a photograph. She was nearly as fair as Flavia, but her skin was darkened by the South American sun. Her features and expression meant nothing to Harry. He had never looked at children to tell one apart from the other. He never answered the letters. There was no need, since Flavia had never asked for money. Her husband was rich, he understood. It was just that scene which hovered in his consciousness. He and Flavia sitting side by side on the bench while their child sucked gravel at their feet. The memory, although shadowy, was an irritant. Without it, he could have totally forgotten.

Harry stretched in his chair and stood up. He walked to the window. He liked his view, although it might not have pleased everybody. It was a waist-high vision of midtown Manhattan. He saw other blocks of apartments like his own, in which he could imagine, and sometimes even see, other men living out lives, so he presumed, not unlike his own. It gave him the same satisfaction to look at these mirror image lives as it did to drink his coffee and eat his pastry at the drugstore counter. He felt a sense of comradeship with his fellow men, which was a new and comforting experience.

Between the burgeoning waists, he could see a small crack of the East River, a dark ribbon linking his domestic life (such as it was) and his working life. Sometimes he would see a boat passing through the crack. First the front of the boat, then the middle and finally the end. Harry found it a mesmerizing sight. The lack of a whole boat gave it a special fascination. Only the imagination could put the pieces together.

On Monday Harry must start work again. For the first time in his life, it seemed a matter of choice. He went back to his chair and put on a reading light. It was March. Late afternoon. There had been no sun that day and it was now growing unnaturally dark, as if at the approach of snow. The office had sent him a pile of correspondence and notes from various meetings he should have attended. His advice was urgently wanted on one matter, which was flattering. His superior had already grown to depend on his clear mind and infallible memory. "You tell me what to do," he liked to say. "Your memory seems to cope with all the ins and outs more like a computer than a human being."

"Lazy sod!" Harry lifted up a sheaf of typewritten paper and then banged it down again. "International shit!" Speaking out loud had the curious effect of making his head ring. He thought for a moment that his fever was returning. He then realized with some disappointment that it was the doorbell ringing.

"Who is it?" He had eventually learned the New Yorker's suspicious nature.

"Me."

Harry had never allowed Donna a key. Even when he had to crawl sweating to the door, he had remained adamant.

"Wow! Up, dressed and working. Great!"

"My mother rang," said Harry as Donna took off her coat and began to unpack some groceries. "She wanted to know if I was dying. And then when she found I wasn't, she tried to foist on to me some old friend of hers who is."

Donna wished he wouldn't say such important things when she was otherwise engaged. She had pinpointed it as an Englishman's practice. She longed to know more about his mother. The wife of the British Ambassador in Washington was a celebrity. So was the son. The information had affected the way she thought about Harry. He was not only personable and intelligent, but also a *catch.* Donna found it harder than ever to carry out her feminist principles.

"There you are! Pheasant soup, mulligatawny, lumpfish roe, yogurt, eggs, bacon—not streaky—juice, beer, homogenized milk, Oxford's Olde English Marmalade, rye bread, white bread, cheese . . ."

"What sort of cheese?" asked Harry as she paused, not because he cared but because politeness called for a show of interest.

Donna sighed. Inevitably it was the one area in which she'd failed him. "Not very nice, I'm afraid. I ran out of money."

"Didn't I give you twenty dollars?"

"Yes." Donna wondered if his wife had been a good housekeeper. Or perhaps that was where she'd failed him. Since Harry never talked about her she had no idea of their relationship. She would have been amazed to discover how unimportant was the cut of their marmalade.

Donna made supper. In the American way, they ate early. Donna said, "I'm duty translator first thing tomorrow, so I won't stay long." She looked hopefully for signs of regret.

Harry, unusually for him, noticed her expression and, even more unusually, paid some attention to it. "It's no good, I'm afraid."

"What?" Donna blushed guiltily.

"Whatever you expect. You won't get it from me."

"You're just depressed because you've been ill." Donna jumped up and cleared the plates. "I don't expect anything. What do you think I am, some silly girl searching for her life's dream?" Donna, trying to work up indignation, described herself with accuracy.

"Sorry, I didn't mean to insult your independence." Harry failed to keep the irony out of his voice.

"We're friends, that's all."

Harry said nothing. He felt the conversation had curiously

twisted their roles. But somewhere a warning had been given and received. He opened another can of beer. "Anything on the TV?" Perhaps, he thought, life would look different when his urge for sex returned. Donna was thinking much the same thing. In that, at least, they were equal.

Harry went back to work on Monday. Snow came and went. He delivered his report, which was praised. His sex urge returned. He felt the need to spread it beyond Donna to an English secretary called Hazel and a very beautiful Canadian model called Roxy. He played a lot of tennis with Hugo and generally came out the winner. He retained the affection of Lizzie, his Puerto Rican cleaning lady, by dint of giving her a small present once a fortnight. He marked when it was due with a cross, as a woman might note her period. He transferred the latest photograph of Cordelia to the back of the same diary in which he kept the earlier ones.

That year New York saw a little light spring. It came in the middle of April, with the air melting sensuously round the high-rise blocks. The water in the East River seemed to flow more luxuriously black. The trees sent out quivering shoots of luminous green. Harry, who had never much attended to weather, was affected by it as by a fever. He even wondered if his flu—he had never been quite satisfied that was all it was—was returning, this time to show its true death-dealing colors. Martin Luther King had been assassinated on April 4.

In the office, Vietnam overwhelmed all other considerations. Harry was among the first to sense that military might would not overcome. And indeed, probably should not either. He did not yet argue the case officially, but it gave him a secret sense of excitement. He knew something those all-powerful Foreign Office mandarins did not contemplate. Even his father, with all the benefit of experience and total informaiton, still harped on about the domino theory. An ally is never wrong, thought Harry wryly.

One Friday morning Harry received a person-to-person collect call from a pay phone in Los Angeles. It was surprising the Foreign Office had let it through. It must have been the American operator.

"Is that you, Henry?"

"Harry Hayes speaking. Who is that?"

"Belinda." A wild laugh. "I can't believe I've reached you. It was just a sudden impulse."

"I just sit here at my desk," said Harry. He tried to remember when and in what circumstances he had last seen Belinda. He had a vague sensation of something disagreeable.

"You were on honeymoon when we last met. Do you remember?"

Harry looked at his watch. "I've got a meeting in a moment. Are you coming to New York?"

Belinda laughed again. "That's why I rang. I'm at the airport now."

The part of Harry that was going to his meeting was not sure he wanted to meet Belinda. He remembered her appearance as vulgar and distraught. But the feverish side of himself gave her his address and promised to be there at seven that evening.

Belinda was now in her thirites. The pony-tailed wife was unrecognizable. She was very thin, brown, either from dirt or suntan, and dressed in the uniform of the West Coast left. This consisted of sandals, many layers of ethnic cotton, symbolizing solidarity with the peasants of the East, and homemade jewelry, symbolizing solidarity with the individual artist against the state. Her hair was plaited up with a trail of off-white flowers. She dragged in a duffel bag behind her and a thick roll of paper.

Harry, still in his diplomatic uniform, felt a mixture of mockery and exhilaration. "Quite a change from the good car salesman's wife," he said.

"Tom was in real estate."

"Was?"

"He made a load of money and left me for something more delectable."

"Before or after—this?" Harry indicated her gear.

"Before. But that's not the reason. I was moving this way anyway. Like a thinking woman must. He just gave me the freedom. And the alimony."

"So you live off the capitalist state?"

"Hey. Can't I even get through the door?"

"Sorry." Harry dragged her bag another yard while Belinda took off a layer or two. She sat down on the sofa and looked round the neat and impersonal room.

"If it comes to that, what happened to your wife?"

"Ran away." Harry took off his jacket and sat down too. He thought that this strange creature had known him longer and at more important moments in his life than anyone else in the world.

"Marriage is a bummer." Belinda delivered this view with the satisfaction of a much repeated truth.

"That sounds very definite."

"I am. You have to be. Otherwise you just get swallowed up. You might as well be dead. I was just about dead when you last saw me."

Harry then remembered the horrible sight of her in the stuffy house, with the air-conditioning and the drink and the television. And the little boy. "You had a son?"

"Pollock prefers to be with Tom. You have to pay a price."

"For independence?"

"For doing what you've been put here for."

Harry stood up. "Like a drink?"

"I don't. I'll have a smoke, though, if you don't mind."

It was clear what sort of smoke she meant and Harry did mind, but he was too cowardly to say so. He poured himself a beer in the kitchen. When he returned Belinda wore a determined expression which suddenly reminded him of her as a very young girl. It was an expression that even her mother never dared balk.

"How is your mother?"

"Dead. Cancer." Belinda's intensity did not alter. "I'm going to be in New York for about a week and I'd like to stay here. But I think I'd better warn you that I'm organizing a protest. Women Against the War. And I might be arrested."

Harry saw that she was a militant. The flowers, symbols of peace, did not reflect her mood. She was under orders. A militant against the military. The idea struck him as ironic. He could see if he said no to her staying, she would march out of his life without a farewell salute. "You wouldn't have to give my name or address, would you?"

Belinda considered this, presumably searching for a principle involved. "No," she agreed with some reluctance.

"That's okay then." Harry was cheerful. "Let's have a puff." He held out a hand to her cigarette.

Chapter 18

Belinda had the energy of someone who knows exactly what she should be doing each moment of the day. Sublimating herself to her mission of peace, she had found happiness for the first time in her life. Despite her community fellowship, she actually felt gloriously self-sufficient, also for the first time in her life. She looked round her group of workers, gathered in a small room on the East Side, and glowed with tender dedication. They, too, were reborn into a world where the problems of everyday women had been banished. There were other, new problems, of course. To the outsider they might have seemed more frightening than the old. There were the "pigs" who hated them doubly for being anti-old-style ladies and anti-patriotic. The "pigs" were a physical threat. But then, as some of the girls said, "Better a 'pig' who breaks your arm with hate than a husband who does it with 'love'." There were the politicians who attacked them with words. And there was the continual battle for enough money to keep the whole show on the road. That was the worst anxiety.

But put these against their previous preoccupations—the sterile round of the young married with the young baby, the demeaning patronage of a young husband, the conformism of looks and behavior expected by their (usually small-town) society—and they were riding in the sky. They had a purpose. An unselfish ideal. They were iron-clad against the worst enemy of all—boredom. They were women fulfilled!

Belinda hardly needed to sleep. On Saturday, she came back to the flat at one in the morning, waking up Harry. In his dreams he had forgotten her presence, so he stumbled out of his room waving a stick.

"I'm not a burglar." Belinda flung down her belongings. Her eyes glittered excitedly.

"However did you get a key?" grumbled Harry.

"I took it. Some day!" She slid down onto the sofa bed. "I don't think I've got the strength to pull this out."

"I'll pull it out. But you're not talking. I want to sleep."

"Okay. Okay."

But Harry had woken up now. They sat side by side on the pulled-out bed. "It's going well, then?"

"Going well? The country's a mess. Assassinations. Forced elections. You don't understand the strength of the feeling. Of course it's students and kids who're afraid of the draft. But it's more than that too."

"Mothers of the kids who're afraid of the draft."

"Don't be cynical. The point is people have suddenly grasped that this is one war we'll never win. No matter how many soldiers and helicopters and billions of dollars we pour in." Since Harry suspected this was a correct view, he made no comment.

Belinda continued. "It's a form of crazy capitalist empire-building gone mad."

"Do you think the West should try and influence events in any way outside their own boundaries?"

"They should give aid." Belinda's reply was prompt. "The Peace Corps was the right way, even if it was run mostly by the CIA. We should be humble. Learn about other people's cultures before we try to change them. Particularly before we start to send in bombers and napalm. What do the Vietnamese themselves want? What are they really like? That should be our concern. Not self-interest. That's the only reason we're there. Self-interest. Just like the British in India a hundred years ago."

Harry thought she might at least have attacked the French, who'd started the mess in Vietnam. But her proselytizing attitude made him unwilling to begin an argument. Sitting here with her reminded him of long evenings with Wiggins. He seldom argued with Wiggins either, except as a kind of intellectual exercise.

"But what about you?" Belinda was sharp, her face back to that childhood determination. "This is your business, after all. Foreign affairs. Where do you stand?"

Here was the difference between Wiggins and an American. An American asked questions. "This is my night off. No dice." Harry spread his hands defensively.

Belinda leaned forward and looked as if she might bite him. Then she gave up, sighing, "That's the matter with you English. Terrified of saying what you think."

Harry stood up. "We're not all like that."

"You are. And you're the one I know best. Of course you've always been the same. Even as a little boy. You were always determined to see both sides. Never saw what was at the end of your nose."

"I don't think I'm strong enough for an attack."

"I admired you very much when you were a child. You were so clever. You knew everything."

"I worshiped you. I had a mad passion for you." Harry was glad to change the subject from Vietnam. He felt safe in declaring his passion to his middle-aged Joan of Arc. He thought she had eschewed sex along with her feminity.

This was a misjudgment. Belinda looked at Harry. He was twenty-eight to her thirty-two, tall, handsome, wearing blue-and-white-striped pajamas. The pill she had taken earlier in the evening to keep her going through a long meeting was still operating. She put her hand out to Harry's chest.

Harry immediately saw his mistake. A musky smell of Eastern promise rose from Belinda's clothing. He felt they were a very mismatched pair.

Belinda felt no such thing. She was enjoying straightforward desire of the sort that used to overwhelm Harry a few years earlier. She unbuttoned the mesmerized Harry's pajama top. It was a role reversal that had never occurred to him before. He felt extremely vulnerable but too weak to take evasive action. He reminded himself that this was his old friend who'd looked after him twenty years ago in New York. Then it was a matter of ice-cream milk shakes and dressing up; now it was something a little different. But all on the same lines. Good friendly stuff. Lie back and think of England.

In the next few days life became complicated for Harry. Donna discovered Belinda's presence and was not convinced by Harry's "childhood friendship." His pajama bottoms, folded into the sofa bed, were an unfortunate clincher. Hugo's arrival for a beer after tennis, coincided with Belinda's exit. She wore a flower behind her ear and carried a large poster declaring "U.S. G.I.'s OUT." Very realistic blood dripped down the letters.

"Who's that?" He waited to ask until the door was closed.

"A childhood friend." Harry's casualness carried an edge of bitterness. He had told Belinda to be out of the apartment before they returned.

Then on Thursday, poor Bridget appeared without warning at the United Nations building. She seemed surprised Harry had received no call from his mother. "But she assured me you could put me up for a night. Otherwise I wouldn't have come."

"I already have a houseguest." Harry's tones were stiff. A glance at the woman in front of him had been enough to assure him that he would have to leave the apartment if she entered it. The once black-haired, loud-voiced more-man-than-woman had now become a gray cadaver tied together by a navy blue suit.

To Harry's horror the suit shoulders began to shake. Casting another glance, he saw a wave of pale purple coat the gray face. "Of course you must come!" he cried hastily. "I'll get my secretary to arrange it."

That evening Belinda brought someone back to the apartment. It was the first time she had done so. Donna also dropped by. Harry, not without forethought, didn't get back until late. Since he had given his key to Bridget, he rang the bell. He rather hoped there'd be no answer.

Donna's face appeared. To his surprise, it smiled. "Oh, there you are. We're having a sort of party. I hope you don't mind."

Harry came in. On the sofa sat an American of a smooth and prosperous appearance whom he had met somewhere before.

"So here's the hero himself!"

Belinda sat at his side. She was even more animated than usual. She wore a flower behind either ear, and across her bosom were pinned a string of badges which together spelled out "U.S. MURDER."

"Shouldn't it be MURDERERS?" suggested Harry.

"Her boobs aren't big enough," laughed the man. This jogged Harry's memory. It was Julián's film producer friend, Phil Sieger. His Six Day War project forgotten, he was now planning an experimental short on the peace movement. It was in this connection that he had met Belinda. "Youth," he explained. "Youth is the key to the sixties."

Harry noticed that his elegant beige had been decorated by a medallion round his neck and made more casual by the sleeves being pushed up to his elbows.

"In my business you've got to be aware of the trends."

"And Belinda's a trend."

Sieger laughed at this, but uneasily, while Belinda herself looked irritated. "I'm not part of the youth movement and I'm not a trend."

"It was only a joke."

"You can't joke about life and death."

"Sorry." Harry went into his bedroom. There he found Bridget. She sat propped up in his bed wearing a pale blue fluffy dressing gown. "Sorry." He went out again.

"But Henry, dear!" she called after him.

Harry passed through the living room on his way to the kitchen. "This apartment's not big enough," he commented. In the kitchen he found Donna. She was mixing him a martini. She had never looked more charming.

"What a madhouse!" He sat down at the table.

"Who is he?" whispered Donna, pleased at their confederacy.

"I met him in England. He wanted me to advise him on a script."

"How exciting!" Donna was now overdoing the enthusiasm. She knew it but felt a heightened sense of drama was needed to compete with Belinda. "And who is the lady in your bed?"

"I assumed you'd put her there."

"Oh, no. She was there when I arrived. So were the others. I think he was disappointed I supported the Vietnam War."

"Do you?" Harry sipped his cocktail.

Phil Sieger had appealed to him more in England.

"What's Sieger getting out of Belinda, beyond my liquor?"

"It's more the other way round. She wants him to film her rally."

"I expect she'll succeed."

"Yes." Donna looked gloomily into her glass. She took Harry's comment as a criticism of her own lack of initiative.

"I suppose this is what people call living," said Harry, standing up and heading back for the living room.

Donna followed him, a little puzzled. Surely Harry, with his experiences round the world, had done more real living than anyone else in the apartment?

That night Donna and Harry shared the sofa bed. Belinda had left with Sieger, presumably for his hotel bedroom.

In the morning Donna took breakfast in to Bridget. She had realized with some guilt that they had not fed her the night before. She lay as if stunned, although she greeted the breakfast tray with a peep of pleasure.

Harry dressed slowly in the bathroom. He put on his diplomatic uniform resentfully. He did not feel like going to the office. On the other hand, he could not stay in the apartment while it was held in the grip of the Bridget specter.

"Come and sit on my bed," whispered Bridget to Donna, "and I'll tell you about Henry as a little boy."

Harry walked out in the bright May morning. His hair was well brushed, his shoes polished, he swung an expensive leather attaché case backward and forward. Only his face expressed a lack of solidity, an unhealthy pallor and vacant eye.

Opposite Gristede's, he was hailed by a woman of a quite opposite demeanor. While her clothes suggested disorganization and lack of care, her face was sharp and determined.

"How was your night?"

Harry stopped. "Not half as interesting as yours. How could you—go off—with someone like that—that ape?"

Belinda laughed. "He's sweet, honestly. Very vulnerable. Between marriages. Couldn't believe I had no designs on him."

"No designs?"

"Not that sort anyway."

"So will he film your rally?"

"He's promised. Shall I walk with you to work?"

"If you like. It's such a beautiful morning."

They took Harry's usual route. A few blocks East and then downtown beside the river. They stopped at his usual drugstore and Belinda shared his usual breakfast of coffee and pastry.

"Why are you walking with me?" asked Harry about Forty-eighth Street.

"It's such a beautiful morning, like you said. No particular reason."

"You're not planning to buttonhole someone at the UN?"

"You're so suspicious."

"You're so motivated."

"Is that an insult?"

They continued walking. When they reached Forty-fifth Street, Harry had the brilliant idea of asking Belinda to marry him. This would make sense of his whole life. Just then, she stopped. "Don't!" she said.

"What?"

"I don't believe in it, you see."

There was no good pretending that he didn't know what she'd so cleverly divined. "You can't just not believe in something which exists."

"Don't play with words. Marriage is fake, phony. Games grown-ups play because they don't dare stand on their own two feet."

"What about children?"

"Children are tough. And more independent than adults."

"You do talk bunk." Harry thought he must be really disturbed to have seriously considered proposing to this ragbag of popular jargon.

When they arrrived at the UN Donna was just jumping out of a taxi.

"Hi!" Belinda waved.

Donna did not wave back. She gave Harry a sloe-eyed look and dashed into the building.

"She's late," commented Harry. "They're very strict about time in her department."

Belinda stretched luxuriantly. "Tomorrow's the day," she said. "One hundred thousand in protest." She looked round at the row of flags fluttering above their heads. "Which one is Vietnam, I wonder. . . ."

Harry strode firmly into the building.

Twenty floors up, Donna clipped her translator's earphones over her head and heard again Bridget's confidences. And of course, after poor Beatrice's breakdown, Lionel was a little more sensitive, circumspect, but what a childhood for a boy. And then never knowing where he'd lay his head from one month to the next . . . The shock to discover the daughter of the very worst actually in his flat . . . Her mother came between Beatrice and me and nearly caused the break-up of their marriage . . . Like mother, like daughter, I'd say . . . I mean, just look at the way she dresses . . . Poor dear Henry, or Harry, as you call him . . .

"Donna, don't you want the technical sheet on French fishing terminology? I assure you, your job will be a whole lot harder without it."

"I was miles away."

"That's news?"

Harry planned to sneak into Central Park when Belinda's rally, as he continued to think of it, was well under way. He had earmarked a pair of old trousers and a checked shirt so that he would not look too like a CIA agent.

Friday night he spent alone on the sofa bed. Donna was not invited and Belinda did not return. On Saturday, morning broke between the tall buildings as bright and blue as it had the day before.

Harry ate his breakfast in the kitchen and then took a tray into Bridget. So far he had managed to avoid any conversation with her. As usual she presented a stunned appearance, as if rescued, perhaps, from drowning or some other awful experience.

"Here you are. You must get some strength up for your flight back to Washington." He drew the curtains with a minimum of aggression.

He was about to leave the room when his subconscious, more acute than his outer eye, forced him to turn back to look at her again.

"Oh, God. She's had a stroke!" Harry leaned against the wall and put his head in his hands. Why had this woman washed up in his bed? Did she have no one who loved her enough to look after her? Surely she had possessed a whole load of ugly children like herself? What was she doing in his bed? What was she doing dying in his bed?

Harry was galvanized enough to reach forward and touch her. She was cool but not entirely cold. "Oh, God!" The kiss of life. He pushed aside the inappropriate blue fluffy dressing gown and pounded the heart. Such moments of anguish for someone he felt nothing for but the merest quiver of pity. He had allowed her to stay because he was too cowardly to take the responsibility to say no. He had thought by doing that he could absolve himself from any further involvement. He hadn't talked to her, he hadn't looked at her.

Harry put his mouth over her gray orifice and tried to give her breath. He banged her brittle chest, knowing that if he was to do any good he must break a brittle bone or two. As he labored, he watched himself with disbelief.

Order an ambulance. Pass her on with horror and relief. He looked at his watch. It was still only nine o'clock.

After ringing for the ambulance, he put a call through to the British Embassy in Washington.

Beatrice lay in bed. She was in her favorite state, halfway between sleep and waking. She had allowed the tea on her bedside to grow cold. Harry's voice came to her as if in an echo chamber.

"But her heart was very strong, she told me that. It was the cancer that was the problem."

There was a silence. Neither mother nor son could understand why this woman from the past had come, bringing them death. Harry, more closely involved, now saw it practically, as a matter of efficient organization. Beatrice, from her remote standpoint, could afford to be philosophical. Besides, her dark nature and religious convictions encouraged her to see death in a not altogether unfavorable light.

"Poor Bridget, one might say, dying alone and on foreign soil.

But then something as grand as death can hardly be expected to slot neatly into one's diary."

"Does she have a husband? Children? Relations?"

"Divorced. But don't worry about all that, darling. I'll get the staff here on to it. People are very helpful in crises. Even on a Saturday." Beatrice now felt awake and ready to talk, but the conversation was interrupted by the arrival of the ambulance people.

There were a man and a woman. They seemed brutal for such a delicate mission, grumbling coarsely about the interruptions to their journey. "Goddamn pinkos, peaceniks and weirdos!" They continued even as they arranged poor Bridget with supreme efficiency. "Goddam fat-assed hippies!"

Gradually Harry, absolved of any action other than executive, realised they were referring to Belinda's rally.

Harry hired a car and drove out of Manhattan. After about an hour he found himself beside a great river or perhaps an inlet from the sea. He turned off the main road and at the same time the water curved sharply and formed a large lake or a small sea in front of him. Lying in the water, and lit brilliantly by the sun as if on some giant film set, were twenty or thirty vast battleships. They were mostly black, dating back to the Second World War. They sat in the water, not floated, as if their hulls were set into a muddy floor.

Harry turned off the engine of the car and got out. In the back he had a bottle of wine and a pastrami sandwich. This seemed the perfect place for a picnic.

About twenty yards behind him and up a rising slope of grass stood a stone. It was formed in a most convenient stool-like shape and received full sunlight. Harry sat on it with a sandwich in hand and a peaceful smile on his face. In front of him lay the battleship graveyard.

It rained on Sunday, flattening into the grass the wastepaper scattered across Central Park. A few flower petals, symbols of peace and love, received the water thankfully, their limp edges revived and glistened.

Belinda flew straight back to Los Angeles. Harry drove her to Kennedy. She was still exhilarated, probably still high. She had not slept for two nights. The rally had been covered by network television, nationwide. There had been few arrests and those mostly for smoking pot. "It was a love-in," she told Harry. "A huge celebration of love."

"But what about Vietnam?"

"You can't fight wars if you're filled with love."

They kissed as they parted, although Belinda's mind was not on it. "I'll be back soon," she said. "So keep that sofa bed oiled."

Somehow Harry did not find the moment to tell her about Bridget's death. He was not even sure that she had noticed her presence in the apartment.

Belinda left an odd legacy to Harry in the shape of Phil Sieger.

"I thought you'd be back on the Coast," said Harry, receiving his first telephone call.

"Films are made there. Documentaries are made here. And my sort of film-documentaries are made here and there."

Sieger, apparently, was keen to employ Harry as political adviser for his new film. He took him to lunch at the Oak Room in the Plaza. Despite his better self, Harry was seduced by the surroundings and his host's enthusiastic wooing.

"Politics is the new high. It's taken the place of sex. The young are all too doped up for sex anyway."

"That's not what I've heard."

"""Listen to me. Or better still, listen to them. Pop songs. Are they about romance? No. Unless you count the romance of world peace and love."

"But how do you make a film about that?"

"I don't know. I just don't know. You tell me."

After their lunch in the Plaza, Harry gave Sieger drinks in the United Nations bar. He was as excited as a schoolboy, wanting to know who everybody was and which country they represented and what was their position in the hierarchy. He showed so much interest that Harry took him on a full guided tour, ending up in the Assembly Hall. There was no debate but Sieger was still impressed by the size of the hall and the technology used for simultaneous translations. "What I want to know is why the young don't get into this place as a forum for peace."

"They don't believe in it," said Harry. "They think it's just a lot of old right-wing windbags earning inflated salaries."

"But every country in the world is here!"

"Most of it. But I'll give you a bit of political advice for free."

"What? What?"

"Leave out all mention of the UN if you want your film to be a success."

"Ri-ight. Ri-ight." Unsmilingly Sieger turned away from images of international co-productions.

After he had gone, Harry routed out Donna and took her to the canteen. "Can you think of one reason why I should continue to devote my life to this place?"

"Of course you don't belong here." Donna's reasonable voice successfully covered her panic. What did he *mean?* "You're just visiting from your own Foreign Office. You're on a temporary assignment. Secondment. You won't stay here forever." She valiantly resisted the temptation to add "like me." In moments of crisis (and indeed in most of her dealings with Harry) old-style selfless programming won over feminist self-importance. Her sacrifice was naturally useless. She watched as Harry piled his cup with sugar lumps. Brown tears trickled down the sides.

"Whatever are you dong?" she cried eventually.

Harry looked down. "Oh, sorry." He pushed back his chair and stood up. He walked out of the canteen.

Lionel surveyed various reports about the growing antagonism to the Vietnam War by the youth in the United States. And not just the youth either. He wondered why he found it so hard to put across in quite the right perspective to the British government. Possibly it was something in his own nature which made him unwilling to take seriously popular expression. Popular expression was usually a matter of emotion and emotion was usually foolishly based. On the other hand he could see the power of strong popular feeling in a democratic country.

But the British government couldn't see even that. They simply saw a bunch of weirdos and cranks, probably whipped up by left-wing agitators. They could not conceive of it as any threat to the policies of their great Western ally. Governments made policies, not people. Certainly not those sors of people.

Lionel sighed. There he agreed with them again. Yet you still could not ignore what was going on. Perhaps a succinct telegram might make the point better than a pile of long reports. "Ten thousand gather in Detroit." Was it Detroit yesterday?

The telephone buzzed on his desk. "Your son to see you, sir."

"My son?" With some relief Lionel put his papers back into a folder.

"What a surprise! A nice surprise. You will stay for luncheon? Oh, where would we be without luncheon?"

Harry had stopped considering Lionel as his father. It had happened gradually, unnoticed over the years, although hastened along when he became Sir Lionel Middleton-Hayes, insulated, as

Harry saw it, by the grandeur of office. However, he still regarded him as a figure of ultimate authority and influence in his life. Not necessarily for the good.

"I'm planning to leave the Foreign Office." His words, delivered over lunch, made less of an impact than he expected.

Sir Lionel took a second lamb cutlet. A look of guilt passed quickly over his face. Beatrice had remarked on his expanding waistline only that morning. "Planning to leave the FO, you say?"

"Yes." Harry was a little sulky. He could see his father was not putting his whole mind to him. He turned to his mother. "I see no point in continuing."

Beatrice narrowed her eyes sympathetically but said nothing.

"Is that why you came to see us?"

"Yes." Harry pushed his plate so hard that it shot off his mat. A servant retrieved it with a look of reproach. "You can't go on doing things if you don't see the reason!" Again he caught his mother's eye. This time she was smiling secretly. It was disconcerting.

"I see." Sir Lionel put down his knife and fork, with deliberation. "So what will you do instead?"

Was there to be no argument? Harry floundered. "It all started in Jordan, you see. I want to go back there."

"Jordan. Allah. Royal Hashemite Kingdom of . . . The West's unfortunate little creation. How is it we manage to draw all our boundaries in the wrong places?"

"I have a friend there"—Harry was not to be drawn into wider issues—"who had half his land annexed by Israel . . . "

"Hardly annexed. Controlled, supervised. The land you speak of is the West Bank, I assume?"

"The Palestinians . . . "

"But your chap hardly sounds like a Palestinian."

Beatrice pushed back her chair. "Shall we?"

Lionel remembered with regret that they were eschewing pudding on the few days when they lunched without guests. He looked at his son's irritable face and for a moment it seemed to represent all the protesting youth he couldn't make sense of in his report. But Harry was too old for that, too well-educated, too English. Nevertheless, he leaned forward. "You're not on drugs, are you?"

"Oh, father."

They went to a little rose-colored sitting room. Harry refused to sit down, "I want to go and sit on Rahat's land under the Golan Heights and meditate."

"Meditate?" Beatrice at last showed some interest.

"Think," said Harry.

"Ah."

"Which side of the border will you be?" asked Lionel. He asked himself why he could not take Harry's undoubted dissatisfaction more seriously.

"Jordan."

"What you need is a holiday. Have you got any leave coming?"

"Yes."

"There you are. Go to your farm. Meditate. Think. And then decide. Afterward, not before." He turned to his wife. "Isn't that sensible?"

"Very sensible, dear."

"I think you owe us that," added Lionel after a pause. His words had the resonance of a first and last appeal.

Beatrice and Lionel prepared for bed. They had attended a dinner in honor of a Hungarian pianist. Afterward he had played. This had encouraged introversion.

"I believe Harry is entering a period of crisis."

Lionel, halfway into his pajama top, halted in an attitude of shock.

"After all," continued Beatrice, "his wife did run off with his child. He's probably just feeling it now."

"Nonsense!" Lionel recovered some energy. "He's just fed up with the UN. Quite understandable."

"All the same, I think I'll consult Father Bernard. Get him to write a letter or something."

"What? Who?" Lionel was now touching his toes.

"Father Bernard. You know, my nice priest in London."

"I do not know."

This, of course, was true, as Beatrice was perfectly well aware. However, she had long ago discovered the best way of getting her husband to digest something new was to pretend he'd known all along. Quite often he did not even bother to deny it. "Oh, yes," she said vaguely. "Such a sweet man."

The Hungarian pianist's fingers stabbed at Lionel's head. "I'll see if there're any more postings coming up."

Chapter 19

Harry lay on his back in warm pearly-gray water. The water gushed up in a natural spring about a hundred yards away and was channeled down into a large pool. The pool was edged by huge smooth-edged rocks left over from splendid Roman constructions. Around the edge stood various busts, lintels, pillars and carved blocks coming from the same source. They stood against a background of flowering shrubs and trees. Paradise could hardly be more enticing.

Harry had been staying on Rahat's country estate for two and a half weeks. Although the pool was so grand, the house consisted of two rooms with no electricity, only one faucet and no kitchen. In the evening a servant lit a fire outside and cooked rice and chicken. At lunchtime, Harry ate olives and white goat cheese and fruit. All week Harry was on his own, but on the weekend Rahat appeared, bringing elaborate picnics and cosmopolitan friends from Amnan. Harry preferred it during the week. For one thing, he suspected Rahat's friends thought he was a spy. It was an odd place to find a solitary Englishman so securely lodged.

At night when he was sipping his whisky and waiting for his chicken, he listened to the Israeli patrols above him along the border. Night or day he would look up to the starry sky and see one star bigger than the rest that moved deliberately and he knew it was the light from an Israeli plane. And yet it was so peaceful. He had never known such peace.

In the daytime he read or went out to the orange and lemon groves which Rahat was planting and tending so assiduously. They were marked by lines of irrigation cutting the farm into thousands of small segments. There were olive trees, too, these older and casting Harry back to the days when he could visit the slopes around

Jerusalem in a jolly day trip. Now that period of his life seemed as far away as the stars.

When he lay on his back in the pool, he thought of time and change and couldn't conceive of a future.

Nevertheless, after eight weeks, which was not much more than the leave due to him, Harry returned to his career in New York.

While he was in Paradise he had received several letters. They came as rather a shock. The advent of a letter at all in such a remote place was a surprise. Father Bernard's was the most surprising.

Dear Henry,

I apologize for presuming to write to you. But sometimes one must dive in uninvited. Particularly if you're a priest!

You are a young man of such potential, educated to a level most of us could never hope to achieve, that you must at times find it difficult to see the point of it all. The most intelligent ask the most questions, as they used to say at my college. I never found too many to ask. But that, too, can be a blessing.

Enough of this rambling . . . the point of this letter is to invite you to ask me questions. I may not be able to answer them but I am the representative of someone who knows it all.

Don't bother to answer this letter. But pop in to see me next time you are in London.

Yours sincerely,
Father Bernard

For a moment Harry wondered if this was a practical joke, written perhaps by Julian, but then he had a letter from Julian himself.

Old Thing,

You're the rock of my life, so don't start exploding all over the place. However, if you do, remember the film industry. Money, sex and money.

Cheers,
Julian

The next, much longer missive came from Wiggins. It was not so much a letter as a report on the prevailing political conditions in England.

Finally his mother wrote.

> Darling Henry,
>
> You seem so far away now that I wanted to send a little greeting from Father and me. Things can look so black when one's all on one's own. I know the feeling so well. But remember we're always here to love and support you . . . .

Harry read none of these letters with care. But he found Wiggins's the most interesting and least mysterious. He had always had the urge to communicate information and, although boring, it did serve that purpose.

His other correspondents seemed to be more or less off their heads. After all, the one thing to be said about his parents was that they were *not* "always here" and never had been. It wasn't their fault and he didn't mind, but those were the facts. Unquestionably, Wiggins's was the only letter worth reading. Even so, he skipped over the passage subtitled "The National Health Service Under Threat."

The day before Harry left Jordan, Rahat gave a particularly grand luncheon party at which most of the Royal Family were present with the exception of the King himself. Champagne was offered to those who were not strict Moslems and everyone became very noisy. Harry knew it was Rahat's message to the West. That, and the young orange groves of which he was so proud. Yet the message he had received lying in the silken pool surrounded by the past had been very different.

When they parted, he clasped Rahat in his arms. "Thank you," he said emotionally, "for giving me a little moment of eternity."

Rahat sighed and turned away. He still would not meet Harry's eyes.

Harry worked for two more years at the United Nations. He moved to a new flat which was more to his taste. His Puerto Rican cleaning woman followed him, grumbling. He continued to play tennis with Hugo but carefully limited his contact with Donna. He found an ugly but clever English girl working in the mission who helped to host the diplomatic dinner parties he was expected to give. Julian visited once or twice on the arm of a shrew-faced actor with bleached blond hair. Wiggins also came with a Labour Party delegation inquiring into American industrial relations. He had a tremendous argument with Harry's opposite number at the British Embassy for which Harry gave him full marks. He himself had lost the habit of saying what he thought.

Harry continued to please his superiors at the Foreign Office, who marked him out for high-flown things. This meant First Secretary at an early age and a posting to somewhere important. Secretly, they felt it a pity that he had specialized in Arabic. For they were mostly old-school snobs and still thought of Europe as the center of the world. Of course, oil had not yet made its power properly felt.

By the time it did, it would be too late for Harry's future.

In the winter of 1969 he visited England for two weeks. To his own surprise he found himself at the church where Father Bernard worked. The priest was even more surprised and took some time to work out who he was. They stood in a dark corridor. "Beatrice Hayes-Middleton's son. Of course. It was the Hayes alone that confused me."

"I dropped the Middleton years ago."

"Come in." He did not say this with much conviction. Indeed Harry now saw that he was wearing bicycle clips and that a bicycle lurked behind him.

"You're on your way out?"

"Nothing that can't wait." He peered around Harry. "Look, it's started raining."

They sat in a little room with a tiled floor, pale green walls, a table, two chairs, one very small window and a crucifix. Father Bernard did not take off his bicycle clips.

"How is your mother?"

"Very well."

"She's a most energetic correspondent. Unlike me, I'm afraid. But then a sympathetic ear can be helpful in itself."

Harry now recognized the style of his correspondent. "Do you remember you wrote to me? More than a year ago."

"So I did." The priest suddenly leaned forward and snapped off his clips. He popped them on the table between them. A new expectancy gave him a sharper, more intelligent air. Harry's case had returned to him. This was the clever Foreign Office lad who, according to his mother, had been on the edge of a nervous collapse. He certainly did not look it now. "Spruce" was a word one might use to describe him. "Are you in England long?" He placed his red hands beside the bicycle clips.

"No. Just a short break. I don't like to get too out of touch."

"England's certainly changed in the last few years."

"Yes," agreed Harry.

There was a pause while both men considered the obvious lack of rapport between them. Then Father Bernard, who was more used to this situation and had less time to spare, said determinedly, "Not for the better, I'm afraid. This is a Godless era we're creating."

It was a provocative statement and Harry roused himself. "I've always found the idea of God appealing. As long as he stays in the background."

"A sort of divine backdrop?" suggested Father Bernard, smiling.

"Well, once he gets mixed up in politics, he causes nothing but trouble."

"Ah, politics . . . "

Harry found this line extremely irritating. "You're Irish, after all, you can see what's happened over there."

"Yes, indeed. Man's capacity for evil is infinite."

This annoyed Harry even more. "But the Church is responsible. They attack with crucifixes like the one on your wall there! Even the priests are involved!"

Father Bernard sighed and sneaked a look at his watch. He didn't feel up to the argument which he would clearly lose. He should have got on his bicycle and visited poor old Mrs. O'Grady, whose reheumatism had corkscrewed her head into her shoulders."

Harry saw him look at his watch and felt apologetic. It was not natural for him to be rude, particularly to tired old men. "I'm sorry."

"No. I'm sorry. A lot of what you say is right. But it's not absolutely the point. Is it?"

"I don't understand."

"Well, you haven't come here to throw brickbats at the Catholic Church."

"I don't know why I've come here."

The priest smiled at Harry's sulky face. "It's very nice to meet you anyway. I'm only sorry I haven't got more time." He stood up. "Perhaps you can pop back another time?"

Harry stood up too. When they got back to the dark corridor the priest bent down and put on his bicycle clips again. "Incidentally, do you have a lovely wife when at home?" Harry stared over his head, apparently not hearing. He straightened up again. "I'm afraid I've disappointed you."

"Not at all," said Harry in the sort of polite tones used after an unsuccessful party.

As befitted his now grown-up status, Harry stayed in his club. It was a grand club, which wore its chipped gilt and threadbare towels with pride.

On his last morning in London Harry sat eating his eggs and bacon opposite a large fair man. He was reading the *Telegraph* and coating his toast with slabs of butter. He wore a tweed suit and had innocent blue eyes. After a while Harry realized it was Salmon. He decided to finish his breakfast before making contact. If indeed he wanted to make contact at all. He unfolded his *Times*.

"Excuse me . . . I just wondered. Hayes-Middleton!"

Salmon's delight was so great that Harry could hardly demur. "Salmon, old chap!"

"It must be ten years. What a coincidence! I'm hardly ever in town now. And you round the world, so I hear."

"How do you hear that? Sit down."

Salmon sat down. He was not just large, but overweight. His waistcoat bulged out stiffly. "From the old school mag. Heard about your marriage and divorce too. Sorry about that."

"Wiggins. Wiggins must have written in."

Salmon laughed. "You'd think he'd be satisfied with his own entry. It lasts a page or two."

"How are you? Married? Working?"

"My father died. Ages ago now. So I ran the farm. I married soon after. Seemed like a good idea at the time."

Salmon's face looked suddenly so lugubrious that Harry found it hard not to smile. "What do you mean?"

"My mother's still in the house."

"Oh, I see."

"Then there's the children."

"That's nice."

"Yes. Except Johnny, that's the eldest, is mentally handicapped. Not bad enough to send away, if you know what I mean. Although we wouldn't want it anyway. But needing a lot of attention. Has terrible rages. Wets his bed. Shouts. Breaks things. It's a terrible strain on my wife. And then my mother has ideas on how we should manage him." Salmon's voice suddenly was swallowed up into a gulp.

Harry watched. It was difficult to believe that Salmon of all people should be facing tragedy. "I'm so sorry."

"No. No. It was just seeing you. After so many years. Telling you. Usually I'm a tower of strength. We've got the sweetest little girl, Emily. And the farm's thriving. Do you remember how we used to storm about on our bicycles? Those were the days!"

"And tease your sisters."

"Oh, yes." Salmon looked at his watch. "I've got an appointment with my accountant. Could we meet later?"

"I'm flying back to New York today."

Salmon sighed. "Sometimes I feel more like sixty than thirty. But then you were always clever, ready to grab opportunities."

"I don't know. I'm following in my father's footsteps, just as you are."

"It's a pity we can't meet. I'd like to have heard about the big world outside. Vietnam and all that sort of thing. The English Home Counties haven't changed in a hundred years."

Harry looked at Salmon's red-face and tweeds. "But you like it."

"Sorry. Going on a bit, am I? Come and stay with us next time you're in England. I've introduced some really good fishing. Makes a mint in the season."

"Yes, I'd love that," said Harry, lying. He couldn't find it in his heart to be really sorry for Salmon. Despite his child and his mother. Good fishing, slabs of butter on his toast and a congratulatory visit to his accountant. He imagined the women would carry the real burden for him.

During the last year of his posting at the United Nations, Harry visited his parents every other weekend. Often he took a girl with him but seldom the same one. Even Donna had found a man who seemed more likely to marry. It was she who started the rumor that Harry Hayes still carried a torch for his wife. This did him a service because, New York being a small gossipy place, it saved him the trouble of embarrassing demands which he couldn't meet. His girlfriends began to have a certain uniformity in that they themselves were unavailable, either through marriage or design, for more than a sexual friendship. They were also fair with long hair.

Harry didn't know why he went to Washington so often. His mother invited him, of course, but he did not go out of filial duty. Nor out of pleasure, exactly. He went, perhaps, in a spirit of inquiry. Who was this man called Father?

Lionel was also surprised by the resurgence of this grown-up son. He had never seen so much of him. He said to Beatrice, "Henry's quite all right now, would you say? Not heading for another breakdown?"

"He never had a breakdown." Beatrice's voice was unusually sharp. She was the one who talked about things like that. Lionel's role was essentially formal, ambassadorial. "Bachelors like being looked after. Meals cooked for them. He brings his laundry, too, you know."

Lionel was headed off. The idea of traveling with a bag of dirty washing was too much for him to contemplate, as Beatrice knew it would be.

"Yes. One would go a long way for a good lunch."

"Quite," said Beatrice.

What Lionel did not mention to his wife was Henry's exhausting keenness for an argument. It would have shown weakness to admit it but he had reached a point in his life when he preferred people who agreed with him, particularly over Sunday lunch, when he was usually off duty. It was not just Henry but his girlfriends who seemed to have been trained to probe in delicate political areas. Thinking back to when he had been a young man in the company of a distinguished Ambassador, he couldn't believe he would have questioned the way they did. Times had changed. Could it all be put down to the unfortunate matter of Vietnam? Perhaps it wouldn't be so bad to retire after all.

There was Henry to carry on the family name, although Henry himself showed disconcertingly little interest in his future. For example, he would not take part in that most entertaining of games—speculation on the posting of contemporaries. Nor was he typical of his friends. Young Hugo, who visited now and again, liked nothing better than a good diplomatic gossip and tried constantly to worm out secrets from Lionel, a ploy which he found understandable and attractive rather than otherwise.

Henry never tried to worm out anything. He was too busy with his other kind of questions. "Why has the West turned its back on the East?" Surely Henry's whole education and upbringing had been designed to stop him asking ridiculous questions like that?

Harry had only a few months left before he would be moved on to another part of the world. Probably some dark-suited gentleman in London already knew which part it would be.

Summer had recently burst upon New York. The city rattled with air-conditioners. They competed with the cries of the anti-Vietnam War protesters who now spread across the country. Gone were the flowers of peace and love; now they were a declared militant anti-military force. Every weekend there were marches, demonstrations, meetings.

Partly to avoid them, Harry had joined a group who rented a beach house on Fire Island. They were a mixed group, American and English, male and female, who shared a certain dullness of spirit which Harry enjoyed. The girls were efficient secretaries, the men efficiently in business. Harry was a bit of a star, glittering but remote and cold.

This suited Harry. He walked along the endless dunes watching how the wind whisked the sand into twirling pyramids. He swam for long periods, lay on his back sunbathing, read Samuel Pepys, followed by Proust, and drank large quantities of beer. Each Sunday it became harder to return to Manhattan and work.

Harry now recognized two sides of himself. There was the inactive, contemplative side, which had surfaced in Ireland and Jordan and now in Fire Island. And there was the hardworking, well organizied scion of the Foreign Office. There didn't seem any way to reconcile the two. He felt, on occasion, like a mere outline which moved between his two selves but had no reality of its own. This sensation grew very strong as he walked along the flying sand. The pyramidal slopes had more substance than he did. When he swam, his mind seemed to dissolve in the water so that he felt as if he were dreaming.

In this mood, he began to read the Bible.

"Proust first, the Bible after," he joked to friends who caught him at it.

He began on page one and inched his way slowly through. He read it daily, however much work he might have or however late it was. He was addicted to it, needing his daily fix, as an addict pants for his heroin. While he was reading it, his two selves seemed in abeyance and the third self, his silhouette, usually fated to eternal movement between the two, seemed settled and strong. Soon the word "God" gave him a shiver of excitement and made the hair prickle on the back of his neck.

This God was new to him. He had nothing to do with the school variety (Harry of course had already studied the Bible at school). This God was a huge magnetic force around whom the whole world and all its inhabitants circled. He gave out power like vast electrical waves and it was these to which Harry's body reacted. They gave his silhouette strength and substance. In his mind's eye, Harry saw himself as an electric light bulb, waiting for God to switch on the current.

Harry talked about this to no one. He continued working as usual during the week and going to Fire Island on weekends. This schedule meant he no longer visited his parents.

One morning Beatrice telephoned: "I thought I might pay a little visit."

"New York's very hot, Mother."

"I'd just stay for Saturday night. Go back on Sunday."

Harry was surprised to find how much he hated missing a weekend of sand and sea. It was there he thought about what he had read during the week. There he had the space and time which made it possible for him to continue working.

He met Beatrice at the airport. They both needed a shower when they arrived back at the flat.

"It is hot." Beatrice's skin was extraordinarily sallow against her son's beach golden. She was not much more than fifty. She looked much older.

"Are you all right, Mother?"

"Oh, yes."

"I've booked us lunch at the Four Seasons. You'll need a fur coat there."

"How grand!"

"It's not every day I entertain my mother."

There was an air of escape from the headmaster about her which appealed to Harry. He suddenly found himself wondering whether he might not confide in her about the new world opening up for him.

The restaurant was indeed cool and high-ceilinged, but Harry found it not conducive to revelations of the heart. Silvery water trickled in the center of the room. Instead they talked of Vietnam and Lionel's retirement plans—he and Beatrice would go back to the London house.

The lunch seemed to take a long time. Their words had a colorless, almost transparent quality which Harry found disconcerting. His mind wandered away to the passage of the Bible he had been reading the night before: 'When you go forth to war against your enemies, and see horses and chariots and an army larger than your own you shall not be afraid of them; for the Lord your God is with you."

Beatrice was dazzled by her son's sun-bronzed beauty. He did not at all look like a man who was approaching an inner crisis. He looked like a film star or, perhaps too conventional for that, a rising politician. She had not been feeling well lately and had begun to worry about Harry. But now she saw him so glowing and healthy, so sweet and attentive to her, she was reassured.

That night Harry lay in his bed reading his daily quota. "You shall not abhor an Edomite, for he is your brother . . . "

Next door his mother also was awake. It was so seldom that she slept apart from Lionel that she found it difficult to adjust. Again her fears arose. How could Harry spend the rest of his life alone? And yet he seemed to be taking no steps to find a partner. Surely it was a mother's duty to guide him in such areas? Eventually, unable to bear her thoughts anymore, she got out of bed and tiptoed out of her room. There she saw the light under Harry's door. The temptation was too great.

She tapped gently on the door and then opened it.

Harry put his finger against Deuteronomy, Chapter 23, Verse 9, and looked up at his mother. The bedside light shone full on him, showing a face that seemed transfigured. The word "transfigured" popped into Beatrice's head.

"Mother?"

"I'm sorry. I couldn't sleep."

'I'm reading." His voice too had a different timbre, higher, with a kind of excited vibration. "Come in." In his joyous state, he felt endlessly generous, endlessly welcoming.

Beatricie sat gingerly on the end of the bed. "You're reading."

"Yes. The Bible."

"The Bible," repeated Beatrice, bewildered.

"I started just a few weeks ago and now I can't stop. I try to ration myself so I get a good night's sleep. But it's very difficult to cut off the voice of God."

"The voice of God?"

"Oh, yes. Yes! I know you've felt it. Not the same. But something. Do you remember, all those years ago, bringing me that picture of the Virgin and Child? Sitting on the bed at night just as you are now? You lifted the edge for me but I didn't understand. It's taken all these years. So long. Such a waste."

Beatrice felt her head spinning. She couldn't see very well, as if the room had got darker. She must have drooped forward, for Harry leaned forward anxiously. "Mother, are you all right?"

She pulled herself together. "Yes. Just tired. I'm glad for you." She tried to choose appropriate words but it didn't matter, for Harry interrupted her anyway.

"It's like a revelation! A divine revelation. I can actually feel God reaching out to me directly. He makes sense of everything. He makes me feel like a whole man. A new man!"

Beatrice saw that there were tears in her son's eyes and found answering tears in hers. It was too much. She felt too tired and old to hear such things. It frightened her. It was all so sudden and emotional. Even with the greatest love and understanding, which she could not really command, this "divine revelation" seemed nearer madness than true religious belief. Nevertheless, she cleared her throat and patted his hand. "I'm glad for you," she said again. She stood up. "We'll talk more in the morning."

In the morning Beatrice felt stronger. She dressed carefully.

"You're up early."

They met in the kitchen. Harry lounged in his dressing gown. He looked so very physical and ordinary it was hard to believe anything could move him other than a hard game of tennis.

"I thought we might attend Mass." Beatrice spoke firmly.

"You go, if you don't mind. I've got a bit of work to catch up on." His voice was casual. Clearly Mass rang no bells in his God-filled world. Beatrice's resolve to have everything in the open weakened.

"I would so love it if you came with me. Your father never will."

"Okay." He flung some papers together, drained his coffee. "But let's make it brief."

Beatrice never managed to get everything into the open. When she returned to Washington she said to Lionel, "Harry seems to be having some sort of religious conversion."

"Don't tell me you've been at him again."

"Absolutely nothing to do with me, I promise. Although I do wonder if I might not get Father Bernard to write to him again."

"You do that." Sir Lionel was very preoccupied lately with the retiring Ambassador's valedictory report. It was traditionally expected to contain not just diplomatic and political information but a form of biographical commentary. It was also a competitive exercise, read critically by all the important Foreign Office staff. Lionel felt he, in particular, who had started his career in the Indian Political Service, that bastion of Empire, and ended it in Washington among what seemed to be a disintegration of diplomacy as it was, should have something important and personal to say. But the words would not come. He had taken to sitting up late at night with a bottle of whisky and a pad of American yellow paper. This was where Beatrice had approached him about Harry.

Finding so little interest in the matter, she wrote a long letter to Father Bernard.

Unfortunately Father Bernard was busy with a retreat which had the theme of "Personal Conscience: A Concept of the Past?"

He was expected to give a good hour's lecture on the second day. But, like Sir Lionel, Father Bernard found it hard to put pen to paper. It was partly that he distrusted the written word, preferring human contact to dictate his lines, and partly because he was mixed up on the whole subject of personal conscience. He wished now that he'd objected more strongly when the Bishop had suggested it. The Bishop, he thought with admiration rather than disapproval, was an intelligent, highly educated man who enjoyed meeting conflicts head-on. On the other hand the retreat drew mainly on older ladies, who were hardly likely to raise that most awkward of questions in the personal-conscience field—birth control. Father Bernard cheered up a little. Sometimes he found the mantle of Christ a heavy weight on his only too human shoulders.

For this reason, his letter to Harry did not arrive until the day Harry went in to the office to tender his resignation. Harry put it in his pocket along with the small Bible he now carried. He had been determined to resign for so long that he hardly noticed the real consternation with which the news was received. It was the resignation of a Crown Prince. Worse still, he was not leaving to take a gainful job in either American or British business affairs—that route was fairly well trodden and understood—but in order to do nothing.

After he had left, one of the men in the office turned to the other. "Daddy won't be pleased about this."

"Daddy's retiring today," said the other, realizing the fact with some surprise.

"What a coincidence!"

Harry sat in a very hot Central Park. Scrofulous pigeons pecked in the dirty gravel. Diseased squirrels scurried over the burnt-out grass. He held a once-cold can of Coke, which dripped through his fingers. After a while he remembered his letter from England.

Dear Henry,

Your mother is a little worried about you. Yet what she tells me seems hardly worrying. You are reading the Bible, which can do nothing but good. You have a firm belief in God, something for which we must give thanks. You feel his presence coming to you directly as a "divine revelation." Perhaps here there is a slight lack of humility. Only the most spiritual, the saints, can hope to have direct access to our Maker on this earth. However, I cannot share her disquiet. All contact with God is good in whatever form it may take. Just one word of warning: the Devil is a wily adversary and on occasions may disguise himself in God-like form. Be sure it is the voice of God you hear.

With all my blessings and prayers,

Father Bernard

P.S. Come and see me when you next visit London.

Chapter 20

Everyone thought Harry had gone stupidly mad. With the exception, apparently, of Julian. Julian who, as a longtime unbeliever, should have found his friend's preoccupation with the spiritual only explicable in terms of lunacy, was understanding. "You always were too good to be true. You had to break out some time. God. Sex. Drugs. It's all the same."

After his resignation, Harry quickly got rid of his flat and moved back to London. He stayed in a small semi-residential hotel in the Paddington area. It was just round the corner from the hotel previously run by Mary Ann and her Italian husband. Harry went round there soon after his arrival, only to be told they had sold it and bought a bar in Ireland. "They said it was too rough round here," said the new owner derisively, "which makes you laugh when you think what's going on over there."

"In the name of God," said Harry.

"Popish. That's right. Both of "them," agreed the man after a pause for surprise.

Harry returned to his room, not altogether disappointed. He remembered the tall spire in the center of Mary Ann's town and the black-suited men and gaily-colored women who gathered at its foot every Sunday. And the little children, scrubbed and buttoned like children from another country. He understood why they would prefer it to Paddington.

Paddington was, however, just right for him. The transitory nature of most of its inhabitants, arrived from the railway station or even farther afield, suited his mood. He was in no-man's-land, outside the normal structure of society. Here he felt free, without pressure. He also liked the presence of a very large hospital with its reminders of the transitoriness of life. Not an hour passed without a siren-wailing ambulance speeding toward its wide gates.

Harry visited Julian.

"Do you remember at Oxford . . . ?" he began.

"Not very well."

"When we were taking Schools . . . ?"

"Not at all."

"I forgot. You were sent down."

"What did you want to say?" Julian looked at his watch. Although he didn't think Harry mad, he did find him tiresome. Harry had all the time in the world in which to conduct long, self-explanatory monologues. Julian, although incurably curious about other people, which was why he became such a good agent, was trying to run a business. Evenings would have suited him best, but Harry seemed at his most compulsively introspective in the middle of the afternoon.

"I've got someone coming in five minutes."

"When I was taking Schools"—Harry rose and began walking up and down—"I had a kind of breakdown."

"Are you sure?"

"What do you mean, 'Am I sure?' "

Julian looked at his watch again. His visitor was a Los Angeles agent with whom he hoped to make a liason. It could open many new doors.

"My kind of breakdown took the form of trying to make a new structure of the day. I made time follow my rules instead of following its."

"I don't quite understand."

Harry sat down again. "It's quite simple. I worked at night, slept in the day. That sort of thing." He was endlessly patient in his explanations. "What it symbolized was my dissatisfaction with the organization of the world."

Julian stood up. "I'm afraid . . . "

"I wanted to break it down so that I could see how it works. Like a child takes a toy apart. I was trying to find the spring. Or if I couldn't find the spring, watch it all fall apart."

A buzzer sounded in the room. "There's your visitor!" Harry jumped up quite cheerfully. "I'll go now. I just wanted to explain to you that my present situation hasn't come out of nowhere. See you soon!"

He bounded away.

The agent came in looking dazed. "Who was that maniac who nearly knocked me down?"

"He's found God recently."

The agent, whose name was Judy, groaned. "Not one of those!"

"No, actually. He's unique."

After that they got down to business

Harry's room was as unlike Julian's large, expensively bare studio as it was possible to be. It was extremely small, with heavy furnishings and carpets in clashing orange, brown and green. It always took Harry a moment or two to adjust to its supreme ugliness. It was on the first floor, and very little light came in, which was perhaps just as well. He couldn't say he liked it, but it provided an appropriately unappealing launch pad for his spiritual questing.

Harry had not yet told to Julian or anyone the main line of his present thinking. It was very painful and had been caused by Father Bernard's letter. "Be sure," he had written, "it is the voice of God you hear." Harry understood: it was because he had come to this position of belief so suddenly, without any apparent period of prayer or preparation. Such precipitate behavior smacked of the Devil.

"The Devil is a wily adversary," the priest had written, "and on occasions may disguise himself in God-like form." These words rang in Harry's ears, causing at first confusion, fear and anger. But then he came to see them as a challenge. He had to prove that the God who had brought light was the True Light, and to do that he must look back over his life and see the steps that had led him toward it. What he needed was time, a clear head and solitude. Apart from the Bible, he did not turn to books of theology. This would have been the automatic approach of his old self. He was not writing a report. He was not looking at both sides of the question.

He had belief. A purely personal belief. And now he wanted to find the purely personal facts to support it. Nevertheless, he was very disturbed and at night woke to find tears on his face.

Beatrice and Lionel had taken some time installing themselves in London. Beatrice, who found everything took longer these days, wanted to make perfect the home of their retirement. Some of their possessions had been in storage for so long that she hardly remembered them. Among the last batch was Harry's picture of the Virgin and Child. She popped it on the chest of drawers in the bedroom.

"You're not leaving that in here?" said Lionel, feeling no need for emphasis.

"No," agreed Beatrice, also without rancor.

She took the picture along to the spare bedroom—where Harry might have slept if he ever visited—and propped it up there. She couldn't help feeling it might provide a clue or a key to Harry's state of mind.

She had discussed his case with Wiggins and Wiggins's charming wife, Julia; and although they had both been most helpful and Wiggins had invited her and Lionel to lunch at the House of Commons, they had not been able to throw any light. In fact Harry had not contacted them at all and their efforts to contact him had failed. They were both, of course, busy people and Harry had no direct telephone line.

Just as she was leaving Wiggins did remember one thing. "At school, you know, there was a period when he used to badger the poor vicar."

"What do you mean, badger?"

"The usual sort of schoolboy nonsense. 'What is the meaning of life?' 'What is the point of doing anything?' We all go through it. But he had it worse than most of us."

One autumn afternoon Beatrice set out from her house with a large brown paper parcel under her arm. By the time she found a taxi she felt quite weak. The sun was low, shining through the trees in Hyde Park and only just clearing the buildings along the Edgware Road. As she arrived at the Devon Court Hotel it dropped out of sight completely. Beatrice got herself and her picture out of the taxi and thought what a cheerless place her son had chosen for his home. No. Not his home.

Harry's window faced on the street, so he was able to see his mother's arrival. She seemed to have taken another step into old age, moving with a stiff weariness. Harry was filled with pity for the human condition. He dashed downstairs and out to the forecourt of the hotel.

"Oh, darling! How lovely!"

He hugged her warmly and then took her arm and her parcel and helped her up the chipped steps.

"How kind!"

"My mother," he explained to a woman behind the counter. They went upstairs.

"How did you know?" said Beatrice when they stood outside his room. "I felt quite feeble down there. Just for a moment."

"I'm afraid my room's very small and very ugly. But I've invested in an electric kettle for tea."

When they were settled, Beatrice's spirits sank again. What was her handsome and clever son doing in such a frightful place? Lionel was right. He was mad. She must persuade him to see a psychiatrist.

"Thank you, dear." She accepted the tea gratefully. "So how are you filling your days?"

"Reading. Thinking. Cinema. Concerts sometimes."

"Oh, I see. Having a nice time. Of course it's a long while since you were in London." Her spirits rose again. Perhaps he was merely enjoying an eccentric holiday. "And do you see many old friends?"

Harry jumped up without answering. "What's in the parcel? Is it a present?"

Beatrice became a little flustered. She had forgotten about the picture. She had meant to lead up to it cleverly. "Not a present. Not anymore."

"How intriguing! Not anymore? What can that mean? Perhaps you've decided not to give it, now you see just how nasty my room is."

"It was a present."

"But no longer."

"Now it has an owner." Beatrice's expression became firmer. "Although he may not want it."

"Me?"

"Yes. You."

Harry took the brown paper off the picture. "I should have guessed." He traced his finger over the clear contours of the Virgin's face. He said seriously, "Why have you brought this to me?"

"It had been in storage with all our things. I unpacked it last week."

"But why did you bring it to me?"

"Well, it's hardly your father's taste, is it?" Beatrice attempted a laugh.

"You brought it here for the same reason you made me go to church that morning in New York after I'd told you about my beliefs. For the same reason you keep poor Father Bernard dogging at my footsteps. You want to rein me back into your faith. You want to stop me using words like 'divine revelation' and get into line with the rest of the flock. You want me to become a member of your Church. The Catholic Church."

Beatrice sighed. "And why not? You'd be happier. There's nothing wrong in it."

"It's perfectly normal on your part, I agree. But I can't line up and be counted just to please you."

"No. No." Beatrice looked distressed. This introduction of their personal relationship was beyond her ken? Besides, it frightened her. She was his mother. Further than that it was not necessary to investigate.

"Do you remember that historical novel you wrote?"

"Novel? I never wrote a novel." Truly, she had forgotten.

"You showed me it in Madrid. One holiday. Romantic stuff set during the French Revolution. Full of romantic longings."

"Yes. Silly stuff." This was horrible.

"Not at all. You aren't a writer, of course. But it expressed very clearly your dissatisfactions with the world. I thought of it again the other day and it made me understand why you tried to commit suicide."

Beatrice felt her head spin and the blood in the top of her body drain downward. She kept very still. She was like someone faced with a stamping bull. If she kept still and pretended she wasn't there, it might just go away again.

"You see, I think I've inherited a lot of your character. But until now, I've always tried to mold it into something else. You were trying to do the same, which is why you broke down. But now you've been successful. I don't quite understand, but I think women are different from men. Ultimately they prefer to follow. You've followed Father. Quite right too, I expect. After all, someone's got to compromise in a marriage or it would soon cease existing. Like mine and Flavia's." Harry laughed.

The laugh gave Beatrice a line. "You're very excited. Your head's buzzing."

"I know. There's so much to work out. So much to think about. For example, do I really have a daughter?"

A slightly vicious look came over Beatrice's face. "Really, you seem hardly normal."

"Oh, Mother!" Harry leaned back with an "Et tu, Brute" expression.

"Well, what about this picture?" Viciousness had brought back blood and life to her body. She quite felt like grabbing it and popping straight out for a taxi. Thinking the word "popping" reminded her of Father Bernard. Perhaps he would have managed it better. "Do you want it or not?"

"I'm sorry I've upset you. I hadn't finished explaining about myself." Harry's face now wore the same expression of obstinacy that Julian knew well. "I wanted you to see this is a temporary phase . . . "

"That's good news, at least. When shall I tell your father you'll be back in the world of ordinary human beings again?" Beatrice stood.

"I'm sorry."

"And what are you living on? What about money?"

"I saved some."

"And this horrible room."

"It doesn't cost much."

"That's not what I meant."

Beatrice went downstairs in a highly irritated state. She had gone to meet her son and he had not come to her in any way. Except at the very beginning. That embrace. They did not kiss now as they said farewell.

"I'm sorry, Mother," repeated Harry. To Beatrice's ever increasing anger, she saw what appeared to be tears in his eyes.

"No, you're not!" Rejecting his offer to find her a taxi, she walked away briskly down the road. After about ten paces she thought of something else she wanted to say. Glancing backward, she saw he was still standing in the front yard, so she returned with equal briskness. His face was open, welcoming, but she hardened her heart. "The teaching of Christ, which is the teaching of God, is based on charity, ordinary human charity. Love, in other words. And the greatest love should be between a father and a son, a mother and a son." Dark eyes flashing, she stamped off again.

"So did you unravel the mysteries of God?" Lionel, although unwilling to see his son himself, was keen for a detailed report of his wife's visit.

Beatrice's spirits had sunk again almost as soon as she arrived home. She was ashamed of her anger, her outburst. It was not an image of herself she liked. "He hugs God to himself," she said coldly. "I did my best to raise the subject. But my best was not good enough."

"You're disappointed." Lionel responded with a polite interest as if they were not discussing the mental state of his only son. "I saw old Fordingham today. His son's following a guru and disappeared off to an ashram." As Beatrice, sunk in gloom, made no comment, he continued. "He's shaved his head and wears saffron robes."

"I should think an ashram's healthier than Paddington."

Lionel looked at his wife with concern. It was unlike her to make bitter comments.

"Fordingham's decided to leave him alone to work through it himself."

"I don't know what that pompous Fordingham's got to do with Harry."

Since returning to London Lionel had found a new world of old colleagues, now mostly retired, like himself, from around the world to the Motherland. The end-of-career report which had originally given him such trouble had ended in victory. It was spoken of by the inner circles as one of the best pieces written by a retiring Ambassador since Sir Ronald's in 1948. Word had spread and Lionel had been approached by a publisher to write his memoirs. This gave him a reason for an interesting social life, long visits to the Foreign Office archives and quiet mornings at his desk.

It was not that he didn't care about Harry but that he was deeply embroiled in the business of "putting things in perspective." From a personal point of view, of course.

"I'd hand him over to your priestly friend," he said. "After all, it's his job to care for the soul."

Harry was stumbling. He could neither move backward or forward nor stay still. He had been distressed by his mother's visit. When he lay down to pray, he was no longer filled with warmth and light. Instead he saw the reproachful eyes of the Virgin and Child. It lay under his bed, facedown, but this did not curtail its power. He tried reading aloud from the Bible, but the New Testament took over from the Old and paraded the women in Jesus' life. His mother's parting exhortation to Christian charity rang in his head, driving into second place Father Bernard's letter, although a fear of the Devil still lurked behind every thought.

In order to escape thought, he went to a liquor store and bought a bottle of vodka. He drank it steadily until evening. Unfortunately it seemed to have more effect on his body than on his mind, which tenaciously clung to awareness. Feeling hungry, he wove his way to a late-night grocer's. It was on the way back, with his belly full of bread, that he had the idea of visiting Father Bernard. At last he felt perfectly prepared for confrontation. He started to hail taxis and, after two killjoys, managed to find one prepared to take such an obvious drunk.

"Going to confess everything, are you? With a little bit of Dutch courage to help out?"

Harry ignored such nonsense.

Father Bernard was called by the night porter. He was watching a very good episode of *The Avengers.* It was his once-a-week relaxation, allowed to himself on grounds of keeping touch with current taste. Occasionally, he dreamed of Diana Rigg.

"There's a very drunk young man here," said the night porter, who was Irish and unimpressed by such sights.

"Breaking things?" inquired Father Bernard apprehensively. A gunshot shatteringly close on the television screen made him jump.

"No," said the night porter, adding dourly, "not yet."

"I'll be down."

Harry sat waiting in the same little room he'd visited before. It now seemed very like a padded cell. The old Irishman hovering in a watchful way at the door added to the impression.

"I'm not dangerous, you know. Though I could do with a piss."

Harry followed the porter through dark corridors. The walls seemed very close on either side and he bumped into them several times. "Bloody walls!" He punched out with his fist.

Coming back, he shut his eyes for part of the way, which made everything swirl about him as if he were riding on an amusement-park train. He hoped he would not be sick.

Father Bernard waited for him in the little room. He recoiled at the sight of the blood on Harry's fist but then cheered up when he recognized his face.

"Ah, Henry Hayes-Middleton." He held out his hand but Harry ignored it.

"Do you remember what you wrote to me in your letter?" he began intensely. "About the Devil? Beware of the Devil! Well, the Devil had been nowhere near me before that. But you put him into my head and now he's stuck there. I can't get him out. . . . " Harry held his head and began to shake it.

Father Bernard came to him and put his arm round his shoulders.

Harry recoiled. "I'm not in the fold yet, you know. I've come here for a theological discussion, not for a bit of your old comfort and succor. If it comes to that, how do I know the Devil hasn't crept under your venerable robes? He worms his way everywhere, you know. Not a respecter of office. Absolutely not!"

Father Bernard nodded calmly. "I'm sorry you're so unhappy."

"Unhappy! That's rich. Unhappy, he says. Happy, unhappy. Don't tell me a man of your spiritual cloth sets store by such dangerous nonsense. Is that what you think it's all about now? You holy chaps! Happiness? I thought as much. Corrupted like everyone else." Harry's voice fell to a mumble and then grew again, with indignation. "I come all the way to the center of God's teaching for a theological argument and what do I get but a whole lot of crap about unhappiness. Or happiness. It's all the same. All about the self. Do you think Jesus went about asking whether he was happy? I can see now—I thought as much before—the Church has nothing to offer. Just a few worldly platitudes. A little bit of saccharine succor!" Harry turned on his heel. "You can count me out. That's definite. The Devil, you say. He's here, all right. But what about God, that's what I want to know. What about God?"

This question, probably rhetorical and pitched in a grand tone, should have been Harry's exit line. But on reaching the door he was overcome with the urge to vomit. He would never find his way through the maze of dark corridors.

"Get a bucket and warm water, would you, Paddy?" said Father Bernard resignedly.

Harry stood shivering by the doorpost.

"You'd better sit down."

Harry sat down. The room was dark before him.

"Where are you living?"

Harry raised just enough energy to be irritated by the priest's constant preoccupation with the practical. "Where I'm living isn't the point."

"What?"

" 'Consider the lilies of the field, how they grow; they toil not neither do they spin: And yet I say unto you, that even Solomon . . . ' "

"I'd better telephone your mother."

Harry sat indifferently. It hardly mattered where he went. He must have slept for a moment. He was awakened by a firm voice saying, "We'll wait for your mother in the church."

He followed obediently. His sickness had made him docile and very sleepy.

Father Bernard and Harry knelt side by side in the church. Harry rested his head on the bench in front. When he opened his eyes he could see the darkness was pierced by a few points of flickering red.

"Oh Lord," began the priest, quietly, "may we be given the grace to approach you in all your glory. May you show mercy on our sins and teach us how to lead our lives in the image of your son, Jesus."

"Did you write that prayer yourself?" Harry raised his head and looked at the dark shadow beside him.

"Prayer is just a name for talking to God. I was trying to say something appropriate."

"I suppose you have something appropriate for every occasion at this point in your career?"

Father Bernard was overwhelmed by a longing for Lady Hayes-Middleton to remove her son. He prayed inwardly for strength. "Oh, Lord, let me be your true pastor and find the strength and right way to help this lost sheep." It did not sound very elegant but he was tired.

"Are you praying again?" asked Harry curiously. "Why don't you do it aloud?"

"Don't you pray?"

"I listen. I wait. I don't use words."

Father Bernard felt his prayer had been answered. "Listening is the most important thing of all," he said.

"Not for answers," said Harry suspiciously. "I just lay myself open."

At the back of the church a door opened loudly. Regular footsteps came up the center aisle.

"Your father's come for you," said Father Bernard.

Harry lifted up his head and gave a wild laugh. "My father in church! That's rich! You know, you can get right to the top of the establishment tree these days and be an honest-to-God atheist. You'd never think it for a moment!"

"I'm sorry, Father," Lionel whispered. He took his son's arm. The priest followed them down the aisle. Now that relief was at hand he felt a new surge of spiritual enthusiasm. He also felt in awe of Sir Lionel's commanding presence. It was a terrible thing to get such a man out so late at night.

They stood on the pavement. "Thank you, Father. I apologize on my son's behalf for all the inconvenience."

"Not at all. Not at all. I apologize for inconveniencing you."

Harry stood between the two, smiling. The scene struck him as quite ridiculous. "Our Father who art in heaven, hallowed be Thy name . . . "

"He's very troubled," said Father Bernard.

"He's very drunk," said Sir Lionel.

Harry wanted to say the two were not incompatible but had the sense to know the word was beyond him. He allowed himself to be bundled into the back of Lionel's car.

As they moved off, he was struck by the loneliness of the priest's long dark figure. He wound down the window and yelled out, "It's a cruel world, Father! But we God-fearing people must stick together! In the name of the Father, Son and Holy Ghost!" He waved energetically.

"Shut that window and stop making an exhibition of yourself."

"I was only trying to cheer him up. Poor old blighter."

"He wants his bed. As I do."

Harry wound up the window and laid himself across the seat. The motion of the car was soothing.

"Really, this is the kind of behavior one expects from a boy of fifteen, not a man of thirty."

Harry grunted. He tried to remember what he'd been like at fifteen. As far as he could remember he never touched anything stronger than watered-down wine until he left school. "When I was fifteen, I was a paragon," he said aggressively.

"I didn't say you behaved badly at fifteen, I just said you're not behaving like a thirty-year-old now."

But Harry's mind had been set on track. "When I was fifteen, you were pulling the chicks like a fine old cock-a-doodle-doo!"

"What?"

"I said you were having it off like an old bull. . . . "

"You're drunk. You're disgustingly drunk."

"I know. It is disgusting. I was sick in there too."

"What! In church?"

"Not exactly. No. I don't think so. Not actually in church. More like a sort of prison cell with a crucifix. Probably where they torture sinners."

Both men lapsed into silence. Lionel was trying to pretend to himself he had not heard his son's sexual accusations. Although he had never found much difficulty in justifying himself on grounds of Beatrice's limited interest and his powerful passion, he did not at all like the idea of being judged by Harry. Cock-a-doodle-doo, indeed. Still, he was drunk. He would have forgotten all about it in the morning. In the interests of accuracy, he would have liked to point out that the major part of his womanizing was over well before Harry's fifteenth birthday.

"Your mother is most upset," he said, feeling once more ready for attack. "She hasn't been well, you know."

Harry came to from a gentle doze. It struck him at once that he no longer wished to remain in the car. At the next red traffic light he opened the door quietly. Lionel didn't realize he'd gone until he started up again.

He saw Harry in the rearview mirror. He was jumping up and down making the V sign. Lionel drove on with a grim face.

Chapter 21

Harry's money began to run out. On the whole he liked the feeling. It gave a sense of purpose to his drifting. He advised the hotel he would be leaving in a week's time.

Julian said, "Sieger's in town. You'd only have to behave a little more like everyone else and he'd give you a job."

"Who's Sieger?"

"Your American producer friend."

"That shark!"

"You admired him so much."

"I must have been mad."

"No comment."

Julian made an appointment for them to meet. The day before, Harry took a plane to Cork. He caught a train and walked from the station to his uncle's farm. It was now December and he was struck afresh by the overwhelming wealth of Irish mud. He sang as he walked: "Mud, Mud, Glorious Mud" to the tune of *To Be a Pilgrim.* It took a great deal of concentration.

He decided to buy himself a secondhand bicycle and ride about the roads singing. When he was not working on the farm, of course. His visit had the strictly practical and charitable purpose of helping his widowed and elderly relation.

The farm seemed unchanged. It was dark as he arrived. The light was not on in the porch but a lamp shone through a front window. Tripping over the usual gumboots, the household gods, as he thought of them affectionately, he banged on the front door. There was no response. He banged again.

He went round to the window. There sat his uncle, legs outstretched, television blinking, eyes closed, a bottle of whisky and a glass at his elbow. The room emitted waves of boredom and despair. At a different level its decor could have taught a thing or two to the worst of Paddington. Harry's resolute spirits, though not broken, were diverted. He walked round to the dark farmyard. Mud and slurry reached new heights. There were no cows in the milking shed, but there were signs that the shed had been fairly recently used. It was not very clean, either.

Harry turned on the hose and began washing out the stalls. The water sluiced out with enormous force. Soon the stone floors were shining, the whitewashed walls dripping with cleansing liquid like the sides of a bath. Harry stood back a moment to admire.

"What the hell do you think you're doing?"

Uncle Johnny stood behind him—a fearsome sight. Not in body, for he was thinner, red-faced and swaying, but for the twelve-bore gun he pointed.

"Uncle Johnny!" cried Harry with not unreasonable alarm.

"What are you doing in my milking shed?" The fierceness was unabated. Recognition had not been effected.

"It's Harry!" The finger trembled on the trigger. "I was trying to help!" What a way to die, mistaken by your own uncle for an IRA gunman . . . "Look, I was trying to help!" Harry waggled the hose in a helpful manner.

"I don't know any Harry." This was delivered in a mumble and although the sense was not encouraging, the gun was now pointing at Harry's feet, not his heart.

"Henry Hayes-Middleton," said Harry loudly and clearly so there should be no mistake.

"Oh, you." At last understanding came to Uncle Johnny's dazed and drunken face.

Harry hung the hose back on the wall. "I'm sorry to have given you such a fright."

"I have to be careful. Living here on my own."

"It'd be a funny sort of IRA man who'd wash down your walls," said Harry, attempting to lighten the atmosphere.

His uncle didn't smile. He led the way back to the house.

"Wouldn't it be an idea to break the gun?"

His uncle didn't seem to hear. When they got inside the house, which smelled of damp, cigarettes and not very clean clothing, he leaned the gun just inside the door. "Like a drink, would you?"

"That would be nice."

They sat down in the living room. Harry felt unwilling to explain his presence. He sipped his whisky. After all, he had come here like this once before.

"Funny. I saw that girl you used to go with in town the other day. Pretty girl. Three children she had with her. Three or four. All with her red hair. Funny you should turn up. I thought of you then. Wondered what you were up to. Round the world. Going to the sort of places I only see on television. It made me feel jealous. Ridiculous, of course, at my age. I'm good for nothing but the scrap-heap now. Which is just about all this farm is. I don't see any point in going on. But then what do I do if I stop? I have to earn money. And there are the cows to think of. The cows are all I've got, really. But I don't treat them very well. Cows like regular on-the-hour milking, you know. But I milk them when it suits me. Never in the evening anymore. I like to finish with them by five so I can come in here and drink myself into a stupor. That's what I was doing when I saw a light in the yard. From the upstairs lavatory. The downstairs one's given up functioning, like most things round here. Are you just passing through?"

The question coming at the end of such a long, unexpected and depressing monologue caused Harry to start. "I thought of staying a little," he said with inexplicable guilt.

Johnny poured himself another drink. "You always were an odd boy."

Harry moved into a large bedroom upstairs. His uncle seemed to more or less live in the sitting room. After that first night he talked very little. Harry realized he had received the pent-up thoughts of years. The death of his wife had left Johnny almost completely solitary. He had even given up hunting, saying it reminded him too closely of Anna. Hunting had always been her first love—before him, he sometimes thought. His first action after her death had been to sell the horses. It was only afterward he realized this had cut him off from the main source of social life in Anglo-Irish society. By then he felt too depressed to do anything about it. Drink had seemed the only alternative.

When Johnny was drunk, slumped comatose in his armchair as Harry had found him, the world seemed an exciting, accessible place. The television gave him a sense of participation. He imagined that on the following day he would sell the farm and buy a ticket on an intercontinental cruise. Of course on the next day the cows needed milking and afterward he felt far too ill to do anything more than look forward to his first drink at nightfall.

"I never drink till after dark," he reproved Harry, who had opened a bottle of Guinness to liven up their lunch of bread and cheese.

"Guinness is a food," said Harry.

They had soon fallen into a routine agreeable to both. Harry got up early and did the morning milking. There were not many cows in milk, so it did not take too long.

"I had a chap here for a bit," explained Johnny gloomily. "He insisted on putting the cows in calf."

"Well, that's the purpose of keeping cows, isn't it?" Harry was enthusiastic. He had started reading *The Farmer's Weekly,* which lay in unopened piles around the sitting room. "If they were never in calf they'd never give milk."

After milking Harry cleaned the stalls and yard, fed the cows and took them back to the fields. Then Johnny took over till lunch. After lunch they worked together. Spreading muck, mending fences and other jobs. They did the afternoon milking together.

Harry fixed up a speaker to a radio so that the cows could listen to loud music. His uncle was at his happiest at this time, the hard road to the bottle nearly covered. Sometimes he even sang along in a loud and surprisingly good bass. Darkness fell outside the shed, making them spotlit against the white walls as if they were on a stage.

In the evening, while Johnny got drunk, Harry cooked supper and read. He had set himself to study the metaphysical poets, with particular reference to John Donne. He became fascinated by Donne's apostasy from Catholic to Anglican and by the tensions between his worldly self and his awareness of God. He learned a great many of his poems by heart and took pleasure in shouting them above the noise of the tractor. Driving a tractor was a pleasure in itself but the introduction of the divine sometimes gave him a feeling near ecstasy.

> Batter my heart, three person'd God; for you
> As yet but knocke, breathe, shine, and seeke to mend!

He did not answer worried letters from his parents or friends. Wednesday was market day. The town was full and Harry knew many of the faces. Some would stop and ask him about his uncle. He always told them he was lonely, but no one ever called. He always looked out for Mary Ann. Eventually he met her in a grocer's shop.

She recognized him immediately and blushed, pushing her children in fronst of her as if for safety. "Buying potatoes, are you? No self-respecting person buys potatoes in Ireland."

The attack, Harry assumed, was due to nerves. A respectable

Catholic matron with three children might well recoil when faced with evidence of her youthful immorality.

"My uncle didn't plant any last year, I'm afraid."

"What a shocking story!"

On the other hand, thought Harry, she might have changed over twelve or thirteen years and become this positive, almost aggressive woman, instead of the tentative creature he remembered. In appearance she seemed unaltered.

"And how's your wife?"

"I'm afraid we're divorced."

"Divorced!"

"Actually, annulled."

"Annulled? But you had a child?"

"That's true." Harry nodded. "Cordelia."

"Cordelia?"

"She was called Cordelia out of *King Lear.*"

Harry became aware that the grocer's shop, which had filled up since the start of their interchange, was throbbing with the intensity of listening. He felt they were taking sides and, since his English accent was hardly unnoticeable, they must be on hers.

"What lovely children you have!" He patted the nearest on the head. "You must bring them over and they can play in the farmyard. We're always there." He virtually ran from the shop.

"You've forgotten your potatoes!" shouted her voice after him.

On Sundays Harry came into town. The bells ringing from the churches drew him in. But he did not at first attend a service. There were two major churches, both large granite constructions with tall spires. One was Catholic, one Church of Ireland. They were so similar in appearance that a visitor might have easily found himself worshiping under the wrong roof. The surest way to tell the difference was by the congregation. Not, however, by the quality but by the quantity. While the Catholic services were crowded to overflowing into the porch and the areas round the doors, the Church of Ireland fielded no more than thirty or forty, even if those thirty or forty tended to include the bank manager, the owner of the largest hotel and the head of the local police force.

On the Sunday after meeting Mary Ann, Harry joined this select band. He had come because he wished to consider the question of marriage, of Flavia, of Cordelia, but he was immediately put off by the woman in front of him. She had one of those broad fixed backs which irritate unreasonably. Whichever way he moved she seemed to block any hope of vision. Filled with despair, he found himself banging with clenched fist on the back of the seat in front. The woman turned round in surprise.

Her face, despite the sacred precinct, made him burst into laughter. It was so red, so open-mouthed, so filled with a sense of moral respectability. The laughter following the banging added up to a disturbance. Other heads turned and the prelate, a tall distinguished man, appeared for a moment suspended in his prayers.

Harry decided it was time he left. As he stood, the woman who'd provoked it all turned again and snarled under her breath, "Henry Hayes-Middleton."

He mounted his bicycle and rode back to the farm singing gustily, "The Lord is my Shepherd."

He was touched, on his arrival, to find his uncle halfway through preparing the Sunday lunch. The potatoes were peeled and in a pan, the joint salted and ready for the oven. He was now shredding cabbage with earnest precision.

"I was thinking about Christmas," he said when Harry complimented him. "It'll be upon us soon. I was thinking I might invite myself to my sister's in Scotland. If you could manage here?"

Harry sat down. It was one thing to help. Quite another to take full responsibility. He was not a farmer. He knew nothing about tetanus, brucellosis, foot-and-mouth, silage explosion, grazing rotation. He was a diplomat, trained to size up situations and report. He knew about political initiatives, cultural exchanges, financial tariffs, pressing the boundaries of purely national interests.

"How long will you be away?"

"A week perhaps."

"I expect I could manage."

Beatrice begged Harry to come home for Christmas. "Home" struck no chord in the wet fields of Cork.

"I fear the cows have greater need of me than you," he wrote. "They bellow terribly if they're kept waiting for milking. Something to do with the pressure on their udders, I understand. No doubt you as a mother will sympathize."

"Harry's going quite off his head," Beatrice said to Lionel.

Lionel, seeing the tears in her eyes, forced himself not to turn away. "Is he still with Johnny?"

"He writes about cows." Beatrice looked down at the letter with a hopeless expression.

Christmas Eve was an exceptionally beautiful night. Cold and clear. Harry walked round the farm with his arms upraised to the stars.

At about eleven-thirty a car drew up. Harry had seen its headlights and retreated into the house. There was a bang on the door.

"Mr. Hayes-Middleton. It's Major Gormley." Harry opened the door. "My wife thought you might like a lift to church." Mrs. Gormley was the woman who had blocked out vision.

Harry smiled and said he'd just lock up. As he sat in the Gormleys' old Rover, he considered the programming of the human animal which made association with its peers so inevitable.

That night the church was very peaceful, the carols nostalgic and soothing. There was no sermon but Harry supplied one for himself about motherhood and birth. He thought of Flavia and his daughter, Cordelia. It was seven years since he had seen her in the flesh and four since he had even seen her photograph. The arrival of her latest face had used to be a mark of Christmas. He supposed Flavia had given up because he had never made any contact in return. It was the unreality of her existence which had made this impossible. But perhaps that too was his fault.

Harry groaned and struck his head, causing Mrs. Gormley, standing gamely at his side, to flush in anticipation of another scene.

It was ten days before Harry realized his uncle would not be returning. It was the imminent birth of a calf which brought the matter to a head. The cow, bellowing, raised huge reproachful eyes to her ignorant attendant. Harry rang the vet.

"You don't need me," he said when he arrived. "The cow's doing fine. Where's Johnny?"

"I don't know. Gone, I suspect. Fled."

"Oh. Perhaps you do need me, after all."

Harry hired a lad from the next-door farm to help him. They stayed up night after night with the cows. Often as not, they had the vet out in the end. At the end of a fortnight he received a letter from his uncle.

> I had to go while I had the strength. My apologies. I've sent instructions for the farm to be sold. And the house. You'll get ten percent of the proceeds as something of a thank you. I shan't come back to Ireland.

There was no address.

The animals went first in a market the following week. Then the land went, to the same neighboring farmer who had lent Harry his lad, and finally the house. It was bought by an estate agent with plans to modernize.

Harry was given a check in an envelope.

He took a boat to the Aran Islands in celebration. It was very wet and cold but he was used to that now, and even enjoyed it. He stayed in a square room in a square house painted in squares of pink and yellow and lilac. Above his bed hung a picture of a Madonna and Child; the lips of Jesus were as red as strawberries, the eyes of the Madonna as blue as a periwinkle.

"In the summer we have visitors in plenty," said the woman of the house on his first desolate morning.

Harry walked out through the fields marked by stone walls, like a herringbone stitch in a patchwork quilt. The sea, flattened by the rain, streamed in silvery gray sheets beside his path. He headed for the most westerly point, the stone fortress of Dun Aengus.

There the grayness of the scene had a majesty of gloom. Gray skies, gray seas, gray granite rock on which he stood looking outward. Next stop America.

A voice at his elbow piped high above the rush of rain and sea, "Frightful, isn't it?"

"No. I like it."

"You must be daft." It was a small boy, about seven or eight.

"My mother thinks I am."

"My mam's daft. She's been taken off to hospital. I'm staying with my auntie. That's why I'm not at school. What are you doing here?"

"I'm too old to go to school."

The serious expression on the boy's dripping face did not heighten. "You're very wet."

"I like looking."

"There's nothing to see."

"No. But I like that."

The boy sighed. "I think you're daft like my mam. She used to look at nothing for hours. And she'd cry."

Harry began to think the boy was right. He was very wet and there was nothing to see. He turned round briskly. "Do you want to walk back with me?"

"I would that."

They walked together, not talking. But Harry now found the

scene made a different impression on him. Instead of luxuriating in the majestic desolation, he saw it through the little boy's eyes. It was the desolation of banishment from life. The sea held no fish, the granite rock grew no vegetation, the sparse grass would hardly feed a single cow. Instead of hedges thick with growth, there were the sterile lines of balanced stone. He took the boy's hand.

"What's your name?"

"Sean Bradey."

"And how old are you, Sean?"

"Seven. Last week. The day after Christmas. I should have had two presents, but the farm set didn't arrive because it was too rough for the boat."

They walked along in companionable silence. The rain trickled inside Harry's collar. The boy's hand was hot and felt boneless. Harry had never held a child's hand before and it gave him a mixed sense of power and humility. It seemed terrible, too terrible to imagine, that this little boy had been cast alone onto such a bleak island.

"I was sent away to school when I was about your age. My parents were way across the sea too. A bigger sea than this one." Harry waved towards the gray water. They both stopped to look. The clouds split horizontally, allowing a thin shaft of light to shine across the surface of the water.

"The rain's stopped," observed the boy. A desultory row of whitewashed houses started in another hundred yards or so. He looked at the houses and looked at Harry. "My auntie might be in."

"Busy, I expect."

"She might not be."

They walked on. Outside the second house Sean stopped. Harry looked up over the tiled roof.

"The sun's smiling." He wanted to make the boy smile.

"No. It's not. It's sticking its tongue out. Right down to the sea. It's trying to lick up the sea."

A woman came running out of the house. "You mustn't go off like that without telling anyone! I've told you and told you." She stopped and looked at Harry. "Thank you for bringing him back. Would you care for a cup of tea, now? You look soaked through."

The house was identical with the one in which Harry stayed.

"You're with Mrs. Murphy, aren't you?"

The woman was efficient and knew everything. She gave Harry a towel, made tea, dried Sean, made him change his clothes. She talked all the time. In the course of this, Harry realized she was Sean's mother.

"Schooling must be a problem?"

She seemed surprised. "Of course it's school holidays now."

The boy sat demurely. His skin was very white, with pale freckles, his cheeks very pink. His hair was combed back from his forehead. He dipped ginger biscuits into milky tea with a virtuous air. Behind him a farm set filled an entire table. "That's a beautiful lot of machinery you've got there." Harry smiled at him, but he still wouldn't smile back.

"Sean's second name is Jesus. He was born on Christmas Day. So he always has a mighty present."

"It must be difficult getting things over in this weather."

"I had it burning a hole in my bedroom carpet months before. And will you be staying here long?"

"I was helping on my uncle's farm in Cork."

"And you an educated man from England!"

"But now he's sold up."

"So you're having a rest?"

Harry didn't answer. The warmth in the room, the hot tea, the woman's bright voice were in such contrast to his wet stance at Dun Aengus on the edge of the world. It was Sean who had pulled him back from that cold glory with sham tales of daft mams, recalling images of his own childhood.

"I'll be off now."

Harry lay under the garishly colored Virgin and Child and wrote a letter to Flavia.

Dear Flavia,

This will come out of nowhere.

He crossed this out and wrote instead,

I am sorry I have not been in touch before.

This displeased him too.

I'm afraid I've behaved very badly.

Too self-centered.

Dear Flavia,

It is four years now . . .

Was it four?

It is several years now since I've heard from you. I know I didn't answer your letters but I liked receiving them. I liked the thought of Cordelia . . . .

This sounded too insulting. She must be more than a thought.

Cordelia looked so beautiful and so happy. It was difficult to believe I had anything to do with her.

Although this represented the crux of the matter, he saw it was open to misconstruction.

Dear Flavia,

It is so long since I have heard from you. How are you? How is Cordelia? Please send a photograph. If you ever come to London, let me know.

The idea of a meeting was so fantastic, so extraordinary that Harry could no longer lie still. He rolled off the bed onto his knees. Lately he had taken to doing his praying in that position. "Dear God, I am listening to you for guidance. Dear God, I am talking to you although I have no words. Dear God, Dear God, Dear God."

Harry put his face on to the bed. After a few moments he returned with more composure to his letter.

Dear Flavia,

It is so long since I have heard from you. How are you? How is Cordelia? Please send a photograph. Or perhaps we could meet if you pass through London? Your husband, if I remember rightly, is in the Argentinian Foreign Office, so you must travel a certain amount. I have left the FO but you can contact me through Wiggins at the House of Commons. I will send this letter to your parents' address.

With love,

Harry

Chapter 22

Harry returned to London and went to work for Sieger.

"At least he's earning money," said Lionel dourly.

"A good deal. So I understand from Wiggins."

His lunch with Wiggins at the House of Commons had been a great success. Lionel reciprocated with lunch at his club. The two men complemented each other. They were both successful men of the world with an unselfish ideal. If Sir Lionel had not been at the top of his professional tree and Wiggins still clawing up the trunk, the balance might not have been so equal. Then the politician would have been despised by the diplomat as an ignorant front man with a big mouth and the politician, an elected member, would have seen little to admire in the dreary logic of a civil servant's mind. As it was they understood each other and felt secure in each other's company. Particularly when discussing Harry.

"Do you understand him? Because I don't."

"My wife is very fond of Harry," said Wiggins.

"Is that so? A pity his wife didn't feel the same."

"They were very young." Wiggins wondered just why Julia continued to defend Henry. He was not her type, he thought, basing this view on her presumed predilection for a man in his own image.

"What he needs is a good woman to set him straight," said Sir Lionel. "Get his head in order again. Get him back to doing a decent job of work."

"He's very stubborn." Wiggins held his hand over his glass as Sir Lionel offered the bottle. He had not retired yet.

"Perhaps a friend of your wife's?" Sir Lionel filled his own glass. "My youthful contacts are limited. Living abroad so much, you know."

"I'll ask her." Wiggins leaned forward with more intensity than he'd previously shown. "Do you think this Cambodian business is going to be the final disaster?" One can only talk about human emotions so long.

Harry lived in a grand bachelor flat in Albany. It had been offered to Julian for six months by a titled ex-Guards officer. It had bed-posts carved out of holy wood brought from the olive groves of Jerusalem. On the wall there was a Victorian painting of the raising of Lazarus. His naked, thin and white body was painted with all the attention to detail which marked someone under the influence of the Pre-Raphaelites. However, at least in Harry's view, it did not share their spiritual purpose. After a day or two he turned its face to the wall, only to discover on the back another version of the same theme whose purpose was quite openly pornographic. Harry, who had always liked pallor in the female body, found it quite revolting in the male. He decided to sleep in the living room.

Sieger was impressed by Harry's new surroundings. Harry sometimes wondered if the American was not in love with him, he was always so appreciative. But since he was either accompanied by a nubile female or attacked any not already at hand, it seemed his admiration was based on something sterner. Harry represented the Old World, true Englishness. He did not seem to mind his newly acquired eccentricities, such as sandals and a habit of sudden, fixed and total silence. If anything they convinced him further of Harry's uniqueness.

"They don't make them like you now," he would say meditatively.

"You should meet my father," replied Harry.

"I would like to." Sieger leaned forward earnestly.

"My father's only seen one film in his life."

"What was that?" Sieger's eyes were hopeful.

"The Bridge on the River Kwai."

"For Sieger read Spiegel. I might have guessed." Sieger sighed. "You're the right man to have on my team. You know that, Harry?"

"I'm very glad of it. Although I wish you'd given me more to do."

"Conversation like this. Serious discussions are invaluable to me. You don't suppose your father would like to meet me for a drink sometime?"

Harry laughed at his dog eyes. "You don't need my father. He's the past. Gone. Over. You don't need me either. I need you for the money. You don't need me at all."

Harry had first spoken like this out of a guilty sense that he was taking a lot of money for very little work. About once a month Sieger would ask for a page or two commenting on a script (usually a thriller) or on the political situation in some far-off place or other. But his protestations seemed merely to encourage Sieger's determination to have him on his payroll, so now he spoke jokingly.

"You're a wonderful fellow!" cried Sieger.

"Do you think the frightful Sieger works for the CIA?" Harry asked Julian.

"He's your friend," said Julian peevishly. Despite effecting the introduction, he was rather jealous of Harry's relationship with the American producer. He, Julian, had to bend like the proverbial willow to get on with these people, while Harry behaved exactly as he felt and yet had them eating out of his hands.

"I expect he is," said Harry, "but I don't really care. The reports I write wouldn't interest a grasshopper."

The two men were walking round a spring-fresh Green Park. Julain, pale, tall, long-haired and fashionably dressed in the style of the early seventies, turned a blank eye on twirling leaf and expectant duck. Harry, brisk, bright-eyed, dressed in cords, sweater and sandals, had the look of a country monk out for a constitutional.

"Actually, I write just the same sort of things I used to write for the Foreign Office. I like to keep them to a decent sort of length, or Sieger might be tempted to read them."

Julian snorted. Really, Harry had become cynical far too quickly. He would have preferred him to stay cruelly unhappy a little bit longer even if his long gloomy discourses had been inconvenient at times. "How's the religious life?"

Harry didn't answer.

His inner life had entered a new phase with his return to London. He no longer needed to loose his unconscious on reluctant listeners. For one thing he was no longer so unconscious about his unconscious. He had begun to read those theological books that he had previously spurned. He filled one spiral exercise book with notes and quotations and another with questions. He took long walks through Richmond Park in which he silently addressed the questions to the newly clad trees.

On one of these walks he rescued a small child from drowning. He saw her face down at the edge of the lake, apparently lifeless. It was very early on Sunday morning, a bright still day with no one else in sight apart from a herd of gently cropping deer. The child was about two, with brown curls now dripping into a soggy pink anorak. Harry pulled her from the water and began to pump the water out of her. Soon she was crying loudly.

"Oh, God! I fell asleep." A girl, white with shock and visibly shaking, threw herself down beside the child. "Auriole, Auriole, are you all right?"

"She's all right now," said Harry, trying not to sound too severe. The girl, who he assumed to be the child's elder sister, looked so piteous. Huge tears were rolling down her face. "She's all right," repeated Harry, his voice louder to rise above the child's yells. "I think she looked more drowned than she was."

"Drowned. Ah!" The girl also began to scream.

Harry felt at a loss. Here was tragedy averted. Fate had placed him between the tanks and helicopters of death. "You should be happy she's all right," he said.

The girl stopped screaming and began to cuddle the child properly. Soon there was peace again. Harry now saw the sun had risen high and strong but they were under the shade of the trees. He led the girl toward a grassy patch in the open. "You'll dry out here." Since she still seemed too shocked to do anything, he undid Auriole's anorak and took it off. Surprisingly there was quite a lot of dry underneath. Already her hair was turning yellow and springing up on the top of head. He saw a bag and a rug spread under a nearby tree. "Is that yours?"

"Yes. We were going to have a treat. Breakfast in the park. She'd been awake most of the night. Teething, you know. That's why I fell asleep, I suppose."

Now that the girl had revived, Harry saw she possessed the pale mouse-like charms he'd always admired, although she was a darker version than usual, with black eyes recently reddened with tears and long black lashes. "What's your name?"

"Henrietta. But you can call me Hen."

"I'd rather not."

"What?" She blinked at him questioningly.

The child, already recovered from her fright, struggled off her lap and held out her arms to a butterfly hovering above the bracken behind them. Harry was reminded of an unidentified moment when another child had slipped off her mother's lap and reached her arms upward.

"My name's Harry. I'll get your things."

"I don't think I'll ever get over the shock," muttered Henrietta. But in a few minutes they were all making a hearty breakfast.

Henrietta gave a new dimension to Harry's life. She was twenty, a student, living off her grant, unmarried mother of Auriole. She came from Manchester where her parents still lived, but she seemed to have little contact with them.

"They don't mind about Auriole so much," explained Henrietta in a matter-of-fact voice. "It's me living so far away that gets their goat. If they're going to help me, they want daily daughterly contact. So I'd rather not be helped."

The precariousness of her existence shocked Harry. Most of her grant seemed to go on baby-sitters, so there was very little left for food or what he considered other essentials. Instead of detergent she cut up little pieces of soap. Instead of tampons she used balls of cotton wool. Her room was too small for a cot as well as a bed, so Auriole slept with her. "It's good for a child to be near its mother," she told him firmly. "All the anthropologists say so."

Her attitude was just like Flavia's toward Cordelia when they were living in Beirut. Moreover, Auriole was about the same age as Cordelia had been when Harry had last seen her eating Dr. Morton's pathway. The parallel did not strike Harry consciously, possibly because his attitude toward them was so different. His role was a paternal one, of the gentle authoritarian sort who gave advice but never criticized, who supported without expecting a return, who loved without being loved.

Henrietta, sometimes with Auriole and sometimes without, began to visit Harry regularly at Albany. Like Sieger, she was impressed by the Edwardian splendor of it all and by the cloister-like peace in the middle of London. Fairly soon Harry made love to her. She was receptive in a mild kind of way but to get properly turned on, she said, she needed a smoke or something stronger. Harry resisted this idea with firmness.

When on his own, Harry had some doubts about his new relationship. He wondered whether he was a good influence on Henrietta. After all, it was fairly clear that she was simply using him as a convenient source of otherwise unattainable comforts.

From his point of view she gave him nothing more than a bit of low-key sex and human contact. Henrietta, by her presence, had the effect of making him realize that he was lonely. One night he dreamed of Flavia and Cordelia but Cordelia had Auriole's face.

Harry prayed now on his knees, dropping there heavily with hands clasped like a picture from a child's prayer book.

Henrietta caught him there once. He opened his eyes to find her staring at him curiously. "You're not praying, are you?"

"Why not?" He stayed in position, feeling strengthened by his contact with the floor.

"It's silly." A vague apprehension crossed her face. "No one prays anymore."

"Do you mean it's unfashionable?"

"I don't know." She floundered among unaccustomed thoughts and then gave up. "You look silly."

Harry got off his knees. "Sorry. I didn't mean to shock you."

Harry began to experiment with the spoken word in his prayers. "Oh God, let your light shine upon me and give me understanding so that I may serve you as you would wish." This was his own composition and, at first, it sounded presumptuous to his ears, but after a while he could ring it out with true feeling.

He decided to make a third call on Father Bernard. It was now nearly a year since the unfortunate evening when he'd defiled the holy passages with his vomit.

The porter obviously possessed the memory of an elephant. He looked at Harry with distaste. "Father Bernard is not too well today."

"Here I am, Paddy." The priest appeared behind him. He did not look well, Harry thought. The red in his hair had now been nearly overtaken by gray and his shoulders bowed forward unhealthily. Once again he failed to recognize Harry.

"I came to apologize for my behavior on my last visit. I'm afraid I was half mad and drunk."

"Oh, it's you." Father Bernard could not disguise a sigh. He looked at his watch. It would be lunchtime in five minutes. "Come along, now."

"Do we have to talk in that awful little room?"

"We can sit at the back of the church, I suppose. Or the con . . ." He was obviously going to say "confessional" but then, remembering his visitor's non-Catholic status, stopped himself. "There is a little garden."

As they proceeded through dark corridors, a clock struck from one dim direction and a bell rang from another.

"What's that?" asked Harry.

"Lunch. But don't worry."

"It must be nice living with so much order."

They reached the garden. It was September. A second flowering of roses grew up the brick walls. The priest sat down on a grimy London bench.

"Your father apologized for you. Actually he gave an offering to the church. Most welcome. And of course your mother worships here. Now I come to think of it, we paid a chap to sort out this garden with Sir Lionel's money." He looked round appraisingly.

"Most apposite."

"And what have you been doing since?"

"I was in Ireland."

"Ah, Ireland. Mother Ireland. What county?"

"Cork. And then I visited Aran."

"A desolate place. West Meath is my corner. A fine corner if you're a racing man."

Harry saw that their previous conversations had discouraged Father Bernard from further probes into his spiritual welfare. He had never been too keen on it, anyway, as far as Harry remembered. As if to emphasize the dearth of time, the priest's stomach rumbled hungrily.

"Too good a timekeeper." He patted himself apologetically.

"I just wanted a word about prayer."

"Ah, prayer. A most important part of the Christian life. You have been indulging in a bit of prayer?"

"I wondered if people come to church to pray?"

"There's a question. Who can answer but each individual? And He who knows everything, of course." He gave Harry a complicitous smile. Since Harry did not respond he tried harder. Hunger had receded since his stomach's protest so he was more able to concentrate. "I should say that twenty percent come because they've always come. Twenty percent come to please their spouse or their parent. Twenty percent come for a bit of peace—they don't like the new Mass. Where have I got to now?"

"Sixty percent," said Harry earnestly.

"Maths was never my strong subject. Communal prayer is thought by the Church to have a special power."

"What sort of power?"

"To reach its destination. The communion of saints. I expect you've heard that phrase."

"Do you mean I've got to sort of link up with the people in the next pew?"

"Solitary prayer can be a selfish activity."

"But surely all the greatest mystics were solitaries? Jesus himself went into the desert when he wanted to pray. He left the disciples just before he was crucified to be solitary."

"Yes. Well." Father Bernard suddenly felt quite faint. "There's room for both ways. The Church no longer rules as firmly as it used to . . . " His voice faded away.

It took Harry a moment or two before he noticed his companion had keeled over sideways with eyes closed.

"Are you all right?" He touched him. Dust rose from the black cassock and danced in the sunlight. The priest opened his eyes.

"Just hungry."

"I'll help you."

"Love your neighbor as yourself."

Harry left him at a door from which a smell of meat and two soggy vegetables streamed as if tangible.

Walking back to Albany, he reviewed the situation. Communal prayer was a proposition he found eminently resistible. Maybe he would read Newman, who was, after all, an intellectual and a convert. "Love your neighbor as yourself" indeed!

Julia Wiggins and Henrietta sat in Harry's spacious living room. By chance they had both found baby-sitters and spare time on the same golden afternoon. A visit to Harry had seemed a nice piece of daring to Julia and a pleasant chance of relaxation to Henrietta. Julia had arrived first, let in by the porter, and, about a quarter of an hour later, Henrietta had opened the door with her own key.

This had irritated Julia considerably. She had already made certain with probing raids into bedroom and bathroom that there was no female living in the flat and, although she knew of Henrietta's existence, she had ruled her out as peripheral. The key was a distinct blow.

"Oh, hi!" Henrietta, dressed in patched jeans and to-the-knees sweater, dumped a bag, apparently filled with empty bottles, onto the floor.

It is not that I wanted to drag Harry into bed like some rapacious unappreciated housewife, thought Julia, but we do have a very special relationship which I would not like to see disappear altogether. "Hi!" she said out loud, with the smile of a politician's wife.

Henrietta looked round. "No Harry?"

"I'm afraid not. The porter let me in. You must be Henrietta?"

"Yup."

Since she did not ask, Julia felt obliged to introduce herself.

"I'm Julia Wiggins. My husband's Harry's oldest friend. They were at school together."

"Do they still remember school?"

"I'm sorry?"

"It must be so long ago." Henrietta bent over her bag and began to take out the bottles, which were indeed empty and very dirty. She lined them in two rows and began to count them. "Eighteen. Not bad from the tube to here."

"What are they for?" Julia looked down with distaste.

"Money. I get them from the dustbins. The trouble is, they're so heavy." She began to pile them back in the bag. "I'll have a cup of coffee and then be off."

Julia had to restrain herself from saying, "Good!" Nor did she want a coffee made by those dustbin-probing hands. "Not for me, thank you."

Harry arrived back just as Henrietta was preparing to go. He looked at the two women with some surprise. They did not fit into his thoughts on communal prayer. He considered the idea of a pew in which they both figured and he in the middle. He supposed this was behind the idea of Christian unity. He kissed Julia, who held up her cheek and smiled at Henrietta.

"Been bin-hunting again?"

"She'll get cholera or something!" broke in Julia, who could not resist saying unpleasant things about Henrietta.

"Thanks for the coffee. I'll get to the grocery store before it closes if I hurry."

Harry watched his pew empty without regret. Even he could sense a lack of shared communal spirit between the politician's wife and the student unmarried mother.

"Henrietta's just the sort of girl Labour chaps like Wiggins are trying to help," he said when she'd gone clanking off.

"I wish you wouldn't call him Wiggins."

They fell into a silence broken eventually by Julia. "I can't stand that sort of girl! So hopeless. And living off everyone else."

"The Labour Party created the welfare state to encourage the existence of such people."

"Oh, shut up!"

Reluctantly Harry recognized her vehemence as a sign of sexual tension, even jealousy. "Look how hard she was working carrying all those bottles from pillar to post."

"Stuff her bottles!"

Harry went over and looked out of the window. He asked resignedly, "Where's Wiggins?"

"In his constituency." Julia had the grace to look a little shamefaced. "I haven't talked to you properly for so long. Not on our own. Your mother said you'd gone mad. Or perhaps that was your father."

Madness as a subject could provide an alternative to serious activity. "Do you believe in God, Julia?"

"Well, I don't know. I suppose so. Like everyone else."

"Ah." Harry came over and sat close to her. He could see that the mention of God had had a most detumescent effect, if women could be described as detumescent. "What do you believe in?"

"David believes in improving the social welfare through political means."

"David?"

"Wiggins."

"But what do you believe in?"

"Oh, Harry. You never used to ask so many questions." Julia crossed her legs, which remained her best point, so that her skirt slid almost up to her crotch. She then pulled it down again.

Almost absentmindedly, Harry put his hand between her two legs. Henrietta would hardly have noticed such a friendly gesture. Julia stiffened and flushed.

Harry abruptly removed his hand. "I wrote to Flavia just before I left England but she hasn't answered."

Julia was so overwhelmed by the leg-touching that she found it difficult to speak. She had realized all at once that Harry was the only man she'd ever really found physically attractive. This was a horrifying thought and had to be cleanly and efficiently removed before it did further damage to her proper and happy life. She stood up. "Of course, I never knew Flavia." Her voice was cold.

"I wrote to her parents' address."

"And the letter wasn't returned to you?"

"I didn't put my own address."

Julia went to another chair far removed from Harry and sat down again. Her composure returned. "Come to think of it, David mentioned some letter at the House of Commons that belonged to you. Perhaps that's it."

"Quite possibly." With the cooling of sexual atmosphere, Harry lounged into a chair. "I told her to get in touch via Wiggins."

"That's it, then," said Julia.

Harry resisted the impulse to slip onto his knees for a little prayer about comfort and consolation. He had been expecting a letter from Flavia. It had been in his dreams. "That's it, then," he repeated, giving Julia a bright look.

Flavia became a bit of a Holy Grail with Harry. Her predominance in his imagination was encouraged by Henrietta's disappearance from his life. It was almost as if her meeting with Julia had turned her away, although that seemed too ridiculous an idea for serious contemplation. It was far more likely that she had found a more suitable boyfriend. It would not be in her nature to produce explanations or a farewell scene.

Images of Flavia's pale flying walk flashed about Harry's mind. At times she transformed herself into an angel, almost fleshless, her gleaming hair rising behind her shoulders like wings. The truth was he couldn't remember her physical reality. It was nearly eight years since he had seen her and she had never been a very solid sort of person anyway. It was even harder to give a form to Cordelia, who he had last seen as a red and choking baby. He did, however, have photographs of her up to the age of four. These he placed round the room. He had no photographs of Flavia.

He confided his longings to Julian.

"Aren't God and Sieger enough?" said Julian, who had just failed to get a client a very lucrative part playing the Marquis de Sade.

"I don't want her . . . " began Harry.

"Just as well, as she clearly doesn't want you."

"I just want to make contact. Check out her existence. Actually I want to *see* what she looks like. I can't tell you how odd it is having been married to someone and had a child when you can't even remember what they look like. Flavia's a ghost in my mind, driving me mad."

"Not again!" Julian began to smile. The suffering Harry had always appealed. "Track her down through her husband," he suggested.

"I can't remember what he's called."

"He was in India with your parents, wasn't he? They'll know."

"How do you think of these things?" Harry sighed gratefully.

"You've lost all rights to your daughter, of course." Sir Lionel sat at his desk. He did not take off his half-moon reading glasses. "Our granddaughter."

Harry thought that retirement had not brought out the best in his father. He now played a role halfway between a crusty colonel and a crusty academic, although this attitude might just be personal to his son, since it had intensified after the drunken night at the church incident. Forgiveness was never high on Lionel's list of virtues.

"I don't *want* either of them. I'd just like to meet them again."

"I suppose that's reasonable." Sir Lionel scribbled something on a pad. His pen hand felt weary. How he longed for a son to take him from his desk and join in stimulating conversation over a whisky and soda! Henry had once provided that service. He handed over the paper. "There's his name. Their Embassy should track him down for you easily enough."

"Thanks." Harry put away the paper without looking at it. "How's the memoirs?"

Sir Lionel's military bearing slumped into dejection. Harry suddenly noticed he was wearing slippers. He stood up.

"How about a drink?"

"Isn't it going well?" Harry watched his father shuffle irritably among the decanters.

"Your mother *will* mix up the whisky and sherry labels."

"Surely they look different?"

"A book is a very different kettle of fish from a report—however long the report. It requires judgment, description, revelation, all of a personal nature. It requires an awareness of your reader. And of your publisher too." Sir Lionel took a large gulp of neat whisky. The truth was he had serious doubts about the whole project. He had begun with the cheerful concept indicated by his working title, *Out of Empire into the World,* but the more he went on the more he felt that *Out of the Frying Pan into the Fire* would be more appropriate. It was Vietnam that brought all his worries to a head, just as before. It undermined his splendid confidence about the future of the West allied to a democratic great power. It confused his sense of right and wrong, good and bad. Lately he had even begun to wonder whether Truman and the Americans hadn't made a ghastly mistake in dropping the atomic bomb on Japan. More and more he looked back to the golden days of the Empire when Great Britain (then truly Great) ruled half the world with justice and humanity. However, his publishers, who had if anything a left-wing bias, certainly hadn't commissioned him to write a paean of praise to England's historic past. He was supposed to be a man of the present, even the future, with a "wide-ranging" knowledge of diplomacy in Asia, America and Europe.

"What is the point of diplomacy?"

Harry at first thought it best to ignore this question. But since his father, reading glasses off, fixed him with a baleful stare, he began obligingly, "Diplomacy is the art of bringing together . . . " He hesitated and changed his tone of voice. "Diplomacy is lying abroad for your country."

"Yes. Yes." Lionel waved his glass impatiently. "I didn't ask for the catechism or the jokes. What is it to you?"

"To me?" Unable to read his father's self-doubts, Harry saw only rocks ahead. "It doesn't mean anything to me anymore."

"What do you mean? That's a stupid thing to say! It exists. All over the world people are making contacts, doing all the things you said. You must have a reaction." Lionel felt cheered by anger. He drank some more whisky.

"I'm sorry. I just came here to find a way of getting in touch with my ex-wife."

"You're a fool!"

"I expect so."

A flush of pleasure suddenly suffused Sir Lionel's face. "And who do you think would find your precious ex-wife and long-lost daughter if it wasn't for the Foreign Office? Your God? It may not mean anything to you but you sure as hell wouldn't get far without it!"

"There you are, then." Harry put down his drink and got up. "The point of the Foreign Office is to find ex-wives and long-lost daughters for fools like me."

Chapter 23

he Foreign Office tracked down Signore di Stefano quickly and efficiently. Harry sent a letter to his office address and after a few weeks received a polite letter from a secretary informing him that Signora di Stefano was presently in England but would be returning to South America in a few days, at which time she would be informed of his wish to make contact.

Flavia came on a visit to London. She came without her husband, who was being diplomatic in New York, but with her children. They now included not only Cordelia but two little girls who looked as English as Alice in Wonderland but spoke Spanish as their first language. Only Cordelia retained a gawky Englishness with almost no accent. Flavia wanted to continue feeling English. It gave her an expatriate sense of freedom and pandered to her husband's Anglophilia. Were England not her country, her whole existence might tumble like a card-house. However, childbirth had intervened and she had not visited England since her marriage. She came because her father was dying of emphysema.

How can doctors be foolish enough to smoke? thought Flavia.

Flavia was not as ethereal as she had been and certainly not as Harry imagined her in his dreams. She had lived for nearly a decade among the ruling classes of Argentina, which was an extremely materialistic society. She was mother of three children and she had a husband who, although always in love with her, believed a wife to be property. In this, he was the opposite of Harry, who had never given her any status as wife.

Flavia was not searching for Harry on her return to England. When Cordelia asked about him, she answered in a dreamy, unconvincing voice as if he had no real existence. "He'll be round the world somewhere, representing his country in a very special British way."

"But what does he look like, Mama?"

"Dark." Flavia was vague, turning away. But "dark" was enough to inspire Cordelia. Her hair had darkened as she grew older. Now she was the only brown-haired one in a family of golden halos. She was dark and sturdy and determined. One day she would meet her father.

Dr. and Dr. Morton no longer lived in the country. The house to which Harry had sent his letter had become kennels for dogs whose owners had gone on holiday. Flavia pointed it out on the drive to the small town where her parents now lived. Her mother still practiced. Her father lay in a hospital bed in a large town nearby.

The barking of desolate dogs haunted Flavia. "People are so cruel," she said. Her three daughters, sitting in a row on the back seat, stared solemnly but without understanding. They did not share the English sentiment for dumb animals. Or even vociferous ones. They could not know that Flavia saw their howls as echoing her own. Now she had no home in England.

Patricia Morton was no surprise to the children. She had visited them twice in Argentina. But the house with its thick stone walls, small windows and low ceilings disappointed them. It was not even warm enough to be cozy. Reluctantly, Cordelia gave up the idea that her father would be waiting to welcome her.

"What a sad little bunch!" The children were pale after their long flight and car journey. To Dr. Morton, living in the shadow of her husband's imminent death, their air of vulnerability was almost unbearable. She began to bustle about pulling off their coats and offering biscuits, which they refused. The smallest, Maria, shivered continuously, yet again reminding Flavia of the dogs.

"What a horrid thing! To have our house filled with weeping dachshunds."

"Oh, you drove that way. Actually Mrs. Scott-Price adores dogs. They're all very very happy. Everyone says so."

"Then why do they wail?"

A possible argument was avoided by the second daughter, Lucia or Lucy, having an accident. "Oh, Mama, like a *niñon!*"

"And there's a lavatory just here." Flavia looked near tears.

"It's the cold!" cried Cordelia, hugging her sister defensively.

Now Dr. Morton's lips trembled. "It's a warm spring day."

Four pairs of blue eyes stared at her uncomprehendingly.

Harry walked through the crowded streets around Piccadilly—it was only a few yards from his grand apartment—expecting to meet Flavia at any time. He had only twenty-four hours, he reckoned, before she would leave, according to the secretary's timetable. Since he did not know of the existence of Lucia or Maria, he looked for a slim fair-headed young woman for whom he allowed no aging and a clone in the eight-to-eleven age group. He was unsure of Cordelia's exact age.

In fact it was Wiggins who spotted Flavia. He was hurrying back to the House of Commons, having spent lunchtime at Liberty's buying a wedding anniversary present for Julia. He knew her at once, that irritating, swaying walk, which had seemed affected among all the affectations of Oxford and now seemed positively outlandish. Her hair, too, still floated in an obvious bid for attention. He wanted to pass by unnoticed, but by sheer bad luck they crossed a road at the same time and found themselves all alone on an island in the middle.

"Hello, Flavia," said Wiggins with a carefully apportioned smile.

The look she gave him, the vacant rolling eye, made it clear she had no idea who was addressing her. This was doubly annoying. He was in a hurry and had no wish to meet her, yet he it was who had initiated contact.

"David Wiggins. Harry's friend," he said, giving the traffic a look of reproach.

"Oh, Wiggins. I was thinking of Harry last night."

The cars around them at last reached a standstill. There was no more reason to stay. Wiggins put a foot off the island and then hesitated enough to leer at Flavia. At least Flavia thought of it as a leer. "Quite mad, of course. Should never have left the Foreign Office!" And then he was gone, hopping between the cars with the perfect coordination of a man with all his wits about him.

Flavia stood on the island and watched him for a minute or two longer. Had he always been so abrasive? She couldn't remember. She thought he might have made a rejected overture to her in Oxford, and certainly he had always been jealous of Harry. She wished she had refuted his "mad" with a hearty stamp of the foot, but he had given her no time. Harry had been mad once before.

Flavia's spirits were low. She had left the children with her mother. Lucia and Maria had colds, Cordelia was bored, her mother was nervous and her father still had not died. It was true that she had been thinking of Harry.

The night before, after a dismally silent supper, Dr. Morton had pulled out an old box from under a cupboard. "Oh, darling. Do see if you want anything here. I saved them when we moved."

Flavia opened the box. A strong smell of burnt paper made her recoil in disgust.

"They were on the bonfire with all the rubbish," said her mother. "When I saw they were letters, I raked out what I could. Actually it was quite a memorable scene. Dusk, the red fire, and me fighting the flames with a rake."

This was an unusually emotive speech from someone of Dr. Morton's practical nature. Flavia felt obliged to look at the papers. Her mother went to bed and she rummaged about in the crisp fragments. In the midst of a soft nest of ashes she found intact the tight white bundle of Harry's letters just before Schools. She had forgotten just how mad he had been.

> It is two A.M. and the moon is beaming through the window. Sometimes I think it's the eye of God sending a message by night. Donec Diversas praecurrens luna fenestras . . .

Flavia now remembered that one of the deterrents to a proper reading of Harry's letters was his habit of breaking into Latin or Greek. She turned over the letters, looking for English. It seemed an odd legacy of a proper public school education that when you felt emotional you broke into a language no longer spoken and largely unintelligible to ordinary mortals.

> Six A.M. I've just come in from a walk around London. My parents are still sleeping. When the sun came up it reminded me of you. I sat on a bench in Hyde Park and cried for a moment or two. Then a tramp came and peed on my foot. How terrible it must be to lead a life unmoved by beauty . . . .
>
> . . . Mary Ann is marrying a Papist wog. She is not the same. My mother goes to church. Ave Maria gratia plena. But she does it secretly, almost guiltily. I noticed that when she returned she was more vivacious than usual. . . .

The letters, Flavia now saw, were written in the form of a diary.

> . . . Today I worked for twelve hours. I drank water twice and passed water three times. Otherwise my concentration

> was unbroken. I can now do Paper I. Deo gratias. . . .

The frequency of reference to God surprised Flavia. She did not remember them from her previous reading. Then they had seemed to revolve round his love for her in a form which was more embarrassing than flattering.

> . . . A daisy opened under my eyes this morning. The sun came streaking down and it fluttered open. How sweet you are when you wake! So virgin!
>
> My parents walk about with their eyes shut and their hands held out in front of them. They're very frightened of bruises. My father begrudges me a glass of sherry.

Flavia tossed the letters back into the box and the following morning told her mother she could burn the lot. It was only then she remembered her own incendiary efforts in a bucket. The bucket had burnt but not the letters.

Flavia had thought of Harry. So when Wiggins, with his self-importance sprayed over him like after-shave, broke into her meditations in the middle of the road, she couldn't quite throw him off again.

She did not wish to see Harry, even for Cordelia's sake, but there was unfinished business. She went to a telephone booth and looked up Sir Lionel Hayes-Middleton.

Beatrice was nervous about seeing Flavia and couldn't understand why she was not bringing Cordelia. Always supported by appearances, she chose to wear a gray silk dress and three strings of pearls. She sat in a chair beside a vase of white flowers. Light, from the tall London window, came in across her left shoulder. On a nearby table she placed a bottle of white wine and three glasses. She sat waiting, with her hands in her lap and thought about Flavia and Cordelia and Harry.

Lionel was at a meeting with his publishers. Beatrice didn't know he was having a little retirement fling with an assistant from his agents called Carol. She was a sharp-faced blonde whose affection for him was openly based on his importance as an ex-Ambassador and future author. Lionel found not being wanted for himself quite a compliment. It also gave him a sense of security. She would make no trouble.

Flavia came off the streets with her head buzzing from traffic and people. Beatrice was startled by the creases above her nose and round her mouth. She had not imagined her aging or weary. Nevertheless she remained cool, neither friendly nor unfriendly.

Flavia took off her coat and sat in a chair opposite Beatrice. For a moment both women seemed in a kind of trance.

"Would you like a drink?" Beatrice asked eventually.

"Oh, tea!" Flavia smiled for the first time.

"I'd thought wine." Beatrice gestured at the bottle.

"Oh, wine," responded Flavia with not quite the same enthusiasm.

"And how is Cordelia?" asked Beatrice when the wine was poured.

"With my mother. In the country."

"I suppose she is hardly English now?"

"Oh, but she is!" exclaimed Flavia without explanation. She had forgotten Beatrice's close resemblance to her son. It brought back memories and made it seem impossible that she could be a sympathetic ear. "I haven't seen Harry," she said abruptly. "Is he well?"

"He wanted to get in touch with you, I believe." Beatrice leaned forward a little. "It depends what you mean by well. He is healthy." She sat back again and remembered how she'd liked this girl in India. She had thought of her and the child as a happy lifeline to the future.

"I met Wiggins in the middle of the road. He said Harry is mad."

"Wiggins." It was time for Beatrice's first smile. "He is terribly irritated by Harry. It undermines his life, you see. His successes."

"So Harry isn't mad?"

"Really, I can't think why you use such a childish word."

Beatrice spoke with such severity that Flavia blushed quite red and tears came into her eyes. "I'm sorry." She bowed her head.

Beatrice relented. "It's Wiggins's fault. You probably caught it off him. Harry has altered his values, that's all. Change always upsets people, so they shout "mad." Personally, I have very high hopes of him."

There was a pause. Flavia wiped her eyes surreptitiously. Beatrice looked out of the window. Her placid expression was hiding the sudden annoyance she felt with Harry for making everything so difficult. For some reason an image of the long dead and forgotten Otto came to her. He had been difficult.

"What's he doing?" Flavia's tone was humble.

"Working for a film producer. At least that's how he earns his money. What he's doing is another matter. Looking for you, last time I heard."

"Oh, I can't see him."

"That's your business. Have some more wine?"

"We were never properly married."

"I heard the marriage was annulled."

"I didn't mean that. That was for George. He's Catholic, of course. As a matter of fact, I became Catholic, too. When the last child was baptized."

Beatrice looked at her wineglass. Her own Catholicism was so private that she felt little desire to compare a faith with this girl. Flavia seemed very young to her again, despite the lines. "Do you believe in the Church?" she asked idly.

"I believe in God. Most of the time. But I can't think about things like that. When the priest was instructing me, my mind wandered. Sometimes I planned the entire week's menus. I suppose, my parents both being doctors, I was born with a load of non-religious genes. I like dreaming but that's not the same."

"No," agreed Beatrice. She wondered whether to tell her about Harry's position re his Maker. But then she wasn't at all sure she knew what his position was. "I suppose there are those who wish to believe and those who prefer doubt," she said. "Happiness is simply a matter of deciding which you are."

"Then I'm doing the wrong thing," said Flavia anxiously.

But Beatrice had lost interest in her idea. Besides, she could hear Lionel at the front door. "It's not a question of wrong or right." She rose briskly to her feet.

Flavia realized she must be drunk when Lionel came into the room. His bulk loomed over her in undulating outline. She had eaten no lunch and taken breakfast early. Her cheekbones were spotted with red.

"How d'you do," bellowed Lionel appreciatively. He had no idea who she was. He was feeling joyously young. He could even consider the penultimate chapter of his book, on the tricky question of French agricultural policy within the Common Market, without shuddering. Carol had suggested that his next book should be an examination of the effect of the class system within establishment institutions. It was not that he was a dirty old man but that, at sixty-five, he was still filled with vim and vigor.

"You remember Flavia, of course," said Beatrice in such a soft voice that Lionel failed to hear the name.

Flavia, trying to clear her mind of alcoholic mists, gave no clue either.

"Cheers!" cried Lionel impartially, lifting a glass of wine.

"I mustn't stay long," said Flavia. "I promised the children I'd be back for their bedtime."

"Many children, have you?" said Lionel.

"Three now," said Flavia.

"I have one." Lionel, who still had not sat down, took a stride or two across the room. But he's enough trouble for three. First he marries a silly girl who runs off and leaves him, taking their child, mind you. Then he throws up an extremely promising career in the Diplomatic Service because he hears the voice of God! What do you say to that, eh?"

"My children are all girls," replied Flavia faintly. She had heard Lionel's slighting reference to herself distinctly but it had not penetrated her consciousness. She didn't feel as if he were reproving her, which of course he wasn't, although she had no idea of the real reason.

Beatrice, who should have taken command of the situation, was staring calmly ahead. Her face was very pale. Perhaps she, too, had drunk too much on an empty stomach.

Flavia stood up. "I should go . . . " Her sentence was not finished. She crumpled to the floor at Lionel's feet.

"She's fainted!" He looked down in surprise.

"Poor child. I never could see why Harry married her."

"So that's who . . . ?" Lionel looked even more surprised.

"I thought you were being unusually rude."

"But I didn't . . . "

Further explanation was curtailed by Flavia's returning to life. "I'm so sorry." She sat up, apparently once more composed. "I'm hungry, that's the problem."

"Oh dear. I should have thought."

"It's entirely my own fault. I expect I can get a sandwich on the train." She stood up.

"Certainly not!" Lionel took her arm gallantly. Preceded by Beatrice, they proceeded down to the kitchen. The house was too big for them now, but Lionel would only relinquish so much ambassadorial grandeur.

They sat round the kitchen table, eating bread and cheese. Lionel and Beatrice's supper had already been laid out by a daily woman. A white cloth covered salad and peeled potatoes. Flavia felt a moment of longing for the peace of old age.

"I must be going."

"Even though you don't wish to see Harry, I shall tell hm of your visit."

"You are the only daughter-in-law we've got!" cried Lionel in hearty tones.

Beatrice frowned.

"Not anymore," said Flavia on her way to the door. Her head ached. She felt Lionel's hand on her shoulder. "I'll send you photographs of Cordelia," she said.

"It must be her birthday soon." Beatrice looked at Flavia directly.

"Yes, yes, next week." Flavia was disconcerted. "She's getting very grown-up. Tall."

"I'd like to see her." Beatrice's tone was matter-of-fact.

Lionel squeezed Flavia's shoulder. The warmth and heartiness of his hand reminded her of her husband. She managed to meet Beatrice's eyes. How cool she was! How remote! But she had said she wanted to meet Cordelia. "We're leaving tomorrow." And then she would be back with George, who would comfort her and make her feel safe.

"I'd like to see my granddaughter."

Why did she repeat it? Flavia backed away.

"I'll make her write. We'll keep in touch."

"Good, good." Lionel escorted her to the door.

He kissed her under Beatrice's silent gaze. The two women did not kiss.

"Strange girl," commented Lionel as soon as the door closed.

"Not particularly."

"Oh, yes." Lionel smiled. "Ice and fire, I'd say." He stroked his mustache. "Tricky mixture. Consumed poor old Henry. Now he's on to the fires of hell."

"What utter nonsense!" Beatrice swung about and took neat but brisk steps in the opposite direction from her husband. "They were still children when they married. That was the only problem."

Lionel continued to smile.

The next day Beatrice telephoned Harry: "Flavia came to London. We had quite a chat. She has two more daughters now. They were all here with her, staying at her mother's house. Poor Dr. Morton is very ill. The children weren't too well either, so she didn't bring them with her. But she has promisied to send photographs of Cordelia. And make her write. Won't that be nice?"

"Did she ask after me?" Harry's tone carried sepulchral echoes.

Beatrice continued in the same chatty vein. "Oh, yes. She wanted to know how you were."

"And what did you say?"

Now Beatrice hesitated. "She had met Wiggins in the street."

"Who said I was mad."

"I said I had high hopes of you in the future."

"That was nice of you, Mother. If I may ask, in what sphere do you have high hopes of me in the future?"

"If you're going to be sarcastic . . . "

"Not at all. I was asking for help. A lead. In this great human drain known as life."

"I was speaking in general."

"I would have liked to see her. Maybe I'll go to South America."

"Her plane leaves this morning."

Harry strode out of Albany and picked up a taxi in Regent Street. "Heathrow Airport, please."

They sped out of London with a delightful ease that gave Harry a sense of real achievement. Within half an hour they were at the airport and it didn't take long for a well-traveled chap like Harry to find Flavia's flight. It left in ten minutes. The passengers were already aboard, the gate closed.

Harry bounded up to the observation deck and peered out across the runway. There was the huge airplane, engines just starting to turn. In a moment it would move slowly backward, turn in a dignified half circle and crawl toward takeoff position.

Harry looked up at the sky. It was essentially blue with strips of white dragging slowly across it. He would have felt at the center of a majestic revolving stage except that the clouds did not move at a coordinated pace. Some hastened, however gradually, to overtake those ahead, and others lagged so that the sky stood still behind them. It made the scene confusing instead of uplifting. It was like riding on an escalator whose handrail is not keeping proper pace.

When Harry looked down again, the airplane was no longer visible. It queued somewhere, he supposed, among all the others. He left his position.

"Harry! This is great! Where's the car?"

Since Sieger traveled constantly between London and Los Angeles it was only a small coincidence that he should be at the airport.

"I've got a great new project. We can talk about it on the way in." He gripped Harry's arm excitedly. "It's a thriller but no ordinary one and Lee Marvin's expressed interest. Hey, Harry, why are you wearing pajamas?"

Julian had become so successful that it became necessary to leave England for America. He came to inform Harry. He was sad but philosophical. "You've got to grow, Harry, grow. Or you might as well be dead." He had brought his new constant companion, Richard, pronounced in the French manner with an "sh." Richard was half Indian and very beautiful, with huge black eyes and slender hands. Despite his slave-boy good looks, he had been educated at Eton and Oxford and was far better informed than Julian.

"What does he see in you?" inquired Harry admiringly when Richard left the room for a moment.

"He's using me," sighed Julian, "for his own ambitious purposes. Oh, the torture of being in love!"

"I've never been in love!"

"No. Women were nice to you so early. Of course it's never too late to start. Richard makes everything else seem like mere dalliance."

Julian wanted Harry to take over the English end of his company. Harry was astonished.

"But you know how I live! How can you possibly imagine me running an office?"

"I've got an excellent girl who does that." Julian became nonchalant. "I just want someone with a bit of class if any big fish swim out of my American net. Perhaps a bit of wining and dining. After all, Sieger thinks the light shines out of your eyes."

"He saw me during my Foreign Office days. He thinks I'm going through a "self-discovery revelatory situation phase." He doesn't take the present me seriously. He knows my father's an Ambassador. He thinks I'm an English eccentric like, like Oscar Wilde."

Julian snorted. "Not like Oscar Wilde. Like George Bernard Shaw."

Harry sighed.

At this point Richard came back into the room. Julian caught his arm and swiveled him to face Harry. "How would you describe this rotten old layabout? Honestly."

Harry looked interested.

"Tall, a little flabby round the middle. Good features, thinning dark curly . . . "

"Not that sort of description. The inner man. Honesty. Integrity, that sort of thing."

"Searching," said Richard briefly.

"Searching," cried Harry as if exhilarated at the idea.

Harry decided it was time for a fourth visit to Father Bernard. By chance he chose a time of the evening when a service was in progress. It was Benediction. Harry could hear the Latin singing coming through the church door.

"Tantum ergo Sacramentum
Veneremur Cernui . . . "

It surprised and delighted him. He thought all Latin had been banished with the Second Vatican Council in the sixties.

He slipped into the back of the church and knelt down with his head in his arms. This was his favored position for prayer in his flat, but it felt strange to be doing it in a church. He paid little attention to the service, which seemed to pass very quickly. At school he had a memory of church periods stretching into an eternity of time. In what seemed like a few minutes the dozen or so worshipers came sliding down the shadowy aisle toward him. The last made such slow, almost tottering progress that she caught his attention. It was his mother.

Since Harry had looked up as she came level, they came almost face to face. But as in a dream Beatrice made no sign of recognition, and Harry was too startled by her blankness to react. Perhaps she was a ghost.

Father Bernard came whisking out of the sacristy. Benediction always gave him a feeling of satisfaction. He felt it as a warm glow in his solar plexus. It was a link with the past, the church's past and his own. Whenever he thought of changes that had wrenched apart the attitudes of thirty years in his case, hundreds of years in the case of the Church, he was amazed that it had survived with as few breakages as it had. It showed the strength of Catholicism, of course. However, just once in a while it was a delicious treat to relax into the old ways.

"O Salutaris Hostia!"

The priest's good humor was only slightly jolted by the sight of Harry in the corridor. The eye of long practice had picked him out in the church and noted that his mother was also present. Although they did not sit together, they prayed under the same roof. This must be a cause for thanksgiving.

"Hello, Harry. Hello." Harry, although a troublesome visitor, was not a frequent one. Father Bernard's charity was being strained deeply at that time by a young man who called twice a day, threatening suicide if he was not admitted.

"Hello, Father." Harry was pleased by the priest's welcoming manner. It was the first time he'd got his name straight off.

"Like a word, would you?"

"That would be kind."

"Now you don't like my little room, do you? Prison, I believe you called it."

"Please don't worry."

"It's a fine evening. We can watch the sun set in the garden."

Indeed the sun set above the dark brick wall. Harry watched its progress with a reflected calm. He couldn't remember why he had been so angry on his previous visits.

"Have you been making out all right with the books I suggested?"

"I read them." There was a pause. "But they're not the point, are they? I mean, what other people believe is largely irrelevant."

"It can be helpful."

"It seems to be that a true understanding of death, of the certainty of non-existence, is the only way to a sensible life. Without that belief, the whole of life becomes a charade."

"Death is a very painful subject."

"Surely not for you."

Father Bernard scratched his ear. The truth was he had always been terrified of dying. It was the terror which had led him toward a vocation. Becoming a priest had alleviated it less than he had hoped. When he had been ill a few months ago, the thought of dying had increased his blood pressure and delayed his recovery.

"Personally, I've always found death a very hard nut indeed. Of course, Christ himself found it pretty difficult. That's comforting. . . . "

"I'm not in the slightest bit frightened of dying." The sun was now a red arc resting on the red bricks. "I imagine death like that sun. One minute you're there and the next you're gone."

Both men watched as the arc reduced itself to a slither and then disappeared altogether.

"Yes. But where's it gone?" The priest leaned forward intensely.

"Behind the wall." Harry laughed loudly. And then looked ashamed at the priest's shocked face. "Sorry. The sun's a silly image."

"It rises again." The warmth in Father Bernard's solar plexus had vanished. "You feel you lack an awareness of death. Is that the problem?"

"An awareness of anything, really," Harry muttered. "Death. Life. Love." His face had become abstracted. He rose as if the priest no longer existed. But then, remembering him again, he held out his hand. "You've been most kind. Thank you."

"Not at all." Father Bernard's voice was gloomy. He stood up.

Harry suddenly took a step toward him so that he was close enough for the priest to see his bloodshot eyes and unshaven chin. "You never had a child."

"No." Father Bernard retreated, winding his hands together. "Not part of the deal." He tried a smile.

"They say a child gives you a future."

Before the priest could think of any answer to what was only possibly a question, Harry had turned his back on him, staring upward with concentration. He saw a broad-leafed tree with a thick gnarled trunk. Among the leaves stood flowers curling upward like delicately molded cups. It was these that had caught his attention. "What's that tree?"

"What?" The priest looked up, surprised.

"That tree. The one with those tall pale flowers."

"That's a tulip tree, I believe."

"Tulip? Tulip!"

"So I believe. Not very convincing tulips, I do agree."

Harry followed Father Bernard back through the dark corridors. "You mustn't judge yourself too harshly," the priest said over his shoulder. "That's the sin of pride."

"I might take a trip," said Harry. "I was brought up to travel, lived all over the world, you know. I was brought up to believe in England as the center of all the other countries in the world. It was a matter of total confidence. When I showed my U.K. passport, I was showing myself."

"I've never had much chance to broaden my horizons," began Father Bernard, feeling out of his depth. "Ireland, of course, and Lourdes, every few years or so . . . " His voice trailed away. The porter had appeared and was signaling a message. Besides, Harry was paying no attention. "Have a good trip." He raised a hearty voice and opened the door to the street. "And come and see me when you get back." Too late he realized he hadn't mentioned Lady Hayes-Middleton. He had planned to slip in the advice that the relationship between mother and child was fundamental to Christian teaching.

Chapter 24

Harry looked up his old girlfriend, Donna, the morning he arrived in New York. She was still working for the United Nations and received him in her office. The city was suffering from an early heat wave and it was thirty degrees colder inside the air-conditioned buildings than it was on the streets.

Harry took a crumpled sweater out of his carryall and pulled it over his head.

Donna stared at him with a shocked expression. He looked no better than a tramp.

"What's the matter?"

"Nothing." She crossed her legs and then folded her hands on top of her knees. All round there was evidence of neat folding.

"Tell me, Donna dear, what purpose do you find in this life?"

"Oh, Harry."

"Seriously." Harry leaned forward and covered her hands with one of his. He peered into her eyes. They were expertly encircled by black eye pencil which separated them from the rest of her face. "Windows of the soul," murmured Harry.

Donna was a sensible girl who recognized that Harry represented danger. But she had also been brought up a Catholic in South Carolina. "There is no purpose, is there? Not like you mean. One just keeps on, trying to do a little good. Not hurt too many people. Be a little successful, a little happy." She stopped and shook her knees so that Harry's hand slipped off. She flicked at her skirt. "And now I must put on my earphones and dash off to a discussion on international germ warfare." She stood up. "Goodbye, Harry, and very good luck."

Harry had never been brushed off by a girl before. Literally brushed off in this case. He felt the flick at her skirt reducing him to a mere speck of dust. "Ashes to ashes. Dust to dust. *Vita brevis, ars longa. Ars brevis vita longa.*" Harry walked along Fifth Avenue, talking to himself in a gentle way. Since it was lunch hour and the streets were crowded, it would have taken at least a scream to attract attention.

Harry had taken off his sweater again and rolled it back into his carryall. The hot clear skies and the brilliant sun gave the scene an air of festivity. *"Nunc pede libero pulsanda tellus."* Harry was on the way to a Horn and Hardart he had always favored on Fifty-seventh Street. There, in anonymity and cool, he expected to make a plan. "Death be not proud." Donna might turn out to be a mere preliminary skirmish.

Thinking such thoughts, Harry looked up to see Flavia approaching along the pavement. Her undulating motion was unmistakable. In the enormous heat she seemed to shimmer above the ground in the manner of a desert hallucination. Was she a product of jetlag, of fevered imagination, of wishful thinking? Surely he had seen an airplane fly her away to South America?

Harry looked again. She was dressed all in white, her hair like silver wings on her shoulders. At either hand floated a small attendant, also dressed in white, also bewinged. Were they angelic beings, approaching him with heavenly intention? Or, oh tragedy, had Flavia's airplane crashed and were these beings her spirits, all that was left of her, saying a last farewell?

Such ideas occupied Harry for several seconds, during which the glorious trio continued to make progress toward him. He now saw their feet were touching the ground and that the shimmering impression was produced because they were running quite fast.

Harry stood solidly in front of them.

Flavia stopped, panting. Her expression said: Not a lunatic, please, not now.

"It's me, Harry."

"You!" Her expression changed to a childish one of shock. She looked as if she might burst into tears. "What are you doing here? Oh, it's so hot. And we're late. George will be furious!"

Her animation disconcerted Harry. He looked at the two little girls, who stared at him with unusually dark blue eyes. "How do you do?" The girls made no response.

"I can't stop," said Flavia, her voice impatient.

"You can't stop?"

"Look. Give me your address. We're here another day or two. I'll get in touch." Even as she spoke, she began to edge round him.

One of the girls, Harry noticed, was holding on to her skirt with a tight fist.

"I haven't got an address."

"Oh, Harry." She was on the other side of him now, the excitement in her face turned pale and rigid. She would be away in a second, thinking that he didn't really want to see her or Cordelia.

"I'll be here tomorrow at this time. At the same time." He looked at his watch. "One o'clock."

"One o'clock! Oh God!" She fled away. Soon her feet and the feet of her two little girls had lifted off the pavement again.

"At the round earth's imagin'd corners, blow
Your trumpets, Angels, and arise, arise . . . "

Harry ate a pastrami sandwich and a slice of pecan pie in the Horn and Hardart. He decided to cadge a bed off dull old Hugo, who used to be his tennis partner.

To his surprise, he found Hugo had married Mona. "She's preggers, can you believe it, feet swollen bigger than her stomach. But please come just the same. It'll cheer us up. We might even get good old Donna along."

"I wouldn't do that," said Harry seriously.

"Better not, you think. Nice girl, though. They're still friendly, Mona and Donna. Do you remember our first double date? Little did I think then I'd found my life's partner." Hugo laughed contentedly.

Mention of the double date reminded Harry that he'd always disliked Hugo. However, it was too late for alternate plans. "I'll be with you at six."

When Hugo opened the door to his flat, Harry recognized the expression on his face. He had worn it himself when letting in Belinda to his New York flat. She had been draped in the paraphernalia of a sixties peace protest. What could there be in his own appearance to provoke such a mixture of surprise and, perhaps, secret admiration in poor staid old Hugo?

"Hi, Hug! Kind of you to have me."

"You certainly did leave the Foreign Office." Hugo followed him into the bleakly clean living room.

"How do you mean?" Harry dumped his carryall with relief.

"You look different." Hugo had never been a whiz with words. He raised his voice. "Mona! He's here."

"How do you mean, different?"

"Your clothes."

"My clothes. What about my clothes?" Harry was beginning to get excited.

Hugo moved back a little. "Dirty. And to be quite honest, you smell."

"I smell! I smell!" Harry shrieked with laughter. He fell backward onto the sofa, still laughing.

Mona came in. She held her fat stomach in a way Harry found unconvincing. "What's the joke? Hey, give me a chance to laugh."

"Your husband says I smell," gulped Harry.

"He does." Hugo's face was very red. He couldn't think how this extraordinary situation had arisen. He had imagined a calm chat over slightly stronger than usual gin and tonics and then a jolly old-times dinner at the Italian place round the corner. He had never made a personal remark before in his life. "He does smell."

Harry's paroxysms of laughter had squeezed tears from his eyes. He, too, was red and gleaming with sweat. Mona picked up his carryall. "I'll show you to your room. It's going to be the baby's, so you'll have to forgive the pixies on the wall. Pixies seemed appropriate for either a boy or a girl."

"Unisex pixies!" Choking over the words, Harry followed Mona's sturdy bulk. But at the door he couldn't resist turning round for another glance at Hugo's obstinate, angry and bewildered face.

"Don't worry," cried Harry, "I'll use the bathroom before I reappear."

Harry sat on the edge of his bed wearing underpants. He was freshly washed, comfortable.

Hugo appeared at the door, frowning. He folded his arms. "You have upset Mona."

With an effort Harry managed to suppress further hilarity. "Sorry. Really, I'm sorry." The truth, of course, was that Hugo was upset, not Mona. Mona had always been as tough as old boots. But he was sorry for upsetting Hugo even if he was behaving like a silly ass. "It was just relief, Hugo old chap. That's why I laughed. It's so nice here and you're so kind. And I did smell. You were absolutely right. You were quite right to say so. I don't anymore, though. I've had an excellent bath in which I poured some of your Fleur de Lis bath essence. In a moment"—Harry stood up—"I shall be a truly charming English gentleman. I am sorry."

"I accept your apology." Hugo bowed stiffly.

"Perhaps I should extend it to Mona in person?"

"I don't think that will be necessary." Hugo spoke a trifle hurriedly, afraid, apparently, that Harry would approach Mona in his underpants. He and Mona had agreed that they could not kick Harry onto the streets tonight but first thing in the morning he should be sent on his way. They were both into pre-birth influences on the womb and fully agreed that Harry gave off the very worst vibes for a sensitized fetus. Neither reiterated the word "mad." "Unstable" was as far as they allowed themselves to go.

Considering such a bad start, the dinner was a success. Harry told them very amusingly about his work for Sieger. "Corruption," he said, "is so endemic in the world of films that they have no standard of right or wrong. Success or failure is the nearest they get to it. Quite a relief, in a way, although I know I should disapprove."

Inspired by Harry's example, Mona told several amusing translator's tales in which the poor delegate invariably came out looking a perfect fool. Even Hugo drank enough Bull's Blood to bring a softening to his handsome cheek and a few office jokes to his lips. "Did you hear the one about Nixon and the Irish lavatory attendant?"

That night, in bed, Mona and Hugo revised their estimate of Harry. At least Mona did the revising and Hugo assented sleepily. "He's much livelier and less patronizing than he was before. Quite honestly, he used to be a conceited prick."

"And what is he now?" mumbled Hugo.

"A crazy fellow. Fun, though."

Harry was not yet in bed. He knelt beside it with his head in his hands. "Dear God, why? Why? Why?" Tomorrow he would meet Flavia. Perhaps Cordelia too. His daughter.

The next morning over breakfast—Hugo had already left for the office—he asked Mona why she was bringing a new life into the world.

Mona was touched by his concern. She put her hand across the table to his. "Oh, Harry. I'm just a woman, biologically programmed to continue the human race. A few years ago, when I first met you, in fact, I was resentful about it. I had all kinds of strong feminist views. But once I fell in love with Hugo . . . Well, then I wanted to marry him. And the next thing I knew was this terrific urge for a baby. We're programmed, like I say. It's no good fighting."

"Then to whom should I put my question?"

"Whoever programmed us, I suppose!" Mona laughed but Harry remained serious.

"Who's that?"

"Some would say God."

"What would you say?"

"I don't believe in God."

Harry took up where he'd left off with his toast and honey. "As I understand it, programming apart, you're having a baby because you fell in love with Hugo."

Flavia approached along Fifth Avenue. Her steps were slower than the day before. She wore a sharply defined navy suit. Harry looked at her and felt nervous.

"You didn't bring the children today?"

"No."

"Not Cordelia?"

Flavia seemed surprised. "She's away. Staying with friends in Nantucket."

They were suddenly separated by a large man wearing a tartan shirt and straw hat. As he passed between them, he swore and his hand shot out to pinch Flavia's thigh. She flinched away. Harry clenched his fists. But it was all so sudden. Flavia held him back. "Don't!" The man had gone.

"Would you like to have lunch?"

"I've got till two." Flavia swiveled her watch on her wrist but did not look at it.

Sitting in the very nice Italian restaurant, Harry was struck by the impossibility of throwing a bridge to this stranger. He put his elbows on the table and stared downward with unutterable gloom.

"I'm sorry about Cordelia. I didn't know you were here."

"You were in London last week."

"I didn't know you wanted to see her."

"My mother told you."

"We were leaving then. You never answered when I wrote."

"No."

Harry noticed a slight foreign intonation in her voice. Also a trace of American.

"Do you come to North America often?"

"It's closer than England."

Harry wanted to ask her all sorts of questions but frankly hadn't the nerve. He ordered one martini and then another. Flavia, not drinking, watched him with an inscrutable expression. She was trying to remember moments of happiness in their marriage. This would have interested Harry, since his questions began: Were you happy? Were we happy? Was there love between us? Why did we have Cordelia? Why did we marry? Why did you leave?

"I hear you've become a Catholic," said Harry.

"My husband . . ." Flavia did not continue further. For her marriage to Harry, she had worn silver and decorated the church with white daisies.

"But you've become a Catholic?" His voice was loud. To Flavia it seemed like bullying. That was why she had left him.

"Yes. He wanted it."

"What did you want?"

Flavia would not answer.

"We were married, you know," said Harry irritably. "We had a child together." He poured wine into both their glasses.

"Hardly."

"What?" She had spoken quietly, barely above a whisper and, besides, Harry's emotion was blocking his hearing.

"I said we were hardly married." Flavia looked at him for the first time. Her small, not very pretty eyes stared at him accusingly. "You never loved me. Never."

"Love. Love." Now the word had been spoken, Harry fell back, battered. "We were speaking of marriage, not of love." His heart had begun to beat like a child's faced by authority. Surely he had loved her? Why else had he married her? Surely he had loved her when he had taken her to lunch at the Ritz? When he made love to her in New York, where they were now?

"Oh, well." Flavia sighed. "I loved you. But there was absolutely no point. It was a total waste of time."

Harry revived. "What about this husband of yours, then? This Catholic husband. He pours love all over you, I suppose."

"You wouldn't understand."

"Does he love you or not?" Harry drank some more wine. "That's not too much for an ex-husband, an annulled husband, to ask, is it?"

Flavia had become very pale. "He respects me."

"Respects you! Respect, is it now? But I thought it was love you wanted. Love you missed from me!"

"He does love me."

"Ah," Harry collapsed again. He muttered. "I thought as much."

"Not romantically . . ." began Flavia and then saw Harry's face. "What's the matter? You look so unhappy."

"Nothing."

"But you can't care about me anymore. You never did care even in the past. So why should you care now if my husband loves me? Anyway it's not like that. It's very hard. We try not to hurt each other." Flavia stopped again. She didn't know what she was saying. It upset her seeing Harry slumped so dejectedly over his glass. "You're drinking too much."

"There's no way out."

"What? What do you mean?"

"Nothing. There's no place for me in the world."

Flavia laughed. Harry the strong, Harry the clever, Harry the selfish, egocentric invincible, could not mean to say a thing like that. "What is the matter?"

"I had a spiritual experience when I was last in New York. That's why I flung up my job."

"I see." Flavia remembered what Wiggins had told her. Harry was mad. Till this moment it had been wiped from her memory. His physical presence had taken her back ten years with no idea of change.

As if Harry saw her thoughts he said, "Didn't my mother tell you?"

"Yes. I'm sorry."

"Sorry?"

"I don't know. Shouldn't we eat?"

Harry crumbled a bread roll. " 'Take this bread and eat of it, for this is my body . . .' Don't you want to know about my mystical experience?"

"I . . ."

"Don't worry. I'm used to it. Even the priest prefers talking about supper. But then we got off to a bad start. I was sick all over his corridor. Drunk."

"You're drinking too much now."

"Panem nostrum quotidianum."

Flavia signaled for the waiter. "I'll have the grilled veal, and my friend will have vermicelli as a main course."

"Tomorrow morning I'm going to jump off the Empire State Building."

"You can't. It's enclosed." Flavia poured herself a glass of wine.

"If that proves to be the case, I shall find somewhere else more suitable."

"Oh, Harry, why do you talk such nonsense?"

Harry waved his glass in the air. "To amuse you. To catch the attention of a happily married woman, a loved woman."

"Don't start that again." Flavia sighed and smiled with relief. For a moment she had almost taken his intensity seriously. But now she recalled his drunken exaggerations, he and Julian bounding about with youthful carelessness. He was still childish. "You should settle down."

Harry gulped his wine without acknowledgment.

Harry continued to drink after his lunch with Flavia. He went to two films, about which he remembered little. Between them he walked from midtown to Washington Square, where he sat among the chess players with a bottle of vodka. He even played a game and, irritatingly for his companions, won it easily. It seemed wiser than to pick up his bottle and leave. "Bloody know-all limey!" shouted his vanquished adversary.

It was about eleven when he arrived back at Hugo's flat. In a parody of a drunk, he banged on the door with the bottle. Hugo came anxiously, wearing pajamas and neatly sashed dressing gown.

"Sshh. Mona's asleep."

"I'm afraid I'm drunk, old boy." Harry collapsed in a chair. "Saw my wife, annulled wife, that is, for lunch and it didn't go too well. She tells me her husband loves her. Advised me to settle down."

"If I might advise you . . ."

"Advise, advise. You don't even know me. No one knows me. You're lucky, though. You're so lucky."

"Yes. Quite. Now if you would . . ." Hugo took Harry's arm in an attempt to lead him to his room.

"Don't you want to know why you're lucky?"

"Yes. I . . ."

"You're lucky because your wife loves you. That's why you're going to have little noggins surrounded by its unisex pixies. Because Mona loves you. Not because she forgot to take the Pill or the Dutch cap went back to Holland but because she loves you. Now what I want to know, what I must know . . ."

"Harry. Please!"

"Do you love her?"

"Of course, I do. Now . . ."

"There's no of course about it. I've never loved anybody. Ever. Not even Flavia. She told me that. Nobody. No one. *Niente. Nulla.*

Fucking nil." Harry fell back in the chair so suddenly that for a moment Hugo thought he had passed out. He leaned over him.

"Get out of it!" Harry's arm caught him a blow on his shoulder. "Can't you leave me alone, damn you!"

Hugo shot backward, not for fear of another blow but because Harry was crying. Stumbling against the sofa, he made for the safety of his room.

Mona sat up in bed, her eyes round and excited. "What is it? What's the matter?"

"He's drunk, that's all." Hugo rubbed his shoulder. "And now he's crying. Blubbering. It's pathetic, that's what it is. Pathetic!"

From the next room came a loud bellow, making them both turn nervously.

"I'll fucking well jump off the World Trade Center! That'll show you!"

"It's impossible," whispered Mona.

"Of course it's impossible. I told you. He's pathetic. A load of parceled-up fantasies."

They both listened again, this time to the sound of the sofa being pulled out.

"I think he's going to bed."

"Blubbering," repeated Hugo as if the word gave him pleasure. "Blubbering like a great big baby."

Chapter 12

Mona and Hugo had already left the flat when Harry staggered out of bed. He put on the same clothes he had worn the night before and gone out into the streets. He remembered it was his birthday when he bought a pair of dark glasses from a drugstore. The date was printed on the *New York Times,* but he didn't buy the paper.

Today the sky seemed unpleasantly blue. The color had intensified, but it represented the center of a storm cloud. Dark, menacing—except that the sun still shone.

Harry took off his birthday dark glasses and the sky resumed a more moderate blue. He had promised Flavia to jump off a high building and that remained his ultimate objective. Meanwhile he could not resist once more the prancing crowds of Fifth Avenue. He thought, sentimentally, that there was nowhere else that could be so accurately called "the melting pot of the world." You could meet the whole world on Fifth Avenue. You could meet your whole life.

So far he had met only Flavia, but who knew who might be next? Belinda? New York was where she'd last appeared. But now Belinda had no use for him anymore. Julian? Very likely. Wiggins? He was everywhere. His mother? She had been at her most cheerful shopping in Bergdorf Goodman. His father? The world was his oyster.

Sir Lionel Hayes-Middleton. It was not Harry's habit to contemplate his father. The only moment he could recall with real delight was his drunken escape from the car, leaving Sir Lionel driving impotently forward. Harry put on his dark glasses again, hoping to lessen the banging in his head. Then he had been drunk, now he had a hangover and the thought of a drink was nauseating.

Unfortunately he had never trained himself to drink through his hangover like other, better regulated sots.

Before entering the flood-stream of Fifth Avenue, Harry felt the need to sit down. He found a low parapet in front of a grand glass building which proclaimed itself as leader in the communications industry. He hadn't been sitting long before a policeman passed by. Harry had enough left of his respect-for-authority background to make him sit up with a guilty smile. The policeman was black and very well turned out. There were creases in his shirtsleeves as well as his trousers.

What a disgusting sight I must seem to him, thought Harry, shutting his eyes momentarily. A middle-aged Englishman, lounging in drunken idleness on a parapet. If I were him I'd feel like hauling me up and propelling me along the pavement.

The policeman passed on, impervious, but Harry, encouraged by his imagined scenario, rose shakily to his feet. "Onward, Christian soldiers!" The image of a soldier recalled Sir Lionel. Sir Lionel was a correct man, a man to whom behavior, appearance, were all-important. Lunch, for example. He believed in lunch, or rather luncheon, as an all-important pivot of the day. Harry remembered him giving a long explanation of the importance of lunch when he was still a child. He must have wanted to skip the meal. Perhaps it was during their posting in New York. Perhaps Belinda had taught him the excitement of snacks, of food snatched without ceremony, of unpremeditated eating, of non-communal guzzling, hamburgers, pizzas, pretzels and peanuts.

Harry looked for a restaurant.

The one he chose was small and Italian, a humble little trattoria in appearance. In fact its fishing nets, plastic lobsters and scenes of the Bay of Naples played a complicated game of American snobbery. It was a very expensive and fashionable restaurant.

Had the headwaiter not heard Harry's English accent he would never have permitted him across the threshold. But the English were hard to assess. Sometimes the grandest were the scruffiest in appearance.

"I'd like a double martini!" Harry tossed the words over his shoulder.

"Certainly, sir!" The headwaiter ordered his subordinates into action. Since it was early and the Englishman still the only customer, he took over the menu himself.

"I can recommend the shad roe today."

"Isn't it a bit late for shad roe?"

As he had thought, a man of the world. "We have a new source of shad that breeds a week or two later. There are some who believe it has more taste, almost a bouquet as of the waters of the Potomac."

"Potomac . . ." Harry leaned forward. "Is there a kind of battleship graveyard there? A sort of funereal dump of naval warfare. A black corner of dark water."

"Battleships. I don't think my shad roe . . ."

"Of course not." Harry leaned back again.

"One shad roe." The waiter hurried away. Battleships? Battleships? He was soon diverted by the usual twelve-thirty rush of arrivals.

Harry enjoyed his meal, for the martini had immediately returned him to drunkenness. Life seemed agreeably removed once again, the pain of his thoughts subdued into bearable dullness. A half bottle of white wine added to this sensation.

For this reason he was less disconcerted than he might have been when he found he was not carrying enough money to pay the bill. He had given up credit cards years ago and his checkbook was English and in his suitcase. He stabbed the bill accusingly.

"This is a ridiculous sum! There must be a mistake."

The restaurant was full. The waiter bowed. "I shall have it checked for you, sir."

The headwaiter returned. "The total is correct, sir."

"Impossible! A few fish eggs and a glass of booze!" Harry stood up belligerently.

The headwaiter's heart went cold within him. How had he been deceived by this impostor, this madman, this drunk? Was he no longer a good judge of appropriate clientele? What could he do now? Such a disturbance would not be appreciated by the other diners. He glanced round nervously.

Harry pulled out what dollars he found in his pocket. He was walking from the table, expostulating, gesticulating. "These little Italian bistros certainly get above themselves!"

The headwaiter, eyes black with defeat, held out his hand. The notes, few as they were, were bundled into his palm. One dropped to the floor. Allowing a moment of emotion, he ground it under his heel. It was only one dollar.

Harry strode out into the heat and glare and worse. He was indignant still, unaware of any triumph. The world was against him. He took up again his journey to the World Trade Center.

After a few more blocks he turned east. Looking toward the

East River, he could see the image that had always excited him—the tall buildings and the slice of river in between. It was less dramatic now because he was farther away and at ground level but still he longed for that moment when a ship passed, piece by disjointed piece. At last it came. Prow, funnel, bow. Never joining, the reverse of the conjurer's box. A bit of magic that only the imagination could put together.

Harry received some very funny looks from passersby as he stood on the pavement staring and smiling from ear to ear. He didn't notice. He was back on course for the Trade Center.

Harry's was almost the last ticket sold that day for the top of the Trade Center. Luckily he had taken the precaution of emptying only one pocket into the waiter's hand. He went up against the stream, breasting his way through crowds of chattering tourists, like the prow of a boat through rough waters. By the time he reached the top of the last escalator, there remained only a small backwash of Japanese and a fat girl eating popcorn.

It was exhilarating to be standing so far into the sky. His head spun and he put on his dark glasses. The sky was no longer glittering bright but a dull Prussian blue, thickening to gray. He walked to the midtown view, where a clutch of turreted buildings poked into the sky like a Disney wonderland. Between them, far below, threaded the ruler lines of road, filled, at this rush hour end of day, by scarcely moving lozenges of color. On either side moving faster in tiny black procession were the homeward-going workers. Little black wriggling things, thought Harry, with a thankful sense of dissociation. Like sperm rushing up in tail-wagging enthusiasm for the womb.

How grand he felt standing up so high above them, king of his own castle! How enormous he was compared to them! Above the whole world, nearer his Maker, a God of a sort himself. Harry looked closer in order to identify Fifth Avenue. There it was, a channel of endless, useless movement, along which the whole world swam. Now his eye was more accustomed to the looking he felt almost capable of spotting individual characteristics. Boy or girl? Was Flavia there, with her silly gliding walk?

Suddenly disgusted with the prospect of writhing humanity, Harry walked briskly round to the other side of the tower. This was better. He expelled breath and lifted his head. Here was space and peace, the Statue of Liberty, a noble image of Liberté, Fraternité, Egalité. But what was that at its feet? A crinkle paper of water, its creases catching the dull gleam of late sun. And just above its rank and oily depths were little boats speeding like black beetles. Behind them they left a spider web of silver but that was soon dragged under and despoiled. Where were they going? How hot it was! Stifling. Harry grabbed at his shirt collar and gulped for air.

And now even peace was threatened. For from the horizon and approaching rapidly came a mosquito's buzz of noise. A trio of helicopters or perhaps more, circling over the water as if it were a jungle swamp. Fetid, steaming . . . Harry put his hands to his head. Why did nothing make sense? At the beginning he had asked no questions. And now he asked questions and got no answers. He was given only the stink of the world, the stench of humanity. The fact of birth with nothing to alleviate the blood and pain.

Harry threw up his hands in diving position and opened his mouth to scream. . . .

There was no way Harry could jump off the top of the Trade Center. First, there is a smallish fence leaning inward. Then there is a moat-like runnel about five feet deep, and finally there is a second, much higher parapet. Only then comes the edge. Besides that, there is a guard on constant duty. Harry could scream, however, which he did very loudly. The guard was instantly alert (even though it was the end of a long hot day) and bounding toward him. As it turned out, he was not first on the scene.

"Here, I say."

Dazed by his own scream, Harry took a moment or two before he recognized Hugo. Hugo was, after all, spectacularly unimportant.

"Are you crazy or sumpin?" The guard arrived. He gripped his nightstick pugnaciously. He was only doing his duty.

"It's all right, officer." Hugo wore a tailored suit, and his handsome face suggested sensible concern. "His mother's died. I just told him."

"His mother . . . You chose a great location for that piece of news."

"I was trying," muttered Harry, standing dazedly between them, "to jump off."

Neither guard nor Hugo paid any attention to such idiocy.

"At all events you should go down now. We're closing."

"Fine. Fine. I appreciate your understanding."

The two Englishmen were ushered off the roof.

"You didn't have to say that about my mother." Harry and

Hugo stood alone in the elevator, which was dropping at a slightly slower rate than its prerequisite twenty miles per hour owing to a blustery wind recently arrived.

"The guard might have arrested you."

"I didn't know what you're doing here anyway."

"I came to tell you."

"What do you mean? I think I might be sick."

"Mona guessed you'd be here."

Harry put his head between his knees. The position gave him an odd sense of security—despite an upside-down view of the Statue of Liberty.

"I got the message at the office. You know what it's like. I'd said you were staying. So when the news came through they knew who to tell."

"What do you mean?"

"She died late last night. English time last night. She never recovered consciousness. The time change makes it awkward."

The elevator came to the bottom with a high-tech lack of reverberation. Harry recalled his head from his knees. "Are you telling me my mother is dead?"

"Yes. Of a heart attack."

"You weren't just making it up to pacify that gorilla on the roof?"

"That's correct."

"I must go home."

"I took the liberty of booking you a flight."

"Thank you. Thank you for everything. I hope all this hasn't disturbed Mona in her delicate condition."

"Not at all. She's very fond of you. She was determined I should find you."

"Very kind indeed."

The two men got into a yellow taxi.

Harry presented a respectable and orderly appearance on his return journey. Mona saw to that. But his head was anything but orderly. It whirled with confused images. Like a kaleidoscope set to favor one scene, it constantly returned to that evening in Cairo when Beatrice had been carried out on a stretcher to the hospital. How old was he then? He couldn't remember. A child, already separated from his parents by boarding school, but still a child, a boy who in that moment had felt himself utterly abandoned by his mother.

Harry borrowed three aspirin from the stewardess and ordered two bottles of soda water. Why should his mother commit suicide now? Father Bernard would not be at all pleased.

The first thing Harry noticed when he arrived at his parents' house was the absence of his mother. It made him realize that he had never seen his father at home without his mother.

Lionel had a terrible expression on his face. Harry remembered it from those displaced refugees he had seen in Jordan. He hardened his heart a little. There was nothing he could offer now, any more than he had been able to then.

Father and son stood on either side of the mantelpiece.

"Have a drink?" said Lionel.

"No thanks."

Uncontrollable whirling stars burst in Harry's head. "Why did she do it?"

Lionel took a step backward. His face contorted as if he were going to have a stroke. "Why did she do what? What do you mean?"

"I don't know." Harry wanted to bang his head against the wall. He wanted to smash away all the pain, the stabbings and crashing. Instead he laughed hysterically. He saw the sound coming out in a stream of light and color like exploding fireworks. "She did commit suicide, didn't she? Like she tried to before? But this time she succeeded. Unlike some of us. Unlike some of us. Lucky her, that's what I say! That's what I say!"

"What? What?" Lionel's face twisted and writhed in a quite extraordinary way. "What do you mean? You think Beatrice committed suicide? But of course she didn't. She was ill. She died. Late last night in bed. She had a heart attack. Her heart had been bad for a long time. But we never thought . . . Why should she commit suicide? She was happy with me. She loved me!" As Lionel produced the last words his face formed one last surge and then dissolved into a shimmering mass of emotion. "Oh God! Oh God! Oh God! I loved her too. I loved her . . ."

The fireworks inside Harry's head ceased abruptly. His father was crying in front of him, an elderly man of distinction and some pomp, crying like a child in front of him. Blubbering, heartbroken, talking about love.

Harry sat down on a chair.

Lionel's eyes, innocent like a child's, looked at Harry.

There then appeared in front of Harry an image of himself with his arms round his father comforting him. The distance between them was only a few feet.

Harry was aware he was playing for time, hoping for some kind of escape.

But as he registered these thoughts, a new sensation, like a heavy mass inside him, forced itself slowly and painfully to the surface. In a moment Harry found tears were running down his face, accompanied by a convulsive heaving of his own body. He thought of his mother as chalk wiped from a blackboard.

So it was Lionel who came over to Harry and put an arm round his shoulders. It lay there, warm and heavy, the comforting yoke of paternity that he had never felt before.

Chapter 26

It was early morning. Lionel was making tea in the kitchen. He carried two cups upstairs and knocked on Harry's door. He opened the door to a quick scuffling as Harry got back into bed. He had been on his knees. Lionel did not notice this, presuming Harry's startled expression referred to the sight of the tea.

"Your mother liked a cup fairly early." He approached the bed. "So I supplied it. Since my retirement, that is. Your mother was not at her best in the morning."

Harry had been praying. "Make me understand, O Lord." He took the tea and put it on the bedside table.

"I fear I made her very unhappy."

"I wouldn't say that. She was frightfully upset that day she came to see you in Paddington. But that was unusual. I think she was angry with herself for being angry. She didn't like showing emotion."

"No."

"She didn't take responsibility for you."

"No."

"She was quite in awe of you, actually."

Harry sat up stiffly. He felt his face turning red like a child's. "But she was my mother!"

"There's nothing that says you can't be in awe of your own child." Lionel took a firmer girp on his cup and saucer and walked to the door. "I'll see you in about an hour."

Although Beatrice had died at home in her bed, her body had been immediately removed to a hospital. Harry wondered at the idea behind this pointless procedure. It was presumably to avoid the macabre presentation of death. Yet how much harder it made the necessary realization. He was reminded of the death of Bridget in his bed in New York. Then he had waited anxiously for the ambulance.

Harry and Sir Lionel went to see Father Bernard about arrangements for Beatrice's funeral. Lionel, as a non-believer, hoped to feel supported by his son's presence—however unorthodox his views. Lionel was fighting a desire to see his girlfriend. He needed someone to comfort him for Beatrice's loss. He found it a strain being with Harry, whose face and emotional density reminded him more and more of his wife's.

"Welcome! Welcome! A sad time for you, of course, and yet we must remember that your wife believed in eternal life, not eternal death." Father Bernard was more animated than Harry had ever seen him. He glanced to catch his father's reaction and caught him glancing too.

"Good afternoon, Father. As you see, my son has flown back from New York."

It was extraordinary, thought Harry, that these two men managed to communicate in any way. They had age in common but almost nothing else. One had tried to serve the world, the other the spirit.

"I know nothing about the Catholic funeral service," said Sir Lionel.

Father Bernard took them along to his little visiting room. There was no talk of the garden, although it was a pleasant autumn morning.

"Your wife was perfectly clear. She wanted a full Requiem Mass. She even chose the hymns."

"What hymns?" asked Harry curiously.

The priest looked vague. "I have it written down—there is a French one, I believe. Or did she abandon that finally?"

"Was she so certain of her death?" Lionel's hands trembled slightly as he brushed them over the top of his head.

"We all have to die. At any rate, you need not worry about arrangements. Except, that is, for the twofold question of a homily and an address."

"I'm afraid I'm not quite clear . . . ?".

"A homily is in the nature of a sermon. The theme is death, naturally, the outlook Christian. One hopes to touch the heart. It is usually delivered by one in holy orders."

"And an address?"

"An address is traditionally delivered by a family friend, someone who . . ."

"Father, you know what an address is! 'Friends, Romans, Countrymen!' "

Sir Lionel seemed curiously unmanned by this meeting with a priest.

Sir Lionel revived as they left the church. "A man like that is beyond my understanding." His voice boomed out so that Harry glanced behind him nervously. But the door was already closed. "Do you understand him?"

"I understand nothing."

Lionel ignored this. "To put all your eggs in one basket quite so completely. It smacks of stupidity. Or at very least a limited intelligence."

"Intelligence isn't everything."

Again Harry was ignored. "Come to think of it, in my long career around the world, in the course of which I've met a huge variety of ecclesiastics, all apparently at the top of their chosen tree, I've never, not once, met a really outstandingly intelligent man. That can't be a coincidence, can it? Educated minds occasionally, inquiring minds even more occasionally but true socking intelligence, alpha double plus, Fellow of All Souls, standing ovation at your viva, never. Never!"

"Their Church was founded by a carpenter."

"Quite." Lionel's spirits were much restored. "The Church has a place in society, of course, though probably a diminishing one, but it must be seen for what it is."

"What is that?"

"What?"

"What is the Church?"

"A temporal institution. All Churches are the same. Staffed by second-raters with a penchant for mysticism. No doubt it attracts a higher rate of good men. I have no doubt Father—what's he called?—is a good man."

Harry sighed.

"Certainly your mother thought so. She wrote to him from around the world. She relied on him. She visited him. As you see, she confided in him her belief that she would die."

Now Harry understood his father's dejection when faced by Father Bernard. He was his only rival. Beatrice's secret lover in a spiritual sense but no less emotional for that. Lionel was suffering from jealousy.

"Mother believed a priest spoke with the voice of God."

"How do you know?" Lionel's voice was sharp. "Did you talk about it?"

"All Catholics believe that. She was a Catholic."

"Catholic! Catholic! We weren't even married in a Catholic church."

"Oh, Father."

"Huh." They walked on several silent paces. Then Lionel turned to confront Harry. "Your mother was fond of this essentially Irish cleric, so we'll give her the sort of funeral he says she wanted. And that's an end to it."

"Yes," agreed Harry. "We must do what she wanted now."

After an announcement in *The Times,* the postman began bringing packages of letters. Harry was amazed. He had thought of his mother as a solitary woman. He had never taken her role as diplomat's wife seriously, seeing it as a kind of façade, a game which people played to pass the time. But now it seemed this game had been her life. People spoke of her sympathy, her support in charitable projects, even her energy. Harry saw that she was one half of a relatively public Figure, that the church would be full and that this required organization which must be his responsibility.

Father Bernard's image of the occasion, his hymns and homilies, was only one side of the picture.

Harry invited Wiggins and Julian to act as ushers and then, sweeping further, found Salmon and, more remarkably, his deserting Uncle Johnny. Johnny appeared at lunchtime in a pub on the King's Road. Henry was waiting to meet Julian. Standing with half a pint of bitter, he became aware of a spot of intensity somewhere on the other side of the bar. His mind on funeral arrangements, he did not pinpoint the face for a while. There was just a sense of something turned tensely toward him.

Julian was late. Harry put down his glass, focused on the world around and recognized his Uncle Johnny—last seen fleeing the Irish homestead.

"Uncle Johnny!"

The face contracted and ducked almost below the counter.

Harry hastened round to him. "What a coincidence!"

Eyes blinked at him, as if tearful. Harry saw he was consumed with guilty anxiety. "Don't worry. I'm not angry with you for leaving me in the lurch like that. I'd have done the same."

"It was my chance, old chap. My last chance." Johnny's face expanded a little, though he remained wary.

"And not a bad price you got for it," said Harry heartily. "I was glad of my cut."

"Your cut?"

"Yes. You generously gave me a percentage."

"So I did. So I did." It was apparent Johnny's guilt had wiped out its antidote. He smiled with relief and called out at the barmaid, "Shirley, another glass for the both of us and allow me to introduce my favorite nephew—a queer enough fellow but possessing a stout heart!"

Harry noticed that whereas in Ireland his uncle had been gloomy and English, here in England he was ebullient and Irish.

Julian and Harry were meeting in order to visit the church. Salmon had promised to join them also but it seemed unlikely Wiggins would be able to leave the House. When Johnny heard the afternoon's plans, he insisted on coming along.

"There's no one who knows more about death than myself! Didn't I lose my own dear wife in the prime of life? Her prime, that is. Mine is yet to come!"

Julian thought he was great fun. "Of course you must come! You're family. I can't think why Harry's kept you hidden all these years. I never understood before now why he kept sneaking off to Ireland."

The church was dark but not empty. To Harry's surprise, Wiggins was already there, pacing up and down at the back with an impatient expression. As they appeared, he turned back the cuff to his gray suit. "You are half an hour late. Over half an hour late."

"Wiggins! How very nice of you!"

"Do not call me that."

"What?" said Harry, who had turned back to find his uncle, apparently lost in wonder over a holy-water font.

"Wiggins. My name is David. Of course I'm here. I was very fond of both your parents. I saw them only a couple of weeks ago. This is a very sad occasion."

This last remark seemed to be aimed particularly at Johnny, who was now sliding along the polished parquet.

"I'm afraid he's had too much to drink," said Harry, "but he insisted on coming and he is my uncle."

"Your uncle."

"My father's sister's husband. She died a few years ago and I fear it may be bringing back memories." This seemed a brilliant stroke to Harry, but Wiggins remained unconvinced.

"Of ice-skating in church, apparently."

"He wants to be an usher," contributed Julian, who up till now had contented himself with the satisfactions of a spectator.

"Hello, Julian," said Wiggins unenthusiastically. Why had he cut a meeting of a subcommittee on Urban Commercial Renewal to be with this bunch of dropouts? Why? An image of Beatrice's face floated before him. The calm, the beauty, the elegance. That was why. And then Julia had told him he must. It was not for Harry anymore. Harry's behavior, his lack of serious purpose, had put him beyond the pale a long time ago. And now this drunken uncle!

Johnny skated to a halt in front of the assembled ushers. He addressed Wiggins as the obvious leader. "There is something remarkable about this afternoon. Something which I wish to share with you. A sense in which this occasion is unique."

Although his wispy gray hair stood on end and his face was swollen and red and his jacket lacked buttons, there was a reverence in his tone. Even Wiggins was convinced. All three men waited respectfully. Here, after all, was a man, however disreputable on the surface, who had gone through the agony of losing a beloved partner. Wiggins inclined his head to indicate close attention.

"Despite a lifetime spent in the Holy Mother Ireland, a lifetime minus five percent or perhaps ten percent allowing for an English education, this is the very first, the very first time that I . . ." his voice slowed, deepened and became filled with awe . . . "that—I—have—crossed—the portals—of a Papist church!"

Reaction to this inappropriate personal revelation was interrupted by a loud bang as someone entered the main door of the church.

"Sorry. Sorry. Kept you waiting. Thought it was the grand St. Mary's by my club. So sorry."

Everybody had forgotten about Salmon. He too looked as if he'd had a glass or two at lunch but the well-tailored tweeds, the smoothed-down hair, the genial expression, now a little anxious, inspired confidence. Here was another man of the world. Wiggins, who had despised Salmon at school, welcomed him with relief. "Good to see you, Salmon. Looking prosperous as ever."

"I don't know about prosperous. Fat is true enough. Hello, Harry. I am sorry about your mother. Must have been a terrible shock. Wish mine had dropped off instead." He turned to Wiggins. "She lives with us, you know."

This sentiment also struck Wiggins as shocking bad taste, but

Harry was not there to hear it. He had wandered a little way up the center aisle, where he stood, apparently deep in thought.

"Shall we get started, then?" called Wiggins.

"Hear! Hear!" said Johnny.

Harry lifted his head. He said with an air of surprise, "This is where I last saw my mother." The others came closer. "She walked down the aisle. I was kneeling here." He demonstrated. "When she was level with me, she stared straight at me. Unfortunately she didn't recognize me." He looked up. "Or if she did she pretended not to."

There was a silence. Salmon rubbed his chin and then his eyes. "Women are very deep."

Wiggins looked at his watch again. He couldn't bear the sight of Harry on his knees, hunched over, possibly praying.

Julian lifted Harry to his feet. "Upsy-daisy, old chap. Everybody's waiting."

Harry, who'd been about to enjoy the luxury of prayer, pulled himself together. He extracted a piece of paper from his trouser pocket and began to explain their various duties. Wiggins on the door, he thought. Salmon as his first lieutenant. Julian and Johnny on either aisle and himself somewhere near the front.

Wiggins took notes. He was pleased with the idea of himself under the porch welcoming men of importance in the diplomatic world. There might even be a Minister or two. "That seems pretty straightforward."

"Just fill up the pews, eh!" said Johnny cheerfully. "Like peas in a pod."

"Putting the most important people at the front," added Julian, "or they'll be furious."

"And someone should take names for the *Telegraph,*" said Salmon. "You know, we could do with another couple of ushers."

"I don't know anyone else."

"Richard would help. Just think of him in tails!"

Harry turned away from them and walked back up the aisle. Father Bernard appeared from behind a pillar. He looked uneasy, almost shifty. "Going all right, is it?"

"Yes, Father. None of them is Catholic."

"Well, that is a little unusual."

"We won't know when to stand or sit or cross ourselves."

The priest allowed a small pause. "It's what your mother wanted. A full Requiem Mass."

"Frankly, it might all turn out to be rather embarrassing. I mean, no one knew my mother was Catholic."

"Embarrassing? I can't quite accept that a Mass could ever be 'embarrassing.' "

"As a social event, it might be embarrassing."

"Ah, well. As a social event. That's not my field. Perhaps you're right. As a social event. Perhaps your father should have taken that into account."

Harry saw that for the first time in a conversation with the priest he had met conviction. He glanced back at where his friends waited restlessly by the door. "I must introduce you to my Uncle Johnny," he said. "He used to own a farm near Cork."

"Cork! Cork!" Father Bernard clapped Harry on the shoulder. "Now don't tell me a Cork man doesn't know when to get down on his knees!"

Lionel's sense of loss increased. The suddenness of Beatrice's death, the return of Harry, had at first put him in a bearable state of shock. But after three days and with two more before the funeral, he began to suffer a dangerous sense of dislocation. He no longer slept, his hands shook, he could not read and he could not concentrate long enough to finish a sentence or even listen to somebody else's sentence. He no longer thought about visiting his girlfriend. When she telephoned he did not recognize her voice. His main occupation was a kind of blind shuffling of the letters of condolence—blind in the sense that, having read them once, he did not reread them but laid them out around his chair in carefully ordered yet changing piles.

It reminded Harry of his childhood when his father had always sat surrounded by "papers" needing constant and urgent attention. There had been the famous occasion when the papers had lifted themselves off the deck of the ship and flown out to sea. Their attempted rescue had nearly caused the death of several young seamen. Now the papers had no life except that given them by Lionel.

On the day before the funeral Harry found him playing with the guest lists in the same compulsive fashion. Harry had just picked up the printed order of service. He showed one to his father. "I'm afraid there are errors," he said. "There was so little time. But I think, in general, they've done a good job."

Lionel took the paper but Harry could see he wasn't properly reading even that. "Beatrice Hayes-Middleton," he murmured. "We were very close most of the time. About most things."

"Yes, you were."

Lionel's face lightened fractionally. "You were aware of that?"

"Yes," repeated Harry.

"She was so young when I married her. And naturally I don't believe in an afterlife."

"I'm afraid I don't quite follow."

"It's unfortunate to be separated by belief after so long."

"But if you don't believe in an afterlife then you've accepted the idea of being separated anyway, in death."

"But she does believe in it. If it comes to that, I suppose you do too." Lionel heaved himself up in his chair and stared accusingly. "Do you?"

"I don't know."

Lionel slumped down again as if disappointed. His attention was caught by one of the piles of letters. He picked it up and read out the first two lines: "Dear Sir Lionel, Beatrice was a woman of supreme beauty."

He tapped the paper. "There's a letter for you. Number one. 'Of supreme beauty.' That was your mother. Not only of face, it goes without saying, but of disposition also. This is an excellent letter!"

Harry bent over the piles. There was nothing from Flavia, although she had been informed of Beatrice's death. He looked at his father. "Are you putting them in order of merit?"

But Lionel wouldn't answer. In order to get his attention again, Harry said in a firm voice, "I have a very strong belief in God, as I presume Mother did, and I am also convinced of"—he paused, "the possibility of eternal life."

Since there was no response Harry had begun to withdraw in the direction of the drinks table when he was surprised by a wild cry from his father. "Stubborn! Stubborn! Stubborn! Both of you. Why can't you be like everyone else and be satisfied with the world!"

Harry stood still.

"With the whole world. The whole world." His voice shuddered into sobs.

Harry looked at his father and looked at the drinks table. He went over to the table and poured two whiskies.

Harry took a look at the manuscript of his father's autobiography. It was piled on a table in the spare room where he slept. Although unfinished, it already made a substantial monument to his life. "Chapter One. *Empire Made.*" He flicked to the bottom. "Chapter Twenty. *Common Market for Common People.*" He was nearly at the end. Why did such a formal man reach for such popularist titles?

Harry sat down at the table and tried to read it. "Chapter Four. *A New World in New York.*" But instead his mind wandered to his mother's one effort at self-expression. Where was that manuscript? *Flight from the Guillotine.* It might be in the cupboard or the chest of drawers.

Harry banged about the spare room. But what he found was a box of very decrepit lead cars and a painting of the Virgin and Child wrapped in brown paper. The painting must have miraculous qualities, he thought, since he had certainly abandoned it in his little room in Paddington. Or had his mother gone there secretly and removed it? It looked no better than it ever had. Indeed the patina over the print was wearing thin in places, giving it the vulnerable look of the recently balding.

He wrapped it back in its brown paper and returned it to the cupboard. The cars, though less than in the past, made a very respectable traffic jam on top of the dressing table. He remembered how he had forced his mother to drive a Bentley with one door. It had probably been the peak of their emotional contact, certainly from his point of view. And it had happened in this very room. Harry stretched out on the bed with his arms behind his head and stared at the row of battered little cars.

Johnny had moved into the Hayes-Middleton house. He had arrived with his case. When he addressed Lionel he used a thick Irish accent. This enabled Lionel to treat his brother-in-law as if he were a long-established house servant. He ignored his presence in any positive sense but accepted cups of tea with polite detachment. Johnny took over the kitchen.

Harry said to him, "I don't mind your staying. But you can't be drunk all day."

"I do not drink till five. It is the rule of my widowhood." Johnny was dignified.

"You were drunk in that pub at lunchtime."

"That was an exception. I was under the weather."

"Whatever do you mean?"

"I was fighting a cold."

"You haven't got a cold."

"I won the battle." Johnny laughed uproariously. It was after five o'clock.

Chapter 27

The church was not very welcoming, nor, perhaps, grand enough for the friends of Sir Lionel Hayes-Middleton. It was built of concrete, an early postwar example of new brutalism. Inside, the insignias of faith, the statues, plaques, candles, flowers, gave it a livelier, more agreeable air. Outside, the spirit of the Lord failed to shine.

The Mass is a celebration, thought Harry, who was standing on the steps outside. A gray sheen of damp road, pavement and houses stretched in front of him. He was waiting for the hearse.

"It should be here any minute." Wiggins had taken over. As visitors arrived he whisked them past the ruminative Harry and up the aisle. There the other ushers bounded into action, making, at a snap, long-reaching decisions about the appropriate pew. Harry had watched for a while and then come outside to wait.

Behind him he heard the organist swing into a brisk rendering of Bach's Fantasia and Fugue in G minor. He was a student, recommended by Father Bernard, and he too seemed filled with energy. Harry hoped he would not be too much for the choir, who had been described by Father Bernard as "loyal but no longer young."

Diverted by such thoughts, Harry failed to notice the funeral procession—if two cars could be called that. They had crept up on him, black and glistening like two huge slugs encouraged out by the rain. He had seen them just like that on Irish country roads.

The first car halted in front of him with a long sigh. The second stopped. Inside it sat Lionel and Johnny. That was unexpected. Surely Johnny was to be an usher? Yet there he sat, or rather now rose, as close to Lionel as if he were holding his hand. The driver opened the door for them.

Four men had appeared from the first car. They were preparing to take out the coffin, which was topped with a froth of flowers reminiscent of a well-risen soufflé. Harry wondered which impossibly large bouquet was Sieger's. A telegram had arrived from him that morning.

> My deepest sorrow, Harry, for the passing of a great lady.
> My flowers will be there even if I may not.

He had never met Beatrice.

There was still no word from Flavia.

The men lifted the coffin onto their shoulders. Harry's heart gave such a lurch that it seemed the steps, pavement, road and cars had moved around him. The undertakers' contact with the coffin had produced an image of his mother's body lying inside. He swayed forward and stumbled.

Father Bernard caught his arm. Harry shook him off. The coffin passed. He joined his father and Johnny and walked behind. Those guests already there rose as they entered the church. His father appeared completely emotionless.

The coffin was set in front of the altar rails. Sir Lionel took his seat in the front pew.

"Three minutes." Wiggins appeared at his side.

"I'll go now," the priest whispered. "Got your reading safe?"

"Yes, Father."

Sir Lionel looked sideways at his son. In his hired morning dress, he appeared once more as he used to be: an intelligent, well-educated man with a distinguished future, though no longer quite so young. Like his father. Lionel's diplomatic mask twitched a little as if someone pulled at the corner. He wished the service would start. He remembered with a wrench in the region of his heart how he had picked Beatrice out of that crowd of pink-cheeked debutantes in 1939. He had loved her because she was different and remained so, never quite fitting in wherever they might travel. Always a little secret and a little unhappy (sometimes a little more than a little unhappy, but Lionel did not dwell on that) and now dead. Far before her time. She was hardly over fifty.

A bell rang in the side aisle and Johnny laid his hand on Lionel's arm. They stood together and the congregation followed their example. At last the service was beginning. Lionel raised his eyes above the flower-decked coffin, which reminded him of a funeral pyre on the ghats at Benares. He looked firmly toward the altar. Four young boys entered with downcast eyes. The hems of their robes bounced off their brightly colored trainers. Behind them came Beatrice's priest, his thin tufty hair smoothed sideways, his vestments making him impressive in a way he could never be in life.

"Wonderful turnout!" whispered Johnny.

Lionel inclined his head in acknowledgment. It was his turnout. Diplomats, peers, politicians, publishers and businessmen. Only last week he had been offered a useful directorship in the city. But the service, the Mass, the priest with his boys belonged to Beatrice.

"In the name of the Father, Son and Holy Spirit . . ." The English came as a surprise to almost everyone in the church. They had been expecting something more foreign, more distinguished. The few Catholics crossed themselves in a self-conscious manner. Julian's friend Richard was one of these. So he comes from Goa, thought Harry, cast back for a second into the role of diplomat with global understanding. Unusual for one so educated.

The mass proceeded. Harry took out his reading from his breast pocket. He had chosen it himself. He smoothed out the paper, and, as he did so, remembered the visit his mother had paid him in his New York bedroom. He had been studying the Bible and had confided in her his sense of Divine Revelation. But she had been angry. Or had seemed angry. Why?

Harry went up to the pulpit.

"A reading from the prophet Isaiah. 'On this mountain . . .' "

Harry looked up to see the black costumes of the world." " 'This is the word of the Lord.' " He returned to his seat.

To his surprise Julian now rose, clutching a piece of paper. The idea of Julian in a pulpit was absurd.

"A reading from the letter of St. Paul to the Romans."

He read heroically, as if auditioning or trying to reach the hard-of-hearing. "For I am certain of this: neither death nor life, no angel, no prince, nothing that exists, nothing still to come, nor any power . . ."

He, too, looked up at the finish and he waited as if for applause. But the silence of the old, the sad, the unawakened, was only disturbed by a cough and a whisper.

Father Bernard crossed briskly in front of the altar. The four boys in their white surplices got cheerfully to their feet and the congregation rose, too, gathering momentum like a badly rehearsed chorus.

"Jesus explained, 'I bless you, Father, Lord of heaven and

earth, for hiding these things from the learned and the clever and revealing them to mere children . . .' "

Harry glanced at his father and saw an expression of stoicism. It was a face he recalled from as far back as Ceylon when white-uniformed schoolgirls paraded before His Majesty's representative. It suggested a wall-like strength of endurance, which was not unhelpful.

Beyond Lionel, Johnny folded his arms, possibly in protest.

" 'Come to me, all you who labor and are overburdened,' " read the priest in unemphatic tones—although the Irish in him turned up the sentences—'and I will give you rest.' "

After the gospel, thought Harry, comes the homily. The congregation sat down. At last an air of expectancy charged the pews. Wiggins leaned forward, hands clasped, eyes bright. This was a speech, something he understood.

"A-hem." Father Bernard muddled anxiously among his notes. Then he bowed his head.

"Lost his way, poor old fellow," Johnny whispered loudly to Lionel.

"He's praying," hissed Harry.

Lionel's stoical face did not change. Nor did Wiggins's attitude of expectancy. He was used to every kind of speaker, the slow starter, the pause-for-emphasis, the lowering, raising, altering-of-tone-for emphasis, the anxiety-to-express-concern. Sometimes a speaker fulfilled every one of these criteria in a single performance. Wiggins himself favored the direct man-to-man approach. But then he was a socialist. Leaving aside Latin America, the Catholic hierarchy could be safely categorized as conservative. Conservatives believe in the slow start as an indication of confidence and superiority. In this case, the priest seemed to be making a combination of the slow start and anxiety-to-express-concern.

At Wiggins's side, Julia had recourse to the Order of Service. She felt protected against the threat of death by the baby growing inside her. Nevertheless, she still made a conscious effort to eschew morbid thoughts for its sake. How handsome Harry looked in his morning suit!

"I will give you rest." Father Bernard's repetition of the last line of the gospel was unconvincing. He raised his voice. "John Henry Newman." He paused. "Cardinal Newman." He paused again. Now he had collected some listeners. The words of a Prince of the Church were a vastly different matter from the utterances of a humble parish priest.

"Newman wrote, 'Here we are tossing upon the sea, and the wind is contrary.' " The priest looked up now, reciting by heart. " 'All through the day we are tried and tempted in various ways. We cannot think, speak or act, but infirmity and sin are at hand. But in the unseen world, where Christ has entered, all is peace.' "

Father Bernard looked down at his notes. The quotation was ended. The congregation relaxed. "Peace," he said again.

Repetition-for-emphasis, noted Wiggins, plus pause.

Harry remembered the priest's admitting to a terror of death.

"Beatrice Marie Hayes-Middleton has found that peace. She is no longer of this world. We have here in front of us her body, the poor vessel in which she tossed upon the seas."

" 'Tossed,' " Julian mouthed the word to himself. What a truly Victorian word! What a truly emotional word. If only modern writers dared to such heights of bathos.

"We honor it now," continued Father Bernard, making some wonder to what the "it" referred, "as we loved it in life. But we should not feel pity. For we too are left behind, still troubled, still tempted, still living in infirmity and sin. Yet we, like her, can achieve peace, rest. How can this be?"

Oh ho! Wiggins' eyes glinted. Rhetorical question. Unexpected this. Not easy to pull off.

A lecture, thought Lionel. Do I need a lecture? One of Beatrice's virtues was that she never lectured. She did not even acknowledge what she disliked. She simply removed herself. Yet she had left this deputy to lecture. Over her dead body.

This'll show them, thought Harry, and quickly rejected the idea. How fumbling Father Bernard looked. How uninspiring!

Johnny blew his nose and Julian raised his eyes to heaven. Richard, catching the upward roll, smiled ironically. He knew Julian's doubts, desires and sentimental core. "Poseur," he whispered. "You know you love it."

"Death, you may say. By dying you will find peace. Death is the answer. But that is not the peace that Cardinal Newman meant or the 'rest' about which Saint Matthew wrote. Death is merely the gateway, the fearsome gateway to something quite else."

Now he's lost them, thought Harry. Why couldn't he talk about love and eternal bliss?

"The spirit," said Father Bernard without much enthusiasm. "It is our spiritual nature about which Matthew and Newman write and it is the travails of our spiritual nature which find peace after death. God the Father gave us his son in death and resurrection to see that this should be so."

"Pity he doesn't talk more about Beatrice," commented Johnny in his loud whisper.

Captive audience, replied one part of Lionel's mind, but he said nothing.

"He does, however, demand our cooperation."

There was a slight heaving at this word, as if the congregation recognized the switch to active participation. Those who were less in touch hoped vaguely that they would be able to avoid this "He," whoever He might be.

"First of all, He demands we recognize our spiritual nature."

In the second row a distinguished Ambassador hiccoughed in unambiguous protest.

Lionel fixed his eye on Beatrice's coffin. Why had she made this happen? Why these sudden demands? In life, she had been a most undemanding human being, almost selfless.

"This sounds easy," continued the priest in his unassuming yet inexorable way. "But for many the recognition of a spiritual nature is an impossible leap into the unknown. It fills them with terror. They would rather face emptiness and despair than plunge into the vastness of the infinite. They try to imitate the animal, the dog, the cat, the cow, and find happiness in certainty. For them death is the certainty. Death is the end." He paused.

"But Beatrice Hayes-Middleton was not one of these."

"At last!" Johnny nudged Lionel, who gave a small grimace.

"Beatrice Hayes-Middleton bravely sought the shining spheres of heaven. And now she has found them!"

Rhetoric, thought Wiggins, almost impressed. Genuine rhetoric. "Wow!" he mouthed to Julia.

"Endless," Julia mouthed back. They were seldom on the same wavelength.

"Infinite," said Father Bernard, his head rising like that of a horse which knows it's on the home straight. "Infinite happiness, satisfaction, fufillment is what she has found. For she has found the love of the Lord! The love of the Lord. So let us not mourn but rather rejoice! In the name of the Father, Son and Holy Ghost."

The end had come quickly, almost abruptly. Those older members of the congregation who were accustomed to a longer wind-down felt cheated of a final sentence. They liked to be able to quote a final sentence.

Now the organ struck up again, pounding out the beat.

"Lead, kindly Light, amid the encircling gloom,

Lead thou me on!
The night is dark, and I am far from home . . ."

But by this time most people's attention had wandered and the sound was thin. It wound upward into the high concrete dome and was almost drowned out by the rustle of paper as the bored took refuge in energetic turning of the page. It was a relief when the choir, who had somehow missed the first verse, came in for the second and third.

Harry, however, sang loudly. So did Johnny.

"I was not ever thus, nor prayed that thou
Shouldst lead me on;
I loved to choose and see my path; but now
Lead thou me on!
I loved the garish day . . ."

Their voices, strong and bass, made noticeable Lionel's silence between them. Despair, thought Johnny. Arrogance, thought Harry, out of habit. And then remembered his father's passionate tears.

Father Bernard was busy preparing the bread and wine.

"Pray, brethren, that our sacrifice may be acceptable to God, the almighty Father."

How ugly this modern English is, thought Julian. Really, if I had any interest in it all I'd find a twentieth-century Newman to translate the lot properly. Actually it's not such a bad idea anyway. . . . His mind dispersed into a well-tried groove about whether he should include writers in his agency.

The English doesn't mater, Harry told himself, even though it's so ugly. It's a ritual. The form of any ritual soon becomes automatic, only remarked for its sameness. Of course, if that is true, they should have kept the Latin. I wonder why they didn't.

Father Bernard took the central part of the Mass at high speed. He was filled with cowardice as bells rang and the servers bobbed up and down. However, he found new strength with the transformation of the bread into the body of Christ. He slowed down again and became immune to his congregation.

The familiar feeling of well-being came over him as the choir sang.

"Tantum ergo Sacramentum Veneremur Cernui."

The classicists in the pews sighed nostalgically.

"Arma virumque cano," murmured a shriveled gentleman on Harry's left.

"*Troiae qui primus ab oris*," replied Harry.

I am coming to the end again, thought Father Bernard. Another Mass imperfectly celebrated. Or is it the sin of pride to think this way? I am but the instrument. And the bread did change into the body of Christ.

High in the organ loft, the student, who up till now had reined himself in, lost control. He flung down great cascades of notes which overflowed onto the heads of the congregation. Those who had been somnolent jerked once more into life. Was this the last hymn? Should they stand? They looked for guidance. But the priest sat, arms folded.

Harry too jerked upright. He shut his eyes and something like a smile stretched his lips. When he opened his eyes again, they were bright, almost joyous. As suddenly as it had started the music stopped, leaving behind a high note vibrating shrilly.

The priest stood. In another few seconds, another few words, it was over.

Lionel, Harry and Johnny walked out behind the coffin. As they passed beside the pews one voice whispered, "Terribly long," and further down the aisle another, even more heartfelt, could be heard. "Dreadfully cold."

Harry stared at his father's stern profile. The mustache was thinner, paler. Now his mother was to be burnt up under her husband's solitary gaze. Her ashes and bones would join the indiscriminate piles in the Kensal Rise charnel house. His father had not wanted a burial ground and she had made no reference to it. Harry had said he would not go to witness such a pagan end.

Father and son stood once more at the doors of the church and thanked people for coming. Harry's face and eyes glowed. He moved from foot to foot. Soon Father Bernard joined them. His spirits had risen. A few lines in his sermon had come back to him and they seemed good. Better than good. "Joy." "Rejoice." Perhaps he would conquer his own fear of death.

"Thank you, Father," said Lionel.

"It all went well enough," agreed the priest, rubbing his hands together. The Irish in him longed for a bit of a party now, a drink or two.

Harry gradually became separated from his father and surrounded by his friends. There were Wiggins and Julia, Julian and Richard, and Salmon and his wife, wearing a headscarf tied as if to remove her nose, and there was Uncle Johnny. They moved restlessly, hunching their shoulders against the damp gray air. "Garish day," murmured Harry. "Wonderful image."

Father Bernard nodded. "Of course, Newman pinched the idea from Milton's 'day's garish eye.' "

Harry didn't seem to hear. He spoke intensely.

"It reminds me of my first consciousness of the world. I was in Ceylon. I was watching some sort of parade with my parents. But what I saw was a tree. It was dazzling. It had very dark green leaves, lustrous like a rhododendron, and, sprouting out of them, so big that they stood clear up into the sky, were enormous scarlet flowers. Gigantic scarlet flowers."

"The tulip tree is quite common in southern India and Ceylon," said Richard politely.

"Within the equatorial band," agreed Wiggins.

"Amazing Mother Nature." Father Bernard took a quick look at his watch. What a strange young man Harry was! Tulip trees indeed! If there wasn't to be a wake, then he didn't want to miss the priory lunch. "Amazingly fertile."

Julia smoothed her stomach tenderly. She felt hungry. Pregnancy had that effect.

"I bet you don't know what makes trees different from humans," said Salmon.

"Leaves?" Wiggins looked at his watch. He had taken the precaution of reserving a table for lunch in a Greek trattoria nearby.

"Oh, it's much more interesting than that." Salmon ignored his wife's attempts to shut him up.

"No soul?" Father Bernard's voice was jocular.

"I wouldn't know about that." Salmon's face beamed.

"I have booked a table for lunch," volunteered Wiggins.

Father Bernard's face brightened and then fell again. He could not go to lunch. He had a meeting with the parish treasurer at two-thirty P.M. He offered up his disappointment and received in return a quick flush of satisfaction.

"You haven't guessed the answer yet," insisted Salmon.

"I booked the table for one o'clock," said Wiggins, thinking with sudden viciousness that Salmon was exactly the same silly old bugger he'd always been.

"Trees are taller than human beings," suggested Julian good-humoredly. Why should Harry look exhilarated at his mother's funeral? He was bouncing about as if preparing for a race.

"They never stop bloody growing." A gloomy voice came from the fringe of the group.

"Who said that?" Salmon dropped with disappointment.

"Me," muttered Johnny. "You should see them in Ireland. They grow and grow and grow and grow. Growing heavenward, I wouldn't be surprised. Like everything else in Ireland. And just look where it gets them."

"That's the right answer," Salmon said bossily. "Trees never stop growing until they die. Humans stop growing less than a quarter of the way through their lives."

"Lunch?" Wiggins took Harry's arm. He had the look of a keeper.

Harry shook him off.

"No!" he said loudly.

"No," repeated Wiggins stupidly.

"We must always look to the future," suggested Father Bernard. He was beginning to be positively glad not to be attending lunch. He too had noticed the odd expression on Harry's face. His explosive qualities, particularly after alcohol, were known to him. He remembered there was jam roll for dessert on Tuesdays.

"Lunch-lunch-lunch," insisted Wiggins. Harry must not be allowed to go off his head again, on today of all days.

"And I shall slip away." Father Bernard produced a key for the sacristy door from under his robes. He waved it, wand-like. "God bless you all!"

"And God bless you, Father," responded Johnny.

"We are all priests!" cried Harry, striding off suddenly down the silvery-gray pavement. Above him the clouds descended another notch.

"Trees!" shouted Salmon, catching the spirit but mishearing the word.

"You would think they were drunk already." Julia clutched Wiggins's arm.

"The loss of a mother is a dreadful thing." Johnny stared at Julia's swollen stomach with solemnity.

"Trees traveling the world," laughed Harry, "but getting nowhere."

"Stunted now and to eternity. Unless . . ."

"Unless one fine day out pops a scarlet tulip." Harry's words flew over his shoulder.

Salmon chased after him.

"I thought his mother's death might calm him down," said Wiggins crossly. Was he really expected to follow the two rushing figures?

“Drat!” said Johnny. “I never finished preparing Lionel’s lunch.” 310

“They’re like children,” commented Mrs. Salmon with no sign of sentiment. “I suppose that’s why they were such good friends at prep school.”

“Lunatic.” Julian smiled. “Extreme conventionality, such as Harry displayed until a few years ago, is almost certainly a cover for total insanity.”

But Harry, with Salmon close on his heels, was out of earshot. Indeed they now turned a corner and were also out of sight.

Once round the corner, however, Harry stopped abruptly. Since he gave no warning, Salmon, who was at his heels, collided with the force of 225 pounds. Harry bent double. Salmon saw tears in his eyes.

“Oh, I say. . . . Why were we running?”

“To get away.” Harry straightened up. But Salmon noted with embarrassment that the tears had increased. One stood quivering on the top of his cheek.

“Look, I’m sorry.”

To Salmon’s relief Harry smiled. “It’s not your fault. I was just thinking.”

“Ah, yes.” Salmon paused and became greatly daring. “Your mother?”

“That sort of thing.” Harry put his arm round Salmon’s shoulders. “You’re not such a bad old sod.”

“Thanks.”

“Do me a favor. Wait here for the others, and when they catch up, say I couldn’t make lunch.”

“Couldn’t make lunch?”

“Apologize.” Harry started to walk away.

“But where are you going?” Salmon called after him.

Harry walked more briskly but shouted over his shoulder, “Father, Son and Holy Ghost. I’m going to see the bones of my mother enter the charnel house.”

Salmon watched him go.

Soon the others arrived.

“Where’s he gone?” asked Wiggins, looking round suspiciously.

“To honor his father and his mother,” replied Salmon, showing a previously untapped intelligence.

Chapter 28

It was raining heavily when Harry and his father returned to the house. Harry brushed the drops off his father's shoulders and led him into the sitting room.

"Of course your mother didn't care about death," Lionel said.

"Sit down, Father. I'll get you a drink."

Lionel rubbed his hands together. "Just look at the way she behaved when poor Anna came her everlasting cropper."

Harry understood he was still wrestling with Beatrice's belief in the afterlife. "I'm sure she would want you to mourn."

Lionel looked unconvinced but now he allowed Harry to settle him into his chair.

"You would like a drink, wouldn't you?" Harry asked.

"What I'd like is a spot of luncheon." The "luncheon" sounded feebly like a gong improperly struck. "Where's Johnny?"

"You said you wanted to be alone. He's gone to a restaurant with Wiggins."

"Drunk, I suppose." Lionel closed his eyes.

Harry made him a whisky and then went down to the kitchen. There a tray was neatly set with everything his father could want. Harry took a slice of ham, ate half and put the rest back. He sat down at the table. Why was his heart pumping like a power station, making the whole room rock? Oh God, is my mother's death a cause for rejoicing?

Above his head, he became aware of movement. Not the dogged steps of one old man but a purposeful to-ing and fro-ing. Then there were voices. Listening intently, Harry recognized Johnny, although he couldn't understand what he was saying. He sat back in his chair. For a moment he had been poised for something, he didn't know what.

Johnny's steps came to the top of the stairs. He bellowed, "Harry! Come up! I've got something for you." His voice was loud but unthickened by drink. Even for Johnny, not noted for his tact, it seemed odd behavior under the circumstances.

Harry came up the stairs slowly.

Johnny stood at the top impatiently. His grizzled hair, rather damp, fell over his forehead. He took Harry's arm. "Come on, old chap. Your mother wouldn't want you to turn catatonic. Wouldn't do at all." He paused and pushed Harry through the sitting-room door. "Not at all. You must buckle to and give a proper welcome to your long-lost daughter. She's flown all the way from South America especially to be with you.

"Stiffen the swines!" he continued as Harry failed to move farther forward. "She's only a little girl and very tired and nervous too."

There must be a mistake, thought Harry. The girl standing in front of him was not a bit like Flavia. Surely Cordelia had been fair as a little girl? But his recollections were bleached by imagination. This girl had brown hair, thick and bristly. She was not very tall and stood quite stockily with her legs apart. She reminded him of a Shetland pony for, despite the pallor of exhaustion on her face, she had a plucky and determined air.

"My mother sent me," she said now, blushing slightly under Harry's gaze and his continued silence. "But I think she got the time change wrong. She's never very good with time changes. My father usually . . ." She stopped, gasped and blushed so deeply that tears came into her eyes.

Horrified, all three men spoke at the same time. "I'll get you something to drink," began Johnny.

"Sit down, my dear," pleaded Lionel, who, up till that moment, had seemed detached from the scene.

"I'm so glad you've come!" cried Harry, at last finding himself able to move toward this extraordinary stranger.

But it was too late to stop the tears. They swelled out of Cordelia's eyes while she stood helplessly, arms dangling.

"Don't cry, please! We're so happy you're here." Harry, half-crouching, flung his arms round her. "Please, don't cry!"

"But I'm all alone. And the flight was so long. And I couldn't sleep. And I didn't think anyone would meet me." Her voice was overwhelmed by her sobs.

Her shoulder writhed under Harry's fingers so that, unused to childish emotion, he imagined she was on the verge of some terrible seizure. "You're not alone! We're here! I'm here. I'll look after you." He spoke passionately into her ear.

"She's quite right," said Johnny in disapproving tones from the door. "She's much too young to go on a great flight like that on her own. How old is she? Ten? Eleven? Twelve?"

"I don't know," said Harry distractedly. The writhing continued, but she turned a little toward him so that the sobbing was less vociferous.

"And what if I hadn't got that telegram and met her? It was unnatural virtue that brought me back here to check poor Lionel's lunch."

"Mama said," Cordelia's voice emerged with a little more strength, "that my, my father would meet me but I didn't even know what he looked like."

"She thought I was you," Johnny nodded, grinning. "Gave her a nasty fright. And now I'll get us all a drink."

"I'm your father," said Harry gently as Johnny receded swiftly down the stairs. He stroked her bristly hair with shaking fingers. "He's your great-uncle."

"I know that now." The girl nodded seriously and Harry realized she had stopped crying.

Feeling foolish but determined not to mind, he got up and led her over to the chair. "Sit down and now we'll look after you." He pointed to Lionel. "That's my father, your grandfather and if he looks sad, it's because of the funeral. You mustn't be upset."

It seemed against nature that such a young girl had been brought to the house by an old drunk and received by another old man whose heart was filled with death. But her face looked at him with clear bright eyes.

"I'm all right now," she said, giving an ordinary cheerful smile. "Mama says I cry much too easily." She shook her mane of hair. "I was so excited to come to England again, even though we've just left, because I wanted to meet you. I've always wanted to meet you."

She seemed about to say something more but then a movement from Lionel caught her eye and she flushed guiltily. "I'm sorry it's such a sad occasion."

"Oh, but it's not!" began Harry, then stopped himself as his father rose slowly from the chair.

"I shall lie down for a moment," he said, "in my room." He passed by Cordelia and gave her a light tap on the head, as if in approval. "Tell Johnny to bring me up a bite. Just a bite. I might drop off for a moment. Didn't sleep too well last night."

"I'll bring you up something, Father."

"No. No. Johnny will do me. You've got other responsibilities."

Cordelia stood up again and watched gravely as he left the room.

Harry stared at the carpet. He wanted to ask why Flavia had sent her. There must be some catch somewhere. But before he could think how to phrase the question, Cordelia began to rummage in the bag at her feet. She seemed quite recovered now, energetic and excited.

"Mama gave me a letter for you. She made me swear not to forget it, although she's the one who forgets. I never forget." She handed a long cream envelope to Harry.

He held it in front of him and looked at her. She looked back sympathetically, as if she understood the kind of emotion he was feeling.

"Is there a lavatory?" she said, eventually. "I'm bursting. And then I'll go down and see how Uncle Johnny's getting on with our drinks."

She was leaving him alone to read his letter, Harry realized. She was not such a little girl as the tears had made her seem. Her expression was kind, almost patronizing, as she crossed the room and carefully closed the door behind her.

Harry sat down and opened the envelope.

Dear Harry,

I promised to send Cordelia to your mother. But I didn't realize how ill she was. So now you have your daughter. It's probably what Beatrice intended all along.

Flavia

Oh God, is my mother's death a cause for rejoicing?

From downstairs, Harry heard voices. The girl's high excited tone, answered by Johnny's deep drawl. He went down and saw Cordelia again.